Delicious

An MM / MMM Charity Anthology

Volume One

Contents

Content Warnings

Your mental health is important and for that reason some of the stories will have content warnings displayed.

Hot Dish

Annabeth Albert

Chapter One

Stu

"A paramedic guy came to check on you," Shelby reported as I emerged from an unplanned afternoon nap. In my defense, I'd had a heck of a week, and I'd been up late last night finishing a painting.

"Who?" I blinked, brain bleary from the too-long nap.

"The one who is our neighbor." Shelby rolled her eyes at me. My daughter was getting all too good at that skill as we approached her freshman year of high school. "He's also on the ambulance crew that helped the night of Magnus's fire."

She kicked up a leg, showing off her healing scrape. Our next-door neighbor, Magnus, had suffered a catastrophic house fire earlier in the week. Shelby had been the one to discover the fire when she went to her job as Magnus's dog sitter, and we'd both suffered minor injuries prior to the arrival of the first-responder crews.

"Oh right. Percy." The night of the fire had been so

chaotic I'd almost forgotten that our neighbor had been one of the paramedics to respond to the call.

"You know his name?" Soren scoffed from his seat at the kitchen table. Our house was small but cozy in a neighborhood of other older, working-class homes, and the kitchen shared space with the dining room. From the looks of his ham sandwich and chips, Soren was having a late lunch or a giant snack.

"Mount Hope is a small town." I resisted the temptation to roll my eyes like Shelby. Soren was about to be a junior and was so very, very sixteen these days. "Tony, your football coach, is dating Caleb, a firefighter. Percy works with Caleb, hence we've been at the same event a couple of times. And he's our neighbor."

Those were facts, but I hadn't mentioned Percy was a major silver fox, maybe ten years older than my forty. Even if we'd lived in Manhattan, I would have made it a point to know his name. And if I spent way too much time looking out the window when he did yard work, well, that was another thing I'd keep to myself.

"This is why we should have stayed in Berkley." Two years into living in Mount Hope, Soren had yet to forgive me or his mother for the move. However, when my ex-wife needed to return to Oregon to take care of her aging parent, I hadn't hesitated to move as well. Keeping our blended family together was more important than mine and Soren's love of the Bay Area. "Too much small-town gossip. It's weird, everyone knowing everyone else's business."

"Well, I like it here." Shelby was ever our peacemaker.

"We should do something to thank the first responders from the fire."

"We should." I agreed, if only to have an excuse to ogle Percy's lanky muscles up close, along with whatever other eye candy was lurking around the fire station. "What were you thinking? Take cookies by the station?"

"Everyone else likely sends cookies." Shelby had a typical teen fixation lately on "everyone else" and not wanting to be "boring." "How about we do a casserole? Like those stuffed pasta shells I made last week. Everyone loved that one." She smiled hopefully at me.

"That sounds like a decent idea," I allowed. Shelby had spent the summer binging cooking competition shows and honing her culinary chops. Not only were the results tasty, but she usually doubled the recipes to split them between households, giving her a chance to practice her math skills as well. "You can make two casseroles again, so we get dinner out of it too."

"And you could drop the second one off with Percy to take in on his next shift." Shelby was also a born organizer, but I didn't hate the idea of a reason to knock on Percy's door.

"Good plan."

Thus, one trip to the grocery store and one marathon cooking session with Shelby later, I found myself knocking on Percy's front door. Like my house, his had a narrow concrete front stoop rather than a porch, and I felt more than a little silly and exposed standing in the open, holding the wrapped casserole. And that was before Percy opened the door wearing only a pair of loose-fitting athletic shorts and rubbing his eyes.

"Oh no." My shoulders dropped. "Did I wake you?"

"It's okay." Percy waved away my concern. He was tall and lean with rugged features and closely cropped silver hair. If not for the shorts and bare, fuzzy chest, he could pass for an old west sheriff. "I sleep weird hours. As do you, apparently."

"Apparently." My face heated more than was reasonable for the July evening. "Sorry that I was napping when you stopped by earlier."

"No problem." He opened the door wider. "Come in so I can grab a shirt before I give the neighborhood something to talk about."

"Okay," I said in lieu of what I really wanted to say, which was that he didn't need to put a shirt on for me. I was only too happy to look at his fuzzy chest and flat stomach. However, Percy was already pulling on a T-shirt advertising the annual Mount Hope first responder pancake breakfast. "And the nap comes with the territory of being an artist. And an art teacher with the summer off and a lack of routine."

"Understandable." Percy gave me an easy smile. His extroverted, chatty nature had been on full display at the social events we'd both attended. "I'm glad to see you up and around. No lingering effects from the fire?"

"No. But Shelby and I wanted to say thank you to your crew. You saved us a trip to the emergency room." I'd been treated on the scene for smoke inhalation while another paramedic had bandaged Shelby's leg.

"You're welcome." He shrugged, an easy roll of his broad shoulders. "That's what we're here for."

"Well, we made you a casserole." I held up the metal pan. We'd forgotten to buy a disposable pan, so I'd simply used one of ours. "Stuffed shells. You can take it with you on your next shift if you want. It freezes well."

"You brought me a hot dish?" His forehead creased as he cocked his head.

"It's cold now, but I put the heating instructions on the top."

"Sorry, I'm from the Midwest." He chuckled, and had I been paying attention to more than his chest, I might have noted his slight accent. "Casseroles or, as my mom always said, hot dishes are a way of life. After my dad died when I was young, we had a full freezer for months."

"That's good that the community helped you." I nodded, unsure how to express sympathy for a loss I knew only too well. "Another advantage of small-town living, not that my older kid agrees."

"The football player? He's lucky to be at a small school." Percy finally took the casserole from me but seemed in no hurry to send me on my way as he walked through the small living room to the kitchen/dining room combo that mirrored my own. He stuck the wrapped casserole in the fridge. "I grew up in a small Minnesota town, but went to a county high school that pulled from all the other area small towns. Getting a starting spot on our team wasn't easy."

"What position did you play?" I hadn't played myself, but I'd turned a lifelong football fandom into a volunteer position helping with Soren's team when the previous coach had experienced some health issues.

"Running back. I wanted to be a quarterback, but there was too much competition for that spot. I settled for scoring in other ways." He gave me a wink that went straight to my suddenly way-too-interested dick.

"I see." I cleared my throat. "Well, I should probably let you get back to sleep."

"That's all you came over for?" he asked, giving me a blatantly long once-over. He had a reputation as a flirt with all genders, a trait I shared. I was drawn to confident, take-charge personalities more than a particular set of body parts, and a commanding voice like Percy's was an added bonus. The air grew thick, not simply from the lack of air conditioning.

"To drop off the casserole and say thanks, yeah." My voice came out ridiculously husky. "Why else would I come by?"

"Oh, I don't know. I've seen you looking when I mow or run." Voice light, he offered another of those devastating winks. "I was hoping you might be here for the neighborly equivalent of a booty call."

I gulped, doing a fast set of calculations. Soren was at a friend's house while Shelby had walked the couple of blocks to her mom's house with the leftovers from our casserole. "I could be."

Chapter Two

Percy

"I could be." Stu, my neighbor, looked the part of an art teacher or possibly an aging surfer. He wore his dark-brown hair in a messy ponytail, had what seemed like a whole collection of colorful T-shirts and board shorts, and usually sported paint smudges in a few spots on his person. Today's shirt featured a joke about Van Gogh I didn't quite get while his shorts had red chili peppers on them. I wasn't the artist, so I lacked the precise color label for his warm skin tone, which made me think of Hawaii and other tropical locals. And his lips, rosy and sinfully full, inspired far more X-rated thoughts. He nodded again, like he'd come to some sort of agreement with himself.

"Thought so." I smirked. I'd been waiting for an opportunity like this for months now. I opened the fridge and extracted two bottles of a local microbrew I'd discovered since moving to the area. "Beer?"

"Yes, please." Stu accepted the second beer and followed my lead in opening it and taking a long sip. And lord, those lips wrapped around the cold glass bottle transformed my already active imagination into a steady stream of pornographic thoughts.

"Kids expecting you back?" I asked, using neighborly concern to disguise a necessary fishing expedition before this little visit went further.

"No. I share custody with my ex, who lives nearby." Stu followed me back to the living room. "Shelby will likely sleep there tonight, and Soren's with friends."

"Excellent." I flopped on the couch. I had been dozing in my recliner earlier but the couch suited my purposes here better. "Have a seat."

"Thank you." He perched next to me, not relaxing but not retreating to the far side of the long leather sofa.

"You still seeing that artist?" Having established that he didn't live with the co-parent to the kids, I still had a couple of questions. The previous fall, Stu had been seen at a couple of local events with a glass artist who had worked in several area galleries, but I hadn't seen them together all winter. Now it was July, and I hoped like hell Stu was fair game.

"Gotta love small-town gossip." Stu gave an eye roll that made him look far younger than his actual age, which was likely his early forties. I liked his maturity. Around here, the local singles scene tended to be a lot of younger folks, which was a no-thank-you from me. I wanted sex, not a babysitting gig. Stretching, Stu finally relaxed a bit against the couch. "No, that was a brief fling. Mika wasn't up for the whole dating a single dad thing, not that I blame them."

"Their loss." I took another leisurely sip of my beer. One of his many colorful T-shirts featured a goose holding a pan Pride flag, so I'd been fairly certain he swung my direction at least some of the time, even before he'd dated the nonbinary artist.

"Thanks." As before, Stu mimicked my actions. I did like the potential here, for sure. Hot and able to follow directions well? Yes, please. Stu set his beer on a nearby end table I'd picked up at a neighborhood yard sale. "You're single as well? I'm not opposed to casual, but I don't do cheaters."

"Single. Divorce cured me of any settle-down urges I might have had." I met his gaze, trying to convey that I wasn't the dating type. Hookups, yes. Flings, sure. But picket fences? Been there, got the heartbreak, no thank you on a repeat.

"Ah. My divorce wasn't so bad, but we were college friends first." He gave a vague gesture. "We've made it work for the sake of the kids."

"That's good. I moved across the country to escape the fallout from mine." I was an open book by nature, but I also wanted to reinforce that whatever happened here wasn't the start of some grand romance. "Hector, my ex-husband, was also the mayor."

Stu winced. "The mayor. Ouch."

"Told you. The aftermath sucked." I left out the part about Hector leaving me for his much younger administrative assistant. Somehow, despite the cheating, he'd managed to keep the bulk of our friend group and town support, and I hadn't been able to stomach staying and starting over in the same area where I'd lost my parents, my marriage, and my hopes for the future.

"I imagine so." Stu nodded sympathetically.

"It's been a couple of years, but feel free to console me." I stretched out farther, legs falling open, arm snaking out along the back of the couch.

"What did you have in mind?" Stu's dark-brown eyes flared with heat. I'd made the suggestion open to whatever ideas he might want to run with, but the way he tossed the ball back into my court for direction made my cock pulse that much harder.

Reaching out, I ran a thumb over his lower lip. "I've been a fan of these lips of yours since I saw you at Caleb's birthday party at the Heist."

"Yeah?" He scooted closer.

"Watching you sip that beer gave me all sorts of ideas, but you feel free to share your own." I left him an out in case giving oral wasn't his thing.

"I like how you think." He laid a hand on my bare knee. "And I'm happy to follow your...*suggestions*."

The way he drew the word out made the tent in my shorts that much bigger. I did enjoy giving orders and having them followed, and if Stu was into that too, so much the better for this little encounter.

"Is that so?" I drawled. "Anything you really don't like? Kissing okay?"

"Kissing is great." Nodding, he licked his lips. "Don't come on my face, and I'm not into pain, but feel free to get as bossy as you like otherwise."

"Come here." I started with a simple command, yanking him into my lap. No protest from Stu as he arranged himself to straddle me on the couch. He bent forward, close enough to kiss, but waited for me to make that move.

I happily obliged, pulling him into a kiss with a hand tangled in his thick hair. He moaned approvingly. Since Stu wasn't under a time crunch, I intended to fully enjoy those lips of his. I traced them with the tip of my tongue before sucking on the lower one, which earned me another groan. He wasn't a passive kisser, but he did let me lead. I moaned as well when he welcomed my tongue into his mouth, sucking on it in a clear imitation of where this was headed next.

He clutched my shoulders and rocked against me, eager for everything I wanted to give him. Tightening my hold on his head, I deepened the kiss. His hands roamed from my shoulders down my arms, and I took the opportunity to shrug out of my shirt. Stu said he liked direction, so I put his hand where I wanted it, on my pec over my left nipple. He took the hint perfectly, playing with my nipple as I continued kissing him.

"You can go harder," I suggested when he stuck to light caresses and careful teases.

"Yes." His eyes went molten at the permission, and he tweaked and fiddled more aggressively as I pulled him in for another kiss. My cock throbbed in my shorts, and the pressure of him on my lap, grinding, turned me on that much more. I pushed on his shoulder, and he followed that unspoken direction, sinking to his knees in front of me. Bracing his hands on my thighs, he gazed expectantly at me, so I moved his right hand to cover my cock.

"Damn. You're packing." He moaned softly as he

explored. I wasn't much longer than average, but what I did have was thick all the way down. He squeezed and stroked until he apparently reached the limits of his patience and tugged at my waistband.

"Think you can handle it?" I hadn't bothered with underwear when I'd pulled on the shorts after my shower, so they were easy enough to shimmy out of. Being naked with Stu still dressed felt rather indulgent.

"I'd sure like to try." He fisted my cock, giving a slow, firm stroke.

"Good answer." I let him play a few moments more because his hand felt damn good, but I was only so patient. "Kiss it."

"Mmm." Stu gave an excited hum like he'd been waiting for that command. Following the letter of my instruction, he dropped soft kisses all over my cockhead and shaft before teasing the underside with the tip of his tongue.

"Oh, you can do better than that," I gently chided, playing into the game more. "Suck." He responded by sucking my cock into the warm heat of his mouth, shallow bobs that went deeper when I put an encouraging hand on his head. "That's it. Nice and deep."

"Yes." Stu reached up and patted my hand on his head. "Love it if you drive. And playing with my hair is a turn-on."

"Noted." I kept my grip on his head loose, letting my fingers thread through the silky strands of his hair, the ponytail elastic having gone missing sometime during the kissing. Watching his reactions closely, I directed his movements, learning how deep he could go and finding an angle that worked for us both. And he could go pretty darn deep, an admirable skill given my girth. "We're gonna go faster now, okay?"

Stu moaned his agreement and moved one of his hands from my thigh to his shorts. I reached down and batted his hand away.

"Nope. No touching yourself. That's mine for after."

As I'd expected, that proclamation got a louder moan. I sped up my thrusts. Stu went right for extra credit, increasing the suction and using his tongue on the upstroke to milk my cock. Damn, he was amazing at this, and I wasn't going to last long with his combination of eagerness, skill, and submission.

"That's right. Suck hard. Show me you want that come."

Moaning again, Stu bobbed his head faster even without my urging, and the way he kept the tongue action going had me on the edge in record time.

"You ready? Gonna swallow?" I made sure he heard the question there. I wasn't going to presume.

He pulled back exactly long enough to groan, "Gimme. Please."

"I like it when you ask nice." *Please* was absolutely the magic word as far as my dick was concerned, and as soon as Stu resumed the speed and suction, I lost myself to his determined mouth.

"Get ready, baby," I warned, tightening my grip on him, which made him moan that much more. "Here it comes."

He sucked hard, clinging to my cock, and that hunger tipped me right over. I came what felt like gallons, but Stu swallowed it all. Finally reaching that too-sensitive place, I pulled him off my dick and up next to me on the couch. I wrapped an arm around him, holding him close.

"Kiss me." I had no idea why, but kissing after oral was a huge turn-on for me, tasting it, knowing he'd swallowed. Stu hesitated, glancing up at me for reassurance. "I like it. Keeps my cock hard."

I doubted I could go for doubles, but staying turned on enough to focus on getting Stu off was my goal. He wriggled against me as I kissed him, showing him who owned that mouth. He shuddered.

"Mmm. Someone liked sucking me off." I palmed his cock through his shorts.

"Yes. God." He tipped his head back against the couch.

"Nuh-uh." I made a warning noise. "Can't send you home with a mess in your shorts. Clothes off."

"Oh. Yeah." His cheeks went dusky as he quickly stripped with unsteady hands before settling back down next to me.

"Gonna come fast for me?" I asked as I got a hand on his cock right away. He was longer than me, though not as thick, and his cockhead was uncut and more oval, whereas mine was more bluntly rounded.

"Uh-huh." He made a needy noise, arching into me. "Please."

"Ask me for it." I stroked him hard and fast, upping the ante by fiddling with his nipple with my free hand. Not everyone had hardwired nipples like me, but Stu seemed to like it well enough, moaning and leaning into the touch. "Come on, say please again."

16

"Please let me come. I need it." Stu moaned as his head fell onto my shoulder.

"Yeah, you do." I heaped on the praise as I jacked his cock with a practiced grip, using the slide of his foreskin to speed up my strokes. "And you did so good, sucking me. Made me feel so good."

"Please." He made a sound that was close to a whimper. Yeah, he was right there.

"Say my name," I ordered. A bit power trippy, but I got off on my partner knowing exactly who they were with.

"Percy." Stu gasped and released a fountain of come that hit his collarbone before painting his chest and belly. "Fucking hell."

I gave him one last kiss, softer now, a sweet reward for coming so good for me. Releasing him gently, I used my discarded shirt to clean up his chest and stomach.

"That was amazing." He sounded more than a little come-drunk.

"It was." I offered a bemused smile before offering him a hand up. "I'll show you where the bathroom is if you want to clean up a little more."

I liked the afterglow as much as anyone else, but there was no sense in dragging out an awkward parting.

"Yeah." He followed me to my hall bath, pulling on his shorts as we went. "Thanks."

By the time he emerged a few minutes later, I had a fresh pair of shorts and a T-shirt on and had returned to my recliner.

"You're welcome to finish your beer." I gestured at his

half-empty bottle, knowing full well he wouldn't take me up on the offer. "I can put the sports news on if you'd like."

"Nah. We should..." He paused near my front door, making a vague gesture. "I mean, if you want to."

I chuckled. "We should definitely do that again, Stu."

And we hopefully would. For all the inevitable stilted goodbyes that followed a first hookup, I was already craving a repeat. I trusted he'd be back for more.

Chapter Three

Percy

I waited for Stu to come back around for a second helping.

And waited.

And waited.

The stuffed shells casserole was delicious and enjoyed by the whole crew, and now Stu's metal pan sat clean on my counter, waiting for him to stop by.

Only he hadn't, and it'd been over two weeks since our little escapade, and I was more than a little miffed that Stu hadn't so much as waved to me from his driveway. Also, I was approaching DEFCON levels of horny, with zero desire to go hunting on the apps or in person. For all I was known as a flirt, I could be rather picky about partners, and Stu checked every last one of my boxes. There had been something...else to the encounter with him, something I didn't care to name but made him linger in my brain.

I glanced out my front window yet again. His place was

across the street and two houses over, but I had a pretty good view of his driveway, especially now that the house on the other side had been lost to the fire, creating a gap in the street.

"See you Monday!" A cheery, forty-something woman with short teal hair and silver glasses stood next to a large, loaded-down silver SUV. I'd seen her around and was reasonably certain she was Stu's ex. Both kids emerging from the house with backpacks and other bags and climbing into the SUV added to that assumption.

"Have a great weekend." Stu waved to them from the porch.

What was this? Stu home alone? Possibly bored and also horny?

I glanced over at that empty pan. Returning it was a rather obvious excuse, but it wouldn't be neighborly to keep his pan. A distant memory tingled in my brain. My mom sometimes returned a casserole dish with something in it as a thank you. I had a wicked sweet tooth, so I easily found a box of brownie mix in my pantry and some parchment paper for lining the pan. I could make brownies in my sleep, so I had them baking in the oven in short order, allowing me time for a quick shower.

Now, I had the pan to return, and if Stu wanted to take the hint and invite me in for a brownie, I wouldn't complain. With one eye on Stu's driveway to make sure his car was still there, I let the pan cool to a point where it was easy to carry but still had a hint of fresh-from-the-oven warmth.

Showered and with brownies in hand, I headed for his place which was close to a mirror of mine—slightly different exterior styling, but same window placement and roughly a similar size. Confident, I rang the bell, but then Stu kept me waiting. And waiting. Now, I was less sure and a little irritated, but before I could retreat, the door finally opened.

"Hey, Percy." Eyes squinting, he looked a bit confused at my presence. "Sorry, I was painting in the back garage."

"No problem." I offered the lie cheerfully like I hadn't been worried he was avoiding me. "I've been meaning to return your pan. Thought you and the kids might appreciate some brownies."

Another lie, but I couldn't reveal that I'd been watching his house.

"The kids are camping for the weekend with my ex and her new partner, but thank you." He accepted the pan. "Way too much chocolate here for just me. Would you like to come in?"

"Sure. I'm in no hurry. Not on duty until tomorrow." I followed him into a near-identical layout to my house, but where my walls were bare, his were a riot of colorful paintings on large canvases. Even his end tables and kitchen chairs were painted in bright shades with geometric accents. "Nice place."

"Thanks. It's a rental, but way bigger than what we had in San Jose." He set the brownies on the counter before fetching two small plates.

"I like the art." Surprisingly, I wasn't just being polite. While it wasn't what I would have chosen for my place, I did like his bold style, which managed to be both striking and welcoming.

"Eh. That's what you get with an art teacher." He gestured at the walls. "A lot of these are samples I've done for student projects but didn't feel like painting over so I could reuse the canvas."

"Well, I'm glad you didn't. It works for the space."

"Hey, you want some art for your walls? I'll cut you a good deal," he teased, marginally more relaxed than when he'd opened the door. He handed me a plate with a fork and a large slice of brownie.

"Might take you up on that." I glanced at the table and his couch, unsure exactly where he wanted us to eat.

"Sit." He pointed at the table, which was closer but decidedly less cozy than the couch. "If you're serious, I can show you some of what I've been working on after we eat."

"I'd like that." I'd like him on my lap again more, but we could start with a tour of his art. And the brownies, which were surprisingly decent for a mix I'd grabbed on sale.

"How's work been?" Apparently, Stu was in small-talk mode. He had a way of asking questions that made it seem like he truly cared about the answers. "Is this a busy season for you?"

"It can be." I was going to leave it at that, but Stu leaned forward, intent on listening. "The tourists climbing all over the Gorge, summer sports injuries, and idiots on ladders attempting home repairs all add up. I can't complain though. I'd rather have a full shift than be bored."

"I feel that. I don't like sitting around either." Stu took a delicate bite of brownie, licking the crumbs off his lip in a motion that went straight to my already over-eager dick. But Stu seemed in no hurry. "Have you always been a paramedic?"

"No, I was a firefighter for years, but I liked getting to put my EMT certification to use on calls with medical emergencies. After my divorce, when I was looking to move, it seemed like an ideal time to try something new." For all that I liked talking, I tended to keep most conversations surface level, but opening up with Stu felt good, warm and comforting like the brownies. "And honestly, I'm getting older. My back thanks me for less heavy equipment to carry."

"Getting older sucks." Stu stretched before taking another bite. "I can't pull as many all-nighters painting these days, and I have to run twice as far for half the results."

"You run?" Maybe I needed to look out my windows even more.

"Yeah." He made a vague gesture with his fork. "Mainly late at night. I'm not a morning person like you."

"Eh. I'm an any time of day person." I delivered the line with a wink. "And if you ever want a running buddy, holler."

"I might." Stu's tone was cagey like he didn't quite believe the offer.

"I'm serious. I'm still new in town. I wouldn't mind adding a new friend." For all that I didn't want a relationship and all the associated heartbreak, I was a social guy, and the long stretches of solitude could bring me down. Having someone to pal around with could be nice, and Stu was remarkably easy to spend time with. "Benefits would be an added bonus but not required."

"So that mention of a repeat wasn't simply you being nice?" Stu leaned forward again.

"I don't make offers I don't mean." I held his intense gaze.

"Ah." His cheeks flushed dusky. "I couldn't tell, but then again, I don't have a ton of hookup experience."

23

"That's why you didn't come back over?" I pushed aside my empty plate.

"Pretty much." Stu shrugged, uncharacteristically shy. "The sex was spectacular. I just didn't want to presume."

"Presume away." I leaned back in my chair, legs falling open, invitation clear.

"Good to know." Stu cleared his throat before gathering our plates. "You still want to see my paintings? And then maybe stick around a while?"

"Absolutely." I nodded. And while my dick was delighted at the second half of the invitation, I honestly did want to see more of his art. The more I learned about Stu, the more I enjoyed spending time with him. "Nowhere else I'd rather be."

He led me to a detached garage he was using as a studio. Various completed paintings leaned against the unfinished walls. His style ranged from abstract, with more of the geometric elements he'd incorporated on the furniture in the house, to more realistic landscapes. Several spoke to the California connection with big waves and beachy scenes. I stepped closer to admire one that featured a line of colorful surfboards.

"You surf?"

"I used to when I was younger." Stu gave a weighty sigh. "I was born in Hawaii, then my mom moved us to California after my dad died. I still surfed some, but it was hard to enjoy surfing without him along."

"I feel that." I nodded. The list of things I'd given up after my father was lost in the line of duty was long. My chest tightened, an unfamiliar sense of kinship with Stu. "My dad

24

and I used to camp. Haven't had much of a taste for it in years. He was a firefighter. Good guy."

"I still miss mine too." Stu held my gaze, and the moment stretched out. In addition to being a good listener, he was talented at making me feel seen and understood in ways I hadn't in years. Stu stepped toward another painting, this one a sunrise over a beach. "This one is from a photograph of the Oahu town where I grew up."

"It's beautiful." I wasn't sure what else to say about such a deeply personal piece of art, the way the sunrise conveyed nostalgia and longing. "You're really talented."

"Thank you." Stu bent to reveal a canvas behind the sunrise painting, this one more abstract with floral shapes and colors. "Teaching is my first love, but painting is my favorite creative outlet and stress relief."

"Well, you're damn good at it." I bumped his shoulder with mine. "That the only form of stress relief you like?"

"No, but not a ton of opportunities for that." He offered me a flirty smile. "The other day notwithstanding."

"No time like the present."

Chapter Four

Stu

"Indeed," I agreed easily with Percy. I'd wanted a repeat as soon as I'd spied him on my front step. To be fair, I'd wanted a repeat moments after we'd finished last time, but Percy had been none too subtle about sending me on my way. I hadn't wanted to presume his "we should do it again" had been anything other than parting nicely. I'd decided to let him seek me out, and while it took him long enough, he had. And he'd brought brownies, so I was in a giving sort of mood. I glanced at the dusty, scarred garage floor. "However, I'd rather not get busy in my studio. Besides, I'm too old to kneel on concrete."

I gestured for Percy to follow me back toward the house.

"Amen to that." Percy shut the side door to the garage behind us. As we entered my kitchen, he drew me against him from behind. "Is oral your favorite pastime? You said you like me leading, but I'm happy to indulge special requests."

In case I missed his meaning, he gave my ass a firm

squeeze before nuzzling my neck. I inhaled sharply, weighing my desire to make the most of this rare opportunity for sexy fun against prudence.

"Are you tested? It's been a while since I bottomed, but I've got condoms and lube if you're interested in fucking." Both items were mainly for use with my hidden toy collection, but I was craving the real deal at the moment more than toys.

"Oh, I'm interested." Percy drawled before nipping at my neck. "And yes, negative for everything, and I always play safe."

"Good." Decision made, I led him to my bedroom at the back of the house, wincing at my unmade bed, pile of books next to the bed, and full laundry hamper in the corner. I pushed the heap of covers aside and tossed a clean towel onto the bed. "I wasn't exactly expecting guests, so apologies for the mess."

"I'm not here for the decor." Percy pulled me in for a kiss. He was an even better kisser than I remembered. Decisive and in charge without being overly controlling and exactly possessive enough to get me fully hard in a matter of seconds. He pushed at my T-shirt, so I broke away to strip off my clothes as he did the same with his own shirt and shorts. As before, he didn't wear underwear.

"Do you always go commando?" I had to ask.

"Nah. I showered before bringing you the brownies and didn't see much point in bothering."

That and the dude was seriously packing some heft, and perhaps briefs strangled his assets. Either way, I had to smile as we both got naked. Seeing his cock again, which was a blunt, thick battering ram with a wide head, made my mouth water.

"Really want to taste you again."

"I'm not stopping you," Percy chuckled as I sank to my knees on the fluffy rug beside my bed. I rubbed my face against him, breathing in the scents of him and his spicy old-fashioned soap.

I was way too impatient to tease overly much, so I guided his cock into my mouth, sucking hard to savor his weight and taste on my tongue. His width was the right sort of challenge for my jaw, keeping me focused without being painful. Setting a slow rhythm, I slid my mouth up and back down his shaft.

"Goddamn." Whistling low, Percy freed my ponytail and fisted his hand in my hair, more of that possessive guidance that made my cock rock hard and throbbing. I sucked harder, wanting him as wound up as I was, and it wasn't long before he shoved at my shoulder. "Bed. Now."

He yanked me to standing before manhandling me onto the bed. The display of aggression made my stomach quiver and my cock leak as he arranged me on my knees, him behind me.

"I'm a fan of prep." I looked over my shoulder to meet his gaze before reaching into my nightstand for the lube and condoms. "Love the initiative, but I will need some help to work up to your girth."

"Noted." Percy chuckled again as he accepted the items from me and set the condoms aside. "Don't worry. I plan to take my time."

"Excellent news." I joined his laughter. The vibe was

surprisingly easy and fun between us. I'd figured he wouldn't try to go for it without any warm-up, but it never hurt to be clear. I was also very glad I'd taken advantage of the empty house to shower after the kids left. Percy rubbed my shoulders and stroked my back, not quite a massage, but the touching went a long way to helping me relax into the encounter. His caresses felt more affectionate than I'd expected, a gentleness behind his strong hands. I groaned, stretching into his touch. "Oh, that's good."

"You're like a cat soaking up the sun." Percy's tone was fond. He moved to squeezing and groping my ass, getting me so relaxed that when he ran a thumb down my crack, all I did was shudder. The bed shifted as Percy reached for the lube. He returned with a slick finger to circle my rim. "Tell me if I go too fast."

"Not nearly fast enough," I countered. I moaned as he teased my rim, working one long finger inside. "More."

"Arch your back more," Percy ordered, encouraging me to take a second finger. He stroked his free hand down my spine, a subtle pressure to rock backward. "That's it. Ride my fingers."

"Fuck." The groan came from somewhere around my toes. Simply listening to Percy's deep voice made me ready to go. "Love when you talk."

"Yeah?" Percy sounded mildly intrigued as he continued to work me open. "Just wait till I'm inside you. Gonna make you beg for it."

"Please. Want it." The more he played with my rim, delving deeper to press on my prostate, the less concerned I became about accommodating his size.

"Nah. You said prep, and I'm not nearly done playing." Percy gave a lazy yawn. I glanced back to see his hard cock bobbing in front of him and his eyes hot with desire. The dude was an Academy Award-level actor, making me think for a moment that he was disinterested. Seeing his arousal, though, made me bolder as I squeezed his fingers, using my internal muscles to show off until Percy was the one to groan next. "Look at how that greedy hole sucks my fingers in. Think you can take my cock?"

"Need it." I wasn't faking my urgency. The more Percy played, the more I wanted. I'd never come hands-free, but the way he thrust his fingers over my prostate had me aching to reach for my cock.

"Yeah, you do." Withdrawing his fingers, Percy took care of rolling on the condom and slicking himself.

"Yes." Relief laced my voice. I wasn't known for patience at the best of times, and it had been a long couple of weeks daydreaming about doing this with Percy. "Please. Now."

"Please, what?" The laziness was back even as he lined up behind me.

"Please." I hesitated, unsure what game he was playing, but then I remembered how much he liked the sound of his name last time. "Please, Percy."

"That's it." Percy teased me with the head of his cock. "Show me how ready you are."

The order allowed me to go at my own pace, which I appreciated. I rocked against his blunt cockhead, letting it slowly stretch my rim. Percy had been extra generous with the lube, which helped. His cock was wide, but the weight of it felt so good filling me up. Moaning, I pushed back more.

"Holy fuck." I gasped when his cockhead slid over my prostate for the first time.

"Good?" Percy's voice was a low, seductive whisper as he stroked my sides. "Want better?"

"Yeah." I was happy to follow that voice any damn where. Plus, I had a thing for the way Percy liked to manhandle me. I wasn't a small guy, but Percy was stronger than his lean frame would suggest. He used that strength and height advantage to arrange us both on our knees, me in his lap, my back pressed to his chest. He wrapped his arms securely around me, one hand settling on my dick. I'd only ever seen this position in porn, but it was my new favorite thing on earth. "Oh, that's good."

"Told you." Percy nipped at my neck and jacked my cock with a slow, practiced grip. The position limited my range of motion but allowed Percy to nail my spot with every thrust. It didn't take long before I was writhing against his tight hold, taking everything he wanted to offer.

"More. Please."

"This?" Percy sped up his thrusts, pulling me into him, creating the most intense prostate pressure, damn near guaranteeing I was going to come soon.

"Yes. Yes. Percy."

"That's it. Say my name." He rewarded me with faster stroking of my cock as he pounded me from below. "Gonna get me off the way you beg so sweetly."

"Please. Please come with me." Simultaneous orgasms were a porn staple, but not in my real-world experience. However, Percy made such a feat seem not only possible but probable.

"Yeah. Wanna feel you come on this cock." Percy rubbed his rough thumb across my cockhead on his next stroke. That, combined with the command in his tone, had me bucking against him as come bubbled up out of my cock, running down his fist.

"I'm there." I rode the orgasm out, moving hard and fast with him, using those internal muscles again to extend both our pleasure. "Percy."

"Fuck. Goddamn. Here it comes." Apparently, my squeezing did the trick because a few more clenches and Percy hammered hard as he came. He thrust twice more, then simply held me for what felt like an eternity, stroking my chest and whispering nonsense words of praise. The slow float back to earth was galaxies better than the abrupt ending last time, and I luxuriated against him until he gently untangled us to take care of the condom and pass me the towel.

"Well, that was fucking amazing." I collapsed back on my pillow, gazing up at him.

"Or amazing fucking." Still on his knees, he returned my gaze, head tilting to one side. "What?"

"Waiting for you to dash toward the door." I chuckled but let my pointed look do the talking.

"I was a bit...hurried last time. Sorry." Moving with far less certainty than usual, Percy gingerly stretched out next to me. "Didn't mean to make you feel bad."

"If you want to be friends and have more of these benefits, act like it." Apparently, the sex had made me bolder. I also really did want more of this. If he wanted to be running buddies or whatever else, I was game, but I would demand certain minimum standards.

"Point taken." Percy rolled onto his elbow before brushing the hair off my face. "And I'm in no hurry."

"No?" I grinned at him. "Stick around, see if we can manage a round two?"

"That's gonna take more than five minutes for me." He groaned, and I waited for the excuse, but to my shock, he lay back on the other pillow, hands behind his head, comfortable as could be. "Maybe we could order food?"

"How do you feel about spice?" I asked, using his trick of sounding disinterested when inside, I wanted to dance around at how easily he'd adopted my suggestion of staying.

"Generally, the more, the better, but I wanna be able to feel my tongue for that round two." He leered over at me.

"I found a local place with amazing Szechuan Chinese." I made no move to find my phone, which was likely on the floor in my shorts somewhere. "How about we order some food in a bit, and I'll show you this first-person shooter game Soren has me hooked on."

I'd noted the gaming console in Percy's living room last time while blowing him, so I was hopeful he was a fellow casual gamer.

"Sounds great. Warning you, though, I'm pretty competitive."

"You think I'm not?" I sat up precisely so I could stare him down.

"Look at you all cocky." Percy chuckled, more of that unexpected fondness from him. "Bring it on."

Chapter Five

Percy

"Take that!" Two young firefighters were gaming on the station's TV. It was a slow afternoon in a slow week, so all the chores around the station were done, and I had nothing better to do than watch the young guys duke it out.

"Try executing a roll maneuver next time," I advised from my position on the other couch.

"Hey, Percy! Didn't know you gamed." Caleb grinned over at me. "You want a try?"

"Nah. I'm not that good." I stretched. Stu was a better gamer than me. The guy had a teen son for a sparring partner, so he got more practice, but I spent all of August trying to beat Stu at the video game he'd hooked me on. Stu, however, was crafty and devious and bought an expansion pack as a back-to-school present for himself. So, September found us gaming on the nights he didn't have his kids and I wasn't on call. And fucking. And eating piles of spicy noodles. And some epic post-fucking conversations.

This friends-with-benefits idea of mine was going spectacularly well. We hadn't even managed to squeeze in a run yet. The list of things I wanted to try with Stu in and out of bed kept getting longer, and adding to my mental list was more fun than watching the guys' game. I closed my eyes, content to daydream the last few hours of my shift away, only to be jolted awake by Tate, another EMT, jostling me.

"Gotta go. Come on." He raced ahead to the rig, filling me in on the way. "Football practice accident of some kind. Player ran into a coach, knocked both their wind out, and another player called 911."

"Eric's kid?" Our lead paramedic had a senior on the football team, and the last thing I wanted was for him to walk into a situation with his own kid.

"He's the one who called 911." Tate gave a tight smile. "Thoughtful enough to tell dispatch to tell his dad he's okay."

"Good kid." I nodded as I hopped into the rig where Eric was already waiting. "We good to go?"

"Let's roll." Tate pumped the gas, and we sped the short distance to Mount Hope High School's football field. The parking lot was full of players leaving from practice, but several remained clustered around two prone forms on the ground. Tony, the coach, waved Eric over to look at one of the players, leaving me to assess the other—

"Stu?" My eyes went wide. I'd known his kid played football, but somehow, I'd missed the detail that Stu helped coach. My stomach gave a hard, visceral clench. I'd seen no shortage of truly gory stuff in my years on duty, and never once had my lunch threatened to reappear like it was presently.

"Hey, Percy." Stu managed a weak greeting from his position on the ground as I kneeled beside him. He was far paler than normal and looked smaller from this angle as well. Fragile. Human. *Fuck*. Now my hands were shaking.

"Where does it hurt?" I asked, trying my damnedest to sound professional and failing miserably.

"I'm okay." Stu waved away my concern. "I help Tony with coaching the defense, but it was the offense that got me today. Rookie wide receiver crashed into me on the sideline. I'm more worried about him."

"Eric's checking him out." I glanced over to where Tate and Eric were working on the kid. "911 said you got the wind knocked out of you? Did you lose consciousness?"

"Nah." Stu shrugged, then winced as he coughed. "Just couldn't speak for long enough for the team to panic and someone to call it in. Which is good because I think Forest is gonna need that knee looked at."

Continuing to grimace, he reached down and rubbed his ankle.

"What's wrong with your ankle?"

"Twisted it along with a couple of decent scrapes." He turned his calf to reveal a good-sized patch of road rash with grass and dirt sticking to it. "I'll be feeling it tomorrow, but nothing's broken."

It could have been. The thought slammed into me. Stu could have been seriously injured. I'd be concerned about any friend, but the urge to gather Stu into my arms and hold him close was a new one. Hadn't felt that way since...

Oh shit.

No. I refused to fall for Stu. He was a buddy who was hurt. That was all.

"I'm going to check on you later," I said gruffly.

"You do that." Stu glanced around before lowering his voice. "Kids are having dinner with their mom. I'll be home alone with some ice packs."

"Are you sure you don't want to go in?" I reached for my medical kit. "Or at least let me clean those scrapes?"

"I'm fine, Percy."

"Percy?" Eric summoned me before I could push again, and by the time we had the kid and his wrenched knee situated on a gurney for transport, Stu had hobbled off the field under his own power. He'd signed a waiver for Tate, declining transport of his own, leaving me to rush to his doorstep the moment my shift ended.

"I'm fine," Stu said in lieu of greeting me. He looked freshly showered, but the pink scrapes on his legs and one on his cheek made me want to hug him again. To stifle that urge, I held out the paper bag I'd brought. "What's this?"

"Dinner." I'd swung by our favorite Chinese place on my way to his house. "I figured you wouldn't want to cook while juggling ice packs. Got that noodle dish you liked last time."

"Thank you." Stu's expression softened as he ushered me into the living room. "I'll return to said ice and the couch if you want to grab plates from the kitchen."

I'd spent enough time here over the last month or so that I

knew where he kept the plates and silverware. I fetched us each a beer, noting he now kept my favorite brand alongside his. *Cozy.* My stomach twisted again, suddenly none too sure about dinner.

When I returned to the living room, Stu had set the food on the coffee table before stretching out on his couch, ice packs on his ankle, knee, and ribs.

"You should have let us take you in," I scolded as I dished up a plate of food for him. "I don't like seeing you hurt."

"I'm not hurt." Stu struggled to sit up, wincing again as he accepted the plate. "Maybe a little banged up. But I'm okay."

"I'm going to check your ribs." I glowered at him. "What if you cracked something?"

"I didn't. I'm just old and creaky." Stu submitted, allowing me to feel around his torso until he finally pushed me toward my plate of food. "Go eat, Percy."

"Okay." I stayed quiet while we ate, barely managing to choke down half of my usual portion.

"What's wrong?" Stu asked at last.

I opened my mouth, fully prepared to make a joke, but what came out instead was, "You matter to me."

"And that's a bad thing?" Stu blinked.

All I could do was shrug. I pursed my lips. My expression was likely sullen, but I couldn't help it. This was a fucking crisis, and he couldn't see it.

"Look. I get it." Stu patted my jeans-covered knee. "Divorce sucks. Having your heart broken sucks. But discovering it might still work doesn't have to be a bad thing."

"Says the eternal optimist." I huffed. Stu had nailed it, as usual. I was upset to discover I cared about him and all that implied while he took my revelation in stride. "I'm not sure I'm ready for the risk of dating."

"How exactly is dating different from what we're already doing?" Stu's tone was kind yet logical. "You might call it friends with benefits, but you care about my well-being. You're over every night my kids aren't here. You ask how my day went via text even if we don't see each other. You send me dirty memes."

"Oh God." I sank back against the couch. *We're dating. Fuck.*"

"The horrors." Stu rolled his eyes at me before abruptly setting aside his ice packs and standing. He grabbed our plates and gathered trash. His movements weren't exactly upset, but they were far more efficient than I usually associated with Stu.

"What are you doing?"

"Cleaning up in case the kids come back, and so I can show you the door." He gestured toward the front door. "I like you, Percy. A lot. But I like—and respect—me more."

"I didn't mean I don't want to date *you*. I don't want to date anyone." I tried to backpedal, but Stu shook his head mournfully.

"I know my limitations, but I also know my worth. I've enjoyed the last month more than I can say."

"Me too," I whispered.

"But not enough to date me." Stu exhaled harshly. "If you want to run from this being something real and good, I won't chase you."

"Oh." My jaw fell open, and I stumbled toward the door. I needed to say something quickly, but I had no clue what.

"Good night, Percy." And with that, Stu shut the door on our evening, our future as friends with benefits, and on a piece of my heart.

No. He couldn't have my heart. Could he?

The last six weeks or so of my life flashed through my brain. Stu laughing as we played the video game. Stu feeding me spicy chicken. Stu looking blissed out after sex. Stu showing me his latest painting. Stu welcoming me in with a grin.

Oh fuck. I'd gone and fallen for the guy.

I stumbled back to my place, unlocked the door, and threw myself into my recliner. The same recliner I'd been dozing in when Stu had arrived with a hot dish and rocked my world. I surveyed my blank walls, brown couch, and perfectly boring existence. This was what I had to look forward to. I could go back to flirting with strangers, living my life in monochrome, a word I now knew because, apparently, I'd been unintentionally dating an art teacher.

Fuck me.

Or rather, fuck, Stu. Had I ever had a better sex partner? Ever? He was feisty and competitive outside of bed, submissive and pliant in it, and brought the same creativity to sex that he did everything else. He made me feel sexy and powerful. Did I really want to give that up?

Did he want to give that up? He'd been only too happy to show me the door. Maybe he was getting tired of me too. A siren sounded in the distance, and I reflexively reached for my phone, making sure I wasn't getting called in. However, even after I verified there wasn't a missed message, my pulse continued to pound. I felt like I had as a kid after losing my dad, when every siren had made me think of him.

Oh. Stu knew loss and pain too. We shared that early wound. He just hid it better. All the evidence I had from the last month said he liked me as much as I liked him. I was the one being stupid, but we were both running scared.

Well, shit. I glanced down at my silent phone again. How exactly did one ask out the guy he'd been dating for the last month?

Chapter Six

Stu

Lately, all I wanted to paint was trees. Big, bushy, evergreen trees. Pine trees and cedar. Hillsides covered in trees. Mountain valleys. Close-up studies of individual trees. Trees. Trees. Trees. I'd never used so much green paint in a week before. My latest painting was a tall, narrow tree with speckles of frost on the branches. I was attempting to add a squat little pine cone when the doorbell sounded.

Both kids were home, so I wasn't too concerned. Likely a friend of theirs or a salesperson Soren could dispense with as easily as I. Besides, I was in a terrible mood and had been all week. I went back to the pine cone only to hear Shelby behind me.

"Dad. The paramedic guy is back."

"Tell him I'm fine." I didn't bother turning around. And yes, I was being all kinds of chicken, but avoiding Percy had served me well thus far. "Ankle is all healed. I'll text him later."

"Tell him yourself," Shelby shot back, and I whirled to find Percy standing alongside Shelby.

"Oh." I swallowed hard. "Hey, Percy."

"I'm making loco moco for dinner." Shelby's cooking phase had continued after the school year started, and she was now having fun exploring many of the Hawaiian dishes of my childhood. She gestured between Percy and me. "You should ask Percy to stay."

"I don't think..." I trailed off because she was already heading back to the house, undoubtedly as sick of my mopey mood as I was. And now that Shelby was gone, I was alone with Percy, who looked at me expectantly.

"So, you're fine?"

"Yeah." I stretched out my healed leg. "All better."

"That doesn't explain why you've been avoiding me." He gave me a harsh stare. And he wasn't wrong. I'd ducked into my car rather than do the driveway wave thing and left two texts on Read.

"I wasn't sure what there was to say." I shrugged, fully aware I sounded closer to Shelby's age than Percy's.

"Plenty." He blew out a breath. "Would you like to go somewhere with me on Saturday night?"

"Go?" I blinked. "Where? Why?"

"I'm asking you on a date, Stu." Percy sounded less than thrilled about this fact.

"Oh." I let my jaw hang open for several long seconds. "You sure you want to do that?"

"I miss you." He spread his hands wide like holding an empty basket. And lord knew I missed him too. I hadn't realized how much we'd fallen into a routine with daily texts, funny memes, and frequent visits until it was gone.

"I've missed you too," I admitted.

"And you're the one who pointed out we've pretty much been dating. You deserve the real deal. Let me take you out."

I nodded, considering this as I stared at my row of tree paintings. Somehow, it was easier to point it out when I'd assumed Percy was bailing on us than to accept his invite. I wanted what we had back, but I remained doubtful that Percy truly wanted to stick around.

"You deserve it too. I don't want you dating me out of guilt or something." I continued to stare at my paintings. Taken together like this, I'd made a whole forest. Funny how I'd thought I was just painting trees.

"I'm not." Percy stepped forward, placing a hand on my shoulder. "I didn't want to let myself miss being in a relationship, but hanging around you the last month reminded me that I like having a person. And I want that person to be you."

"Oh." The air whooshed out of me. It had been so very long since I'd been chosen like that. I'd said I wanted to date, but the truth was I had just as many, if not more, doubts as Percy. "I'm kind of a package deal. Not everyone is up for dating a single dad."

"Do I look scared off?" Percy gently applied pressure to my neck until I was forced to meet his steady gaze. "I like your kids. I'll follow your lead in terms of when you want to tell them we're more than friends, but I'm good with dating you. All of you."

"Okay." That reply wasn't particularly brimming with

enthusiasm, so I let my head fall onto his shoulder. "What if we've both forgotten how to date?"

Shrugging, Percy tugged me closer. "Then we'll remember together. I won't lie and say I've got it all figured out. We've both been burned before. But I don't want to let a good thing go because I'm scared."

Oh. I'm scared. I looked down at my forest of tree paintings. I'd been so focused on Percy's rejection that I'd been running from my own fears. And Percy was right. We couldn't let those worries keep us from trying. I didn't want to have regrets. And I sure as hell didn't want to watch him date someone else, see strange cars in his driveway, while knowing I could have had a chance.

"Good point." I gave a decisive nod. "Let's do this thing."

Chapter Seven

Stu

Saturday, I dropped the kids off at their mother's place, then continued into downtown, where I met Percy at The Heist, a restaurant located in a historic bank building. Neither of us had been able to come up with a better date idea than dinner out, followed by an artsy-looking indie movie at the small downtown theater.

"You look nice." Percy greeted me outside the glass front doors of the The Heist. This might have been the first time he'd seen me in something other than a T-shirt. In deference to this being an actual date, I'd donned a seldom-worn light-teal button-down shirt and khaki pants.

"So do you." I gestured at his white shirt and crisp jeans. Geez. We were reduced to making small talk about our clothing choices. "We could skip all this awkwardness and go back to your place instead."

"We'll get there." Percy sounded unruffled as he opened

the door. "Do us both good to wait long enough to get dinner."

Inside The Heist, we were greeted by the owner, Magnus, who moved in some of the same circles as us.

"Percy. Your usual IPA?" Magnus asked, affable as ever. Like Percy, the guy was naturally charming. I wondered if Percy would flirt with him if he were there alone. "And, Stu?"

"I'll have what he's having," I said as we found a table on the other side of the large, polished wooden bar.

"Are you jealous?" Percy asked as soon as we were alone.

"Of Magnus?" I played dumb.

"I'm pretty sure he's hung up on his new landlord and my coworker." Percy kept a conversational tone. "And I'm a friendly guy. I know I have a bit of a reputation as a flirt, but when I date someone, I date them. Despite how everything ended with Hector, I'm still a one-person sort of guy."

"Good to know." I managed a small smile. "So you're saying this thing could be exclusive?"

"Better be," Percy growled, the first time I'd seen his possessiveness outside of the bedroom. "I haven't seen anyone else since you brought me that hot dish."

"Me either." And it wasn't simply from a lack of opportunity either. "Haven't wanted to."

"Same." He took my hands across the table. "You're all I can think about, Stu."

"Good." I squeezed his hand back. "No one else I'd rather send memes to at two a.m. So we're going to do this thing? All in?"

"We are." Percy nodded sharply. "And, amazingly, I'm optimistic. I think you're rubbing off on me."

"Am I now?" I leered at him.

"You are, and I couldn't be happier." Percy dropped my hand as our beers arrived.

"Me too." The last two months since that hot dish played out in my brain. I was happier than I'd been since landing in Mount Hope. I liked Percy, liked what he brought to my life, liked the potential of this thing between us. He was strong and steady and exactly bossy enough. He did make me happy, and I hoped I could do the same for him. "I think I'm going to like dating you."

"Here's to us." He raised his beer at me, and I did the same.

Us. I liked the sound of that a lot.

Chapter Eight

Percy

Eighteen months later

"To the left. No, right." Stu directed my movements in an awkward dance. A giant canvas served as my dance partner, and only for Stu would I put up with this level of indecisive perfectionism. "Back again. Okay. Perfect."

"You sure?" I teased as I settled the painting in place. "Don't need me to move it again?"

"It's good." Stu gave me a sheepish smile. "I just want everything to be perfect."

"It already is." I gestured at the living room and its collection of boxes and furniture. My recliner jockeyed for space with his couch and colorful end tables. We had a ways to go on unpacking, yet we'd already come so far. "I don't have to cross the street to say good morning anymore."

"True." Stu joined me in admiring the painting, a large

piece commemorating the trip to the coast we'd taken in July for our one-year anniversary. Strolling on the rocky Oregon beach near the Rainbow Cove resort that weekend, we'd first daydreamed about living together. Our places were on the small side, and Stu had already been thinking about buying rather than renting. We'd settled on a plan of him buying and me paying him rent instead of my existing landlord. Practical. But also so much fun, spending the fall house hunting with him, settling on a fixer-upper just off the historic Prospect Place row of older homes in Mount Hope. "I can't wait to see what we do with the place."

"Me too." I pulled him in for a fast kiss, only to be interrupted by footsteps on the stairs.

"*Dad.*" Shelby gave her typical long-suffering sigh. "When you're done kissing, I finally picked the colors for my room."

"Colors plural?" I'd impulsively volunteered to help Stu paint her new room, but the scheme was fast exceeding my modest DIY skills, not that Shelby seemed to mind.

"Yep." She nodded. Both kids had adapted to having me around better than I'd hoped. Shelby liked having us around to taste-test her latest creations, and Soren had warmed up enough to occasionally game with Stu and me. "I'll go grab the paint samples to show you."

"Is it too much?" Stu asked softly, and I knew he meant more than just the painting project. Dating a single dad wasn't always easy, but it certainly was worth it.

"Not at all." I shook my head and held him close. "I like all the color. You've brought so much to my life, Stu."

"Same." He stretched to brush a kiss on my cheek. "I love you."

"I love you too." It wasn't something we said lightly. We'd been months into dating before admitting to the feelings that had been growing from the start. But every time we said the words, my chest went warm with how right it felt to love and be loved by Stu.

The next day, we were finishing up work on Shelby's aqua walls when the sound of multiple teens coming in the front door filtered up the stairs.

"Come see my room," Shelby said loudly, undoubtedly also a warning to not be kissing when she and her friends came upstairs. "My dads are almost done."

Knees going wobbly, I gulped. "Did she just say…?"

"Might have been a slip." Stu's mouth twisted, eyes turning uncertain. "I can ask her not to."

"No. I…I like it." My throat was tight and thick with emotion. For all I'd sworn I'd never marry again, I was already planning to ask Stu—and the kids—soon, maybe on another trip to the coast. "I like it a lot."

"You're part of the family now." Stu gazed deep into my eyes. "No takebacks."

"You're my family too." And he was. I'd updated my emergency contacts at work to include him, and with every shared holiday and milestone, I fell a little more in love and a little more certain of our future together. "You and the kids."

"Good." Stu snuck one last, fast kiss. "We're keeping you."

. . .

I hope you loved Stu and Percy's story and their happy ending, which is part of my Mount Hope universe. You can start the series with the prequel novella *Among Friends* and enjoy the happily ever afters for many of the characters mentioned in this story. Tony, Caleb, Tate, and Eric all have love stories to enjoy. I also sprinkled in a few other Easter eggs for eagle-eyed readers, including a mention of my Rainbow Cove series. If you enjoyed this story, I hope you check out my extensive backlist! There is a story for every mood, each as warm and welcoming as a hot dish.

About the Author

Annabeth Albert is a multi-published Pacific Northwest romance writer. Emotionally complex, sexy, and funny stories are her favorites both to read and to write. Fans of quirky, Oregon-set books as well as those who enjoy military heroes will want to check out her many series. Her critically acclaimed and fan-favorite LGBTQ romances include the Mount Hope, A-List Security, Safe Harbor, Out of Uniform, and other series along with several stand-alone titles. Her fan group, Annabeth's Angels, on Facebook is a great place for bonus content and exclusive contests.

For more info: www.annabethalbert.com

Newsletter: http://eepurl.com/Nb9yv

Fan group: https://www.facebook.com/groups/ annabethsangels/

Piece Of Cake

Beth Bolden

Chapter One

A pomegranate flew through the air, trailing seeds as it arced across the kitchen.

Marco Moretti ducked with plenty of time to spare, but then grimaced as half a dozen plums pelted him next, each of them hitting him on his white chef's coat with a soft squish, leaving behind tracks of pale orange pulp.

"You're an asshole!" Izzy shrieked, launching another attack with a handful of grapes. These hit a lot harder than the plums. Maybe because of the way they resembled small bullets, or because Marco had gotten closer, to try to prevent additional weaponized fruit.

"I'm sorry," Marco said, between clenched teeth. Maybe he *was* an asshole. Maybe he deserved death by fruit bowl.

But he'd certainly never made Izzy any promises, and he'd thought they were on the same page. The page where she worked for him, they were friendly, and that was it. But when she'd announced she'd taken the pastry job at his restaurant because she'd assumed *he* came with the compensation package, he'd needed to set her straight.

"I can't fucking believe you! You flirted with me! We had a drink! Twice!" Izzy was panting now, hands deep in one of the bins of fruit. He hoped to God she didn't find a pineapple or melon or coconut in there. He might not survive that.

His sister Marcella would tell him that he'd deserve it.

Well, a *little*, anyway. When he'd been young and stupid, he'd had precisely two relationships with employees, and he'd long since learned it was 1) a terrible idea and 2) wrong on a fundamental level. But his reputation had only grown, despite every attempt he made to change it.

"I was being nice!" Marco didn't usually get pissed off. That was his eldest brother Luca. Marco *had* a temper, but it was buried deep, under layers of other emotions.

He hadn't meant to do this. He'd thought he and Izzy were becoming friends. And if she touched him more than his other friends, casually, on the back and on the neck, well, that was just her way, right?

It turned out her friendliness had *not* been because it was her way. She'd shown up at Nonna's with expectations and Marco, unaware and trying to be a friend and a good boss, had only exacerbated them, not tempered them.

After family dinner tonight, when he came by the back pastry kitchen to check Izzy's progress with the special order cake, she'd sidled right up to him, kissed him firmly, and told him, "It's time."

Marco had been bewildered. Then incredulous. And then annoyed.

Thus, why he was currently defending himself like a fruit ninja.

"Nice would've been not leading me on," Izzy barked, thankfully crossing her arms over her chest. "Making me *like* you."

Marco winced. He didn't want to explain to Izzy, who seemed like a nice enough girl, that she wouldn't be the first or the last to get sucked in by his inadvertent Moretti-ness.

The whole family possessed it—good looks and some amount of charm were sprinkled generously through their family tree—though Marco was the only one this kept happening to.

Gabe, his younger brother, would tell him that the Moretti genes used him instead of Marco wielding *them*. But Marco had never been interested in that.

He just wanted to put his head down and enjoy the work that brought him so much joy—owning this restaurant in his grandmother's name, one of the three that the family ran.

"I didn't mean to," Marco said, holding out his hands in mute surrender. "I'm sorry." He hesitated for a single second. "Could we get back to the cake—"

"Fuck your cake and fuck *you*. I quit," Izzy said vehemently and ripped off her apron, using it as one last bit of ammunition, hitting him square in the chest with it.

He caught the balled-up fabric and sighed as she stomped off.

"Chef?"

Marco turned towards the hesitant voice in the doorway.

It was Daniel, Izzy's young sous. He was wringing his hands, looking distressed.

Marco tried to marshal his expression into something gentler, less thunderous.

"Yes, Daniel?"

"Did Izzy leave?" Daniel was quiet and very young and had only been around a month or two longer than Izzy, who Marco had just lost in the sixth month of her employment here at Nonna's.

He needed to stop losing pastry chefs.

Especially to *this*.

"Yes, she's gone. I need you to—"

Daniel's back straightened. "I got it, Chef. The special cake for tonight, I'll take care of it."

"I'll see if I can send one of the assistants in to help you during service." Marco stopped at the doorway, next to Daniel. Normally, he'd have put a hand on his shoulder, reassuring him with a touch that he'd take care of him, but maybe that was where things had gone so wrong with Izzy—and what felt like so many men and women before her.

Why he could never convince any of them that he *wasn't* interested.

So he didn't. Marco kept his hands to himself, just gave Daniel a reassuring nod and walked off to take care of filling Izzy's job, hopefully sooner rather than later. Daniel might be able to pinch hit, but he didn't have the experience.

Marcella was in the front of the house, reviewing the night's reservations with one of the hostesses. Bea was younger even than Daniel, and Marco realized, as he shoved his hand through his unruly curly dark hair and waited for Marcella to finish her thought, he was beginning to feel old.

Marcella looked over in his direction finally. "What

happened to you?" she asked, eyeing the stains on his white coat. "And what was that yelling I heard?"

"Izzy quit."

"You make a pass at her?"

Marco shot his twin sister a glare. "I did not. And you *know* I did not."

"Ah, so she quit because you *didn't* make a pass at her," Marcella said knowingly.

Marco sighed. "Doesn't anybody just want to *work*?"

But Marcella only laughed—the calm, certain laugh of someone who was happily married with two kids. "We just need to find someone who's completely uninterested in you."

"Or, maybe, someone who's got the requisite skills and experience."

Marcella shot him an amused look. "You've got a reputation, brother mine."

"I do *not*," Marco said, though she was probably more right than he wanted to admit. Maybe he had cut a swath through Napa during his youth—but Morettis loved hard and often, and nobody could blame them, or *him*, for that. But he'd never really touched anyone at the restaurant—not since he was in his early twenties and that had seemed like a great idea.

But those blowups made Izzy's rage-quit today seem minor in comparison, so he'd learned to keep his hands off anyone he worked with, years ago. Even if he was tempted.

Maybe he should have led with that.

Or maybe Izzy's heart eyes would've guaranteed he'd have ended up with a girlfriend he didn't really want and still no pastry chef.

61

"I didn't say you'd earned it necessarily, but it's there all the same," Marcella said gently, leaning against the wood-paneled entryway. "You're not cold, like Luca was. You're available. You're passionate about what you do and your family and you're good-looking—"

Marco opened his mouth to interrupt her.

But Marcella was too quick. Or knew him too well. "Do not even argue with me about this. You're a catch. Thirty-seven and unmarried."

"I'm not the problem," Marco said sulkily. "And what am I supposed to do? I can't just become different."

"No, I know, darling," Marcella said, patting him affectionately. "We just need to find someone immune." She hesitated. "Did you hear that Andrew is back in town?"

"Andrew?" The name sounded familiar, but Marco couldn't place it off the top of his head.

"Andrew. My best friend from high school," Marcella said, looking amused. "He went to Paris, to pastry school. Remember now?"

"Oh. Yes." He'd been tall and skinny and had always followed Marcella around like a gangly duckling.

"Well, he's back in town. He's thinking about opening his own bakery, but he hasn't found a location yet. I bet you could convince him to work for you for a bit, train Daniel up." Her voice dropped. "That kid is wildly in love with Bea, who barely notices he exists, so he wouldn't be interested in you. Win-win."

Marco rolled his eyes. "Why don't *you* convince Andrew to work for me and train Daniel? He's your friend."

"And your friend, too." Marcella shot him a chiding look. "Surely you remember that."

It had been almost twenty years, but now that Marco was thinking about him, he had a lot of memories with Andrew. Mostly revolving around food or Marcella.

Had he gotten distracted and sort of forgotten about the guy since he'd left and gone to France? Yes, he had—but then he'd been fairly busy himself, graduating from the Culinary Institute of America in Napa and then starting and running this higher-end evolution of his family's restaurant brand.

"Sure," Marco said, because agreeing with Marcella was usually easier than arguing with her.

"Go talk to him," Marcella said. "And be nice."

"I'm always nice," Marco grumbled. He was at least nicer than their older brother Luca.

"Actually maybe . . .maybe don't be *too* nice," Marcella said, wincing. "You don't want the guy to fall in love with you."

"Don't worry," Marco said. "That's not going to happen."

But that was because Marco was already determined to be more careful this time around. More aware, anyway. The Andrew he remembered had not once pinged anywhere on his attraction meter. And he found a lot of people attractive—or at least he used to. It should be easy enough to keep his distance.

This time, Marco would make sure he didn't get too friendly or invite Andrew for a drink. He'd keep their lines clear: he was the boss and Andrew was an employee.

If Marcella's plan worked out—and it was Marcella,

which meant it probably would—today's pomegranate would be the very last he had to duck.

Chapter Two

Marco got Andrew's phone number from Marcella and texted the next morning, explaining who he was and what he was interested in offering.

He hadn't had to wait long for an answer. It had come in less than five minutes later. **Let's talk**, the text read. **11 AM, the Coffee Beanery.**

At eleven, Marco would normally be at the restaurant, prepping for the day's service, but he decided that to fix this whole pastry situation, he could duck out for a few minutes.

After making sure his sous knew what needed to be done, Marco jumped in his car and drove the ten minutes over to the Coffee Beanery, which also happened to be *his* favorite coffee shop in the area.

At least Andrew had good taste in espresso.

When Marco walked in, there wasn't anyone in line at the counter and maybe half of the dozen tables in the quaint, wood-paneled space were full. But nobody who looked even vaguely like he remembered Andrew stood out to him.

Marco glanced at his watch, but he was five minutes late, already, probably because he'd swung by the pastry kitchen on his way out, making sure Daniel was set for the afternoon of prep work.

Had Andrew not even shown up on time? Well, that was disappointing. Marco glanced around one more time and satisfied that Andrew definitely wasn't among the current customers, pulled his phone out of his pocket as he approached the front counter. He'd just send a quick text before he ordered a latte, making sure Andrew was still planning to show.

"Marco?"

The voice behind him made Marco turn.

And the man rising from one of the nearby tables, made him stop—body and heart and brain—in his tracks.

If this was Andrew . . .

Well, if this was Andrew, he was fucked.

Because Andrew wasn't scrawny any longer.

He'd filled out his tall frame, a plain white T-shirt clinging to defined biceps and pectorals. The acne that had dogged him during his teenage years had cleared up and he'd grown into his face, golden-brown scruff covering a jawline that could cut glass.

"Fuck me," Marco muttered under his breath.

"Yeah, you *are* Marco," Andrew said with a charming smile that he *definitely* had not possessed in high school.

He *had* had those eyes in high school, hadn't he? They

66

were a flawless azure blue, and Marco could see himself getting lost . . .so fucking lost . . .

He dragged his brain—and his dick—back to sanity.

"Yes," Marco said, shaking his outstretched hand and getting a brief impression of a firm strength and calluses. Ignoring the sparks that raced up his arm.

What he should do was tell Andrew that he was sorry but he couldn't hire him.

As for why . . .maybe it would be better to be honest?

Sorry, but you're too freaking hot and I'm way too freaking attracted to you for us to ever work together.

But it wasn't going to be forever, was it? No. Andrew only needed to come in, spend a few weeks, maybe a month or two, in Marco's kitchen, not even his *main* kitchen, but his back pastry kitchen, and train Daniel to be able to deal with whatever came his way.

It would be embarrassing to admit, even to practically a stranger, that he couldn't handle that.

"You've seen Marcella since you've been back?" Marco said, taking a seat opposite Andrew.

He tilted his head towards a cup of coffee in front of Marco. "Yeah, a few times. I got what Marcella said you liked," Andrew said.

Great. Marcella knew Andrew looked like this now, and she'd *still* suggested Marco hire him, while also simultaneously lecturing Marco about how irresistible he apparently was, just by fucking breathing.

He and Marcella were going to have words later. He desperately loved his twin, but she could also be a massive pain in his ass.

But first, he needed to *seal the deal.*

Nope. Do not go there.

First, he needed to *hire the guy.*

Better.

"We're looking for a pastry chef, for Nonna's. *My* Nonna's, the high-end steakhouse," Marco said. "Marcella said you were looking for work."

He sipped his coffee and to his surprise, *yes,* Andrew had asked Marcella what his regular order was, because the latte was perfect.

Andrew shrugged. "Yeah, that's true. But I'm not looking for something permanent. You'd want to hire someone who's sticking around. Eventually, I'll be opening my own bakery."

"Well, about that . . .we do have an assistant who I think has a great future, but Daniel's young. Needs guidance. More training than I have time for. That would be the plan. Get us through the next month or so. Get Daniel trained."

Andrew tapped his finger against the tabletop. "I'll give you a week. You're open what, six nights a week?"

Marco nodded, not liking this. He needed a lot longer than a week.

"Okay, six nights of service. And if it's alright, if I like it, if this Daniel is as good as you think, I'll give you two months."

Marco opened his mouth, not really liking how Andrew was acting like *they* needed *him.*

Don't be stupid, you do need him. That was Marcella's voice in his head, lecturing him about the unfortunate realities of the situation.

"Okay," Marco said. He named a figure for each night of

service, and Andrew tilted his head, those blue eyes nearly impossible to read.

"Make it fifty bucks more a night, and I'll do it," Andrew said.

Marco was annoyed Andrew was acting like he was doing them a favor *and* negotiating a higher pay grade, but they did need him. He could call up their staffing agency and get another temp, but it wouldn't be someone he'd trust, or someone who could train Daniel.

And God only knew, it might be someone else who'd fall in love with him.

Marco was *done* dodging pomegranates.

"Fine," Marco said, extending a hand, and Andrew took it, shaking on the deal.

"I'll start tomorrow night," Andrew said.

Despite all his vows to himself, he'd let Andrew handle this whole fucking negotiation. *Because he unsettled you. You didn't expect him to be so fucking hot.*

Marco forced himself to focus. "Why did you agree to meet me if you weren't looking for a job?" He hadn't mentioned the job was temporary when he'd texted him.

The corner of Andrew's mouth—even that was fucking beautiful—tilted up in a smile. "Maybe I was curious how you grew up."

He hadn't been curious at all about how Andrew had grown up.

But that had been his own stupidity, imagining that the guy would still look like a gangly eighteen-year-old, not someone who'd just spent the last nineteen years in Paris.

"Curiosity satisfied?" Marco wondered gruffly.

"Almost," Andrew teased.

Marco needed to get a fucking grip.

The irony was that just yesterday he'd been dodging fruit missiles and he hadn't earned any of those, but this guy . . .well, Marco might deserve to be pelted by a whole fucking orchard if he did half the things his imagination was picturing.

He would keep everything focused on business.

Business was what mattered.

Marco dragged his focus back. "I'll have Dario text you a link to our HR system. Get you set up."

"Dario? Dario works for you now? I remember when he was barely a teenager, obsessed with comic books."

And I remember when you were scrawny and plain and your smile wasn't guaranteed to keep me up at night.

"Ah yeah, he's . . .uh . . .he basically runs the empire now."

"Not Luca?"

"I thought you'd seen Marcella since you'd been back?" Marco wanted to be annoyed by his charm, but he wasn't.

"Oh, but we talked all about *my* exploits," Andrew teased. "She wanted to know all about Paris and Sweden and Barcelona."

"You lived in Sweden and Barcelona?"

Andrew waved a hand. "Oh, I've been all around. Was definitely ready to come back, stretch my muscles a bit. But when I left, Luca had just taken over and I had a feeling even then you'd have had to pry out any control from his cold, dead hands."

"Six years ago, he went to South Carolina to fix my aunt's

deli. Fell in love with the guy who ran the bakery there and basically . . .well, he's not here, so I can say it." Marco grinned. "He finally ran away from home."

"And now Dario runs everything," Andrew said, looking surprised.

"Yep, in his own painfully competent way. Of course don't tell Luca that. He still thinks he's got a finger in every pie here, and he does try, but he's got his own mini empire over in Indigo Bay. A husband. Three businesses. His hands are plenty full."

"I never thought he'd leave Napa. Kind of like I never thought I'd come back," Andrew mused.

"Why *did* you?" Marco wanted to know, even though he had no reason to ask. All he'd probably have to do was ask Marcella. She could squeeze hot gossip out of a dry turnip.

Andrew shrugged. "Same old story. Bad breakup. Lost my job."

He didn't seem bothered by this confession. In fact, it felt a little rehearsed. And Marco couldn't help but notice that he hadn't added any details at all.

"And now you're going to open a bakery back in your hometown."

"Seemed like a good idea, if I didn't want to work for anyone again." Andrew flashed another of those undeniably charming smiles that Marco kept trying to pretend didn't give him butterflies.

Marcella liked to tell him that he loved love, that he *liked* feeling it, indulging in it, liked to get swept away.

And Marco felt that a little now, the urge to do his best to charm this man.

Of course, that would probably only lead to more pomegranates launched at his head.

So he didn't. He straightened.

"Working for me is a bad way to not work for anyone else again." He'd attempted to remind both of them that he was Andrew's boss now, but Marco was all too aware of the flirtatious undercurrent in his tone. He hadn't even meant to sound like that. Maybe Marcella was right and it was too much a part of him to turn off.

"Maybe, but it's only temporary."

"Right. Temporary." It was exactly what Marco wanted, but he found himself disliking this label already.

"Besides," Andrew said, "you need me. I saw a few comments on reviews I read, talking about a 'predictable' and even 'pedestrian' dessert selection. Ricotta cheesecake, Marco? Cannoli?"

"They're classics for a reason," Marco said defensively. "The menu doesn't change."

"Sure," Andrew said easily, and Marco imagined that three or four nights from now, there would be some spectacular new item on the menu and they would argue about it. Marco would pretend that he was annoyed by it, instead of secretly thrilled that this gorgeous, talented, charismatic man wanted to leave his imprint on Marco's restaurant forever.

Leave his imprint on *him* forever.

Marco dragged his attention back to where it mattered. *Business.*

"The menu doesn't change," Marco repeated firmly. They didn't need to get into any flirty arguments and he definitely did *not* need to be imprinted. Not now and definitely not in six nights.

"Alright, alright, I'll pretend those reviews don't exist." Andrew flashed him such a great smile it took the sting right out of what he'd repeated.

"You'd better," Marco said and stood now, because if he stayed, he was going to want to keep talking to Andrew. He was going to want to keep flirting. Ask about Paris. Barcelona. Sweden. About the bad breakup, even.

And of course, because he had a service to prepare for.

"See you tomorrow at ten," Marco said, picking up his latte so he wouldn't do something stupid like offer his hand again, so he'd have an excuse to touch Andrew again.

No more unnecessary touches.

As the door to the Coffee Beanery swung shut behind him, Marco swore he felt a phantom pomegranate sail right over his head. But he ignored it.

Chapter Three

Night One

"**B**ehind!" Theo, Marco's sous, called out as he carried a steaming hot pan from the stove to the prep station.

Marco glanced at the list of tickets in front him, nodding absently as he absorbed the sounds of the busy kitchen around him. Everything was working like clockwork, an hour into dinner service.

He could take a minute to duck back to the pastry kitchen and make sure everything was all set. It was Andrew's first night, and even though he was clearly eminently capable, it would be the right thing to do to check on him.

If it was anyone else, Marco would've done it without thinking.

But Andrew was not anyone else, and he was afraid of what he'd feel if he went back there. Attraction, without a doubt, and the insistent, dizzying pull to give in to it.

When he'd texted Marcella, annoyed that she had still

suggested Andrew, she'd replied obliquely, saying that, **Everyone grows up, even you Marco.**

He'd intended to confront her about it, but when she'd shown up to do her nightly tour of the front of the house, he'd been busy, prepping for family dinner, and hadn't had a second to spare.

By the time he had, she was gone. On purpose, he was convinced.

But none of that changed the problem at hand: Andrew, currently working in *his* pastry kitchen.

They were about an hour into service, which meant he'd be starting desserts shortly, if he hadn't already.

Marco took a deep breath, straightened his white coat, and headed to do his duty.

Except that when he walked in, Andrew's back was to him, his caramel-brown hair covered in a blue bandana, his broad shoulders perfectly framed in white, a matching blue apron tied around a trim waist, and it didn't feel like a duty at all.

Daniel was staring at him. Probably because he was staring at Andrew.

"Uh, hey there," Marco stammered. "Everything going okay?"

Andrew turned. He'd been whipping cream in a bowl, by hand. His coat sleeves were rolled up, exposing tanned, muscled forearms that were clearly capable of whipping cream by hand.

"Everything's fine, Chef," Daniel said. He glanced over at Andrew, and it was clear that even though Andrew had been on the premises for eight hours, he was already competing with Bea for Daniel's adoration. A different kind of adoration, almost certainly. But still. Marco shouldn't have been envious that Daniel could stare at him with that worshipful expression, but he felt an undeniable pulse of jealousy.

"More than fine," Andrew agreed easily. "We've sent out some plates already."

"There's some . . .uh . . .older generation that likes to eat early." According to Marcella, he was a charmer and a heartbreaker without even trying, but he just felt awkward and out of his depth now.

"Right," Andrew said, nodding easily.

"Much earlier than I'm sure you're used to. In uh . . .Paris. Or Barcelona."

"It's fine. I'm adapting." Andrew tilted his head towards the prep counter. "Would you like to try anything?"

It was a normal suggestion. Marco should have even been the one to suggest it, to make sure that every single dish exiting his kitchen was as flawless as the Nonna's reputation.

If they'd been in his regular kitchen, he'd already be cutting a narrow slice of the cheesecake, asking to taste a bite of the tiramisu. Checking the cannoli filling to make sure it lived up to every bit of his Nonna's famous recipe.

Instead, he'd been staring at Andrew like he wanted to eat *him* instead.

"Sure, yes, of course." Marco watched as Andrew nodded at Daniel, who efficiently prepared him a plate with small tastes of every one of their desserts. Handed him a fork.

It shouldn't have felt erotic to slide a forkful of cheesecake into his mouth in front of Andrew, but it did.

The flush on Andrew's cheeks made Marco wonder if it wasn't just him.

Made him *hope* it wasn't just him.

Marco dragged his attention back to the dessert.

It was exactly as he hoped. Silky and creamy, the crust nutty and perfectly browned. But with the faintest hint of something else. Something unexpected and undeniably delicious.

For a single beat and then two, he and Andrew stared at each other.

Every chef put a slightly different variation on recipes. It was inevitable. But when the cheesecake, always delicious, tasted that much better, Marco wanted to ask why.

He should've asked why.

This was his kitchen. His responsibility. One he took seriously.

"It's different," he said mildly.

"I know," Daniel burst out, his voice full of excitement. "Andrew had me—"

Marco held up a hand. "I don't need to know, but it's good. It's . . .it's nice."

But he did want to know. He wanted to pin Andrew to that counter with his body, trapping him, until he was mush under his hands and his mouth and Andrew was not only willing to reveal all his secrets, he was desperate to do it.

"Thought it might be," Andrew said, his words the much milder version of the confidence written plainly across his handsome face.

"And the rest, it's good too," Marco said, once he'd tried

everything. Everything else was the same. Perfectly and expertly executed, yes, but the flavors the same.

"Daniel has been great showing me the ropes of how things are done here," Andrew volunteered, giving Daniel a nod of approval.

Daniel fucking glowed.

Probably the way Marco would glow, if he allowed himself to.

It was a good sign, how well Daniel had taken to Andrew, and even better that Andrew understood how important it was that Daniel felt valued and respected in this kitchen.

It was exactly what Marco himself would've said.

That should have made him feel better, made him feel certain he could return to the big kitchen and put any worries of desserts out of his head. But it didn't.

Andrew resumed whipping his cream, his grip firm on the whisk, the muscles of his forearms flexing enticingly.

There was no reason for Marco to stay, except that he didn't want to leave.

Like Andrew was reading Marco's mind, he asked, "Do your pastry chefs ever help out with the family meal?"

During their initial tour this morning, Marco had gone over the schedule for the family meal all the staff shared in the late afternoon, and how every one of his line cooks had a day of the week.

"Uh, Izzy didn't want to, so I . . .uh . . ." Marco hesitated. This was probably why she'd thought he was right on board with her growing feelings, because she'd complained about it, and he'd conceded, without much argument. He'd been *trying* to be flexible, trying to prevent unnecessary drama, but he could see how she'd taken it a different way entirely.

"I don't have a problem taking a day," Andrew said. "Unless you're concerned I can't cook."

It was ludicrous. The man had spent the last twenty years in Michelin starred kitchens. He was probably a better cook than Marco was, sweet *or* savory.

"No, no, you're . . .uh . . .yes," Marco stammered.

When he'd asked Marcella about Andrew's credentials, she'd simply snorted and told Marco to google him.

But Marco didn't want to find out about Andrew from the computer. He wanted to find out about Andrew from *Andrew.*

Stupid.

Still, even without Marco being intimately familiar with his resume, it was clear he knew his way around the kitchen.

"Good," Andrew said with a firm nod and went back to his whipped cream.

Daniel was busy plating a ticket that had just printed out and there was really no earthly reason for him to stay.

So, Marco left.

Wishing the whole time that he'd found an excuse to linger.

Three hours later, he emerged from the nearly clean kitchens to the main dining room to find Dario doing a run through inspection.

"Hey, little brother," Marco said, patting him on the back. Dario he could touch, freely, without concerns, and it felt good to do that, again. To not worry about watching himself every minute of every day.

"I saw you brought in Andrew for the pastry job," Dario said absently, straightening a gleaming glass on the table, already re-set for tomorrow's service. "How's he working out?"

"Beautifully, but then you probably already know that." Dario knew everything. He didn't run the business with Luca's iron hand, but that was probably better for everyone—including Luca.

"I had Natalia send a cannoli to the office, so I could make sure," Dario agreed, referring to his wife.

Marco revised his earlier thought. Dario had just as much of an iron hand as Luca, he was just less obvious about it.

"Did you try the cheesecake?" Marco was trying to be subtle about it, but he wanted to talk to *someone* about how good it had been because he was still thinking about it, the flavor of it still lingering on his tongue.

"No?" Dario looked concerned. "Was there something wrong with it?"

"The opposite."

"It's always good." Dario straightened another glass. Pulled out his phone and made a note—probably to remind the bussers that when they were re-setting the tables to make sure their lines were straight.

"This was better, somehow. The same, and also different, and also *more* the same."

Dario looked up at him, and Marco was suddenly and painfully aware that he was ranting.

"Is this going to be another Izzy? Or James? Or Meredith? Or—"

"Enough," Marco said stiffly. He didn't need to hear a

recitation of his love affairs—or in Izzy's case, *one-sided love affairs*. "James and Meredith happened over fifteen years ago, and Izzy was . . .well, it wasn't like that."

"I'm just asking. I thought Marcella talked to you." Dario's tone was mild. Unaccusatory.

Marco lowered his voice. "Marcella *did*. Marcella also recommended I hire her old friend Andrew *knowing* what he looks like—"

"What does he look like?" Concern blossomed in Dario's gaze.

"Well, you've seen him now, and you know what he *used* to look like, and Marcella still recommended him, all while lecturing me on how fucking irresistible I apparently am. Maybe she should've thought about that before . . .before . . ." Marco shut his mouth because even *he* could tell he'd said too much.

"And we call Gabe the emotional one," Dario teased.

"I'm not *emotional* about this," Marco straight-up lied.

He was still thinking about —still *tasting*—that goddamn cheesecake. Food always made him emotional, and that cheesecake had made him feel it *all*.

"So he grew up hot. Marco, you are thirty-seven and a great chef who runs this restaurant brilliantly. Don't tell me that a guy you knew in high school showing up hot is able to derail you like this."

Marco knew what his little brother was doing, and yet he stood up straight and played right into his hands anyway. "No, no, *no*. Of course not. I'm only interested in the cheesecake."

"Right," Dario said. The asshole was smiling now.

81

It was official. First Marcella and now Dario. His whole family had it out for him.

"I'll just . . .go ask him about it," Marco said.

"Maybe you should," Dario agreed.

But Marco didn't. When he returned to the kitchen, it was clean and almost dark for the night. He saw a light still on in the back pastry kitchen and assumed Andrew and Daniel were finishing up for the night, too.

Andrew had said he was just out of a bad breakup.

Maybe he wouldn't be affected by Marco's Moretti-ness, intended or otherwise.

But Marco was affected by his *Andrew-ness*.

So he stayed away.

Chapter Four

Night Two

Marco slept like shit.

Tossing and turning, thinking about that cheesecake, parsing every flavor he could remember, and when he did finally fall asleep, blue eyes and golden-brown scruff haunted his dreams. Taunting him with the recipe. Taunting him by stripping down to nothing. To just tanned skin and muscles and a hot smile that promised everything Marco craved.

Marco had taken a cold shower after the alarm blared, and he'd resolutely *not* touched his hard cock, because he knew if he did, he'd think about Andrew, and that was the last thing he needed.

He walked to work in a bad mood, even though it was a gorgeous summer morning. Scowling at the sky because it was the same shade of blue as Andrew's eyes didn't change a goddamn thing, either.

Marco shoved open the back door, walking into the changing room, and of course, he was there.

Sitting on the bench in front of the locker Dario had assigned him, those blue eyes gazing up at Marco as he stopped short in the doorway.

Had Andrew been waiting for him?

"Hey," Andrew said.

You are thirty-seven years old and a great chef who runs this restaurant brilliantly.

"The cheesecake," Marco said, before he could snatch the words back. "What did you do to it?"

Sorry, Dario, I tried.

"You told me not to change the menu." He was teasing again, the corner of his beautiful mouth upturned in amusement.

"Yes," Marco said brusquely. He was annoyed. But not at Andrew. At himself. He shoved his hands in the pockets of his pants and paced. Back and forth. Feeling like he was losing himself. If Andrew looked even a fraction less interested or concerned, maybe he could deal.

But no. He couldn't deal. He *wasn't* dealing.

"Are you alright?" Andrew sounded concerned.

No, he was not alright. Maybe Marcella was right. He was a Moretti, the blood running true in his veins. He wanted to fall in love. He wanted to wallow in the emotion, even as he tried to resist its inexorable allure.

"No," Marco said. "What did you do to the cheesecake?"

Andrew raised a light brown eyebrow. Marco wanted to lick it. Wanted to lick him all over. "That's what this is about? The cheesecake?"

No. And yes.

Marco nodded.

"You could've just *asked*."

And I could've just left you alone.

"I'm asking now."

"Candied orange and nutmeg," Andrew said.

"But there wasn't any—" Marco stopped abruptly. "It was the exact same texture. If you'd put candied orange in, I would've known."

"Would you have?" That eyebrow rose again.

"This one of your fancy Paris tricks?" Marco asked gruffly. He'd come even closer than he'd realized, and he was only a foot away from Andrew now, those blue eyes gazing up at him. He didn't seem bothered—he seemed . . .well, *interested*.

And he didn't seem nearly as torn about it as Marco was.

Andrew smiled. "You *also* went to culinary school. I checked."

"You checking up on me?"

He stood then, pulling himself up to his whole height. He was still an inch or two shorter than Marco. Short enough Marco would have to lean down to kiss him. "Maybe. But it's a trick *you* taught me, actually."

Marco swallowed hard. "I did?"

"I'm sure you don't remember—we were in high school, and I was over at your house. You were making marinara, and you showed me how to smash and paste the garlic so nobody would ever get a big chunk of it."

Actually, Marco *did* remember that now. He'd stood

behind Andrew, guiding his hands on the knife, making sure he'd gotten the motion of it.

"Seemed appropriate to use that trick now," Andrew said wryly. "Glad you liked it though. Assuming you liked it . . ."

"I loved it," Marco admitted. At the time, he'd been more interested in imparting the process than in the man himself. But those tables had turned.

Still, Andrew remembered that day.

Remembered well enough that he'd dug that trick out yesterday, to use in his beloved Nonna's recipe.

"You recognized me in the coffee shop," Marco said.

Andrew tilted his head. "You haven't changed much, Marco. Not in any way that actually matters. I'd have recognized you anywhere." He patted him on the shoulder, and his touch burned. "Still the same handsome, irresistible Marco Moretti."

Marco opened his mouth and then shut it again. "Marcella's been telling you stories."

"About you leaving a swath of broken hearts behind you? A little, maybe. But then, you were doing that in high school, too. Imagine my surprise when I come back home and you're still single." Andrew looked amused by this.

Marco wasn't amused by this. He wasn't someone's gossip entertainment.

"Haven't met the right person yet."

"If Marcella's to be believed, you've met lots of right people," Andrew teased. He looked right now like he wanted to be one of them.

It would be so easy to tuck him in, under his arm, and kiss him.

86

He'd probably let Marco.

But Marco didn't want to be like this. He didn't want to be at the mercy of his own desire. What really stopped him, though, was what Andrew had said before. The words that had been turning over in his head, right alongside the undefinable flavor in the cheesecake.

Bad breakup. Lost my job.

It suddenly occurred to Marco those were connected.

"You dated your boss, before. The bad breakup." He said it, shocked, before he could snatch the statement—*not even a goddamn question, Marco*—back.

Andrew tilted his head. "You looked me up."

"No." *I wanted you to tell me.* "I guessed."

"Yes," Andrew said precisely. Carefully. But with no additional details.

Marco wanted to demand why he was here right now, then? Swaying in front of him, like he was a half-second and the remains of his judgment away from leaning in, pressing his body against Marco's. Taking what they were both tempted by.

But he didn't.

He moved away, instead.

"Makes sense, now," Marco said.

He could be the reasonable, intelligent one.

You're thirty-seven years old and a great chef who runs this restaurant brilliantly.

"Yes," Andrew repeated.

"Well, keep it up." Marco cleared his throat. "The cheesecake, I mean."

"Of course, what else could you mean?" Andrew said and

skirted around him, shooting Marco one last knowing look out of those blue eyes as he exited the locker room.

Andrew had said *Marco* was irresistible, but he was wrong. So fucking wrong.

Marco let out the breath he'd been holding.

Scrubbed a hand over his face. Tried to clear his mind, but it didn't *want* to be cleared.

It wanted to chase after Andrew and tell him he'd never fuck with him and then break up with him and then discard him, like his ex.

But that way lies insanity and possibly flying pome-granates.

So he didn't.

Not until much, much later.

They were halfway through the night, when Jose, who handled the grill, offhandedly mentioned a comment about hoping there'd be some of the new limoncello dessert left, so he could try it.

"Oh yeah, Daniel mentioned it to me," Elijah added. "Sounded fucking delicious."

Marco's hand froze on the plate he was pulling down from the stack.

"Chef? Chef? I got this prime rib," Jose said, from behind him.

"Yeah, plate it," Marco said and wiped his hands on the towel hanging from his apron. "One sec."

It was not hard to ask Natalia, Dario's wife who managed the front of the house when Marcella wasn't around, for a copy of the dessert menu. She shot him a weird look but brought it, sliding it across the pass-through.

Sure enough, there it was. Printed in black and white. *Limoncello Dream*, it said.

This was *his* restaurant and he'd told Andrew that the menu didn't change. He'd been here for what . . .two fucking nights and he was already screwing around?

That was not going to stand. Not if Marco had anything to say about it.

He stomped off towards the pastry kitchen.

Andrew was whipping cream again.

"For God's sake," Marco burst out.

Andrew looked up from his bowl. "What is it?" he asked.

Marco prowled closer, gesturing towards the bowl. "How much fucking whipped cream do you go through?"

Behind him, Daniel said tremulously, "A *lot*, Chef, especially with the new dessert—"

Andrew interrupted him. "Thank you, Daniel. Go take your break."

"But—"

"Now," Andrew said, his tone brooking no arguments. No doubt he'd seen the fire in Marco's eyes.

"What the fuck is this new dessert?" Marco tossed the printed card on the prep counter. "I told you. No menu changes."

"Marcella approved it. What do you think I did to get it printed?"

Marco threw his arms up. "I don't know! Enticed Dario, who's practically a zero on the Kinsey scale—"

"And who's married," Andrew said steadily.

But Marco hated this calm act. He wanted Andrew to get worked up, like him. Like he'd been worked up, since the moment he'd turned in the Coffee Beanery and seen how well Andrew had grown up.

"I made myself so fucking clear," Marco growled.

Andrew set the whisk into the bowl. He'd rolled up the sleeves on his chef's coat again, and *God*, Marco wanted to weep at how gorgeous his muscled forearms were.

He'd seen how many pairs of forearms in his life, and *these* were going to make him lose his composure and even his mind?

Apparently.

"You did," Andrew agreed.

"Then *why?*"

Andrew just shrugged. Still unconcerned about Marco's temper. "Thought I might demonstrate again that nifty little trick. You liked it in the cheesecake."

"That was a cheesecake *on our menu*," Marco retorted.

"You don't even want to try it before you throw a shit fit?" Andrew asked.

Marco told himself it didn't matter how good it tasted. It was the principle of the thing.

What was he doing? Was Andrew intentionally trying to chip away at his self-control one dessert at a time? Did he enjoy reducing Marco to a boiling mess of sugar and emotion?

Maybe it was better if Marco didn't know the answer to either of those questions.

"Fine," Marco ground out.

He watched as Andrew prepared the dessert with expert precision. It had some kind of cookie base, topped with a cloud of pale yellow cream and then more of that whipped

90

cream, a single sprig of thyme and a dusting of baked crumbs resting on top of all that fluff.

It looked like nothing.

But then Andrew handed him the plate and he took his first bite, and he swore in the back of his throat.

Barely resisted gobbling up another bite—or ten.

He hated how good it was. Perfect in every way. Like a flawless Italian summer.

He hated the glowing certainty in Andrew's eyes that he'd love it.

Resisting the urge to demolish the entire plateful, he set it down with a deliberate click on the counter. "What are you doing?" he asked, this time out loud.

The knowing look in those eyes said it all. Andrew knew exactly what he was doing. But he pretended innocence, simply shrugging easily. "Being your pastry chef. Training Daniel to be one. He's got promise. You were right."

Marco wanted to smear the lemon cloud across Andrew's mouth and then devour him.

It didn't matter that this was his kitchen. It didn't matter that Andrew was his employee.

Marco breathed out and then breathed back in. Trying to rein himself in.

"It's a good dessert," Andrew continued, carefully, like he finally comprehended how far he'd pushed Marco. "I'd like to keep it on the menu. It's been popular. It would be a good special for the summer."

"What's that?" Marco barked. He wasn't a barker. He didn't normally give two shits about the hierarchy of the kitchen. That had always been Luca.

But now, for the first time, he had a glimmer of understanding of why his elder brother had said fuck it to everything and had run off to the wilds of South Carolina, to follow love.

"It's a good dessert, *Chef*," Andrew murmured, and Marco swallowed hard.

"Why are you doing this?" he asked again.

"Because I want to," Andrew said, and it made no fucking sense and Marco couldn't understand it, but he could only accept it must be true. "You're probably used to doing the charming, aren't you?"

"According to Marcella, yes."

Andrew turned away, like it was easy, and picked up his whisk again. "We good?" he asked. Like none of this had even happened. Like this was just another night of service.

Marco didn't want to be "good."

He wanted to slide the bowl and the whipped cream and every single other fucking thing on the counter to the floor, lift Andrew up and kiss him.

Even more now, than before.

Because he'd faced Marco's fire, *invited it,* even, and didn't seem all that bothered by it.

The guy was hot. That was a certifiable fact. But *that,* that backbone of steel, was even hotter.

Nuclear hot. Plunging-into-a-volcano hot. Marco-tearing-off-all-their-clothes hot.

"Yeah," Marco said. "We're good."

He turned and walked away.

Chapter Five

Night Three

Six years ago, Marcella had started dragging him to the yoga class she was taking after the birth of her second child. Marco didn't go often, but he'd found he enjoyed the hour of peace carved out of his normally hectic days.

He went to yoga this morning. Practiced his deep breathing.

Hoped that after, when he arrived at the restaurant, that hard-won peace might follow him. Might stick with him even after he was faced with Andrew and his annoying irresistibility.

Today was the day Marco regularly met with Dario and Marcella—and often Luca, calling in from South Carolina.

The purpose was theoretically to discuss the operations of the Moretti empire, though normally it devolved into a bitch slash gossip session.

It only took Marcella four minutes to bring up Andrew.

"We hired a new pastry chef." She shot a knowing glance in Marco's direction. "Or rather *Marco* hired a new pastry chef."

"Yeah?" Luca sounded distracted.

"You remember Andrew from high school? My friend who went to Europe for pastry school?"

"Yeah," Luca said. "He's back in Napa, right?"

Marco couldn't help the frustrated noise he made.

"Someone sounds annoyed," Marcella teased.

"I'm not—" Marco stopped. "He's just pushing me."

"Maybe you need to be pushed," Dario suggested.

Marco rolled his eyes.

"You have gotten stuck in a bit of a rut, haven't you?" Luca said.

Marco rolled his eyes harder. "And you wouldn't know anything about that, would you?"

Luca laughed. "I'd know *all* about that, which is why I'm telling you, Marco. It's good this guy is shaking you up."

"But don't shake *him* up," Marcella warned.

Marco barely restrained himself from rolling his eyes a third time. "Thank you, Marcella," he retorted sarcastically. "I'm attempting to restrain my natural Moretti-ness."

"What?" Luca asked. "What are you talking about?"

"Oh, apparently I can't help that everyone falls in love with me."

Luca laughed again. "Somehow I never had that problem. Except when it counted."

"Or maybe I'm trying to avoid any more pomegranates," Marco muttered.

"The last pastry chef that quit was madly in love with him," Marcella said.

"She was not," Marco protested. "She was just—"

"Madly in love with you?" Marcella suggested archly.

"This is a pointless conversation," Marco said firmly. "Andrew's here. He's doing great. I *do* wish he'd stop changing the menu without my permission, but he's training Daniel and I think in a month or so he'll be set to take over."

"That intern?" Luca asked.

"He's more than an intern," Marco retorted.

"But he's young." Marco could hear the frown on Luca's face.

"But learning," Dario added supportively. "I agree with Marco's assessment. If Andrew keeps training him, he'll be ready, as long as Marco's okay continuing to oversee him."

"The question isn't will Marco supervise Daniel, the question is will Marco keep his hands off Andrew?" Marcella joked.

"Marco is trying," Marco said between clenched teeth.

Thankfully, Luca changed the subject, bringing up the new quarterly figures from the distribution company that sold their line of sauces and antipasto spreads.

After the meeting, Marco avoided heading back to the pastry kitchen. And not because Marcella and Luca had given him shit. Nope. He didn't have a reason to go back there, so he just wouldn't.

Instead, he spent the early afternoon working with his sous, Theo, on the new monthly special, repeating and perfecting it until they were both happy, and by the time he lifted his head, checking on the rest of the kitchen, he realized it was almost four.

Time for family dinner.

"Who's—"

But before Marco could get the rest of his question out, Jose said, "Oh, hey, new guy cooked."

"Paella," Elijah said excitedly. "He said he learned the recipe when he was in Barcelona."

And sure enough, there was an enormous pan of it, sitting right in the middle of the table, and a big bowl of salad currently being passed around, someone exclaiming about the shredded Manchego "he" had grated on top.

Marco didn't need to ask who "he" was.

"He" was standing at the head of the table, smiling and answering questions about the meal he'd just cooked.

But when someone asked directly about Barcelona and the work he'd done there, Marco could sense a shift in him.

"Owned a restaurant there, with my partner," Andrew said, not looking like he wanted to discuss it. "Ex-partner, I guess. He bought me out, and I came back to Napa."

Everyone looked rabidly interested, and like they were about to demand answers about Andrew coming home. Why he'd needed to leave in the first place.

But before they could—honestly, both his employees and restaurant employees *everywhere* were more into gossip than a whole gaggle of old hens—Marco interrupted.

"This looks amazing," he said, patting Andrew on the back, and ignoring the ripple of sensation that washed through him at the undeniable firmness and the warmth of his skin under the white coat. "Thanks for making family dinner for us."

"I wanted to do it," Andrew said, shooting him a look that Marco couldn't help but interpret as pure relief.

He hadn't wanted to discuss why he'd left Barcelona.

Marco had assumed it wasn't a particularly good story, and he hadn't even known that Andrew was part-owner. Now it looked even worse.

He spent the meal making sure nobody else asked Andrew about the end of his time in Barcelona—and enjoying the hell out of the food he'd prepared for Marco's employees. The chicken and shrimp paired with the spicy sausage were tender and delicious, and the rice was flawlessly cooked. Fluffy and perfect.

Andrew was an incredible chef, that much was clear. Much too talented to be bothering with the Nonna's desserts.

He could be doing anything he wanted to be doing. Maybe he'd stick around St. Helena and open his bakery, or he'd go on to something bigger and brighter, but whichever he did, Marco was certain that he'd be brilliant at it.

The thought shouldn't have made him so melancholy, but it did.

Maybe because he was now convinced that the "ex-partner" had massively fucked up in some way, and now Marco wanted to fly to Barcelona and punch him for hurting Andrew. Or maybe systematically destroy his business.

It was a very Luca-like thing to want to do, and Marco didn't quite understand it, not until much later, after service was over.

Elijah and Jose were bickering good-naturedly as they

cleaned the grill, and after checking their work absently, because he trusted them, Marco ignored his good judgment and wandered back into the pastry kitchen.

Andrew was cleaning up alone. He glanced up, seeing Marco walk in.

"Everything go okay tonight?" That was the minimal excuse Marco had prepared to come back here.

After all, he was still the head chef of this restaurant.

Dario's words from the other day echoed through Marco. A good, and necessary, reminder of why he should be able to keep his hands to himself.

Nevermind the reminder from earlier. Andrew's old partner had betrayed him in some way. Romantically? Professionally? Marco didn't know the details, but he didn't have to know the details.

It was enough to know that it had happened. Marco would *never* betray Andrew that way, and if that meant tackling this inconvenient attraction head-on, then he'd do it.

"Yeah. Went fine. Sold out of the special." There was a glimmer of a smile on Andrew's mouth as he said it, but it was fleeting as he went back to wiping down the counters meticulously.

"Heard you nearly ran out of cheesecake too," Marco said.

Andrew gestured towards the fridge. "There's still one piece left. You want it?"

It wasn't cheesecake that Marco wanted, but maybe tasting more of Andrew in his mouth would help him stick to his promises.

"Yeah. I would, actually."

Andrew smiled wider at that. Leaned down to grab it, but Marco gestured him away. "I got it," he said. Grabbed the plate from the fridge and picked up a spoon from a crock of them sitting on the counter.

After his first bite, Marco was no longer convinced this creamy delicious goodness would keep him on the straight and narrow, because it was even better. Tonight, Andrew had garnished it with a sliver of candied orange peel, twisting impossibly and elegantly across the surface, and drizzled a hint of the darkest chocolate around the edge of the plate.

It was even better this way. Impossibly, ridiculously better.

Marco groaned as he took a second bite.

"Good?"

He realized a second too late he shouldn't be making these sounds here—and that it had been far too long since he'd made them in relation to anything but food.

Because Andrew was gazing at him, those gorgeous blue eyes pinned to him, and Marco knew, maybe because he was a Moretti, or maybe because he was a man, that if he walked over and kissed him, Andrew wouldn't push him away.

"It's incredible." Marco set the plate on the countertop. "You shouldn't be here, working for me."

"Why not? Because I push you? Because we're—"

Marco interrupted him before he could say, *because we're attracted to each other,* because frankly it was hard enough keeping his hands off without knowing for sure it was mutual. And if he *did* know it was mutual . . .*well.*

"Because you're really fucking talented," Marco said

instead. "And my dessert menu isn't anything special. You said it yourself."

"Maybe so. But there's Daniel. He does need training. Because he's going to be good. Perfect for you."

Marco realized then that Andrew had heard the whole ugly story about Izzy and the pomegranate. "I don't—I wouldn't—"

"You don't need to excuse yourself to me." Andrew chuckled under his breath. "Daniel's young and impressionable, and I know you wouldn't."

"I didn't with Izzy, and she wasn't young *or* impressionable," Marco said, gripping the edge of the counter and trying to resist the pull to divulge the whole story. Though frankly, there wasn't much to tell.

"You wouldn't overstep," Andrew said with confident certainty.

Sounding a little, though, like he wanted Marco to, with him.

Because like Izzy, Andrew was neither young nor impressionable either. He was the same age, and not only had he been working in restaurants for twenty years, same as Marco had, he'd had everything fall apart on him.

"Not like your ex?" Marco asked quietly.

A flash of hurt crossed over Andrew's features. He turned away, to rinse out his sponge. "Caught him getting a blowjob from our very young intern, late one night, in his office."

Marco let out a breath. It was even worse than he'd expected.

"We broke up, of course," Andrew continued, and there was a very well-earned bitterness in his tone. "I continued to work there. It was my dream. Had been *our* dream, of course, but I thought, I'm not going to give it up just because François couldn't keep it in his pants." He sighed. "But it got too hard. My eyes were opened. He did a lot of things I suddenly couldn't stomach. Threw his weight around—or didn't, sometimes. And I couldn't take it any longer. So I left."

"What are you doing here, now?" Marco had to ask it, even as he took a step closer. Drawn by the mingled sadness and hope in Andrew's eyes. "What are *we* doing?"

Andrew shouldn't want to get involved with another chef ever again. Not one he worked for. Even temporarily. But here he was, flirting with Marco. Not pretending that their attraction was nothing.

"Damned if I know," Andrew said wryly. "I asked you to meet me for coffee thinking, I'd tell you . . .I don't know, not *no*, but *something*. Not yes. I even had this crazy thought of asking you out, instead, but then you looked like that at me, and I just kept saying yes."

"Kept negotiating in your favor, you mean," Marco teased roughly.

He was five seconds away from leaning in and kissing him. Andrew didn't look like he'd hate it. The opposite, in fact.

"Hey, I did do that, at least," Andrew pointed out.
"You did."

Andrew reached out, palm first, pressing it to Marco's thundering heart. Didn't touch him anywhere else, but it didn't matter, because he felt it *everywhere*.

"And I should have left well enough alone, I know that.

But I couldn't, and you just kept *looking* at me like that, and I did want you to stop. But I didn't want you to, even more."

"You're driving me insane," Marco said softly. Aware he was only a few seconds away from just sheer begging. *Kiss me. Ask me out the way you were going to. Anything. Just give me a shred. A crumb.*

But Andrew didn't. He didn't pull away either.

Not until there was a sudden gasp behind them, and of course, that was when Daniel returned to the pastry kitchen, his arms full of clean dishes.

Dumping cold, hard truth all over Marco. *What the fuck are we doing?*

Marco cleared his throat, pulling back. "Uh, excellent work here tonight. Best yet. Very pleased."

He wasn't very proud of it, but he turned and he left. Abruptly. Without looking once in Andrew's direction.

Chapter Six

Night Four

Fridays were always busy at Nonna's.

Marco was counting on the date nights and the big family dinners and the corporate glad-handing to get him through the afternoon of prep and then service.

To keep him from losing the rest of his mind and heading back towards the pastry kitchen, damn his promises to his family, to his employees, to *himself*.

He'd reminded himself half a dozen times on the drive home that Andrew wouldn't work for him forever. It was only ever supposed to be a temporary job. In a month or two, he'd leave, to open his bakery and *hopefully* stay in the general vicinity of the Napa Valley. Then Marco could subsequently ask out Andrew and then kiss him and *more*, so much more, all he wanted.

But for now, he was going to be hands-off. And if he used his job as a distraction to do that, well so be it.

Marco subbed himself in on the line, pushing Jose to the

pass-through as a final check, ostensibly because Jose needed the experience—which he *did*, though he was already good at it—but in reality because it meant Marco's hands and mind were constantly occupied by the revolving line of tickets.

When he finally got a break, he went to Dario's office instead of meandering back to where he wanted to be. Scarfed down a plate of salad and chicken parm and then went back to the line.

When the night finally ended, Marco was exhausted. Hollowed out by the repetitive work.

But ultimately believing he'd done the right thing. It would get easier, he decided, as he helped scrub down the grill and then the rest of the kitchen.

When it was finally clean, he headed towards the locker room. Had just finished pulling off his chef's coat and the T-shirt he wore underneath, wiping himself down with a wet paper towel just so he wouldn't offend *himself* on the walk home, when a noise behind him made him turn.

Andrew was standing there, fingers frozen on the tie of his apron. Gaze glued to Marco's bare chest.

He didn't spend the time in the gym that Luca did. He wasn't chiseled, but he knew he was strong. Lithe too, because of the yoga classes Marcella had introduced him to.

But whatever Andrew saw, he *liked* it. He wanted it.

The heat in his eyes was evidence enough.

Andrew's fingers fiddled with the tie on his apron. "Didn't see you tonight."

"No," Marco said. Hoped that the single word was explanation enough. They'd been playing with fire yesterday.

How else would Andrew know how much he respected

him, if he didn't keep his hands off when it mattered most? How else could he *show* him that he wasn't anything like his ex, who'd blended business with pleasure and then fucked Andrew over?

But of course Andrew wouldn't let it lie. There was a reason he *liked* Andrew, and it was about so much more than just getting him naked.

"You're avoiding me," Andrew said bluntly.

"No. Well . . .a little," he conceded, ultimately not really able to lie to him, to his face. "I'm trying to do the right thing. Not be . . ." He waved his hands around himself. "Not be myself. Cloud your judgment with my stupid Moretti-ness."

Andrew's eyebrow rose. "Your Moretti-ness?"

"Marcella says I can't help it. But I can. I *want* to." Marco shoved a hand through his hair, especially unruly because he'd tied it back for service.

Andrew took a few steps closer, which was plenty close enough. Marco thought it, but didn't quite have the self-control to say it. When he was this close, Marco could almost pretend things were different.

And they will be, just not right now.

"You're trying to avoid being my ex," Andrew stated. His gaze softened, like this was touching. Like he was being seduced, even though Marco had gone out of his way *not* to.

"Yes," Marco said. "And avoid flying fruit, too. I'm not entirely selfless here."

"Flying fruit?"

Marco sighed heavily. "When Izzy quit, in a fit of . . .well, *rage*, she threw half the fruit basket at me. The plums weren't so bad. The grapes made good ammunition, admittedly. But the pomegranates? Difficult to avoid."

Andrew laughed out loud. "What if I promise not to toss any pomegranates your direction?"

It was tempting. So goddamned tempting.

But then Marco remembered the bleak hurt flashing in Andrew's eyes when he'd been asked about leaving Barcelona.

Maybe they still had to get to know each other as adults, now, but Marco knew one thing for sure: he was never going to fuck Andrew over the way his ex had. Blurring the lines until they were messy, then leave Andrew holding the short end of the stick.

"Okay," Andrew said and unexpectedly reached for Marco's hand. "Come on."

"What?" Marco asked, confused. *Come on what? Come on where?*

"Come on," Andrew repeated insistently, and this time he just *took,* grabbing Marco's hand and leading him, still without a shirt, outside the restaurant.

The lot was empty now, or mostly so.

Behind the restaurant was a little grouping of trees, and it seemed Andrew was leading them there.

Why? Marco didn't know.

Maybe he was so tired he was hallucinating this whole thing. But Andrew's hand felt strong and sure and *real* in his.

Finally, they came to a stop, out of the circle of lights from the parking lot, right underneath the trees' canopy. It was still warm outside, the July heat persistent even after the sun had set, but not sticky. Nothing like the South Carolina town where Luca now lived.

"What are we—" Marco began, but Andrew pressed a hand to his lips. It smelled like lemons and sugar and chocolate. An intoxicating combination.

"I wanted to do this," Andrew said, "but considering why I left Barcelona and how you're avoiding pomegranates, I thought maybe we shouldn't do it *in* your restaurant."

And then Andrew leaned in and kissed him.

For a second, Marco let go and just let himself feel it.

Andrew's mouth, firm and lush on his own, tasting like he smelled, like the sharp tang of citrus and the bitter richness of chocolate. Andrew's hands in his hair and Marco's hands curling into the fabric of his T-shirt. Andrew's tongue, flickering teasing touches against his own.

Marco thought he might have groaned.

It felt like it had been an eternity since he'd been kissed like this. Like he wanted to be kissed. Until he lost himself, his body and his mind and his whole heart, in it.

He'd been in love before, in and out of it, throughout his twenties and even into his thirties, but it had *never* felt like this before.

Like he'd just been waiting for Andrew to come home and claim him.

Like he knew it too, Andrew flipped them, so much stronger than he seemed, than he'd been the first time they'd known each other, like it was so goddamn easy to press Marco right into the tree trunk.

Imagine how it might be without all these inconvenient clothes between them.

Marco was breathless when Andrew lifted his mouth. "I don't see how kissing out here changes anything."

"Didn't stop you from kissing me back," Andrew teased.

"I only have so much self-control and your mouth is the limit of it," Marco admitted. *Your mouth. Your hands. Your body. Your cock. Your whole fucking irresistible self.*

"I want you," Andrew said, sighing happily.

Marco could feel it, Andrew's cock hard against his thigh. He was so worked up himself, like he was a mindlessly horny teenager again. But it wasn't mindless. Not at all. There was only one person he wanted.

"I think you know I want you too," Marco murmured and then kissed him again.

Even though he'd been attempting to resist this man for less than a week, giving in felt like peace after a hard-fought battle.

But with Andrew's tongue in his mouth and his hands stroking across Marco's shoulders, it felt less like a bloodless accord and more like a whole body surrender.

"God," Andrew groaned deep in his throat as Marco's mouth found his neck, nibbling at the tendon there. "You're too good at that. Too good at everything."

"It's the Moretti in me," Marco admitted, panting as their hips aligned better. And *yes,* he might actually come in his pants like that randy boy he wasn't anymore.

"No." Andrew leaned back against the tree, putting an inch or two of distance between them. It felt like a mile. Or maybe that was the look in his blue eyes. Hard, suddenly, and determined.

"No?"

"You think I want you because you're a Moretti—"

"Apparently we're an irresistible bunch," Marco interrupted wryly. He didn't *like* it, but he could see the truth in Marcella's argument. Izzy alone made her point, and there'd been many, many others besides her.

"No," Andrew repeated. Then he laughed self-consciously. "You really don't know, do you?"

Marco shook his head, because apparently he didn't.

"I only had the world's worst and *most* obvious crush on you in high school. I couldn't get enough of you."

"But you and Marcella—"

"Oh, we were friends. For sure. She took pity on me, a little, I think. Actually encouraged me to go to Paris, which frankly, *was* the best way to get over it." Andrew's eyes were a fathomless blue now, and Marco wanted to get lost in them. "Though I suppose the jury's out on whether I ever *really* got over it."

"I don't want you to be over it," Marco said gruffly. "Why didn't you just *say*?"

"Because it wouldn't have made a bit of difference back then. And now? Well . . .I didn't know . . .I didn't know I still had it in me. Not until we met at the coffee shop and you looked so fucking poleaxed at how I'd grown up."

"You came intending to say no, and you just . . ." Marco trailed off. Andrew had said it himself last night. He'd come to the Beanery thinking he might ask Marco out. Not that he'd *work* for him.

"Couldn't resist?" Andrew teased and pressed a light kiss to Marco's mouth. "You're very persuasive, it turns out."

"I didn't do *any* persuading," Marco protested. He'd

barely gotten a word in, too shocked at how attractive Andrew was. How attracted to him he was.

Andrew's hands curled into his hair at the base of his neck and tugged in an unexpected and highly arousing way. "You looked desperate and I felt bad. Also, I'm still looking around for a good spot for the bakery, so it seemed like a decent enough way to pass the time. And to get closer to you."

"But—" Marco took a deep breath. "Now you *work* for me."

"That would be very, very easy to remedy."

"But the dessert menu! *Daniel.* I need—" Would he say fuck it to those things? He might. It would not be the kind of thing a responsible and business-minded Moretti might do. But it might be exactly the kind of thing an in-love Moretti might do. Case in point: Luca fucking off to the wilds of South Carolina when he'd fallen in love with his now-husband, Oliver.

"No need to worry about me. I said I'd give you a month or two to train Daniel, and that was before I even knew how promising he was."

"Don't tell me you're going to poach him," Marco warned.

"No. No, of course not. I only mean I *want* to train him. He's perfect for you, Marco. Perfect to be your head pastry chef. Responsible and dependable, without too much imagination."

Marco heard what he wasn't saying. That Andrew would be bored in a week. Less, probably.

"So what, we need to keep our hands to ourselves for a month or two?" Marco wanted to protest that Andrew *defi-*

nitely shouldn't have kissed him then. Now that he knew what he tasted like and smelled like and *felt* like, it was going to be pure fucking torture to not do it again, and *more*.

Andrew laughed. "No. Well. Maybe for a few days. Depending on how good Dario is."

"Dario?"

"You know him. He's your brother. Three years younger than you. An inch taller. Wears glasses. Likes a cannoli while he does the books?"

"I *know* Dario," Marco said. Exasperated and yet totally, completely charmed. "What I don't know is what he has to do with *this*?" He gestured between them.

Andrew tucked himself more fully into Marco's embrace —which didn't feel like a thing he'd do if he was about to counsel them to keep their hands off each other for the next month—or *God*, even longer.

"Easy," Andrew said. "You will fire me, as your employee, and Dario will hire me as your contractor. Contracted to run your pastry kitchen and train Daniel for a set amount of time. Let's say six weeks? You won't be my boss, because I'll be an independent contractor. And we can keep doing this." Andrew laid a lush, insanely good kiss on Marco's mouth. "And after that, I'll be working on the bakery and we'll own two completely totally separate businesses."

"It's hardly that simple," Marco said, even though he desperately wanted it to be.

"Why can't it be?" Andrew shot him a look. "If you weren't so worried about this, and I hadn't just been through the world's shittiest breakup, it wouldn't have even been necessary to go that far. But if it makes us both feel protected . . .why not?"

"You're never going to throw a pomegranate at me?"

"You ever going to lure some intern into your office for a quick blowjob?"

Marco was speechless. Of *course* he wouldn't. Whether he was dating Andrew or not.

"No, you wouldn't," Andrew said, answering his own question. He pressed another kiss to Marco's mouth. "That's to remember me by, until Dario gets the paperwork in order."

"Trust me, I don't think I could forget you a second time," Marco said honestly.

Andrew smiled. "I'm going to hold you to that promise."

Chapter Seven

Night Five

"You've thought this through."

Dario looked up at Marco through his glasses. He looked so much like Luca there, who'd used to occupy that desk, that office.

Sometimes Marco still missed his eldest brother, but mostly, he was happy *he* was happy.

Dario did his job almost better than Luca had and with far less emotional angst about it. But Marco didn't think Luca would have questioned him like this.

"Yes," Marco said.

"We *just* did the paperwork to hire him," Dario said. "Does it really matter to your dick if he's a full-fledged employee and we give him a W-2 at the end of the year, or if he's technically a contractor and we 1099 him? The *IRS* gives a shit, but I don't know what it has to do with your sex life?"

"I know it seems strange," Marco said. "I know it shouldn't matter, but it does. To me. And to him."

"Because of Izzy?"

"And all the others that came before her. I know you don't work in the kitchen or understand the hierarchy of it, but this *does* matter." Marco had lain awake most of the night, tossing and turning over it. Aroused, yes, and not wanting to take matters into his own hands, necessarily, because this erection didn't belong to him, but to Andrew. But also wanting to be sure, absolutely confident, that doing this paperwork would give both of them the peace of mind they needed to pursue this without regrets.

"He can still throw a pomegranate at your hard head," Dario teased, leaning back in his chair.

"Ah, but he's promised not to."

Dario didn't roll his eyes, but Marco could tell he wanted to. "And that's enough for you?"

"I can't say for certain if we'll be together in fifty years, like Mama and Papa. I can't say we'll be wildly in love like Luca and Oliver. Or you and Natalia. Or Gabe and Sean. But I know I want to see. I could wait the month or two, for Andrew to handle our pastry kitchen and train Daniel to do the same, but I . . .I don't want to. I really, really don't want to. And that's what tells me this is necessary."

"Alright," Dario said, nodding. "I'll do the paperwork. It'll take a day or two."

"Two days? Tomorrow night?" Marco remembered what Andrew had initially offered him. Six days. Six nights of service. He'd give him that, then fire him—ceremoniously, of course—and then take him home when the night was over.

"I should be able to get it done," Dario agreed.

"You're the best brother. My *favorite* brother."

"I'm going to tell Luca *and* Gabe you said that." Dario's voice was teasing, but his eyes were full of love. "I'm happy to see you like this. You deserve it."

"Not more fruit tossed at my head?"

Dario shrugged. "Can't say you didn't deserve a *little* of that. But not all of it. You're a good man, Marco. You run a solid kitchen." He grinned. Marco heard what he wasn't saying.

Marco, you are thirty-seven and a great chef who runs this restaurant brilliantly.

And this time it wasn't a reminder, but simply appreciation.

"Thanks," Marco said. "And now I have to go read the riot act to our sister."

"Marcella? Why?"

"Because she is an interfering interferer who interferes," Marco said resolutely.

He found her with Bea again, at the host stand, going over the reservations for the next few days.

There was a single rose in a slim glass vase tucked away in the corner, and Marco smiled. They'd never had flowers on the host stand before—his mother had always claimed it looked "cluttered", but Marco had a feeling that Marcella had let this go because the flower was from Daniel.

Clearly, Andrew was giving him confidence. In more ways than one.

"I need to talk to you," he told his sister.

Marcella looked up. "Does it have to be right now? I'm busy and—"

"Yes," Marco said firmly. "Right now."

"Fine, fine. One minute," she told Bea. "I'll be right back."

"Don't worry," Marco said. "My lecture shouldn't take too long."

Marcella rolled her eyes as Marco led her out the front door. "What on earth is this about?" she asked.

But now that he was looking for it, Marco could see the knowing gleam in her dark eyes. So like his own.

She knew exactly what she'd done.

"You know," Marco said.

"I really don't."

Marco was tired of playing this game, though. Which was why he'd decided to confront her about it at all. "Andrew," he said tightly.

"What about him? Is he not working out?"

"Cut the shit, Marcella."

She huffed in annoyance.

"I know you knew all about Andrew's crush on me. Funny you should recommend *him* for a position here, literally in the same breath as lecturing me about keeping my hands off the staff."

"Which you've mostly always done."

"Mostly," Marco said dryly.

"Alright, in every way that really mattered. You made mistakes early on, but you learned from then. And after that, with Izzy, I know it wasn't all your fault, really, but . . ."

"But?"

"But you were drifting. In and out of relationships, relationships you didn't really care about. And you *do* care about the restaurant, but . . ." She trailed off, hesitating again.

116

"Oh, don't hold back now," Marco said, baring his teeth. "Let me have it."

Marcella laughed. "But it was getting a bit stale. You needed shaking up."

"So you decided to throw Andrew at me." Marco didn't know whether he was annoyed still or actually grateful.

Did he wish that Marcella was less like Luca in that her primary tool was bludgeoning a guy to death with the truth?

Maybe.

"I thought . . .just maybe, it might be worth seeing what happens," Marcella acknowledged.

"You knew about his ex."

Marcella made an exasperated noise. "Marco, most of the culinary world knew about his ex. It was a big deal when he left. A big deal to talk about starting his own bakery."

Well, that answered the question of whether Marco should've googled him.

"You didn't know—" Marcella continued, realization dawning on her face.

"About the whole famous thing, no. About the shitty ex? Yes. I figured it out. But that's why you lectured me on boundaries, before."

Marcella shot him a hard look. "Marco, darling, I lectured you on boundaries because it's the twenty-first fucking century. And no, it's not your fault if your employees can't stop themselves from falling in love with you. That's on them. But you *can* be over friendly with them. I just wanted you to be a little more aware of the potency of your charm." The corner of her mouth tilted up. "*And* yes, there was Andrew's shitty ex. Though I had a feeling he knew you better—at least he *did*—than to assume you would pull that garbage. And I *knew* you wouldn't, ever."

"I wouldn't, no, but . . ." Marco took a deep breath. "I wouldn't ever want to push him into something he wasn't comfortable with. This is his plan. I was willing—not *wanting* but willing—to go the six weeks or two months or whatever."

It would've been hard. Maybe one of the hardest things he'd ever done, but he'd have kept his distance, because Andrew deserved hard things.

"He suggested this because he trusts you," Marcella said and the look in her eye made it clear that if he fucked with that trust, she'd have Marco's ass on a platter. "And, well, he wants you. He always has."

"You're not going to give him the shovel talk? I'm your darling brother." Marco grinned at her.

"Oh, he already got it. When I told him you'd call him about the job."

Marco felt his annoyance soften. It was hard to be mad, not when Marcella *had* been right. "Are you *ever* wrong?" he teased her.

She smacked him on the arm. "Sometimes. I never thought Luca would go out to South Carolina and *stay* there."

"To be fair, I don't think *Luca* knew he'd do that," Marco said. He paused. "But I'm really glad you weren't wrong about this."

"Me too." Marcella pulled him into a tight hug. "Don't fuck it up."

Marco rolled his eyes, and she added, "Not that I actually thought you would."

"So much faith in me, little sister," he teased.

"*Little* by what . . .three minutes?"

"Three minutes or three years, who's counting?"

After leaving Marcella to her conference with Bea, Marco headed back towards the kitchen.

Ran into just who he wanted to see. Andrew had his hand on the door to the big walk-in fridge, and when he saw Marco, his smile dispelled the last bit of annoyance lingering inside.

"Hey," Andrew said. "Imagine seeing you here." He pulled the door open and Marco, feeling safe in the knowledge that in just over twenty-four hours, they would be free and clear—maybe not to make out in the walk-in, but at least to stare gooily at each other all they wanted—followed him.

"I talked to Dario. We're all set."

"You mean, you're set to fire me?" Andrew gazed up at him like this was the greatest thing ever.

"Tomorrow night," Marco said, nodding. "And I thought tomorrow night, after service . . ." He hadn't come up with concrete plans, other than *invite Andrew to something, somewhere, preferably somewhere you can finally be alone together.*

"Yes," Andrew said. "Yes to whatever you were going to ask. *And* I was thinking, I'll bring the dessert."

"I think I've eaten more dessert in the last week than I have in the last six months," Marco said, patting his stomach. "I'm gonna have to be careful."

Andrew flashed him a knowing smile. "Oh, I think we can figure out a way to work it off."

Marco's mouth went dry, and he was suddenly very, *very* glad that tomorrow night, he wouldn't have to rely on his self-control any longer.

It was strong, but his desire for Andrew was even stronger.

"I just want you to know," Marco said, because it was important he knew this, "if you'd wanted to go the whole time you were here just . . .uh . . .being friends, then I'd have been okay with that. It would have been okay."

"Yeah?" Andrew's gaze turned soft. "Just when I think you're nearly perfect, you say something like that. And *God*, I remember—"

"Remember what?" Marco didn't touch him, but he wanted to. He clenched his fist.

"Remember what it felt like when I wanted you so goddamn bad and I couldn't have you."

Marco grinned fiercely. "But you can now. Soon."

"Soon," Andrew agreed.

"What are you looking for in here?" Marco asked. Changing the subject was probably smarter, because he could still remember the way Andrew had tasted last night, and he wanted more.

"Who says I wasn't looking for you?" Andrew's voice was teasing.

Marco raised an eyebrow.

"Fair. I was thinking about working on a new special."

Marco's eyebrow skidded higher. "Think you've got an in now with the head chef, you can do whatever the fuck you want?"

Andrew laughed. "Something like that." Reached up and to Marco's surprise, he pressed a warm kiss to his cheek. "I got this, alright?"

Marco had a feeling he wanted whatever this "special" was to be a surprise—hadn't the last one been, too?—so he nodded and, giving Andrew one last lingering look, exited the walk-in.

Chapter Eight

Night Six

Marco had been afraid that service would pass by, on this last day of Andrew's official employment at Nonna's, like a snail crawling.

Instead, it felt like he could barely take a breath.

Jose called out sick, sounding genuinely awful, and Marco spent most of the evening on the line, in a much closer supervisory role like the one Jose usually held.

Then they ran out of veal.

Then Marco had to duck into the back prep kitchen and whip up a new batch of marinara.

He didn't really have time to stick his head into the pastry kitchen, even though it was right next to the prep kitchen, but he did it anyway.

Andrew and Daniel were both working—this time it was Daniel whipping cream, as Andrew bent over a cutting board, absorbed in a delicate dissection of some fruit.

Clearly, they were busy too, so Marco went back to the prep kitchen and his vat of marinara.

He looked up what felt like only a few minutes later, and it was actually a whole hour later. Nearly close, in fact.

"God," Marco said, scrubbing a hand across his face, "is it almost nine already?"

"Yep," Elijah said. "And there was only a minor riot about the veal."

"We'll get our delivery tomorrow," Marco said. "I called in and double-checked."

Nonna's were all closed on Mondays. Dario always received the deliveries, and he'd already promised Marco that no matter what emergency cropped up, he'd leave Marco be.

He'd been looking forward to sleeping in—hopefully, if everything went well, with Andrew next to him. Waking with him for the first time. Taking him out to his favorite diner for breakfast, their first official date.

"Good," Elijah said. "You go on, Chef. I got this cleanup. I know you've got other things going on."

Marco raised an eyebrow, wondering just how much the rest of his staff knew about his situation with Andrew. Dario wouldn't blab, but they all had eyes, didn't they? And they all talked and gossiped plenty.

"It's all good, Chef," Elijah said with a reassuring nod.

Maybe it shouldn't matter that his staff approved—but it did. They were all a family, because like Marcella had told him, he had absolute shit boundaries.

He was already in the locker room, getting his stuff together, when Andrew walked in.

"Hey, Chef," Andrew said, amusement glimmering in his blue eyes.

"I . . ." Words died in his throat as Andrew walked right up into his space and cupped his cheek.

"Busy night?" Andrew's tone was still teasing.

"Yeah. No Jose and of course, half a dozen problems that I had to take care of—but you know how it is." Andrew would, of course. He'd co-owned a restaurant. He'd always understand if there was some issue that only Marco could solve.

Would it be easy? Marco never assumed that it would be. But even the shitty moments would be worth it.

"I do," Andrew agreed. He put a hand on Marco's chest. Through the thin cotton of his T-shirt, Andrew's touch burned. Made his pulse accelerate. "So, what's the plan?"

You. Me. A bed.

But this wasn't just about sex; if it was just an itch they needed to scratch, they could've done all that without paperwork.

"I was thinking my place," Marco said. "I want to hear all about Paris. And Sweden. Even Barcelona."

"That all?" Andrew's eyes twinkled.

"Well, not *all*. I was promised dessert, after all."

"I did, and I intend to deliver." Andrew gestured down at the white box in his hands. "I was wondering should I bring a bag?"

"Yes," Marco said quickly.

"Good, 'cause I already packed one." Andrew pressed a swift kiss to Marco's mouth and turned towards his own locker, carefully setting the white box on the bench. Unbut-

124

toning his chef's coat, tossing it in the big laundry bin in the corner.

Marco tried not to look as Andrew stripped down, pulling on a pair of jeans and another T-shirt from his locker.

He filled out both perfectly, and Marco's cock throbbed at the thought of stripping him out of them, slowly.

"I'm going to . . .uh . . .go check on everything. Make sure nobody needs anything," Marco said uselessly.

Andrew shot him a grin. "Give me another minute. I'll meet you outside?"

Marco nodded.

Detoured back into the kitchen, finding it clean and dark and empty. Dario's office was equally empty, the man himself in the dining room, adjusting the glasses again.

"You really need to send out a memo about that," Marco said to his brother.

Dario looked up. "I know," he said wryly. "Or I could keep coming out here and doing it every night."

"Whatever floats your boat. The paperwork's all done?"

Dario nodded. "You're free to do whatever you want with him. Just . . . you know, don't tell me about it. And don't make out in the walk-in."

"I wouldn't," Marco muttered. He *wouldn't*.

"I know," Dario said, laughing. "Really, though, we're happy for you, brother."

And Marco realized as he let himself out the back door that they all *were*.

Andrew was waiting there, a duffel bag slung over his shoulder. "There you are. I got exciting news for you."

Marco raised an eyebrow.

"I quit."

Andrew laughed, and Marco had to join him.

Then Marco had to kiss him, cradling his cheeks between his palms, letting his lips say everything he wasn't sure he trusted his mouth to say. *Yet*, anyway.

"You seem pretty happy about it, too," Andrew teased.

"Fucking relieved. Fucking grateful, too," Marco said gruffly. He reached down and took Andrew's hand, tugging him in the direction of the path.

"You wanna go make out in the forest again?" Andrew wondered.

"I actually live just over that ridge there," Marco admitted. "Two nights ago when you brought us out here, I thought for one crazy moment that you were dragging me to my house."

"Oh, why would I do that?" Andrew asked innocently.

But Marco knew nothing about that question was innocent.

"Thought you might want to do more than just kiss me," Marco said. Two of them could play at this game.

"I do," Andrew said in a low, rough voice. "Tell me your house is *close*."

Two summers ago, when he'd started walking this way more often, he'd installed little solar lights every few dozen feet, and he was glad of them now, because he wasn't watching where he was going at all. Too eager to get to their final destination.

"Yeah, right over here," Marco said, gesturing with his free hand.

He could see the front porch light just peeking from between the trees as they climbed over the ridge.

"It's lucky I *didn't* know this was here. I might've said screw the paperwork and well . . ."

"Screwed me?" Marco teased. He tugged him onto the porch and instead of unlocking the door, kissed him again, hard.

Andrew groaned and their hips were colliding as Marco pinned him to the door. Took his mouth with all the frustration of the last week.

They were both breathing hard when Marco finally lifted his head.

"And if I'd known that was waiting for me . . .maybe I would have seduced you in the walk-in," Andrew joked.

"Come in," Marco said, pulling out his keys with trembling fingers and letting them into his little house.

It wasn't anything special, but he'd taken his share of the profits of the Nonna's line of sauces from the last few years and had it built exactly to his specifications.

Open spaces. A living room with vaulted ceilings melting into a spacious kitchen with long bare countertops and top-of-the-line appliances. His bedroom, tucked in the back, a bathroom attached with a big shower and an even bigger bathtub he really enjoyed relaxing in at the end of a long day.

"I really like your house," Andrew said, turning to take in every bit of the living room. "It reminds me of you. All that exposed wood, the lush textures. It's quiet and comforting but challenging too."

"Thanks."

"I was always surprised you didn't leave. I kept thinking,

I'll run into Marco someday in Rome or Marseilles or London. But I never did. Imagine my surprise when I came home, and here you were, still."

"You were thinking about me, huh?" Marco teased.

Andrew shot him a hot look. "Yeah, I was. It's funny. Right now, I think we're both right where we need to be."

It was easy to pull him close then, Andrew pressing his body against Marco's. It was even easier to lean down and kiss him again. The kiss spun out between them, at points soft and tender and at others wild and passionate.

Marco was seriously considering tugging them towards the couch when Andrew finally lifted his head.

"Actually," he said, "I think the place we're both supposed to be is your bed. But first—"

Marco didn't need a reminder that they'd both worked a long, hard shift today.

"You want to take a shower?"

"With you? Yes," Andrew said. "Lead the way."

In the bathroom, Marco flipped on the water nice and hot, and then there was no way to avoid what came next.

Marco expected some hesitation from Andrew—*he* was feeling a little nervous about stripping down in front of Andrew, the man he was rapidly developing complex feelings for—but after glancing around the spacious bathroom, Andrew wasted no time at all toeing off his shoes, pulling off his T-shirt and then unbuttoning and then unzipping his jeans, letting them drop.

Marco nearly swallowed his tongue. Trying not to look. But *looking* all the same, because looking anywhere else was impossible.

"I keep thinking I'll lose my Spain tan, but it seemingly persists," Andrew said, Marco's fingers still tangled in the hem of his shirt, hesitating to pull it up.

Maybe he wasn't self-conscious because he looked like *that*. All lithe muscle dipped in golden sunlight, a trail of hair leading down to his tight blue boxer briefs.

Then, like it was nothing, he tucked his fingers under the waistband and tugged it, no shame whatsoever.

"You look like you're about to swallow your tongue," Andrew teased, leaning over, fingers brushing Marco's, still lingering on the hem of his shirt.

"What I'm about to do is fall to my knees and praise God —or maybe Satan—that you look that fucking good," Marco said honestly.

Andrew laughed.

"You wanna give me a chance to feel the same?" he murmured.

Marco swallowed his worry and pulled off his T-shirt, then his pants, and finally, his boxer briefs joined the pile on the floor.

"Oh yeah, I've only been dreaming about this for almost twenty years," Andrew said, his hand trailing down Marco's chest, heading in the direction of his cock, which was definitely not soft. Not if Andrew kept touching him with that sweet, hot reverence.

"Shower," Marco said gruffly.

In a minute, he wouldn't give a shit if they smelled like marinara and sweat.

He tugged Andrew in, the glass door shutting behind

them, and didn't waste a minute crowding him against the tile wall.

It was one thing to kiss when there were layers and layers of clothes between them, but kissing skin to skin was an intoxicating experience.

"God," Andrew groaned in the back of his throat, his head hitting the shower wall. "I want you so fucking bad."

With shaking fingers, Marco picked up the soap. Made *extremely* quick work of washing himself down. Then, deciding he didn't want to relinquish this opportunity, began to soap up Andrew's body.

His skin was so smooth and perfect under his fingertips, and Marco wanted to explore every inch. Every spot that made Andrew gasp or his muscles quiver.

Then he slid the soap lower, Andrew's cock hard as it brushed his hand. His whole body shook as Marco washed his balls.

"I'm gonna—" Andrew bit off. "You're too good at that."

"Oh," Marco teased, "we're just getting started."

He pulled Andrew under the rain head, water cascading down as it rinsed them off, and a second later, Andrew wound himself around Marco, arms tight around his neck, one leg creeping up the back of Marco's.

"Then let's get started." The way Andrew begged was so fucking sweet. Marco couldn't wait to hear it some more. To hear it all the time. "Come on, let's go. I've only been waiting twenty years for you to finally fuck me."

Marco's fingers were shaking as he flicked off the water, and he didn't bother with towels, dragging them both dripping towards the bed. Andrew had barely scrambled onto it before Marco was covering his body with his own, pressing him down into the mattress.

Andrew reached up, curling his hands into the wet hair at his neck and tugged him down, kissing him hard and insistent, tongue sweeping between Marco's lips into his mouth.

"Want you," Marco murmured into his mouth, grinding his thigh against Andrew's damp, hard cock. "Want you so fucking bad."

Andrew groaned his agreement, and Marco couldn't help it any longer. He drifted lower, his mouth finding Andrew's collarbone. Then his pec, then his lips wrapping around his nipple. Then lower still, coasting across that intoxicating trail of hair, down to where his cock twitched against his abs.

Andrew's skin tasted incredible—like the deepest, darkest caramel—and Marco couldn't get enough. Couldn't get enough either when he finally slid his cock into his mouth, sucking at the head before wrapping his tongue around it and sliding down farther.

Loving the way Andrew breathed out just his name, like it was a vow. Or maybe it was making good on a *very* old promise.

Marco slipped his hand lower, cupping his balls and then went lower still, thumb stroking at the soft sensitive skin of his hole.

"Yes," Andrew begged. "God, yes, give it to me."

Marco wasn't in a position to deny him. Even if he'd wanted to.

He straightened for a second, found the lube and a condom in the drawer, and returned to Andrew's delectable body, enjoying the flush on his chest, the way his cockhead, wet from precome and from Marco's mouth, smeared across his abs.

Marco tucked a lube-damp finger into Andrew's body, loving the way it pulled him in. Like it already couldn't get enough.

One finger. Then two. Andrew was babbling now, and it all sounded good to Marco.

He'd had plenty of sex in his life. Plenty of good sex, even.

But he'd never had sex that felt like this before. Like the first sex he'd have for the rest of his life.

"You want this?" Marco teased, pushing his hard cock, sheathed in the condom, up against his hole. "You want more?"

"I want it all," Andrew said with a hard groan, and Marco didn't deny him—or deny himself either.

He pushed in, loving the way Andrew fit around him, tight and hot and perfect. *Right*, Marco realized. That was how it felt.

When he finally sank all the way in, they were both panting, the sound harsh in the quiet of the room.

Andrew reached down to touch himself, but Marco pulled his hand away, tangling their fingers together as he pushed him back on the bed, trying to find a better angle. Of course, they *all* felt good. But he wanted Andrew to feel the best. To understand that this was how it was going to be from now on.

If Andrew wanted something, Marco was going to find a way to give it to him.

Even if he wanted his heart.

"God, I'm so close," Andrew cried out, thrusting back onto Marco's cock more insistently, needing more, and Marco couldn't help it—he just gave it to him. Long fast thrusts, their bodies rubbing together, Andrew's cock catching on his stomach. A second later he was crying out, coming hard between them, his ass squeezing the orgasm out of Marco only a second later.

Marco collapsed on the bed next to him, but didn't waste a moment to pull Andrew close to him. Andrew got it and curled up, nearly lying on top of his chest.

"I needed that about six days ago," Marco confessed.

Andrew chuckled. "I only needed that about nineteen *years* ago."

Chapter Nine

Their cuddling led to more kissing, which led to another round. Andrew's mouth was tight and hot around him, working his cock like he was born to do it.

When they collapsed after that—really, it was *Marco* who collapsed, spent and exhausted and so fucking happy he didn't think he'd ever felt its equal—Andrew traced patterns on his chest.

"You ever think we'd be here?" he wondered.

Marco wasn't sure if that was a rhetorical question. He'd sure *wanted* them to be here, from the moment he'd spotted Andrew again.

The moment he'd realized that high school Andrew had very much grown up.

"No—but I really wanted us to."

"Yeah, for a whole seven days," Andrew teased, but

Marco could hear the doubt underneath the amusement in his voice.

"Hey, it was a hard seven days," Marco retorted lightly. But he wanted to ask.

How could he say he was falling for him if he *didn't* ask?

"You do this a lot, I know," Andrew said, and it seemed that he was going to say it, without Marco opening his mouth.

"Not that often anymore," Marco said wryly.

"I mean . . ." Andrew waved his hands. "You know what I mean."

Marco was afraid he did. "Really, not *that* often," he said. "You're not one of many, you know, not even close, you're . . ." Marco swallowed hard. He didn't want to say it, it was too soon, even *he,* a Moretti, who as a clan loved love, knew it was too fucking soon. "You're special. As a person. To *me.*"

"Well, that's good," Andrew said. "Because I love you."

Marco froze. Andrew lifted his head, and the truth of his confession was written across his face.

He meant it.

And *God,* Marco wanted him to mean it.

"I know I'm not supposed to say that. I wasn't going to. But . . ." Andrew sighed. "I couldn't not. I feel like I've been half in love with you most of my life, and then the last seven days have been . . .well, you were there. You know what they were like."

"They were great," Marco said. "At least when I wasn't trying to keep my hands off you."

Andrew laughed. "Oh! We didn't have our dessert."

He scrambled off before Marco could wrap an arm around him and forcibly drag him back against his body.

Of course, this guy would say that and clearly mean it and then leave.

Marco huffed out as he lay back in the nest of messy sheets and blankets.

A minute later, Andrew appeared again, carrying the white takeout box in one hand and a fork in the other. "I found your silverware," he said, settling back down on the bed, cross-legged this time, apparently uncaring that he was still naked.

Well, if Marco looked that gorgeous, he probably wouldn't care either.

In fact, even after two very good orgasms, he was having trouble dragging his attention to the box in Andrew's hands.

Then Andrew opened it and Marco made a low exclamation in the back of his throat.

It was a work of art. Each piece of fruit flawlessly arranged across the pristine white surface.

And then Marco realized that he'd picked the fruit specifically.

There were delicate slivers of plums fanned out. Tiny grapes arranged in a cluster.

And a few pomegranate seeds, scattered like precious jewels.

"I . . ." Marco didn't know what to say.

"I made it for you," Andrew said. "Daniel helped, a little. He'd helped you clean up after Izzy, so he knew what she'd thrown at you. Though I wish she'd picked better choices."

He smiled self-consciously and continued. "I said I'd never throw a pomegranate at your head and I figured this was a concrete example of that promise."

"It's beautiful," Marco said. Andrew handed him the fork but he hesitated. "I don't even want to eat it."

"But it's delicious," Andrew teased. "I think you'll like it."

"I know I'll like it. I already do. The only question is how much I'll love it," Marco mused.

He raised his gaze and his eyes met Andrew's. Hoped he understood.

Andrew smiled. "The dessert's not going anywhere—and neither am I."

"Good," Marco said and wrapped an arm around Andrew's shoulders, pulling him in and pressing a kiss to his bare shoulder. "Now tell me, before I destroy the beauty of it, what it is."

"A pavlova," Andrew said.

"A what?"

Andrew laughed. "It's a good thing you're cute. A pavlova is egg whites whipped with sugar and then piped out and baked. Usually with some kind of filling." His eyes were twinkling. "You'll have to eat it to figure out what that is."

"Twist my arm," Marco said and finally dug the fork into the pristine surface. The pavlova was crisp but soft, melting into itself as he cut into it. And in the middle of it, buried deep between clouds of whipped cream and meringue, was a tiny heart of lemon yellow custard.

"I saw your face when you ate the special," Andrew said when Marco looked up at him questioningly. "Come on, take a bite."

Marco did, loving the crystalline sugar crunch on his tongue, the perfectly sour curd, the richness of the cream.

He'd eaten a lot of desserts in his time, but he'd never had one like this.

"You're a genius," he murmured, not hesitating to take another forkful. This one he slipped between Andrew's lips as he opened his mouth, no doubt wanting to argue this inarguable fact.

"Just inspired," Andrew said, after savoring his bite. "By the most delectable muse."

Marco kissed him, the flavor of Andrew mingling with the creation he'd made just for him, and he didn't think it would take him very long to be sure that this was not only love, but *that* kind of love.

A love for the easy Saturday mornings and late Friday nights. A love Marco would embrace and protect with every bit of himself.

The most delicious love he'd ever tasted.

Epilogue

Four *months later*

Marco had never been prouder in his whole damn life.

He'd gotten a front row seat to Andrew balancing the work he was doing with Daniel at Nonna's but also finding and outfitting the space for his new bakery.

He'd found a space just off the main street in St. Helena, a little old-fashioned and he'd leaned into the nostalgia of it.

Curly letters the color of old gold coins adorned the big picture window and a smaller version on the leaded glass of the refinished front door.

"What do you think?" Andrew asked, coming up next to Marco and tipping his head against Marco's shoulder. He sounded tired, but exhilarated.

Marco remembered exactly what that felt like. When he'd opened the steakhouse, he'd been exhausted but so revved up he'd felt like he could go and go and never quit.

Good thing he was around for Andrew, because someone needed to drag him home, to their bed.

"I think it looks incredible. Like the place you'd always envisioned."

One late night during the summer, only a few weeks after they'd gotten together, they'd taken a bath together, and Andrew had confessed that everyone was expecting him to build some kind of very high-end, esoteric kind of bakery. But that wasn't what he wanted.

"I can't believe I'm saying this, but your very pedestrian desserts inspired me," Andrew had teased.

Marco had splashed him but Andrew had only grinned. "I mean it. I walk around the dining room sometimes, and the smiles on everyone's faces? The pure delight and joy? It's wonderful. Nobody's ever worried about how to eat something or what's in it. It's just really delicious food. That's what I want to serve."

"Well, you've got it in the bag then," Marco had said and Andrew had laughed and splashed him again. They'd ended up making out in the tub, water running over the side, and Marco hadn't even minded cleaning it up later.

"Yeah, it really does," Andrew agreed. "Exactly like what I wanted. I know that's not always how things turn out, so I'm gonna take this win."

"You all ready to open this weekend?" Marco asked, even though he knew the truth. Andrew had been ready a week ago.

"Yep, we're all set now. Permits are in. Roger's in the back, inventorying for tomorrow."

"I can't wait to see how this town embraces you," Marco

said earnestly. And it was true. He wanted everyone to see the brilliant, amazing, *lovable* man Andrew was. The one he'd fallen so hard for.

"You think they will?" Andrew sounded nervous, not for the first time, because frankly, starting a new business was *always* nerve-wracking and anxiety-inducing, but it was the first time in probably a month that he'd talked about it.

"I *know* they will," Marco said. "Just like I did."

And he *had*.

After that first night together, Andrew hadn't told him he loved him again, but it was there, in every glance, in every tease, in every kiss. In how hard he'd worked to make sure Daniel had a great foundation to become the head pastry chef in Marco's restaurant.

Marco hadn't said it yet, either, even though he was pretty damn sure he loved Andrew. Had been sure for awhile now.

But Andrew bringing up how many times Marco *had* done this—fallen in love and enjoyed someone before ultimately it ended—made Marco want to be *sure* that this was forever before he said the words.

Because once he said them, they were always going to be true.

It was why he'd waited.

Until now.

"Thank you," Andrew murmured. "For everything."

"I didn't do much," Marco said. He'd wanted to do more. But he'd forced himself to wait for Andrew to ask—a few times he'd intervened but he'd tried not to the overbearing, all-knowing ass that he knew ran in the Moretti genes. Thank you, Luca.

"You did the perfect amount." Andrew sighed happily as he stared out at the bakery, and Marco looked down at him. Loving him, so much that he knew he'd never *not* feel this way.

"There's one last thing I can do," Marco said. "The most important thing."

Andrew looked over at him, blue eyes glowing in the morning sunshine. "What's that?"

"No matter what happens, I'm gonna be proud of you every single day for the rest of our lives. And every single one of those days? I'm gonna love you too."

Andrew blinked, then his eyes went misty. "Oh, damnit, I said I wasn't going to cry but then I am and *ugh*, of course you're a romantic. Of course you saved it for the most romantic moment."

"I just told you I loved you, I think any time would've been romantic," Marco said, grinning.

"But it was *especially* romantic. I guess I shouldn't be surprised. It's just like a Moretti."

"*Your* Moretti," Marco said.

"The Moretti I love," Andrew said.

About the Author

A lifelong Oregonian, Beth Bolden recently moved to North Carolina with her supportive husband and their sweet kitten, Earl Grey. Beth still believes in Keeping Portland Weird, and intends to be just as weird in Raleigh.

Beth has been writing practically since she learned the alphabet. Unfortunately, her first foray into novel writing, titled Big Bear with Sparkly Earrings, wasn't a bestseller, but hope springs eternal. She's published forty-five novels and six novellas.

To learn more information about Beth: www.bethbolden.com/about

You can check out the rest of the Morettis here: www.bethbolden.com/morettis

For a full listing of published works: www.bethbolden.com/booklist

Feeding The Grump

Jax Calder

Chapter One

David

I'm fairly sure that when I'm on my deathbed, I'll still be cursing Benji Gange's name.

"Fucking Benji Gange," I say to my brother on the phone I'm holding one-handed while I try to repair the ancient water trough's third leak this month.

"What's he done this time?" My brother Lance sounds a combination of amused and exasperated, like he's watching a rerun of a show where he already knows the ending.

"He's only gone and painted his gate to the Boundary Ridge paddock."

"What's wrong with that?"

"He's painted it purple," I say.

And not just any purple. This purple is so bright it could probably guide lost sheep home in the dark.

"It's on his land," Lance says mildly.

"But I'm the one who has to look at it! It's a bloody fence, not an art exhibition."

I can too easily imagine the smug smile on Benji's face as he wielded his paintbrush like Michelangelo redecorating the Sistine Chapel. He'll have known what my reaction would be.

I'm fairly sure that's why he did it. My hands clench just thinking about that.

"I'm going to have to go over to his place and talk to him about it," I say.

"Of course you are," Lance says.

"What do you mean by that?"

"Nothing."

"I know your nothings. Come on, spit it out."

"It's just that everything the guy does seems to wind you up. You've been like that from the moment he took over his uncle's farm. Stuff you normally wouldn't care about suddenly becomes a capital offense when Benji's involved."

He's right.

Would I care so much if Bruce and Louise McMillian, my neighbors on the other side, had done the same thing?

But hell would freeze over before Bruce would ever paint a gate that garish purple, so the question is redundant.

Lance is right that something about Benji Gange has rubbed me the wrong way from the first moment I met him.

After his bachelor uncle passed away, rumors flew around the district that his nephew from Auckland had inherited the farm.

I vaguely remember Benji as a kid visiting during the summer holidays, trailing after his uncle like an imprinted duckling, but he was five years younger than me, so I hadn't paid much attention to him.

148

But when he turned up in his city-slicker clothes, his light-brown hair styled with some sort of product that made it shine like a newly polished pickup truck on show day, I'd definitely paid attention.

Mainly to scoff.

The guy would last two months farming if he was lucky.

He's proved me wrong on that one.

Turns out his city-slicker job had been in environmental management, so he understood more about soil composition than half the old-timers who'd been farming since before he was born.

He pissed off quite a few farmers round here by raving on about water conservation strategies, but when he was still managing a good stock load while the rest of us were selling off sheep during the drought, people at the pub began to listen more carefully to what he had to say.

Maybe that was what bugged me about him? The way he'd sauntered into this tight-knit community, all effortless charm and styled hair, and suddenly had everyone fawning over him.

They don't have to be a neighbor to the guy. They don't have to constantly interact with him about shared water rights, boundary fences, and his organic fertilizer experiments that drift onto my land whenever the wind picks up.

I'm not a complete stick-in-the-mud. I'm prepared to learn and adapt.

But some of Benji's experiments belong in one of those fancy agricultural magazines, not in the real world where mud and machinery don't always play nice with computer programs.

Like last spring's debacle with his newly installed automated feed stations. They worked fine until the first proper southerly hit, then the whole system went haywire. Meanwhile, my simple hay feeders kept my stock fat and happy through the worst weather.

I don't have a good comeback to Lance's accusation that Benji winds me up more than anyone else, so I ignore it.

"Need to go so I can finish fixing this bloody trough," I grunt.

"Pub tomorrow night?" Lance asks.

"Yeah. See you then."

I end the call and wrestle with the ancient pipe wrench. The metal groans in protest as I force it to grip the corroded fitting. Water sprays in my face, tasting like rust and minerals, but I don't flinch. Been doing this since I was knee-high to a grasshopper, watching Dad curse at these same troughs while I handed him tools.

The sun beats down on my neck as I methodically work through the repair.

My shirt's soaked through by the time I'm done, but the repair holds when I test it. I straighten, my back protesting.

With the trough sorted, there's nothing left to delay the inevitable.

Time to go into battle with Benji.

But instead of heading straight to my truck, I go via my vegetable garden.

The raised beds are coming alive after winter, with the early potatoes pushing up through the soil like green knuckles. My early variety broad beans are humming with bees despite the spring breeze.

The tension in my shoulders eases as I walk between the beds. There's something settling about good soil under your boots and the smell of things growing.

The rest of the farm might be all about profit margins and stock rates, but here...there are no complicated regulations or fancy modern methods. Just dirt and seeds doing what they're meant to do.

My great-grandfather established this half-acre vegetable garden and acre of fruit trees back in the thirties. It's designed to feed a whole family, but because I'm by myself, I end up giving most of it away.

Benji is a big recipient of my vegetable garden.

It's the neighborly thing to do. No matter how much Benji and I argue over whose stock caused the damage to the new section of boundary fencing or whether his fancy irrigation system sends too much runoff into my lower paddocks, he's still my neighbor.

And in this small corner of rural New Zealand, that means something.

It feels like summer inside the greenhouse compared to the spring chill outside. I check my tomato seedlings first, which are standing tall in their pots, each labeled in my careful handwriting. I used to stick to just Money Makers, but in the last few years, I've grown more varieties. Black Russians, Green Zebras, those fancy Italian ones with the ridges.

I'm a few months away from harvesting tomatoes, though, so I head to the back of my greenhouse, where my cucumbers are showing off, growing faster than gossip at the pub. I pick a couple, along with the last of the winter lettuce that keeps me in salads when everyone else is paying ridiculous supermarket prices.

Armed with the vegetables, I jump in my pickup truck and drive the kilometer to Benji's house.

When Benji's uncle lived here, the house was a testament to bachelor living, with peeling weatherboards that hadn't seen paint since the eighties and a garden of whatever managed to survive without attention.

Now...well...now, the weatherboards are a soft gray that probably has some fancy name like *morning mist* or *coastal storm*. The wraparound porch sports hanging baskets full of natives. And because he's Benji, he's got those windchimes made from old farm tools hanging everywhere. They shouldn't work, but somehow, they do, just like his other mad ideas.

I stride up the path and knock sharply on the front door.

There's no answer.

That's not surprising. Farmers don't automatically clock off after five. There's always more work to be done.

But his pickup truck is out front, and I spot his four-wheeler in the shed, so he must be somewhere around.

I track him down in the cattle yard, teaching his heading dog to work the new cattle he's bought. The dog's young and eager, about as subtle as a brick through a window, but Benji's patient with him. His voice is gentle but firm as he gives commands.

Benji doesn't spot me approaching, which gives me a chance to observe him. Observe how the sun's catching him just right, turning his light-brown hair golden. He's lean, but his shoulders show the results of physical labor three hundred and sixty-five days a year.

Not that I'm paying attention to any of that. I'm just... appreciating his stockmanship. That's all it is.

His head snaps up at the crunch of my boots on the gravel as I reach the yard, a smile spreading across his face.

He's always like this, always acts like he's pleased to see me despite the fact that nearly every interaction between us has some point of friction.

He gives the dog a final pat before striding over, all easy grace and too-white teeth.

"David, to what do I owe this pleasure?"

"You need to repaint your gate," I say.

Benji's eyes dance with amusement. "But I just painted it."

"Yeah, I saw. It's an eyesore."

He leans against the fence post, crossing his arms over his chest, his head tilting to one side as he considers me.

"How is it an eyesore?"

"It's purple," I manage to reply.

"What do you have against the color purple?" he asks.

"Nothing. It's just not appropriate for a gate."

The corners of his mouth twitch up. "Is there some manual about acceptable gate aesthetics that I missed? Was there some report in *Farming Weekly* about how purple gates decrease lamb production?"

This is what makes arguing with Benji so infuriating. His tendency to meet every complaint with that crooked smile and dancing eyes, like I'm simply making his day more entertaining.

"Some things are just done certain ways out here," I say.

"But who says every gate has to be the same color?" he asks, his eyes not leaving mine. "Every time I drive past that gate, it makes me smile. And isn't that worth something? A bit of unexpected joy when you're not expecting it? Besides, last I checked, sheep don't care what color the gates are."

The idea of doing something just to make yourself smile seems frivolous. Wasteful. The kind of thing that has no place on a working farm. But then again, that's exactly what my vegetable garden is, isn't it? Not that I'd ever admit that out loud.

"But I'm the one who's got to look at that gate all the time."

He shrugs. "Maybe I was hoping it would make you smile too."

Inexplicably, heat that has nothing to do with the late afternoon sunshine creeps up my neck.

I scuff my boot against the ground like it's personally offended me.

Because the way Benji's looking at me makes my skin prickle. Better to talk about something that makes sense. Something I know how to handle.

"The thistle paddock's looking rough at the moment. When was the last time you actually ran stock through there?"

"It's mine for another eight months, remember?" Benji says.

The thistle paddock is one of the constant sources of contention between us.

To be fair, the conflict over the five-acre paddock isn't just a Benji and me thing. It's been going on for generations.

Back in the forties, some idiot city surveyor included the paddock on both our farm titles.

The mistake wasn't discovered until thirty years later, and by then, the paddock had already passed through enough hands that unscrambling the mess would've needed King Solomon himself.

My grandfather and Old Jack Gange had knocked back a few beers at the pub before coming up with their solution, deciding to take turns using the paddock in two-year blocks. Simple as that.

"I wish you'd just let me buy it off you," I mutter.

"But I so enjoy sharing custody of a paddock with you." Benji's eyes sparkle with his particular brand of mischief that makes my stomach do something uncomfortable. "In fact, I was thinking maybe we should renegotiate the deal and just split it by days of the week? You get Monday, Wednesday, and Friday. I get Tuesday, Thursday, and Saturday. We can arm wrestle for Sundays."

I roll my eyes because he's just trying to wind me up. But I can't help responding. "Pretty sure it's a paddock, not a timeshare."

His eyes continue to dance. "In fact, maybe we should consider other options for the paddock. We could do a joint tourist venture. Experience authentic rural New Zealand. Stand in a paddock that belongs to two men simultaneously." His mouth quirks up. "We'd make a fortune."

"There's nothing in that paddock except thistles."

"And the view of a purple gate. You can't forget that," he says helpfully.

This is why any conversation with Benji is so infuriating. I swear the blood pressure pills Doc Wilson prescribed me at my last checkup should come with a warning label that reads: *May be ineffective against the annoying neighbor.*

"That gate's about as much of a tourist attraction as my compost heap," I say.

He shakes his head at me. "Still think you're missing out on the potential. We could be great business partners. You could do the practical stuff. I'll handle the creative vision. Picture it: *The Thistle Experience: Where Boundaries Blur.*"

"The only thing blurring around here is your grip on reality," I grumble.

Benji laughs, and the sound does something funny to my insides.

I struggle to come up with another topic of conversation. "We need to talk about the creek boundary sometime. The bend is getting wider every season."

"Nature doesn't go in straight lines," Benji says. He gives me a wink. "In fact, I don't think anything worthwhile is completely straight."

My throat goes dry. Something about the way he says those words makes me wonder if we're talking about boundary lines at all.

After any conversation with Benji, I always spend the next day reviewing everything he said, turning his words over in my mind and silently crafting better comebacks.

I can't think of a reply now, so I turn to go, then suddenly realize I'm still clutching the vegetables.

"Here," I say, thrusting the cucumbers and lettuce at him.

Benji takes them off me, looking down at them with a soft smile.

I don't know how to interpret that smile.

"Thanks," he says, raising his green eyes to mine in that slow way of his, like he's taking his time to memorize something important. "Your vegetable garden never disappoints."

I grunt in reply before turning and striding off.

Chapter Two

David

The next afternoon, I come home from drafting ewes and their lambs into different mobs to find a fresh-baked peach loaf on my doorstep.

I know without tasting it that the peaches will be Golden Queens from my orchard last summer. Benji must have bottled the excess ones I gave him.

This is how Benji has always repaid me for the fruit and vegetables I give him, by baking or cooking something for me in return.

He must've spotted my microwave dinners at some point because once or twice a week, he gives me casseroles, pies, or stews, things I can easily freeze in smaller portions and then reheat.

Our food exchange is almost wordless now, completely unrelated to how we argue over everything else.

But tonight, I don't need to reheat one of Benji's meals because I'm grabbing dinner at the pub.

Before I get ready, I've got one chore still to do.

The orphan lambs are waiting by the fence, bleating their impatience.

"Keep your wool on," I tell them gruffly as I measure the milk powder. They're getting stronger every day, which means they're also getting more demanding about their feeds.

The smallest one, with the black spots around her eyes, still needs some encouragement, so I settle on an upturned bucket, letting her lean against my leg while she drinks. Her soft wool is warm against my calloused palms.

Lambs fed, I head into the house and jump through the shower, grimacing as the hot water hits the fresh scratches on my arms from wrestling with those bloody brambles in the north paddock.

I drag my razor through three days' worth of stubble, nicking myself twice because I'm rushing. My good jeans are folded in my drawer, the ones without any fence wire tears or stains. They feel strange after a day in work clothes, like they belong to someone else.

For some reason, as I get ready, the conversation I had with Lance the night before his and Emma's wedding creeps into my mind.

We'd been having a few whiskeys in the back room of the Royal Hotel—the same place our father had taken us for our first legal drinks—when Lance had started talking about how Emma completed him. It sounded like something from one of those romance movies Mum used to watch, but Lance had said it with such conviction that I didn't take the piss like I normally would.

I'd let his words wash over me while I stared into my glass.

"What about you, big brother?"

His question had forced me to jerk my head up.

"What about me?"

"Don't you want to date, get married? I mean, I don't think you've had a proper girlfriend for a decade now. And you're not that hideous. It's definitely not due to lack of trying by the women around here."

He was right. Ever since I hit puberty and grew to be a replica of my dad, six foot one, broad shoulders, dark hair and eyes, I'd never had a shortage of female attention.

I'd taken another gulp of my drink, but the whiskey couldn't wash away the familiar feeling of somehow being broken. Watching my mates at school fall in lust at first sight, hooking up with strangers at parties, while I never understood the appeal.

"I can't be bothered with that nonsense," I'd replied.

"Maybe you just need the right person to come along," he said.

I'd made a noncommittal grunt and then moved the conversation on by asking about his plans for rotating the winter feed crops. Farm talk was safer than examining the hollow feeling his words left in my chest.

The memory of that conversation rattles in my head as I grab my keys from the hook by the door.

Country pubs in New Zealand are all cut from the same cloth. The Royal's got its share of wobbly tables held steady by folded cardboard, walls covered in faded photos of local rugby teams, and regulars wearing grooves into the barstools. It's the sort of place where your beer appears without you having to order it, and everyone knows whose dog is sleeping under which table.

I arrive and head over to the table where Lance is already deep in conversation with Pete the stock agent and Doc Wilson. Doc's the local GP who's been patching up farmers around here since before I was born. Given the number of times he's stitched me up after farming accidents, I reckon he knows the scar pattern on my hands better than I do.

"'Bout time you showed up," Lance says as I pull out a chair.

There's the usual shuffle of chairs and lifting of pint glasses as I join them, everyone automatically shifting to make room for me.

Tilly the barmaid has barely got my pint in front of me when I spot him.

The sight of Benji's frame in the doorway hits me like an unexpected southerly, only this is something that leaves me somehow both cold and hot at the same time. I take a quick gulp of my beer.

Pete's already standing to shake Benji's hand.

"G'day mate," he says. "You want to join us?"

Benji's green eyes scan the table, and when they meet mine, the usual spark of mischief in them makes my collar feel too tight.

"Sure, I'll join you," he says.

He chooses the seat next to mine. Of course he does.

He smells like the land after rain, mixed with whatever

fancy shower gel he uses. I'm sure the weird flip my stomach does is just my body preparing itself for whatever argument we're bound to have when we're in such close proximity.

"You're looking all dressed up, Benji? You meeting someone?" Pete asks.

I stiffen, my hand clenching around my glass.

When Benji first turned up, it wasn't just his city-slicker ways or farming techniques that caused the gossipers' tongues to work overtime.

It was the fact he openly dated both men and women, which wasn't something our little corner of rural New Zealand had seen much.

Even though he started off dating with gusto, Benji seems to have slowed down lately, like a tractor that's run out of diesel. From what I've seen, he hasn't dated anyone for the past two years.

Not that I care.

My house is on a slight hill that looks down over his place, so I'm aware of the comings and goings on his farm. Same as I notice when his sheep are ready for crutching, or his hay needs baling. Just being a good neighbor, that's all.

Maybe he's simply worked through all the eligible men and women and is waiting for fresh blood to move into the district. Though the thought of someone new catching Benji's eye makes my stomach clench in a way that has nothing to do with my anticipation of the meal the pub is cooking for me tonight.

"Nah, I'm not meeting anyone. I just thought it was time to retire the sheep-dip-stained look," Benji says.

His shoulder bumps mine as he reaches for the beer Tilly puts on the table for him. My muscles lock up tighter than a new fence wire.

What the hell is going on with me?

I scan the room for something to distract me.

A replay of the final of the Supreme rugby competition is playing on a screen above the bar, showing the Auckland Greens losing to the Stallions. I nod at it.

"This must bring back some bad memories for you," I say to Benji. "Watching your team get annihilated in the final."

"At least my team made it through to the finals. Remind me, when were the Marauders knocked out?" he asks with an arched eyebrow, knowing full well the local team, the Canterbury Marauders, hadn't even made the semis this year.

"Talking rugby, who do you reckon they're going to start for the first Australia match. Jones or Bannings?" Pete asks.

This debate has been dominating sports media for the last few weeks. Aiden Jones is a legend in New Zealand rugby, one of the greatest players we've ever produced. He's had a lock on his starting position in the New Zealand rugby team for the last six seasons. But Tyler Bannings is a young Greens player who's had a phenomenal season, and there's lots of speculation that the uppity hotshot might be named to start ahead of the veteran. Bannings has a raw talent that makes spectators forget to breathe, but he's about as predictable as the spring weather.

"They gotta pick experience over the flashy upstart," Doc Wilson says.

"I think they should start Bannings, actually." Benji says

the words with wicked intent, like he knows exactly how much that will irritate me.

I snort. "You'd pick style over substance? Why doesn't that surprise me?"

He slides a look at me. "Sometimes you get both style and substance together in a package."

Fuck. It feels like another one of those Benji comments with a double meaning.

"Is that what you tell yourself when you look in the mirror each morning?" The words slip out before I can catch them, and I immediately regret how they sound. Like I'm admitting I've thought about what he sees in his mirror.

Benji goes still, his glass halfway to his lips.

"Bannings is all flash, no follow-through," I continue quickly. "Man can't hold a defensive line to save his life."

Benji's throat works as he swallows a hefty gulp of beer, and I have no idea why I'm so focused on watching, fascinated by the way his Adam's apple bobs.

He sets his glass down with deliberate care, a smile playing at the corners of his mouth.

"What Bannings lacks in discipline, he makes up for in vision," he says, leaning toward me slightly like he's sharing a secret. "Besides, have you seen his sidestep? He could dodge raindrops in a thunderstorm."

The debate about whether Bannings or Jones should start continues well into our second round of beer, voices getting louder and opinions getting stronger with each empty glass until Pete sets up player formations with the salt and pepper shakers and other condiments on the table.

This is serious.

This is rugby.

What none of the guys here know, not even Lance, is that Aiden Jones is actually one of our neighbors.

Six years ago, I sold off the five acres of land that held the old farm manager's cottage. When I'd gone to sign the contract and seen the purchaser's name, I'd almost dropped my pen.

But Aiden Jones is quite a common name, so I'd figured it must be a coincidence. The odds of a New Zealand rugby player buying my rundown manager's cottage seemed about as likely as finding a Michelin-star restaurant in Old Thompson's hay shed.

It wasn't until I'd gone to drop off a spare key after the possession date and been greeted with those familiar steely eyes and granite jaw that I discovered I actually did have a New Zealand rugby legend as my new neighbor.

Since then, I've kept my distance and my mouth shut.

Because Aiden Jones has one of the most high-stress jobs in the country, constantly scrutinized by everyone from professional sports commentators to the guy behind the counter at the local store. He deserves a place where he can unwind without anyone gawking at him.

I also feel a weird kinship with Aiden Jones.

He's known as the Ice King. Someone who simply gets the job done, doesn't make any fuss, and doesn't waste more words than necessary.

He couldn't be more different from the flashy Bannings.

Of course, the media likes to play up their rivalry and the contrast between them.

You can see Jones's contempt for Bannings every time

he's asked about him in an interview, although he always keeps his comments professional. Unlike Bannings, who often seems to try to bait Jones with some of his remarks to the media.

Benji's still arguing passionately about Bannings' style of play, and it's distracting how he keeps shifting closer to me every time he makes a point, like proximity will somehow make his argument more convincing.

Benji always talks with his whole body when he's excited about something, his hands moving, eyes bright. And even though everyone is listening to him, he seems to focus mostly on me as he makes his points.

The heat from his leg pressed against mine makes it difficult to follow the conversation, but I do my best, arguing back just as fiercely about Jones's tackle success rate and defensive line statistics.

"Bloody hell," Lance cuts through our argument with a knowing look that makes me want to kick him under the table like I did when we were kids. "Last time I saw you this fired up was when the stock agent tried to undervalue your two-tooths at the autumn sales."

"Rugby's important," I manage to reply.

"My brother manages to use up his monthly word quota arguing with you, Benji," Lance says with a grin at Benji.

Benji stretches back with a smile. "Sadly, I don't think the New Zealand selectors really care about our opinions."

"It's a good thing they're not listening to you," I say.

Benji meets my gaze, his green eyes crinkling at the corners in a way that always sends a jolt down my spine.

For a split second, it feels like everyone else in the pub fades away. I can't tear my gaze away from him.

Lance laughs, and it shatters the strange tension. He claps me on the shoulder as he turns his attention to Benji. I clear my throat, looking down at my beer.

"Anyway, what's new with you, Benji?" Lance asks. "Heard at the feed store that you're thinking about going into bees."

"Yeah, I'm putting in some hives."

I whip my head up to stare back at Benji. "You're putting in bees? They're not something to mess about with when you don't know what you're doing."

Benji takes a casual sip of his beer, foam clinging to his upper lip until he wipes it away with the back of his hand. "Don't worry, David. I've done my research."

"Research isn't experience."

"That's why I talked to old Wilson. He's kept bees for forty years."

"Wilson's half-blind and fully mad."

Benji laughs. "He knows his bees. And I'm thinking of starting with just two hives near the manuka patch."

"Two hives means thousands of bees," I point out. "Thousands of bees that don't recognize property lines. They'll be all over my place."

"And you'll get the benefit of a free pollination service," Benji says with infuriating brightness. "Your orchard yields will go up fifteen percent, minimum."

"Or my sheep will get stung."

"Bees don't just randomly attack sheep, David." Benji leans forward, one eyebrow cocked. "I've ordered special

Carniolan queens. They're known for their gentle temperament."

"You've already ordered them?" I straighten in my seat. "Without talking to your neighbors first?"

"I'm talking to you now," he says in this patient tone.

"After you've already made up your mind."

"I thought you'd appreciate the honey. It might sweeten you up." He gives me one of his standard-issue Benji grins, where one side of his mouth quirks up more than the other.

Why the hell do his words and grin send a flush of embarrassment mingled with something else I refuse to name racing up my neck?

"You need to buy proper protective gear, make sure you've got a contingency plan for something going wrong. Those allergic reactions can come out of nowhere, even if you've never had one before."

Benji's eyes switch from playful to something softer. "I appreciate your concern for my safety."

I'm waiting for him to finish his words with one of his typical smartass comments, but he doesn't say anything else. Which sends us into another weird moment where we're staring at each other.

"It's called being a good neighbor," I say finally.

"Right," he replies.

He holds my stare a moment longer than necessary. It's almost like he's waiting for me to catch up on something I'm missing.

I blink and look down, suddenly fascinated with the condensation rings on the table.

The conversation among the others moves on to Bruce

McMillian's new deer fence, but for the rest of the evening, there's a weird tension between Benji and me.

And I don't think our disagreement about his new beehives is why my chest tightens every time he looks at me.

By the time Tilly starts wiping down tables, I'm no closer to understanding the weirdness that has engulfed me.

Chapter Three

David

The next day, the first hint that something is wrong comes from the orphan lambs at their midday feed. Their bleating has a different pitch, like they're singing a song with one voice missing from the harmony.

I count them three times, but the result doesn't change. The little one with black spots around her eyes isn't here.

"Shit."

I pace the fence line, checking for gaps, and find where a fallen branch has pushed the wire down just enough for a determined lamb to squeeze through.

My gut churns. She could have wandered anywhere.

I'm halfway through checking the home paddock when Benji's pickup truck comes bumping down my driveway. Fuck. Just what I need, Benji witnessing me running around like a headless chook looking for a lost lamb.

He gets out holding what looks like a casserole dish.

"Thought you might appreciate some lunch. Made too much beef stew last night," he calls over to me.

"Can't stop right now. Got a lamb missing," I say tersely.

Instead of taking the hint and leaving, he puts the dish on the hood of his pickup truck. "Which one?"

"The little one. Black spots round her eyes."

"Pepper?"

At my incredulous look, he shrugs. "What? She looks like someone sprinkled pepper on her face."

Trust Benji to have named my lamb. Though I have to admit, it fits her.

"How long's she been gone?" he asks.

"Must've gotten out this morning after feeding."

He's already striding over to me. "Right, where do you want me to start looking?"

"You don't need to—"

"Two sets of eyes are better than one." He gives me that crooked grin that always makes arguing with him feel pointless. "Besides, I helped bottle feed her last week when you were drafting, remember? Makes me practically a godfather."

That had been a one-off thing. I'd been running late finishing drafting, and when I arrived back at the home paddock, I'd found Benji contentedly feeding my orphan lambs. I could only imagine the ruckus they'd made when he arrived at my place to drop off his latest casserole.

"Fine," I growl. "But we need to be systematic about it."

We work our way through the paddocks in a grid pattern. The spring sun beats down as we walk, making sweat trickle down my back. Out of the corner of my eye, I catch glimpses of Benji moving through the long grass, his pants getting progressively more damp.

Not that I'm looking.

"Pepper," Benji calls out.

I snort. "You expect her to come to her name?"

Benji shrugs. "I've found my sheep often react to my voice."

"Next, you'll be telling me you read them bedtime stories."

Benji's face lights up. "That's not a bad idea. *The Three Little Rams. Little Bo Peep: A Cautionary Tale.*"

"*The Emperor's New Wool Coat,*" I offer in return.

Benji laughs. "*Little Red Riding Hood and the Big Bad Stock Agent.*"

I can't help chuckling at that one. Benji tilts his head at the sound of my laughter, giving me a satisfied smile.

Like making me laugh is a victory.

But I don't have time to dwell on that thought because I suddenly realize the search has taken us closer to Aiden Jones's boundary. The old macrocarpa hedge there is thick enough to swallow a full-grown sheep, let alone a lamb.

Benji heads straight for it. "Perfect hiding spot for a lamb."

"Leave it," I say sharply. "We'll check the creek bed first."

He turns to me, that familiar spark of challenge in his eyes. "Since when do you shy away from thorny situations?"

Before I can stop him, he pushes into the hedge, the branches catching on his clothes.

"Benji—"

172

"Found some wool caught here." His voice is muffled through the foliage. "Might be recent—shit!"

There's a ripping sound followed by cursing.

"You stuck?" I call into him.

"Not really," he says in a tone that clearly means yes.

I blow out a frustrated breath. "Stay still."

Following his path through the hedge, I find him thoroughly tangled, one arm twisted behind him where his sleeve has caught on a particularly vicious branch.

Of course, being Benji, he still has a grin lingering despite his predicament.

"Don't say it," he warns.

"Wasn't going to say anything," I reply as I move closer, trying to work out the best angle to free him.

But there's not much room to maneuver inside a hedge. In fact, it feels like the branches are deliberately pressing us together, leaving barely enough space to breathe. I can see Aiden Jones's backyard through the gaps in the foliage.

Benji turns slightly, and his chest brushes against mine. Which somehow makes every muscle in my body tense.

What the fucking hell?

"Never figured you for the rescuing type," Benji says. This close, I can see the flecks of gold in his green eyes, something I've never noticed before and immediately wish I hadn't.

"I'm not rescuing you. I'm rescuing my hedge," I retort. We're so close together that I feel the laughter shuddering through his body.

The world narrows to the inches between us, my heart hammering so loud I'm certain he can hear it. His breath warms my neck, sending an electric current zipping down my spine that has nothing to do with the twigs digging into my back. I suddenly forget how to swallow properly, my mouth as dry as summer dust.

I try to focus on the task at hand, but my brain's suddenly rewiring itself without permission. Benji's hip presses against mine as he shifts his weight, and I'm hyperaware of every point of contact between us.

I fumble with the branch that's got him caught, my usually capable farmer's hands clumsy as a newborn calf's legs. The familiar scent of him—soil and that fancy shower gel and something uniquely Benji—fills my nostrils, making it impossible to think straight.

Benji shifts, and our eyes lock.

Bloody hell.

Something passes between us, quick as summer lightning and just as electric.

"Hold still," I command, though my voice comes out embarrassingly rough.

His breath catches as I lean in closer, my fingers working at the stubborn branch that's hooked his sleeve. Twigs scrape against my skin, but I barely notice the sting.

"You're making it worse," I mutter as he tries to twist free.

"Well, if you'd just—"

The sound of a door opening cuts through his words.

Fuck.

We both freeze.

I peer through the branches and my heart climbs into my throat as the familiar form of Aiden Jones emerges onto the back doorstep of his cottage.

I glance over at Benji's face. His eyes widen as New Zealand's legendary rugby player crunches on the gravel path.

Shit. He's coming in our direction.

But he stops at his woodpile thirty feet from the hedge.

Even though I knew Aiden Jones owned the place, it's still surreal to see the Ice King himself, the guy whose poster probably hangs in half the teenage bedrooms across the country, only thirty feet away.

I feel Benji's quickened breathing against me.

Aiden grabs his axe and positions a log on the chopping block.

As he starts to chop the wood, my shoulders unclench. He hasn't seen us.

Benji uses Aiden's distraction to make another attempt to wiggle free, stretching his arm at an impossible angle that forces him to arch against me. His shoulder slides beneath my chin, his thigh wedges between mine, and suddenly, I can't breathe.

Heat pools low in my stomach, my skin suddenly hypersensitive beneath my work clothes.

I'm acutely aware of every point where Benji's body touches mine, like someone had drawn a map of all the places we're touching and set them on fire. The steady thunk of the axe provides a rhythm to my rapidly beating heart.

What the hell is wrong with me right now?

Benji seems oblivious to the effect our enforced proximity is having on me.

Which is lucky, especially as the heat pooling in my

stomach seems to have migrated lower, and my cock is starting to firm up.

Oh my fucking god. This seriously can't be happening. I can't be about to sprout wood while stuck in the woods pressed against my nemesis neighbor.

I shift, angling my hips backward, pressing myself against the unforgiving branches. Better twigs in my back than the mortification of Benji realizing exactly how my body's responding to him.

But then, a sound from the cottage snaps my attention away from my predicament and makes me freeze again.

The back door opens, and a blond-haired guy saunters out, wearing only a pair of track pants that sit indecently low on his hips. His chest is bare.

When I realize who it is, my jaw drops so hard I nearly dislocate it.

Tyler Bannings.

The flashy Greens player. Aiden Jones's fierce rival for his starting slot in the New Zealand team.

My brain short-circuits, unable to process what I'm seeing.

Tyler Bannings. Here. Half-naked. In Aiden Jones's backyard.

When I glance at Benji, my astonishment is mirrored in his face. His eyebrows have shot up so high they've almost disappeared into his hairline.

"Holy fuck," he breathes in my ear.

I couldn't have put it better myself.

The cocky upstart strolls over to where Aiden's chopping

wood, moving with the same liquid grace that makes him such a devastating player on the field.

That part doesn't shock me.

What shocks me is how he wraps his arms around Aiden from behind, pressing a kiss to the back of his neck.

A choking noise escapes my throat.

Fuck. Luckily, it appears Aiden Jones is too busy to notice the strange noises coming from his hedge.

He puts down his axe and turns in Tyler's arms.

"Come back to bed." Tyler's voice carries to our hiding spot.

"Some of us like to get things done before noon," Aiden replies in his usual droll tone.

"I can think of better things to do." Tyler's hands slide down Aiden's back as he eliminates the space between them to kiss him.

Oh my fucking god.

My eyes dart to Benji's face as they kiss, seeking confirmation I haven't completely lost my mind. Sure enough, Benji's eyes are like saucers, and his mouth has formed a perfect O that would be comical if we weren't currently hidden in a hedge spying on New Zealand rugby royalty.

I completely share his reaction. Seeing Aiden Jones and Tyler Bannings kiss is like discovering gravity works sideways or that sheep have suddenly learned to tap dance.

Tyler eventually pulls back, resting his forehead against Aiden's. "You've made your point about being productive. Now come be unproductive with me."

Aiden's laugh is nothing like the short, controlled sounds he gives in press conferences. This is real, unfettered.

"You're impossible," he says.

"Pretty sure you already knew that about me."

Aiden slings his arm around Tyler's waist as they make their way across the yard.

The Ice King and his supposed rival disappear into the cottage.

After the door closes behind them, Benji and I stand there frozen for a few seconds. Then Benji turns his head to look at me, his face inches from mine.

"Holy fuck," he breathes. "I never would have believed that if I hadn't seen it with my own eyes."

"Yeah, I know."

Because it turns out the biggest rivalry in New Zealand rugby is actually a love story. Who the hell could have predicted that?

I can't quite get my head around the fact that Aiden Jones and Tyler Bannings are involved romantically while competing for the starting spot in the New Zealand team.

But I don't have much time to contemplate the complexities of their relationship because I'm currently tangled in a hedge with my own personal rival, close enough to count his eyelashes, trying desperately to ignore how right it feels.

"Right, don't move," I order, my voice low as I assess the branch that's snared Benji. I have to edge closer, my front flush against his side as I work at the gnarled wood that's claimed his sleeve. His breath warms my neck, sending tremors down my spine. Every inadvertent touch between us sparks something that feels unnervingly right, as if my body's solving an equation my brain's been too stubborn to work out.

It almost feels like recognition.

I finally manage to work the fabric free with a small ripping sound.

We back out awkwardly, a strange shuffling retreat where we can't stop bumping into each other.

When we reach the edge of the hedge, my boots are suddenly unsteady on the familiar ground of my own paddock.

My mind spins like the wheel of my old Massey Ferguson when it's stuck in mud—working overtime but getting absolutely nowhere.

Benji gives me a funny look.

"You okay?"

I can't answer him. I can't speak right now.

"Bannings and Jones are just two people, David. It's nothing to get freaked out over."

"It's not...that," I manage to say.

His forehead furrows, but it's impossible for me to explain everything swirling in my brain right now.

Aiden Jones. Tyler Bannings.

Two guys who don't seem to get along on the surface but must be storing up all that friction just to strike sparks off each other in private, like flint against steel.

And my mind is racing, churning through a whole load of things.

My body's reaction to having Benji pressed against me in the hedge.

Years of bickering over stock rotation schedules and water rights and his organic farming experiments that somehow worked better than they had any right to, every argument feeling like practice for something else entirely.

The fact that I currently have eight heritage varieties of tomatoes growing in my glasshouse after Benji once mentioned he liked the old heirloom breeds.

Personally, I don't even really like tomatoes. Unless they're in one of the sauces Benji makes.

Memories of fresh-baked fruit loaves left cooling in the sun and a freezer filled with dinners he's made me.

The fact that, between his cooking and baking, Benji has been feeding me for the past few years.

The time my tractor broke down during hay baling and Benji showed up without being asked, spending the whole afternoon helping me finish before the rain hit. And he never mentioned how I'd told him the week before that his fancy automated baling system was a waste of money.

How he showed up every morning for a week after Dad died, quietly doing my milking while I dealt with the funeral arrangements.

And when he caught a nasty flu last winter, I found myself dropping by twice a day to check on him, telling myself it was just because his dogs needed feeding. Ended up reading him the *Farming Weekly* while he dozed on the couch.

And how having him pressed against me felt like discovering a new paddock I never knew existed on my own land.

My mind works through it all slowly.

Too slowly.

By the time I've realized what it all means, Benji's stalking across the paddock, having spotted a familiar black-and-white spotted face peering out from behind my oldest poplar tree. The missing lamb is standing under the branches, looking about as guilty as a lamb can look, which it turns out isn't very much.

"Here's Pepper," he calls back triumphantly.

I want to growl at him that I don't name my pet lambs, but the words remain lodged in my throat as I stumble after him.

He tilts his head to his side to regard me. "Are you sure you're okay?"

He's standing in my paddock like he belongs there, one hand absently scratching Pepper behind the ears. There's thistle fluff caught in his hair that's catching the sunlight like a halo.

"Yeah, I think I will be," I finally say.

Chapter Four

David

I've never courted anyone before.

It feels like such an old-fashioned word, one that belongs back when blokes actually knew what they were supposed to do in situations like this instead of standing in their kitchen silently panicking about how to make a bloody cheese sandwich.

I spend twenty minutes staring at my wardrobe before accepting that my idea of dressing up means jeans without fence wire tears and a shirt that's never seen the inside of the woolshed. The shirt even has all its original buttons, which practically makes it formal wear in my book.

The drive to Benji's place has never felt longer.

My hands are sweating on the steering wheel like I'm sixteen again, learning to drive stick in Dad's old Hilux. Each fence post I pass marks the seconds until I make a complete fool of myself. I keep the radio switched off because my thoughts are making enough noise.

I pull into his driveway.

The engine ticks as it cools while I try to convince myself to get out or drive away.

There's no point overthinking it now. Not when my truck's probably left a dust trail on the gravel road that's visible from space.

Taking a deep breath, I climb out of my truck, striding up to Benji's front door and knocking.

Maybe he's out? Hopefully, he's out.

Benji opens the door.

"David. To what do I owe this pleasure?" It's his standard greeting, the one he always gives me every time he sees me.

He's leaning against the doorframe wearing dark jeans and a green shirt that makes his eyes look like the sun through spring leaves. His hair's slightly mussed, like he's been running his hands through it, and the half-smile on his face is the one that makes my chest feel too tight for breathing.

"It's a nice evening." I clear my throat. "Thought we could go down by the river for a picnic. If you want."

His eyebrows shoot up for a moment. But the speed at which his eyebrows settle and the happy smile spreads across his face makes me realize I'm the last to work out what's been happening here.

Which I'm sure is something he's not going to let me forget.

"Sure, a picnic sounds great," he says, and I can't take my eyes off his mouth, the way one corner lifts higher than the other. "What do you want to eat?"

"I chucked together some food for us," I say.

His eyebrows rise. "I think in the interest of my tastebuds,

I'd better contribute something edible to this venture. Your reputation with anything more complicated than a sandwich is legendary around here, and not in a good way."

"I made cheese sandwiches," I admit, and Benji's laughter fills his kitchen like sunshine, warming places inside me I didn't know were cold.

"I just baked some honey buns. They'll go great with cheese sandwiches," he says.

I hover awkwardly in the door as Benji bustles around his kitchen, grabbing containers and wrapping things in tea towels.

"Take your truck?" he asks once he's packed things up.

"Yeah."

My pickup bounces down the track to the river like it's trying to remind us why farm vehicles aren't meant for romance.

The air between us feels thick with all the things we're not saying. The rhythm of his fingers tapping on his knee matches the nervous flutter in my chest.

The evening light's gone soft and hazy, making everything look like one of those photographs in farming magazines, all golden grass and long shadows stretching across paddocks.

The river appears through the willows, braided streams glinting like silver wool threads.

I park the truck and grab the picnic blanket and the bag containing our food.

A pair of paradise ducks take off as we approach, their calls echoing across the water. Everything smells of warm grass, river stones, and something else I can't quite name.

I spread the picnic blanket on a patch of grass, and Benji settles next to me, his knee knocking against mine. He unwraps his baking like he's revealing prizes at the A&P Show, which makes me want to roll my eyes and smile at the same time.

"The river level's looking good," he says. "Hopefully, we'll get through summer without water restrictions."

As we eat the cheese sandwiches, we talk about ram prices at the latest sale, the wild pig digging up Thompson's bottom paddock, and whether the Hadfields down the road will really convert their place to dairy like the rumors say.

Then Benji starts to talk about his latest organic trial, and the way he talks about the land reinforces the lesson I've learned over the last five years. He genuinely cares about the same things I do. He just comes at them from a different angle.

I find myself watching the curve of his smile, the way his hands move as he talks about nitrogen cycles and soil struc-ture. *Style and substance together in one package.* The thought rises unbidden, warming my face and making me reach for my water bottle to gulp some down.

Benji licks a smear of honey from his thumb, then wipes his hands on his jeans before splaying his fingers on the blanket between us, just close enough that I can see a small scar across his knuckle.

I can be accused of being many things in life, but a coward isn't one of them.

Taking a deep breath, I slide my hand over to cover his.

He freezes, and for a horrible second, I think I've got this all wrong, and my stomach plummets. The river sounds suddenly too loud in my ears, blood rushing alongside it.

But then Benji flips his hand over, curling his fingers to intertwine his with mine.

He fixes his green eyes on me.

"Remember the time you kept showing up every time I was testing my automated gates, pretending to check your fence line, when really you were making sure I didn't electrocute myself?" he asks.

I keep my voice gruff, trying hard to contain all the emotions swirling inside me at the feel of Benji's hand in mine. "Had to protect my investment in that boundary fence. The last thing I needed was you barbecued against the wire and me having to explain that to the insurance assessor. It was the neighborly thing to do."

Benji ducks his head, a smile tugging at the corner of his mouth as he squeezes my fingers. He shifts his weight, pivoting slightly until our knees touch through worn denim.

My breath catches somewhere between my lungs and my throat as something hot and electric zips up my spine.

The smugness growing in his smile makes me realize he's completely aware of the effect he's having on me.

"Remember the time you insisted on helping me dock lambs even though I said I could manage, then spent the whole time telling terrible sheep puns to keep me from worrying about the storm coming in?" I counter.

"It was the neighborly thing to do. And I object to your categorization of my puns as terrible. I'm pretty sure 'I wool always be here for you' is the height of comedic genius."

186

I snort, but I'm fighting a losing battle against the smile tugging at my lips.

Benji leans slightly closer, his eyes catching the last golden light as if he's gathering it just for us.

"Remember the time you kissed me on the riverbank?" he asks.

My forehead rumples. "I've never kissed you on the riverbank."

"Oh well," he shrugs. "Then I guess you better fix that. If you think it's the neighborly thing to do."

My pulse hammers against my throat and heat surges to my face.

Bloody hell.

I'm lightheaded, my body suddenly unsure how to handle wanting something it never knew it could have.

But I do as my neighbor asks me.

I lean forward and press my mouth to his.

Benji's lips are warm and slightly chapped under mine, tasting of honey from his buns. My heart thunders, but his hand cups my jaw, steadying me.

Fuck.

It's a gentle kiss at first, careful like we're testing uncertain ground.

The stubble on his chin grazes my skin, sending a jolt through me that feels like touching an electric fence, except there's no possibility of me pulling away.

Not when this kiss feels like coming home after a long day of working in the rain. Warm and right and somehow inevitable.

Suddenly, so many of the things I've never quite understood make sense. Those soppy country songs Lance's wife Emma always plays in her car about hearts and forever. The way my parents used to dance in the kitchen to the crackling radio. The way old Joe Morrison's voice still breaks when he talks about his late wife.

I now understand all those things in the context of Benji's lips.

But when he makes a small sound in the back of his throat, hunger roars through me, my control snapping like an old fence wire under too much tension.

His mouth opens under mine, and now our kiss is wilder, like years of bickering and boundary lines and carefully maintained distance are collapsing all at once.

We're crashing together like a downstream surge after the spring melt, powerful enough to reshape the riverbank.

His hand fists in my shirt, pulling me closer as the last light paints everything gold around us. My hands somehow get tangled in his hair, making him groan into my mouth.

When we finally pull apart, we're both breathless and panting.

His pupils are blown out, his lips red and slightly swollen, like the first ripe strawberries in my garden.

I know I'm wearing a stupid, foolish grin. In fact, it appears I can't stop grinning.

The only thing that makes it slightly less mortifying is the matching grin on Benji's face.

"So, my place or yours?" Benji says the words casually, like they're something he's said many times before.

Or maybe they sound so familiar because they're something we're going to be saying to each other for years to come, at least until we finally relent and build our house on the boundary between our land.

It could be a good use of the thistle paddock, come to think of it.

"Mine's closer," I say.

Chapter Five

David

Bumping back up the track in my pickup truck is a completely different experience from going down.

This time, Benji's pressed against me, his hand placed proprietarily on my knee.

Around the time we hit the gravel road, he starts to run his fingers up the inside seam of my jeans, making me grip the steering wheel hard.

"Careful, or this pickup truck is going to end up in Old Thompson's hayfield," I grate out.

It's not until we pull up in my driveway that nerves arrive in my stomach like a swarm of locusts.

The evening light paints long shadows across my front yard as we climb out of the truck. Benji follows me up the path to my front door, and my hands shake so much I drop my keys. Twice. He leans down to pick them up the second time.

"Maybe I should handle the door opening around here," he says, his hands steady as he unlocks the door.

I stumble in after him and find myself standing next to him in my hallway, the familiar smell of grass and sheep dogs and home suddenly seeming different with him here.

When I'm brave enough to glance at him, I find his eyes dark and intent on mine.

Fuck. What do I do now?

It feels like the first time Dad let me drive the tractor alone, that same mixture of fear and wanting so badly to get it right.

Benji steps forward, closing the distance between us.

He reaches up to touch my face, his fingers calloused from farm work but so careful, like I'm something that might spook.

"You okay?" he asks. "We don't have to do anything you don't want to."

At the sensation of his fingertips on my cheekbones, everything I've been denying myself crashes over me like a wave that drowns out doubt and hesitation. My heart pounds a deafening rhythm against my ribs as I pull him closer.

His stubble scratches against my palm as I cup his jaw. He makes a low noise in his throat that unravels something deep in my gut, something that's been wound tight for longer than I can remember.

I catch his bottom lip between my teeth and his hands fist in my shirt like he's afraid I might change my mind. He doesn't seem to understand that I couldn't stop this now any more than I could stop the seasons from turning.

Somehow, we end up with Benji pinned against the wall, me crowding against him.

His back arches as my hands find their way under his

shirt. I'm dizzy with the taste of him, honeyed and familiar in a way that makes no sense. It's like finding a path in real life that I've walked a thousand times in my dreams.

Benji's breathless and panting when our kiss finally breaks.

"Fuck, it's always the quiet ones," he says.

"Didn't hear you complaining," I manage to grind out as I catch my breath.

"Oh, trust me, I'm not complaining about anything right now." He swallows hard, his Adam's apple bobbing before he fixes his green eyes on me. "When did you realize that this was...this?" He waves his hand between us to illustrate what *this* he's referring to.

"In the hedge today," I admit.

He grins. "I'll have to thank Pepper next time I see her."

"My sheep do not have names," I growl, but it only makes his grin grow wider.

"What about you? When did you figure it out?"

"About two years ago."

"Two years?" I grunt the words. I clear my throat, but my voice still sounds rough as I continue, "You never said anything."

He shrugs. "Didn't want to spook you. And you're a smart guy. I figured you'd catch up eventually."

I've never been particularly good with words, so I answer him in what feels like the most logical way—by pulling him closer and claiming his mouth with mine.

To let him know I've definitely figured it out now.

We stagger toward my bedroom, making it to the bed. My bed with its mismatched sheets and the quilt Emma gave me two Christmases ago. The frame groans beneath our combined weight, which I'd find alarming if I could think straight, which I decidedly cannot with Benji's breath hot against my neck.

It should be awkward coming together like this for the first time. God knows I have limited experience with anyone in the bedroom.

Instead, it feels like the most natural thing in the world to unbutton his shirt slowly, kissing every bit of newly exposed skin, methodically, deliberately, making sure I don't miss an inch.

I touch his skin the same way I touched blackbird eggs and four-leaf clovers when I was a kid, when they'd been my most treasured and cherished possessions.

Benji's shirt falls open under my fingers, revealing skin that's tanned golden where the sun catches him working outside and pale as fresh milk everywhere else. I can't help tracing the boundary line between those two tones with my lips.

His breath hitches, and he reaches for my shirt.

When he finishes undoing the last button and pulls off my shirt, he splays his fingers across my chest, rough palm catching on the coarse hair.

When he lifts his gaze to mine, his eyes are molten.

"Holy fuck, David. Why the hell don't you go shirtless more?"

"Pretty sure that would scare the livestock," I reply.

And then Benji is kissing me again as we struggle with belts and zippers, knees bumping, hands fumbling.

Benji's boxers—purple, which doesn't surprise me—slide

down his legs, and I'm suddenly breathless. My underwear joins his, and I feel exposed in a way that has nothing to do with nakedness and everything to do with how he's looking at me like I'm the last green paddock in a drought.

To have Benji Gange stretched out naked in my bed sparks something primitive inside me. The need to possess, to claim, to mark him as mine.

I kiss down his chest, following the trail of dark hair, mapping every muscle and scar with my tongue.

His hands fist in the sheets when I reach his navel.

"This is just another way to torture me, isn't it?" he asks, but his voice is too wrecked to contain much snark.

"You know I like to do things thoroughly," I reply.

And Benji doesn't seem to mind my thoroughness as I head lower. I press my mouth to that crease where thigh meets hip, tasting salt and skin, reducing him to breathless curses and pleas.

His cock is rigid, the head glistening. The desire pulsing through me feels like someone's replaced my blood with lightning, every heartbeat sending sparks through my veins.

How the hell have I noticed every detail about this man except for how much I've wanted him?

I press my lips to his inner thigh, hesitating, feeling his pulse flutter under my tongue.

I've never done this before. My heart hammers against my ribs.

Then summoning my courage, I finally wrap my mouth around his cock.

The unfamiliar fullness makes my jaw ache in a way that's strangely satisfying. He's smoother than I imagined, warmer too. The taste of him, salt and musk, floods my senses, making my hips rock involuntarily against the sheets, seeking friction that isn't there.

The sheer intimacy of him trusting his most vulnerable part to my inexperienced care makes my own desire spike sharply, my body responding to each muffled sound he makes. His hands clutch my shoulders, fingertips pressing into muscle as I take him deeper.

I hollow my cheeks, determined to apply the same stubborn focus to this that I do to everything else in my life.

Then I touch the soft skin behind his balls, feeling him tremble under my calloused fingers.

He grabs my hand and pushes it farther back, and I circle his hole with a teasing pressure that has him cursing my name in ways that would make a shearer blush.

"You've got lube anywhere?" he asks desperately.

"Top drawer." I nod, suddenly grateful for Lance's Christmas joke gift that isn't quite as funny anymore.

"What about a condom?"

"There should be a box in there too."

Benji doesn't comment on the unopened box of condoms, instead ripping through the plastic, his usual precise movements clumsy.

"I'm open to ditching these once we get tested," he says as he passes me a condom.

Fuck. I can't help cringing at his words.

A frown creases his forehead, and he fidgets with the edge of the sheet. "It's going to be just us, right?" he asks quietly.

My cringe fades.

"Of course it's going to be just us." Shit, I didn't mean for that to come out as such a possessive growl.

"Then why did you cringe?"

"Just imagining having a conversation about getting tested with Doc Wilson," I admit.

He laughs, and I watch the laughter transform his face, almost in awe at the quirk of his lips.

I kiss him again, and we sink into the kiss, the taste of his laughter sweet on my tongue as I press him back into the pillows.

Then we're fumbling with the condom and lube, any competence deserting us as we try to coordinate limbs that seem to have multiplied since we hit the bed.

"I have absolutely no idea what I'm doing," I admit, staring at the bottle of lube like it's a piece of farm equipment with missing assembly instructions.

Benji's eyes soften. "It's okay, I'm pretty sure you'll be a quick study with the proper motivation."

And he kisses me deeply, grinding his hard cock against mine, which definitely provides me with the right motivation.

He guides my hand back. "Just go slow. Think of it like... checking a ewe for lambing complications, except with more finesse and significantly less wool."

"Jesus, Benji. That's the least sexy comparison you could have made."

His laugh is warm against my neck. "Sorry. How about, it's like testing soil, but instead of checking for nutrients, you're looking for—"

"If you finish that sentence with any kind of agricultural metaphor, I might reconsider this whole thing," I say.

196

Benji places his hand on my cock and strokes me, making me shudder as pleasure rocks through me.

"I'm pretty sure you're not reconsidering anything," he says with absolute certainty, and he's right.

I'm not quite sure what I'm doing as I press a slick finger inside him, my weathered farmer's hands feeling too rough and clumsy for something this delicate.

"Am I hurting you?" I ask, freezing at the sharp intake of his breath.

"God, no. Just...curve your finger a bit."

I follow his instructions, and suddenly he arches into my touch, gasping my name in a way that makes every hair on my body stand at attention.

The only thing that stops me from feeling embarrassed by my obvious lack of experience is the look in Benji's eyes. I'm pretty sure no one has ever looked at me like this.

"Another finger," he instructs, his voice strangled.

I work a second finger alongside the first, the tight heat making my breath stutter. My hands, usually so confident with machinery and livestock, feel clumsy and uncertain.

"Like this?" I ask, and I barely recognize my own voice, it's so husky.

"Perfect," he breathes.

Benji's eyes flutter closed, his head tipping back against the pillows, exposing the line of his throat. Seeing him like this, him trusting me to take care of him, feels like a gift.

When I twist my wrist slightly, he makes a strangled noise that sounds nothing like his usual articulate banter. His knees fall wider apart, an invitation I can't misinterpret even with my limited experience. His skin is flushed all the way down his chest, and I press gentle kisses along his collarbone as my fingers establish a tentative rhythm.

"Deeper," he gasps. "And angle up a bit."

When my fingers brush against a spot inside him, his whole body jolts like he's been struck by summer lightning.

"Fuck, David," he breathes, voice cracking on my name. His tone is raw, stripped of his usual composure.

"Yeah," I manage to grunt. I can't take my eyes off his face, the way his lips part slightly and his pupils have all but swallowed the green.

"I'm ready," he says breathlessly.

I'm happy for Benji to take the lead, and when he pushes me on my back, I follow without hesitation, grateful for his guidance.

He trails open-mouthed kisses along my neck, finding a particularly sensitive spot that makes me curse under my breath. His chuckle against my skin tells me he's filing that information away for future torture.

Then he pulls back, sitting up to straddle me, and for a moment, I forget how to breathe.

"Oh, holy fuck," I say as he starts to sink down on me. The shock of sensation is so intense my vision blurs at the edges. My entire body feels electrified like I've touched an ungrounded fence wire with both hands.

I grab his hips hard, trying to anchor myself, hoping I'm not leaving bruises.

But Benji doesn't seem to be feeling anything but bliss right now as he continues to take me in inch by inch, his thighs trembling with the effort of controlling his descent, his bottom lip caught between his teeth like he's trying to hold back something that might break us both. His usual perfect hair is a disaster, and absurd pride shoots through me, knowing my hands are responsible.

When he catches my eye, he gives me one of his mischievous smiles, though it wavers when I give a tentative thrust, turning into something more desperate.

This is a sight I'll remember forever. Benji above me, his usual snarkiness stripped away to show something raw and real, something that matches the ache in my own chest.

He starts to move with maddening slowness, and I'm drowning in sensation. The slick slide of skin against skin, the weight of him above me, the way his breath hitches every time I hit just the right spot.

I reach up with one hand, tugging him down for a messy kiss. He moans into my mouth, his usual smartass comments replaced by broken syllables of praise.

I reach out and wrap a hand around his cock. His whole body jerks at my touch, and the sound he makes, halfway between a gasp and my name, sends heat rushing through me.

His hips stutter between thrusting into my grip and grinding down on my cock, like he can't decide which sensation he needs more.

Shit. The need to claim him, to mark him as mine in the most primal way possible, overwhelms me.

Going purely on instinct, I grab his hips and flip us in one smooth motion.

He lands beneath me with a soft 'oof' that transforms into a laugh, then a gasp as I settle between his thighs.

This new angle lets me push deeper, and the sensation nearly blinds me. I brace myself on my forearms, wanting to see his face as I withdraw almost completely before sinking back in.

Fuck. The feel of him around me is better than anything I've known.

The room is filled with the sounds of our breathing, the soft creak of a bedframe that has known only my solitary weight until now. His eyelids flutter shut. Each thrust brings new sounds from him, soft grunts and half-formed pleas that I greedily collect.

I find a steady pace, careful at first, then with growing confidence.

His hands travel up my arms, fingers tracing the work-hardened muscle. When they reach my face, cupping my jaw with unexpected tenderness, something in my chest cracks open as wide as the Canterbury sky.

When I wrap my fingers around his cock, his clever mouth gives a silent gasp. For once in his life, Benji Gange is completely speechless, and the power of that goes straight to my head.

Sweat gathers in the hollow of his throat, catching the late evening light filtering through my bedroom window, and I'm struck by how bloody beautiful he is like this.

And I suddenly realize we've been speaking this language all along. In vegetables left on doorsteps and meals cooked just for me, in arguments that were really just excuses to stay in each other's orbit.

I guess because I was slower to realize what was happening between us, it's fitting that I shatter first.

My usual stoic control deserts me completely as I fall over the edge. Heat surges through me like a current, whiting out my vision as pleasure seizes every muscle. My body pulses and trembles, caught in something so intense I can barely remember my own name.

Benji's eyes lock on mine like he's memorizing this moment.

Fucking hell. Why the hell did it take me so many years to experience this?

I withdraw from him gently, taking care not to hurt him, though the loss of connection makes me ache in ways I hadn't anticipated.

I take care of the condom quickly, then turn my attention back to him because I'm never someone who leaves a job half-finished.

Benji's curled on his side to watch me, his chest rising and falling rapidly, lips parted and swollen from our kisses.

I lean forward to take his cock into my mouth, pushing him onto his back and filling him with my fingers until he gasps a broken sound.

I pull off just as his body shudders and his fingers tangle in my hair as he comes all over his chest.

Satisfaction sweeps through me. I did this. I reduced clever, articulate Benji Gange to a speechless, panting mess.

I press kisses to his trembling thighs as he catches his breath, his skin flushed and gleaming in the fading light.

He looks thoroughly claimed, with marks scattered across his throat, his usual perfect hair completely destroyed, and his green eyes heavy-lidded with satisfaction.

When he pulls me up for a kiss, it's slow and deep and perfect.

We lie tangled together, my heartbeat slowly returning to

its normal rhythm. I brush a strand of hair from his forehead, letting my touch linger longer than necessary, just because I can.

"That was different from what I expected." Benji finally breaks the silence between us.

My stomach drops. All the warmth I was feeling suddenly freezes solid.

"Not sure if 'different' was what I was going for," I manage to say.

"Oh no, no." He's seen the look on my face, and he pushes himself up on one arm to meet my gaze. "That was incredible. Absolutely incredible. I guess I just always assumed that the first time between us would be explosive hate sex after we argued about something."

The relief flowing through me means it takes me a moment to find my voice.

"I'll give you explosive hate sex next time you leave the boundary gate open," I finally say, and he laughs, the sound vibrating through me.

Next time.

The word seems to hang in the air between us.

"I'll take that as a promise," Benji says as he snuggles back into me, his head on my chest.

His weight against my chest feels right, like when the wool press clicks perfectly into place. I never knew I was waiting for this, but now it seems so bloody obvious. His eyes flutter closed as his breathing evens out, and I lie there thinking about tomorrow and the next day and the day after that. Everything suddenly seems so much brighter.

Because I now have a future full of next times.

Chapter Six

David

Waking up the next morning with Benji in my bed gives me the same happiness I usually only feel watching newborn lambs galloping around the paddock in the spring.

I kiss his temple, breathing in the scent of his skin, marveling at how someone who argues with me about everything from sheep rotation to rugby selection can fit so perfectly against me.

Benji's eyelids flutter open, and he stretches like a cat in the sun, all lean muscles and satisfaction, before giving me his crooked grin that always means trouble.

My gaze wanders to where the sheet pools at his waist, and for a moment, I have a flash of disbelief that the man who's driven me mad for years is now sprawled across my mattress like he belongs there.

"Like what you see?" he asks, his voice still raspy with sleep.

"Just trying to figure out how you went from being the biggest thorn in my side to the best thing in my bed."

He huffs a laugh as he shifts closer, resting his chin on my chest. I can't help running my hand down his arm.

Benji's expression turns from playful to something more thoughtful.

"Have you ever been with a man before?" His voice is casual, but his eyes are watchful. "Because I've been in the district for five years, and I've never seen you bring anyone back to your place, man or woman."

"Never really wanted it before," I say truthfully. "With either a man or a woman."

His forehead creases. "You've never wanted to be with anyone before?"

"No. I mean, I was with a few girls when I was younger because that was what was expected, but it...wasn't like this." I swallow. "It didn't feel like this."

Those green eyes study me. But I don't mind his scrutiny. I trust Benji will handle all parts of me gently—except the parts I don't want him to be gentle with.

"Do you think you're demisexual?" he asks. "Like, you only find someone sexually attractive once you've formed an emotional connection with them?"

"Trust you to give a fancy Auckland name to what my dad would've just called being particular about who you let into your paddock."

He laughs again, his warm breath ghosting across my skin.

"Leave it to you to make sexual attraction sound like a livestock management decision. Though I suppose you are letting me handle your prize ram."

His mouth finds mine, and for a while, we're too busy for words. His lips are warm and familiar now as we lose ourselves in each other again, taking our time like we've got all day, like the sheep can wait, like both of our farms can pause while we learn each other properly.

There's a constant war between touching Benji gently to match the feelings swirling inside me and wanting to claim him roughly, to devour him like a man who's been starving himself without even knowing there was food on the table.

Luckily, it seems like Benji is up for both.

After we've finished our exploring to mutual success, Benji untangles himself from the sheets with his usual grace, padding across my worn floorboards.

"Time to make you breakfast. I want my man to go to work with a full stomach," he says.

My man. The words echo in my head as I follow him out of bed.

The sight of Benji standing at my stove in his underwear causes me to crowd closer to him, kissing the back of his neck until he spins to kiss me properly.

I blame the noise of the bacon and eggs sizzling in the frypan and the distraction of a half-naked Benji in my arms for not hearing the crunch of tires on the gravel of my driveway.

Because, suddenly, the kitchen door opens with a squeak.

There's only one person who ever comes into my house without announcing their arrival.

My brother.

It's his childhood home, and therefore, he's never bothered to knock.

He's also never walked in to find me with my arms around my neighbor as we both stand in our boxers in the kitchen.

From the way he stands there blinking rapidly, like his brain is attempting an emergency reboot and failing spectacularly, I'm willing to bet knocking will definitely feature in Lance's future.

He opens and closes his mouth several times without any sound coming out, his expression finally landing somewhere between stunned and slightly hysterical.

"Hey, Lance, want some bacon and eggs?" It looks like Benji's brazening this one out rather than succumbing to the severe mortification I am right now. He nonchalantly pulls away from me and turns his attention back to the frypan.

"Uh...no thanks." Lance's eyes continue to dart between the two of us, still looking like he's just caught Old McMillian's bull doing ballet.

Emma appears in the doorway behind Lance, holding a Tupperware container.

"We brought you some of my leftover lasagna, thought you might be sick of..." Her voice trails off as she spots Benji. Her eyes widen comically.

"Hi, Emma, nice to see you," Benji says.

She swallows. "Nice to see you too, Benji."

"Although we didn't expect to see so much of you." My brother's sense of humor has apparently recovered from the shock.

I send a glare in his direction.

"So, uh, is this a new thing?" Emma asks.

"Me cooking breakfast for David?" Benji asks innocently.

"Ah, yes. That."

Benji glances at me. His lips morph into a smile.

"Yeah, it's a new thing," he says.

I can't help but return his smile.

Which, when I look at Lance, seems to have sent him back into the shock realm.

"Right, well, we've got places to go," Emma says, setting the container on my counter with exaggerated care. "There's a few meals worth of lasagna in there, although..." She sends a sly look at Benji. "It looks like you've got someone taking care of your nutritional needs."

"Thanks for the food," I mutter.

Benji and I are silent after Lance and Emma leave, so their conversation drifts through the open window.

"Oh, come on, you can't tell me you didn't see this coming," Emma says.

"You mean to tell me all that arguing was actually fore-play?" Lance's voice is full of incredulity.

I close my eyes and wince.

When I open them again, Benji's looking at me with concern. "You okay?"

"Yeah, I'm fine."

His concern doesn't fade. "Sorry, that was a shit way for you to have to come out."

"I don't care about that," I say. And I'm being truthful. What other people think doesn't matter to me.

What matters is that Benji's looking at me like I might regret this whole thing when the truth is I've never been more certain about anything in my life. Even if my brother's going to take the piss out of me until the end of time.

"So what are you worried about then?" he asks quietly.

"That my brother is going to think this means he can give me relationship advice."

Benji laughs, then comes over to give me a quick kiss.

"You've got the best boyfriend in the world. You won't need relationship advice," he says.

I roll my eyes at that.

Benji dishes up the bacon and eggs, sliding them onto my mother's old plates with their faded flower pattern. The domesticity of it should feel strange, but it really doesn't.

We eat in comfortable silence, our feet tangled under the table as the morning sun streams through my kitchen window.

"I should head back," he says eventually, though he makes no move to leave. "Got the vet coming to look at that heifer."

"Yeah, I've got a bit to do this morning," I admit. "Those lambs will start a ruckus if I don't feed them soon."

"You won't want to keep Pepper waiting," he says.

When he leaves, he kisses me at the door like he's done it a thousand times before. Like he plans to do it a thousand times more.

I'm humming as I grab my jacket off the hook and head out the door myself.

The rhythm of farm work fills my morning, feeding the lambs, checking water troughs, moving stock. But there's a lightness to it now, like someone's oiled all the rusty gates in my life. And my muscles aching pleasantly from activities that had nothing to do with farming is a nice reminder.

As I'm coming back on my four-wheeler to the woolshed

paddock, I glance toward Benji's property and see the purple gate.

It makes me smile.

I still suspect that when I'm on my deathbed, Benji's name is going to be on my lips.

Although maybe not as a curse.

Epilogue

Benji

Three years later

"I think you should carry me over the threshold," I say.

"I need my back in working order," David replies, his lips twitching into that half-smile that always crinkles the corners of his eyes.

Our new home sits proudly on what was once the infamous thistle paddock, a two-story timber-and-stone affair we've named Thornfield. Not after the Jane Eyre mansion, but because it made David snort with laughter when I suggested it.

The wraparound porch faces both our properties, with matching rocking chairs positioned to watch the sunset.

We're standing on the porch now, debating the best way to mark this milestone.

"Trust me, I have a vested interest in keeping your back in working order," I say with a lewd wink that leaves subtle in another time zone entirely.

David's ears turn that adorable shade of pink. His jaw works in that oh-so-familiar way as he fights a smile while trying to maintain his stern farmer facade. It's been three years, and I still live for the moments I break that stoic exterior.

"That whole carrying over the threshold is meant for newlyweds, and we're not newlyweds anymore," he rallies.

He's right. We're no longer newlyweds, having celebrated our first wedding anniversary last month with an epic trip to Queenstown. Racing each other down the luge, dining out at a top restaurant where David critiqued the quality of the beef, holding hands while walking along the lakefront.

It never fails to amaze me how David has never flinched when showing his affection for me in public. The guy went from being the most stereotypical straight-presenting farmer you could ever imagine—he wore the same polar fleece with a hole in one elbow to every single woolshed party for five years, for fuck's sake—to walking square-shouldered and straight-backed into the Farmers' Collective holding my hand, like anyone who was remotely homophobic could just fuck right off.

Our relationship did cause quite a stir initially. I hadn't realized how much I'd been given a pass for my sexuality due to the fact I wasn't originally from around here. But David was a different story. He was a fifth-generation farmer here, the gruff local institution with his immovable opinions on everything from stock rotation to the correct way to stack hay bales. When he became half of David-and-Benji, gossip ricocheted through Canterbury like a stray .22 round in an empty wool shed, pinging from one farm to the next until even the sheep looked scandalized.

Rumor has it that Old Thompson actually spit out his mouthful of beer at the pub when the news finally reached him.

Pete, the stock agent, had sidled up to us at the pub barely a week after the Farmers' Collective meeting, his weathered face a curious mix of embarrassment and fascination.

"So it's true," he'd said, fiddling with a beer coaster rather than meeting our eyes. "You two are..." He'd trailed off, apparently unable to find the right farming metaphor for our relationship.

David had given him that patented Harrison stare, the one that made members of the shearing gangs quake in their boots.

"Yep. Got a problem with that?"

The way Pete had backpedaled, you'd think David had threatened him with sheep shears.

"No. No problem. Just like... I was surprised, you know, the fact you guys are neighbors..."

"Must be something in the water around here," I'd said airily.

Which apparently had two of our other neighbors frantically cleaning out their water tanks the next day.

The fact we're officially no longer in the honeymoon phase of our relationship doesn't concern me at all. We were like an old married couple long before we ever got together.

"Does not being newlyweds anymore mean we've got no excuse for our lunchtime quickies?" I tease David now.

"I didn't say that," David says quickly.

I laugh because, despite David and I still having spirited discussions about nearly everything, our arguments transform into a different kind of negotiation in the bedroom. The type where we both always win.

"I guess we've got a whole new house to christen," I muse. "And there are lots of rooms."

David's eyes darken, and there's that familiar shift where my practical, buttoned-up farmer transforms into the man who once pinned me against the kitchen counter because I wore his flannel shirt and nothing else to make pancakes.

"There are lots of rooms," he echoes.

Our house is bigger than we technically need for just the two of us. But it's our plan to fill some of the empty rooms with kids, whether it be our own or ones we foster. I can't wait to see David as a dad. I've already watched the way he tends to the orphaned lambs, his gruff exterior melting away as he gently coaxes them to take the bottle. I've seen how he kneels to eye level to talk to Lance and Emma's two-year-old daughter Lily, how he helped her plant carrot seeds in the vegetable garden with infinite patience.

Some people are just natural parents waiting to meet their children.

"Talking about our new house, do you think we should actually get inside?" David asks. The late afternoon sun catches in his eyes, highlighting the tiny laugh lines that have deepened since we've been together.

"Sure. If you're not going to carry me, I guess holding

hands and stepping across the threshold together is the best alternative."

"That works for me," he says, fishing the keys from his pocket. He holds them up, sunlight catching on the metal, turning them momentarily golden. "Ready?"

I place my hand over his, feeling the familiar roughness of his skin. Together, we guide the key into the lock, turning it with a satisfying click.

The door swings open, releasing the scent of fresh paint. We continue to hold hands as we step across the threshold.

Inside, the walls are that soft gray David pretended to hate when I painted my weatherboards and the kitchen window perfectly frames his new vegetable garden. My purple gate has been repurposed as our garden entrance, weather-beaten but still defiantly bright against the Canterbury landscape.

I nod out the window. "Pepper looks happy in her new paddock."

Because yes, Pepper the lamb grew up to be Pepper our pet sheep, who now produces her own lambs for us to dote on every spring.

Lance mocks us constantly about how two farmers with eight thousand sheep between us have sheep as pets, but if it wasn't for Pepper escaping her paddock, who knows how long it would have taken my loveable grump to get his head out of his ass?

Of course not many people can say that their relationship was helped by spying on New Zealand rugby's most bitter rivals kissing each other. Not that we've ever shared that part of our story.

I still love holding it over David's head how I figured out what was happening between us two years before he did.

I'd just broken up with my latest boyfriend, James, the week before. James was a dentist, and he'd been a nice guy, and I was beating myself up again for always falling for people who seemed like a match on paper but couldn't hold my interest past the three-month mark.

I'd been in a bad mood all day trying to figure out why my experimental organic fertilizer was turning my best pasture into something that looked like a nuclear testing site. Three different soil experts had given me three completely different opinions, my online research had yielded nothing but contradictory advice, and I was about ready to admit defeat and go back to the commercial stuff that made my skin crawl with environmental guilt.

I'd just arrived back at the house, and when I saw my grouchy, finicky neighbor had turned up, no doubt to berate me about some farming practice I was doing wrong, my mood had soured further.

David was leaning against his truck, his dark hair slightly mussed and his brown eyes fixed on me with their usual disapproval. Even annoyed and covered in a day's worth of farm grime, the man was unfairly attractive. It was unfair how someone with such a permanently furrowed brow could still look like that.

"Your sheep are getting into my clover paddock again," he'd announced without preamble, following me onto the porch. "Your southern fence line has got more holes than my granddad's socks."

I hadn't had the energy for a snarky reply. "I know. I've

got materials on order, but the supplier's back ordered until next month."

David's eyebrows had knitted together in that way that made him look perpetually disappointed with the world. "I fixed it this morning."

I'd stopped halfway through unlocking my door. "You what?"

"Fixed your fence." He'd shrugged like it was nothing, like he hadn't spent hours doing a job that wasn't his responsibility. "Used some of my spare posts and wire. Should hold until your order comes in."

He'd bent to retrieve something from behind my porch steps. It was a wooden crate filled with vegetables from his garden. Heirloom tomatoes in three different colors, those stubby Italian eggplants I'd mentioned liking once over beers at the pub, and right on top, a bundle of purple asparagus.

"You grew purple asparagus?" I asked, staring at it dumbly.

"Yeah, well." His ears turned pink. "You said at the farming conference dinner last year that the regular kind was boring."

As I stared at the asparagus, something had shifted inside me, like tectonic plates rearranging. I remembered that conference. I'd been drunk on mediocre wine, rambling about how everyone should experiment more with heritage varieties. David had sat there in silence, seemingly uninterested.

Except he'd been listening. Really listening.

I looked at him standing there in his faded work shirt with a smudge of dirt on his cheek, avoiding eye contact as he handed over vegetables he'd grown specifically because I might like them. All while pretending it was nothing special.

The same man who'd lectured me about proper fencing techniques for forty-five minutes last month. Who'd stayed up all night with me during that storm when my barn roof threatened to give way. Who argued with every new farming method I tried and then quietly implemented the successful ones on his own land.

A voice snuck into my head. *This man is the love of your life.*

And the voice resonated inside me with such clarity that I almost laughed out loud. Of course it was David. It would always be David. No one else had ever made my heart pound the way he did.

"You okay?" he'd asked, frowning at my sudden stillness.

"Never better," I'd replied, trying to suppress my smile so I didn't spook the guy. I felt like I'd just discovered gold in my backyard. Which, in a way, I guess I had.

That memory still makes me smile as David and I explore our new home, seeing all the signs of our merged lives. His worn armchair beside my designer reading lamp, his practical wooden coffee table perfectly centered on my wildly colorful Turkish rug that David initially called a hazard to navigation.

We wander through the first floor, my hand trailing along the walls as David, ever the practical farmer, checks the window latches.

We end up back in the kitchen.

"Should we test the water pressure?" I ask, nodding toward the sink, but my smirk means something else entirely.

David gives me that look where he's pretending to be

exasperated but can't quite hide the smile pulling at his lips. "We haven't even unpacked a single box."

"Practicalities later," I say, stepping closer to trace the line of his jaw with my fingertip. "I want to know if that shower fits two comfortably."

He catches my wrist, his thumb brushing over my pulse point in a way that sends electricity racing up my arm.

"Seems like important information for new homeowners to discover," he concedes, eyes darkening.

I tug him toward the stairs, and he follows willingly. Three years together, and my heart still races at the feel of his hand in mine, at the knowledge that this grumpy, wonderful man is mine.

In our bedroom, the late afternoon sun slants through windows that frame the distant hills. His farm is to the left, mine to the right, and this house bridging them together. Perfect symmetry.

David's arms wrap around me from behind as we gaze at our land. His lips find that spot just below my ear that makes me shiver.

"We've got a lot of rooms," he reminds me, his words a murmur against my skin.

I turn in his arms, my fingers already working on his shirt buttons. "Then we better get started on christening the first one."

About the Author

Thanks for reading! I really hope you enjoyed David and Benji's story. If you want to read about how two rival New Zealand rugby players fell in love, make sure you don't miss Aiden and Tyler's story *Playing Offside* here: https://reader links.com/l/4669228

I love writing stories with light-hearted conversations and deeply felt connections. All of my books are available to read on Amazon here or you can check them out on my website www.jaxcalder.com

Deliciously Cookie

Vawn Cassidy

Chapter One

Cookie

"Cookie, are you done with the cupcakes yet?" a soft, sweet voice asks.

"Almost," I murmur, finishing another swirl of rainbow-coloured frosting with a flourish and only then looking up.

"They look great."

I smile at my newest friend, Colin. My best friend Tyler, being kinda prickly, is always bemused at how I can collect people wherever I go, and this impromptu trip to England has been no different. People are fascinating to me, and I just love figuring out their stories. Tyler says that's because I'm too nosy for my own good, and he does have a point.

Take Little Red here, for example. With his bright red hair and swathes of freckles, his neat sweaters and cute bow ties, he's way too adorable for his own good.

I'm also pretty sure he has a crush the size of Vegas on the hot silver fox that builds boats on the other side of this cute

223

little British bay. I can't say I blame Colin though—*ay papi,* Garrett is hot, like full-on scorching. I would have climbed that man like a tree if it weren't for Colin. I don't poach on another man's territory even if Colin is oblivious to the fact that he has a major thing for the sexy older guy. Garrett, on the other hand, couldn't make his interest in my little ginger friend more obvious if he pissed in a circle around him.

I'll give the man his due, he's got a lot of patience. And as I'm so fond of Colin, I'm going to make it my mission while I'm here to help them get their happily ever after...or at the very least, several very satisfying orgasms. Garrett sure looks like a man who knows what he's doing; if it's one thing I've learned, it's to never underestimate a man who works with his hands.

I do seem to drive Ty crazy because I can't resist match-making. Maybe I should've been called Cupid instead of Cookie. I can't help it though, I just like seeing people happy and in love.

"I have something new for you to try." Colin stops beside me and sets a small bag down on the counter.

With eager hands, I open up the bag and pull out a handful of tiny candies. Placing them down on the tray beside the cupcakes, I pick one up to examine it more closely. It's made from a clear hard candy with swirls of edible glitter running through it.

I beam at him as I look up from the twisted cone shape sitting in the palm of my hand. "A unicorn horn?"

Colin nods eagerly. "Taste it!"

Not needing to be told twice, I put it in my mouth and

suck for several seconds before groaning in happiness. "Is that watermelon?" He nods again. "Oh god, so good!"

His cheeks flush with pleasure. "There are other flavours too. I tried to do something a bit different, not just the regular orange and strawberry. There's an apple in there, too, as well as peach."

"You are so talented." I hum and suck the candy harder. "You should spend more time creating stuff like this."

"Maybe at some point." Colin shrugs and starts placing a unicorn horn in the centre of each swirl of frosting. "I usually only make them for the festivals and markets, or as special favours. But I have my hands full with the bakery, so I don't really have time to build up a second business, even if they would complement each other. There's just not enough hours in the day. Sometimes I wish I had a twin, or any sibling at all, then there'd be two of me and I could get more done."

"Honey, you don't need a sib. What you need is a manager and more staff."

"That costs money." He sighs. "Maybe one day. This place does well during the summer months now that tourism is starting to pick back up in the bay, especially since I started adding ice creams to match the flavours of my cupcakes, but it still gets pretty quiet in the off season."

"Are you crazy?" I follow him as he picks up the tray of cupcakes and heads into the bakery. "That's the perfect time to build up your candy empire. You can sell online, and you've got all the best holidays. Halloween, Christmas... Valentine's."

He chuckles as he places the cupcakes in the display case

on the counter, lining them up alongside mouthwatering, sinful-looking cookies and pastries.

"I don't know." He shrugs. "It would take a lot of planning, and that's time I just don't have at the moment. I've got my hands full just with this place, and the Festival of the Sea is coming up soon. Not to mention Nat and Beck's wedding cake, plus all the other special occasion cakes people keep asking me to make."

"Colin, you're going to burn out if you don't take a moment to breathe and figure out a better way of doing things. This place makes more than enough money to support more staff." I glance at the clock and, noting the time, go to unlock the door and flip the sign to Open.

"I know." He exhales slowly and puts the tray away. "I know you're right. It's just..."

"Just what?"

"When I first opened my business, the bay was so quiet. Tourism had dropped off over the years with people heading to bigger towns like Newquay and Falmouth. It was really just the residents and a very small summer crowd. I could pretty much handle everything on my own and still earn enough to cover the bills. But now, with Finn re-opening the old theatre, Nat helping to bring Sully's restaurant back from the brink of bankruptcy, and all the new festivals and markets Nat and Mel have talked the local council into hosting here in the bay, this place just keeps getting busier during the season."

"But that's a good thing?"

"It is." He nods. "I guess I'm just worried because what if we hit a downswing again? Let's say I find the money

226

somehow to take on new staff, open a whole new kitchen off-site, which I'd need to make and store all the candies in quantities to make it profitable, and buy new equipment. What if I did all that and then it doesn't work out? I'd lose the bakery too."

"It's a risk, yes." I head behind the counter and begin to fix him a latte the way he likes it. "But you have a passion and a talent, *mijo*. I know you can do this." My mouth twists as I stare at him thoughtfully. "You know what you need?"

"Besides a manager, new staff, a new kitchen, new equipment, and about twelve extra hours in the day?"

I snort. Colin is so quiet and sweet that I get the feeling not a lot of people get a taste of his sassy side. Except me. I'm so extra most of the time I just bring it out in others, I guess.

"What you need is an investor."

"Sure, because they grow on trees. Have you seen what the interest rates look like right now? I'm not taking out any loans with the bank. I built my business from the ground up on nothing but hard work and my savings. I'm not going to risk that now, especially not with the way the economy is."

"I don't mean a bank. I mean me." I slide his latte towards him.

"What?"

"I'll invest."

"You..." He pauses, his cup halfway to his mouth. "What?" His gaze trails over me, from my faded pink hair and eyeliner to the Colin's Cupcakes T-shirt, which I customised with glitter and rhinestones before removing the sleeves and widening the neck. Continuing on, his eyes track over my tiny little denim cut-offs to my knee-high sports socks and sparkly purple Converse high-tops.

I know nothing about me screams money—not my Puerto Rican by way of Long Beach accent, my clothing style, or, if we're being honest, my whole personality—but I do have money, and a lot more of it than people think, thanks to Tyler.

"That's, er, nice of you to offer, Cookie, but I pay you next to nothing for working here. I'd need a lot of capital just to buy the machinery I need."

I laugh warmly at his wrinkled nose and look of confusion. "Trust me, I have more than enough. I don't even use what you pay me."

"You don't?" If possible, he looks even more confused. "What do you do with it, then?"

I shrug. "I give it to a place that supports at risk and homeless teens." I turn back to the coffee machine and start making a cappuccino.

"I..." Colin frowns and tugs the strings of his apron, the way I've learned he does when he's stressed or overwhelmed. "Okay, putting that aside, which is a really lovely thing to do, by the way, why did you even ask for a job, then?"

"Because you looked so stressed and tired when I walked in here my second day in the bay. I needed something to do while Tyler was dealing with his father's funeral, and I love baking. I had a gut feeling."

"A gut feeling?" he repeats slowly, and I nod.

"Don't you ever just get a feeling about something and go for it?"

"No."

I laugh again. "Well I do, and it has never done me dirty. I

had a feeling about this place and about you. So here I am."
The work visas Tyler insists we always have up-to-date paid
off there.

"And now you want to invest in the expansion of my
business?"

I nod again. "It will all be drawn up legally, this ain't no
shady backroom deal. I genuinely believe in you. It'll all be
aboveboard, Scout's honour."

He huffs in amusement. "I doubt you were ever a Boy
Scout."

"Damn, you got me. I wasn't, too many rules." I lift my
hands and shrug. "Anyway, the offer's there."

"Are you even staying in the bay?" he asks, tilting his head
as he studies me. "Aren't you going back to the US?"

I snort loudly. "Hell no. Not with the way things are at
the moment. Tyler's already moved his base of operations
from Chicago back to the UK. Once he's tied up all the loose
ends here from his father's death, we'll be heading to
London."

"You two do everything together?"

"Mostly." Snapping the lid on the cup, I bag up a pastry.
"He's my best friend." I balance the bag on top of the cup and
look up at Colin who is watching me. "Neither of us had
great childhoods, didn't really have any family until we found
each other. When we met, we just clicked. Kismet."

"That gut feeling of yours?" The corner of his mouth
curves.

"Never steered me wrong." I grin. "Seriously, me and him
are tight, but we don't need to be in each other's pockets
twenty-four seven."

"I doubt anything can fit into those pockets of yours." His gaze drops to my shorts, cut so high that the white linen of the pocket lining sticks out below the hem.

"You'd be surprised." I wink. "But no, Ty and I aren't joined at the hip or anything, just, where one goes, the other tends to follow. Plus, he's a Brit, born and raised, so I always knew he'd come back to England someday. I've travelled all over since I was a kid and have never been particularly tied to any one place. I'm just as happy in the UK as I am back in the States."

"Uh-huh," he muses as he continues to stare at me thoughtfully.

"Just think on it, 'kay?" I pick up the pastry and the cappuccino I've just made and ease around the counter. Still balancing the bagged pastry on the cup, I reach for the door, then turn back to Colin at the last minute. "I'm just going to run these over the street for Dot, although I'm beginning to think her name should be Pot with the fumes coming off her."

Colin chuckles. "Don't breathe too deeply and don't eat any of her brownies."

Laughing, I open the door and start to move through it, only to collide with a big, firm body. The coffee explodes and I lose my balance, windmilling my arms comically as I fall back, hitting the floor with a thud.

"Ow, ow, ow," a deep voice chants, and my eyes lock on a six-foot wall of spank bank material.

He's tall and blonde, with tanned skin and blue eyes, and is now holding his drenched T-shirt away from his body, no doubt in an attempt to keep the hot coffee-soaked material from burning him.

For a second, I don't say anything, just lay there dazed and gazing up at this gorgeous, sun-drenched god.

"Forgive me, Father, for I am about to sin..." I mutter.

"Are you okay?" he asks in concern as those blue eyes fall on my prone form.

"I, uh-huh."

Leaning down, he takes my hand to help me up, but before I can say anything, Colin bustles over with a dishcloth and a roll of paper towels.

"Oh, Quinn, are you okay? Please don't sue."

He rolls his eyes. "Colin, why on earth would I sue you?" he asks in exasperation. "It's just a bit of coffee, I'm fine." He takes the offered dishcloth but instead of wiping himself down, he gently lifts my hands and wipes the coffee from them. "Are you okay? Did you get burned?"

"No, I'm should. I mean..." I close my eyes and shake my head. "Good. I'm *good*. I should clean up this mess." I gaze down at the pool of liquid at our feet, then back up at him. What did Colin call him? Quinn? "Are you sure you're okay? I didn't mean to nail you with a cappuccino the minute you walked through the door."

"I have to admit, I was hoping to drink it, not wear it." He grins, then adds, "I'm fine though. Accidents happen."

"I'll make you anything you want, on me, after I get this cleaned up." I promise, my cheeks heating as I take the roll of paper towels and unravel a load of them to soak up the mess on the floor.

"Here, let me help you." He hunkers down next to me, and I'm treated to the sight of his worn jeans pulling tight on his delectably thick thighs.

"Ay, bendito..." I murmur under my breath.

Shaking my head, I concentrate on mopping up the spill and after a few moments, my hands are filled with a stack of soggy paper towels.

"I'll just get rid of these." I head towards the nearest trash can but as I dump them inside, I hear the bell on the shop door ring and turn to see two familiar men walk in hand in hand.

"Nat, Beck," Colin greets them. "You're early."

"Sorry, that's my fault." The gorgeous dark-haired chef from Sully's smiles. "Mel wants me in earlier to help with the inventory checks because Simon called in sick. Is it okay to do this now?"

"Sure." Colin nods.

Beck looks over and does a double take. "Quinn? What are you doing back?" He strides across the bakery in two steps and wraps his arms around my hot, muscly wet dream in a tight hug.

"Finished up early. I got in last night," Quinn mumbles into his shoulder. "I was going to grab a coffee and a croissant before doing the rounds and saying hi to everyone."

Beck slaps him on the back affectionately. "Whoa, you've put some timber on. You're solid as a rock. What were they feeding you at Uni? You were supposed to come back skinny with a borderline alcohol problem and possible scurvy from a constant diet of pot noodles and beer."

"I've still got a reputation to maintain as the best-looking brother." Quinn grins. "Besides, you're soon to be an old married man. I hate to break it to you, but you're first in line for a beer belly."

"The hell he is," Nat snorts. "You could scrub your pants clean on his abs."

Beck smirks at his—"Brother?" I blurt out. "You're brothers?" Now that I say it out loud, I can see it. Although Beck has the lean, wiry build of a surfer—something I've seen with my own eyes, seen and ogled from a distance on a few occasions when I've wandered down to the beach for a walk— Quinn is a bit taller and bulkier. Although there doesn't appear to be an inch of fat on him. His jeans and T-shirt pull tight over a really, *really* muscled body; seriously, the guy looks like he could bench press an SUV.

"Yep." Quinn grins as he hooks his arm around his brother's neck. "Even though I'm the baby brother, I'm the prettiest."

"Keep telling yourself that." Beck elbows him in the stomach, then frowns and rubs his elbow. "Jesus, Quinn. Seriously, when did you pack on so much muscle?"

Quinn shrugs.

"Just how many Ainsleys are there?" I wonder aloud.

"Six." Quinn turns his attention back to me. "Four boys, two girls."

"Four brothers," I mutter reverently.

"Nat, Beck?" Colin looks down at his watch. "Do you want to come with me? I've got the wedding cake samples set up."

"Sure." Nat heads towards Colin. "Make sure you stop by the restaurant later," he calls over his shoulder to Quinn.

Beck pats his brother's shoulder affectionately, then follows his fiancé. A moment later, the three of them disappear into the kitchen.

"So, I guess we haven't been properly introduced." Quinn holds out his hand. "I'm Quinn Ainsley." I take his hand and stare up into those blue eyes, which are dancing in amusement. "And you are?"

"Oh...uh, Carlito." I blink. "Carlito Rodriguez, but everyone calls me Cookie."

His gaze sweeps over me and a smile tugs at his lips. "It suits you."

My stomach swoops and for a second, I feel like I'm falling.

Chapter Two

Quinn

The cool breeze tugs at my hoodie as I stand and watch the sun rise over the bay. Even though the view is spectacular as always, I close my eyes and lift my chin, tilting my face up to feel the wind ripple over my skin. The sound of the waves soothes my overactive brain.

Don't get me wrong. It's nice to be home, even though I'm not staying—something I have yet to tell my family. I sigh and fold my arms over the railing, looking over the bluff to the sheer drop that ends at the beach below.

Yesterday was hard, being back home with my mum and my sisters. My brothers all have their own places. Jesse's with his husband Deacon, Beck with his fiancé Nat, and our oldest brother Reed, although still single, has his own house too. As a doctor based in A&E at the local hospital, he's almost never there, but he does have a spare room. I wonder if I could stay at his place for a while?

It's not that I don't love my mum and Juni and Joss, my

younger twin sisters who are twenty now. But my whole family is nosy and loud and all up in my business. I know they mean well and they love me, but that just makes it a hundred times worse.

I've been lying to all of them for nearly two years.

That's part of what made yesterday so difficult. As soon as word spread I was back, I was swarmed with well-meaning congratulations on finishing uni and moving home permanently, not to mention peppered with questions about my degree and my future.

I was exhausted by the end of the day. I've couldn't tell anyone what my plans were, not when I hadn't even told my family the truth.

I never meant it to go on so long or the lies to get so deep. They were all so proud of me for getting a place at Exeter University to study environmental sciences. My dad, in particular, who'd been on his deathbed at the time. One of the last things he said to me was how proud he was and how I was going to change the world. Make a difference. Those were his exact words to me.

Quinn, make a difference.

I did choose to make a difference, just not in the way any of them would have thought. To be honest, it surprised me too, but I know I made the right choice. I gave up and left uni after the first year, and that was two years ago. Two years of lying to everyone about who I am and what I do.

I never meant for it to go on as long as it has, but the more time passed, the harder it was to tell them. They were all so busy; in the beginning, we were all grieving my dad, each of us just trying to make it through since he'd been the very heart of our family. Afterwards, it was the restaurant. Sully's, my dad's legacy, had been badly mismanaged in the wake of my dad's passing. The manager Mum and all of us had trusted with Dad's dream robbed the place blind and almost ran it into the ground. We were lucky that my soon-to-be brother-in-law Nat landed in the bay when he did. He's made quite the name for himself in the past two years as a pseudo celebrity chef. Both he and Mum have turned Sully's around, brought more business into the bay, and are closely involved with all the events that have been hosted around here, reviving our local economy and tourism.

I love my brothers and I'm so proud of them, but they and their partners cast a long shadow. Reed is a doctor, Beck is a sculptor well on his way to being famous, his fiancé Nat comes from a lot of money and, in addition to being an insanely talented chef, has just released a best-selling cook-book. Their best friend built his own craft beer company from the ground up and has just been nominated for some kind of beer award from what I hear.

Jesse, Beck's twin, runs his own successful veterinary clinic here in the bay, and his business partner, Wyatt, is with the famous movie star Finn Gallagher. Jesse's husband Deacon is retired now but raced boats for a living and has won just about every trophy there is for breaking speed records across the water. Their best friend is the Oscar- and Grammy-winning rockstar Kyan Amos. It's a lot to compete with.

Sometimes I feel invisible.

Maybe I should have talked to them, but something deep inside always stopped me. A little voice that said—well, it doesn't matter what it said. I tried really hard not to listen to it. Instead, I've spent the last couple of years away from the bay where everyone knows me and my family, trying to figure out who I am. Somewhere I could just be Quinn, not the baby Ainsley brother. I guess I needed to find out who I could be without them. I'm finally in a place where I'm happy, where I'm proud of what I've achieved and what I do.

I let loose a really loud sigh. Now I just have to tell my family the truth.

"Whoa, if you think any harder, *papi*, you gonna give yourself a brain haemorrhage." A soothing, musical accent speaks up behind me.

I turn and see the guy from yesterday, the one who works at Colin's bakery.

"Cookie, isn't it?" My gaze rakes over him.

He's small, maybe five-five or five-six, with a slim build. His hair is almost black at the roots and has a pale faded pink to the ends. A few of the thick loose curls poke out the hood of his purple hoodie, which is pulled up over his head and zipped up to his chin. His hands are buried deep in his pockets, making his purple hoodie stretch at the waist, and he's wearing the shorts so tiny they're pretty much hot pants. On his feet are silver glittery Converse that sparkle in the early morning sunshine.

I can't help but stare at the miles of golden skin exposed. I don't think I've ever seen a guy with legs so long and shapely. They look really smooth too; for one insane second, I wonder what his skin would feel like beneath my fingers, which twitch in an unconscious response.

238

Startled at the errant thought, I tear my gaze away from his legs, only to see him shudder.

"You look cold," I state rather obviously.

"Ay, your country is very cold even in summer," he replies, shivering again.

"Or maybe it's because you're half-dressed. You'll freeze your balls off." Unable to help myself, I find my gaze drawn back to all that golden skin.

Cookie snorts, and my eyes rise to meet his. "My balls are just fine, but thanks for noticing." He gives me a cheeky wink, and I could swear my cheeks heat, which is ridiculous because I don't blush... ever. "Besides, it's warm in the bakery and by the time the sun's up, I'll be sweating." He tilts his head and studies me curiously. "I don't usually see anyone out this early. I thought it was just me and Colin keeping baker's hours. Unless you're a raging insomniac, or worse, one of those crazy people who like to be up early."

"None of the above." I grin. "Just enjoying the peace and quiet."

Studying me for a moment longer, he then lifts one shoulder in a casual shrug. "Okay, sorry to disturb you."

He turns to leave. "No, wait," I blurt out, surprising myself with my outburst. He looks back over his shoulder at me with those dark eyes framed by sooty black lashes. "I just mean..." I shake my head, not knowing what I mean. "I guess I've got a lot on my mind."

Why did I tell him that?

He continues to watch me for a few more seconds, his pouty lips pursed thoughtfully. "You know what you need? Sugar and caffeine."

"Oh, uh." I frown and look down the cliff walk, to where I can just about make out Colin's bakery with its baby blue and white awning at the bottom of the hill. "I didn't think the bakery was open yet."

"It's not."

"But I don't—"

"Colin won't mind, he'll be up to his eyeballs in cookie dough by now anyway." He smiles and something inside me relaxes at the warmth in his eyes. "Besides, we've been trying out some new recipes. You can be our test subject."

"Should I be afraid?"

He laughs, and it's a beautiful, carefree sound. "Depends how critical you are of my new frosting."

He spins around and sashays down the sloping path. I follow along obediently, unable to help it when my eyes track downwards. Jesus, those shorts are *short*, and his bum is... curvy. I've never seen such a magnificent arse on a guy. Although—I frown—have I ever actually checked out a guy's bum before?

I mean, it's not like it's a big deal. Two of my brothers are gay and although I'm straight, I've always been able to appreciate when a guy is objectively attractive.

"So, you've just finished college, right?" Cookie says, tearing my attention from the mesmerising wiggle of his hips.

I hurry to catch up with him. "Um, uni. We call it uni."

"Right." He nods. "Your family must be really proud."

"Hmm," I reply, which seems to be my standard response whenever someone asks me about uni since coming back to the bay.

240

"I never made it past ninth grade," Cookie says conversationally. "Although I did get my GED later on."

"I'm not sure what ninth grade is," I admit.

"I dropped out when I was fifteen."

"That's really young." I frown. "Did you not like school?"

He shrugs. "I didn't hate it, just... things changed."

We reach the bottom of the hill and cross the road to Colin's bakery. White wooden tables and chairs are already set up and the striped awning is extended for shade, which will be a blessing by mid-morning, when the summer temperatures begin to climb.

Cookie opens up the door, and a little bell rings in the shop as we step through.

"Cookie, is that you?" Colin calls out from the back.

"Yeah, Red. I brought a stray back with me, I hope you don't mind. He looked like a sad little puppy."

I glance over to see him grin and wink at me.

"Who has a puppy?" Colin appears in the doorway that presumably leads to the kitchen. With a neatly tied apron over his shirt and signature bow tie and his naturally curly, bright red hair parted neatly to the side in uniform waves, he looks like one of those old-fashioned sweet shop owners from the fifties.

He's holding a large glass bowl that is filled with some kind of whipped cream or frosting, I can't tell which.

"Oh, Quinn, it's you. You're up early. Then again, I suppose you're used to it now, all those early morning lectures at uni."

"Hmm," I mutter.

I don't bother to correct him. Even when I had been at

uni that first year, no one got up early for lectures. Most of the freshers were too hungover to even think about getting out of bed before lunchtime. It's a wonder anyone manages to actually finish a degree with the amount of drinking that goes on.

"I was just going to make him a coffee and get him something to eat before he freezes to death."

Colin blinks. "It's really not that cold."

"Spoken like someone who didn't grow up in California." Cookie snorts.

Waving that comment aside, he lifts the bowl cradled in the crook of his arm. "I've just tried a sample of your frosting." Colin's eyes are wide. "It tastes incredible."

Cookie smirks. "It has been said."

"We should create a signature cupcake for you with a special name, and you get to pick." His eyes narrow a fraction. "As long as it's family friendly."

"You wound me, *mijo*." Cookie laughs wickedly, and my stomach does a funny roll.

Huh, maybe I'm hungry after all. I didn't have breakfast this morning, just crept out before first light so I wouldn't have to make conversation with my mum and sisters once they were up.

An oven timer starts ringing somewhere in the back, and Colin gives a squeak before disappearing through the doorway into the back.

"Take a seat while I get the coffee machine switched on." Cookie leads me to a nearby table. "What do you want to drink, latte? Cappuccino?"

I slide into the seat and smile at him. "Am I going to be wearing it or drinking it?"

His mouth curves. "Depends on how well you tip."

"I hate to break it to you, but we don't tip much."

"I know, that was one of the things I found really weird when I got over here. Y'all actually get paid a proper base wage. I waited tables for a few years and trust me, if customers didn't tip, we didn't make rent."

"That's something I find weird," I reply. "I don't get how low the wages are. How do they expect people to survive?"

"They don't care, that's how." Cookie huffs. "So what do you want?"

"A latte is fine, thanks."

He heads around behind the counter and starts switching things on and getting organised. Before long, the heavenly scent of coffee reaches me, the perfect accompaniment to the mouthwatering aroma of freshly baked... well, I'm not sure exactly what Colin is baking in the kitchen but the smell is delicious, the scent of warm pastry, cinnamon and vanilla filling the air.

My stomach growls loudly, and I hear a laugh as a plate is set down in front of me along with a large cup.

"That's one of the sample cupcakes with my frosting I made last night," he says, nodding to the plate before moving to the next table and beginning to fill the little pot in the centre of the table with little sugar sachets.

I probably shouldn't be having a cupcake for breakfast but underneath the easy smile and bright eyes, there's a hint of nervousness in Cookie's expression. So against my better judgement, I peel back the paper and sink my teeth into a swirl of creamy frosting and the lightest, fluffiest cupcake I've ever tasted. I lick my lip and chew slowly, the delicate flavours bursting on my tongue. I'd expected it to be quite heavy and sickly and, to be honest, too sweet for me, but this is utter perfection in one bite. I'm sure my eyes have rolled back in my head, and I let out probably the sluttiest groan I have ever made in my life.

"Good?" Cookie asks softly, and I turn my gaze towards him as he slides into the chair opposite me.

I swallow and lick my lips. His gaze follows the path of my tongue and once again, I get that strange swooping feeling in my stomach. Maybe I have the beginnings of an ulcer from all the stress lately.

"So good. You made this?" He nods, and I lower my voice. "Don't tell Colin, but I think they're even better than his and that's a high bar."

"I heard that!" a voice rings out from the back.

"Jesus." I turn towards the doorway into the kitchen as his head appears around the corner. "Do you have the hearing of a bat?"

"No, you're just not as quiet as you think. Knowing your brothers the way I do, I'm certain it's an Ainsley trait. But, equally, I can't even be mad at you because I've already had two of Cookie's cupcakes, and even I can admit they're the best I've ever tasted."

He disappears back into the kitchen, and I turn back to Cookie. His cheeks pink up as he bites his lower lip to hide a pleased smile, and for a second, I wonder if that plump lip would taste as sweet as his cupcakes.

Whoa, where did that thought come from?

"Uh, so." I flounder, looking for something to say that

won't make me look like a complete idiot. "Where did you learn to bake?"

Lame.

"When I was little, after we'd moved to the States from Puerto Rico, me and Mama lived in an apartment in Long Beach with my abuelita. Mama had to work two jobs, so to keep me entertained and out of trouble, Abuelita taught me how to cook. I learned all the traditional dishes that came from our homeland, but we both loved to bake so we tried every recipe we could find."

"Sounds like you were close." I take a sip of my latte.

"We were."

"Are they still in Long Beach?" I ask. "Your mum and... abuelita means grandmother, right?"

He stares at me for a moment. "Yes, it means grand-mother, and no," he finally says, a quiet sadness in his eyes. "They're both gone now. It's just me."

"I'm sorry."

He shrugs and looks away. "Some days, it feels like it was a million years ago, and some days, it feels like it was just yesterday."

I open my mouth, although to say what, I don't know. The shop bell rings again and, knowing the bakery is not open yet, I look up and freeze when I find myself staring into the eyes of the girl I've had a crush on since I was old enough to pop my first stiffy.

"Quinn!" Georgie exclaims in delight.

I jump to my feet, knocking the table with a clatter. Cookie steadies my cup as I step away from my chair, and Georgie throws her arms around me enthusiastically. I breathe in the scent of her, board wax and the ocean. It never changes, and it transports me back to those awkward teen years when I pined for her relentlessly.

"Whoa, check out the guns." She laughs and pulls back, squeezing my biceps. "When'd you get so jacked? You're gonna need a new wetsuit. No way your old one is going to get past these bad boys. You're like the fucking Hulk."

I snort as I pull back and study her. She hasn't changed much. Her hair is still dyed blue and green in homage to her love of the ocean, and she seems to have added more tattoos in addition to the full nautical sleeve she had of mermaids and a kraken.

In fact, one of her tattoos now seems to snake up her neck towards her ear, which has a large gauge piercing. When she smiles, the two diamond studded piercings in her cheeks wink like dimples.

"I heard you were back. Sorry I didn't stop by yesterday, but I've been slammed with the Surf Shack. Since things started taking off in the bay, I've had to expand and take on staff so I have the time to work on my custom pieces."

Georgie is insanely talented. She designs and makes custom surfboards, which have become highly sought-after.

"It's okay." I shrug. "It's not like I was doing anything special."

"Well, I know your mum and the others are planning a massive welcome home, congrats on surviving uni, welcome to your future shindig at Sully's."

I groan.

"Come on, it won't be that bad." Georgie grins.

"They've invited half the bay, haven't they?"

"Yeah they have," Cookie says. I twist towards him.

"You know about this too?"

"Everyone knows about it," Cookie says breezily. "Your mama was in yesterday afternoon ordering a whole bunch of stuff for the party."

"Oh god," I mutter.

Georgie looks down at her waterproof watch and sighs. "I better get a move on. Cookie, is the cake ready?"

"Sure." Cookie jumps up and heads around the counter. "I'll grab it for you."

"Cake?" I look at Georgie.

"It's Josh's birthday."

"Josh?"

"He works at the Surf Shack. Lots of new faces since you last came back home. Still, you're back here permanently now, so it won't take you long to catch up."

"Yeah." My stomach clenches. I'm not back permanently, although I'll be closer than I was in Exeter. I'm not staying in the bay, and I have no idea how to tell my family when they're all so pleased to see me.

"Here you go." Cookie reappears and ends over a square cake box.

"Awesome. Gotta run, I'm already late."

"Let me get that for you, it's time to open anyway," Cookie says, flipping the sign on the door before opening it for her.

"Thanks," Georgie calls over her shoulder, and then she's gone.

"You staying?" Cookie asks, and I jolt at the question, but

when I look over to him, he nods towards the table. "Your coffee's getting cold."

"Oh right, thanks."

I take a seat back at the table as a few new people wander into the shop and start to queue at the counter. Picking up my coffee, I take a sip and watch Cookie as he slips off his hoodie and hangs it up. Putting on an apron, he slips behind the counter and greets the first customer with a blinding smile.

It's like pure sunshine and for some reason, I find I can't look away.

Chapter Three

Cookie

I try to force down the surprising disappointment. There's no way I could have missed the way Quinn looked at that surf girl, Georgie. Judging from the look on his face as he held her and breathed her in, I'm pretty sure he's straight.

I'd been hoping to find myself a hot English guy to pass the time with until Ty and I head to London but damn, Lady Luck has not been on my side. That bitch was clearly messing with me when she dangled that fine-ass man in front of me.

It's not like there aren't plenty of gay guys around this tiny little bay, but they all seem to be spoken for. Even Ty's hooking up with his childhood crush while he's back home, though he insists he's not.

Guess I'll just have to handle things myself until we get to London, after all. I'm not sure Grindr is gonna help much around here either. I give Quinn one last regretful glance and sigh. Maybe I won't get a taste of him, but he's definitely being filed away in my spank bank.

Leaving Quinn to nurse what's left of his latte and cupcake, I slip behind the counter and smile widely at the first customer. The next couple of hours pass quickly as the shop gets busy with a constant stream of visitors. The summer season is definitely picking up, and I'm sure Colin's going to have to employ another couple of people before I leave.

I was serious about investing in his business though. Even if I'm not in the bay, I'll still keep in touch with Colin. I adore my little strawberry pop tart and if nothing else, I am heavily invested in what happens between him and his *papi chulo*, Garrett. I bet those two would set the bed on *fire*. It's always the quiet ones.

Dang, I seriously need to get laid if I'm spending this much time thinking about everyone else's sexy times. Maybe I *should* try Grindr.

Finally, the crowd wears thin, with most of the parents fully caffeinated and headed to the beach with their kids. I wipe down the surfaces and check what's run low in the display cases, I glance over and find Quinn still sat at the window table, deep in thought as he twists an empty sugar packet between his restless fingers.

"Hey," I call over to him. He lifts his head and his pretty blue eyes lock on me as I smile back. "I'm not kicking you out or anything, but don't you have something better to do than sit around and stare at the walls?"

He stares at me for a moment, then slides out from the chair and walks over to the counter.

"Are you okay?" I ask as he slips his hands into his jeans pockets.

"Yeah," he replies on an exhale. "It's just weird being back home. Don't really know what to do with myself."

"I guess it's understandable, finishing college or uni or whatever. It's a big change. Do you have a job lined up? Do you know what you want to do?"

He frowns and kinda hunches his shoulders. "It's...complicated."

"Say no more, although it's okay, you know."

"What is?" He fixes those baby blues on me and I lean toward him, propping my elbows on the counter and my chin in my hands as I watch him.

"Not having the answers."

"Oh, I have the answers all right." He sighs. "I'm just not sure my family is going to like them." He shakes his head. "Sorry, I don't know why I said that."

"Maybe it's because sometimes it's easier to unload on a stranger than people who know you and have certain expectations of who they think you are."

He chews his lip and watches me thoughtfully, and I try really hard not to stare at his mouth. Needing the distraction, I turn toward the back and call out.

"Hey, Colin!" My favourite ginger pokes his head around the doorway. "Mind if I take a break while it's slow?"

"Sure. Might as well before we get hit with the lunch crowd."

"Thanks." I untie my apron and hang it on the peg as I round the counter towards Quinn. "Come on." I grasp his arm and tow him towards the door, enjoying his warm skin and firm muscles beneath my fingers.

"Where are we going?" His lips curve in amusement.

"For a walk." We step outside, and I reach into my back pocket for my sunglasses, which I slide onto my face.

"What?" I ask.

"I like these." He grins and taps the corner of my oversized, star-shaped, glitter-encrusted sunglasses.

I shrug. "Life's too short for boring old Ray-Bans."

"Well, they're certainly not boring. You could give Elton John a run for his money in those." He chuckles. "Please tell me you have a whole collection of them."

"Hell, yeah, I do." I huff and wave a hand. "Who doesn't match their sunglasses to their outfit?"

"I hate to break it to you, but I have a boring black pair I bought from Primark."

I press my hand to my chest. "You are literally giving me chest pains right now. You're lucky you met me, you know. We're going to inject some colour and excitement into your life. But for now, we're going to take a walk down to the oceanfront, and I'm going to buy you an ice cream because I may have only been here a few weeks, but I adore those— what do you call them, ninety-nines?"

He grins at me. "I can't remember the last time I had one of those."

"Well, today's your lucky day."

"I'm beginning to think it might be," he mumbles as he stares at me.

"Anyway, I'm going to buy you an ice cream and we're going to stare at the water and you can either stand in silence and just be all zen and shit or you can tell me what's bugging you. No pressure, zero judgement. Plus, as an added bonus, *mijo*, you get the whole cone of silence thing. I won't breathe a word to another soul about anything you tell me in confidence, 'kay?"

He studies me for a moment longer, then nods.

"And put your sunglasses on. It's bright and you don't want to end up with a headache." Chuckling, he reaches into his own pocket and slips them on. "Oh my god, they are as bad as I thought. We'll get you some new ones."

Quinn

I watch him strut away, and for a moment I forget to move as I watch those mesmerising hips wiggling. I scramble to catch up, not sure why I'm following him like he's a sparkly five-and-a-half-foot Pied Piper. There's just something about him, from his sexy accent to his dark, fathomless gaze. Being the object of his focus stirs an unfamiliar sensation in my belly and makes me want to spill my secrets. Maybe he's right, maybe it would be easier to tell someone unconnected with everything that came before. Someone who didn't know me before, or as part of the Ainsley family, or... as Sully's kid. Someone who wouldn't care if I'd actually gone to uni or not.

"Ground control to Major Tom."

Jolted from my thoughts, I look over at the fascinating man I've fallen into step alongside, and I have to admit, I'm a little dazzled by his smile.

"Pardon?"

"You look like you're a million miles away."

I shrug, not quite ready to confess my life story, no matter how much I might be tempted to. "So you're from Long Beach? How did you end up in a little Cornish bay baking cupcakes?"

"Seriously awesome cupcakes," he corrects airily, raising his chin.

"I can't even argue that with you," I reply. "If my family is going to torture me with a welcome home party that I don't want, can you please at least make sure your cupcakes are part of the order?"

"What, instead of the giant sheet cake with your face printed on it?" He tilts his head towards me, and I can't tell if he's being serious on account of being partially blinded by the sun reflected off his glittery star-shaped sunglasses.

"Please tell me you're joking."

He laughs delightedly and my belly does that lazy roll. Jesus, am I getting an ulcer? My stomach is never this jittery.

"I wouldn't want to ruin the surprise for you," he says. I really *really* hope he's just messing with me. "But in answer to your earlier questions, yes, there will be some of my cupcakes at your party, and yes, I'm mostly from Long Beach. Although I was born in Puerto Rico, I moved to the States when I was five."

"So how did you end up here? It's a bit of a downgrade from California for a holiday destination."

"I don't know." Cookie draws in a deep breath of fresh air, his body language relaxed. "I think this place is adorable. Ty grew up around here."

"And Ty is?"

"My absolute BFF, my brother from another mother. We're family. His dad passed away recently, and although he hadn't spoken to Ty in years, there wasn't anyone else. So Ty came back to deal with the funeral arrangements. I wasn't doing anything in particular and, with the way things are back home at the moment, we decided we wanted a change of scenery. Once he's wrapped up his family stuff, we're heading to London."

"He grew up here? What did you say his name was again?" I ask curiously.

"Tyler Evans. I think he went to school with your brothers, Beck and—what was the other one?"

"Jesse," I supply, trying to cast my mind back.

"Yeah, and Ty sure knows your brothers' friend Ryan." Cookies wiggles his brows above the rim of his sunglasses.

"I don't really remember Tyler," I reply as we wander companionably down the boardwalk along the seafront. "But then again, Beck and Jesse are older than me."

"God, I love these little stores." Cookie grins when we stop by one of the little tourist shops at the edge of the sand. "They're so cute!"

He picks up one of the little foil windmills in a display and oohs in delight. Neon-coloured buckets and spades are stacked alongside them, and an inflatable plastic dingy hangs above the open entrance, flapping slightly in the breeze.

To the side of the entrance are two circular stands, one holding rows of postcards and magnets and the other containing sunglasses. Cookie sets the little windmill down and slowly spins the display carousel, humming thoughtfully before picking out a pair and holding them out to me.

Removing my glasses with an amused smile, I take them and slip them on. Cookie immediately frowns.

"No," he declares.

He hands me a couple of others one at a time, and I dutifully try each pair and watch as he dismisses them. I'm not really sure why I'm humouring him. There's nothing wrong with the plain black plastic frames of my other ones.

"Cookie, I'm not sure I need another pair. The ones I have are fine."

"No, honey." He cocks a hip and shakes his head. "You're fine. Your nasty-ass shades are *not*."

I chuckle loudly, my cheeks heating at his unexpected praise. "They literally have one job, turn down the wattage of the sun so I don't sear my retinas. Does it really matter what they look like?"

"I'm going to pretend you didn't say that." He retrieves another pair and holds them out to me.

I stare at them dangling from his slim fingers and then lift my gaze to his. "Seriously."

"Trust me."

Blowing out a resigned breath, I reach out and take them, slipping them on and looking into the tiny rectangular mirror mounted on top of the display.

"Huh." I turn my head one way and then the other. Never in a million years would I have picked these up but I actually really like them. The frames are slim plastic, nicely shaped, and not too big, but they're lime green. "I..."

"Yoooou..." Cookie draws out the word teasingly as the corner of his mouth curves.

"I like them," I confess.

He grins. "You go pay for those, then, and I'm going to get us an ice cream. What do you want?"

He points to a nearby ice cream van parked near the steps that lead down onto the sandy beach.

"Anything is fine," I watch as he practically skips across the promenade towards the van, which only has a couple of kids waiting in line.

I head into the shop and impulsively pick up a little something for Cookie. Then, navigating my way down the crammed aisles of cheap tourist tat, glittery sea shells, sticks of rock, beach towels, and bucket hats, I finally manage to sidle up to the till and pay.

When I head back outside, it's to see Cookie wandering back in my direction with a ninety-nine in each hand. I tuck his present into my back pocket—even though there's no way it will fit—so it ends up sticking out and knocking me in the back. I slide my new sunglasses on and walk across to meet him.

"Thanks." I take the ice cream from him, our fingers brushing as I grasp the wafer cone.

"You're welcome," he says with a soft smile, and I watch, my mouth falling open slightly as his pink *pierced* tongue snakes out and licks a line around the ice cream, which is beginning to melt and drip down the cone.

My dick gives a twitch and I swallow hard. He gives a pornographic moan of pleasure, and it's like he's moving in slow motion as he slowly withdraws the long chocolate flake from the whipped ice cream. I think I actually stop breathing when he slips his pouty lips over the stick of chocolate, sinking down to where his fingers pinch the end, and then he slowly and torturously slides back up, his cheeks hollowing as he sucks the ice cream off it.

He closes his eyes and hums happily.

There's a smear of ice cream on his lower lip and suddenly all I want to do is lean in and lick it up, see if he tastes as sweet as his temperament seems to be.

Holy shit, I'm attracted to him.

There have been plenty of times I've found guys objectively hot to look at but never enough to act on. I'd never once thought about running my tongue along the seams of their lips before kissing them deeply, or sliding my hands up the length of their ridiculously long, smooth legs, or thinking about those legs wrapped around me while I—

Whoa. I suck in a sharp breath at the sudden image in my mind or, more pressingly, my body's reaction to it. My dick gives another enthusiastic throb, and I hope the sudden bulge in my jeans isn't noticeable beneath my untucked T-shirt.

Cookie opens his eyes at my sharp inhale and studies me.

"You're getting messy."

"What?" I squeak, then clear my throat. "Um, I mean pardon?"

He nods to my forgotten ice cream, which is melting in the sun and now runs down my fingers.

"Oh." I startle and lean down to lick the stickiness from my fingers, but my brain, intent on torturing me, starts meandering towards other things I may or may not be interested in licking.

Okay, I'm definitely going to need some time to process this.

I've always thought of myself as straight. Well, mostly. Looking at guys didn't count, or so I thought, because I'd never had the urge to take it beyond that. Until now.

"Are you okay?" Cookie tilts his head and laps daintily at his ice cream, once again giving me a glimpse of that tantalising piercing. I wonder how it would feel against my tongue or my—

Yeah, definitely need time to process, possibly while taking a cold shower.

"I'm fine," I reply, and my voice comes out a little gravelly. "I, uh... I got you a present."

"A present?" He blinks as that sinful mouth widens into a big smile. "For me?"

I nod and turn, cocking my hip and showing him what is tucked into my back pocket.

He laughs in delight and plucks out the long plastic pole topped with a pink and purple foil windmill, holding it up to his face like I've given him a single red rose and he's about to give it a sniff. Instead, he puckers those tempting lips and blows gently to set it spinning. He watches and gives another laugh, and even though my poor dick is very confused, it's also aching.

"You, uh... seemed to like them," I finish weakly, reaching up and rubbing the back of my neck, which feels hot—most likely from the sun and definitely not embarrassment.

"Are you kidding, *papi?*" He grins wildly, his dark eyes sparkling. "This is the best gift ever. I love these, they're so pretty and fun."

"Oh, good." My stomach swoops. It's like, now that I've realised I'm attracted to him, I notice how much I like him calling me *papi* and how hot his accent is.

Oh my god, I'm pretty sure I'm crushing on him. This is really not a good time to have a sexual awakening. I haven't even told my family yet that I'm not staying in the bay, and Cookie isn't staying in the bay either. He said it himself, he and his friend Tyler will be heading to London.

"Come on," Cookie says, nodding along the promenade towards the railings. "Let's get out of everyone's way."

I follow him over to the edge and lean against the metal rail which borders a small drop down to the sand. Lifting my ice cream to my mouth, I lick and gaze out to sea, captivated by the sun glinting on the rippling waves. From this distance, I can see Beck and Nat with their boards tucked under their arms, walking hand in hand towards the surf.

"So, you wanna watch the hot surfers or you wanna tell me what's on your mind?" Cookie asks.

"Well, considering two of the surfers are my brother and future brother-in-law, I guess that leaves me with only one choice."

"There are always other choices," Cookie says. "You don't have to talk if you don't want to, but you seem to have something you need to get off your chest, and I'm incurably nosy, according to Ty."

I turn my head towards him. "You won't tell anyone, not

even Colin? It's just, he's close with my brothers, and I don't want my family to find out from anyone but me."

"Seriously, I won't say a word." He waves his glittery windmill at me like it's Glinda's magic wand. "It's between you, me, and God. Just call me Padre."

"I'd rather not." My mouth twitches and then I sigh, gazing out to sea once more because it's easier than looking at him directly. "I've been lying to my family for nearly two years."

"You kill somebody?"

I snort. "No."

"Okay, so everyone tells little white lies. What could really be that bad? You're not a Republican, are you?"

"No. Also not American, in case you hadn't noticed." I chuckle and finally turn towards him.

"True. Okay, what gives?"

"I dropped out of uni after my first year," I confess.

"Okaay..." He draws the word out, waiting for me to elaborate.

"My dad died."

"I'm sorry," Cookie mutters as he watches me through those wild Elton John glasses and weirdly, it sets me at ease. "That's tough. What happened?"

"Cancer," I reply. "It was fast and aggressive. One minute we were being told, the next he was gone. He was..." I take a deep breath, forcing down the wave of pain that after three years hasn't diminished. "He was larger than life. The lynchpin of our whole family. I idolised him. I'd just been accepted to Exeter University to study environmental studies when he got sick, but he was so proud. One of the last things he said to me was that he wanted me to go out and make a difference in the world. Dad was real big on conservation, especially when it came to the bay and the ocean. I'd also toyed with the idea of marine biology. Then he died and Mum still wanted me to go, said I shouldn't give up my dream. So I went off to uni, still grieving and with his words ringing in my ears."

"That must have been tough, trying to come to terms with his loss. Your family all had each other here, I presume, and you were away from home for the first time, your world upended."

I jolt, staring at him in surprise. "Yes, it was, but no one understood that. No one asked me if I was okay. I get that they were all grieving in their own way. I don't know..." I trail off. "I guess I just felt like they forgot about me. Out of sight, out of mind."

"I'm sure that's not true." Cookie shakes his head. "It's like you said, they were all grieving. Maybe they couldn't see past their own pain."

"Yeah." I nod. "I came to that conclusion myself. Eventually. I know my family love me, but we're all a *lot*. Big. Loud. You have to shout to make yourself heard sometimes. I just didn't feel like shouting much."

"So what happened when you got to uni?"

"It wasn't a good fit." I shrug. "I tried. I tried for nearly a year. It wasn't just that I was dealing with dad's death and missing my family. I didn't belong there. Hated everything about it, especially the course. Making friends was a bit of a struggle too. I didn't want to open up to anyone in case I vomited my unhappiness all over them."

"I can understand that."

"As it got to the end of the first year, there was a local careers fair, so I went along. Not so much with any real expectation of finding answers, more that it was a Saturday afternoon and I had nothing better to do. There was a recruitment tent there."

"Recruitment?" His brows once again rise above the rim of his sunglasses. "Is this where you tell me you're secretly G.I. Joe? Because then the muscles would totally make sense."

"No." I chuckle. "They were recruiting firefighters."

"Firefighters?" His smile fades, his voice soft. "You're a firefighter?"

There's something in his expression that I can't quite put a name to, but it's fleeting, gone before I can figure it out.

"Yeah." I swallow hard, feeling a small weight lift now that I've told someone. Now that I don't have to keep this part of my life secret anymore. "I don't know what drew me to it. It's not something I'd ever considered. But I signed up there and then. Dropped out of uni and started their training program, and just fell in love with the job. I finally felt like I'd found where I belonged."

He pushes his glasses up onto his head, a move that draws back his pastel pink hair and exposes the dark roots.

"A calling?" he says, his dark eyes gentle and filled with understanding.

"Yes, that's it exactly," I reply. "After I completed my training, I was lucky enough to get a place at a fire station in Exeter. One of the other guys who worked there had a spare room to rent, which was great because I could no longer stay in the uni student accommodation."

"Why didn't you tell your family?" Cookie tilts his head and watches me. "Would they have hated it that much?"

"I honestly don't know," I admit. "But I couldn't do it to Mum. She was reeling from losing her husband, and I couldn't tell her that not only had I dropped out of uni but that I also was training for a job that put my life on the line every time I went on shift. I figured I'd just give things time to settle and see if this career would work out for me, but the more time that's passed, the harder it is to just tell the truth."

"I see." Cookie chews his lip thoughtfully.

"But my placement at the Exeter fire station was only temporary. My contract ended just shortly before my uni course would have if I'd stayed. So I knew it was time to come home and be honest. I've got a spot at the fire station in Perranporth, which isn't far, about twenty minutes away. I'm due to start in a couple of weeks. Figured once I've come clean, Mum wouldn't mind me staying at home for a little while until I find a place of my own closer to work."

"Wow," Cookie breathes.

"Yeah," I mutter. "Now I just have to have the balls to tell everyone. I don't know if they're gonna be mad that I lied for so long or that I'm doing a dangerous job–"

"Or maybe they'll be proud of you," Cookie interrupts.

"Not sure about that."

"Quinn." He reaches for my forearm, and I feel the heat of his touch against my skin settle somewhere deep inside me. "I'm proud of you."

"What?" I whisper in shock.

264

"I'm proud of you." His eyes are filled with warmth. "The world needs heroes like you."

I huff lightly. "I'm not a hero."

"Do you or do you not run into burning buildings to rescue people?"

"Well, yes, but it's also getting cats out of trees and kids' heads out of railings." I smile.

"And I bet you're a hero to those mothers and pet owners," he replies with a small grin.

"I guess."

"Do you love what you do?" he asks pointedly.

"Yes," I answer instinctively.

"Then that's all that matters." He squeezes my arm in reassurance and oddly enough, it makes me want to put him in for a cuddle.

Christ, what is wrong with me?

I'm not a cuddler.

"I don't know your family all that well, but they seem to love you very much. Okay, yeah, they might be pissed you didn't tell them, but I'm sure they just want you to be happy."

"I really hope so." I sigh.

His phone pings and he reaches into his back pocket, pulling it free and thumbing the screen to open it.

"Dang, it's Colin. I should head back. He seems to be having some sort of crisis, but knowing him, it could just mean the frosting has come out the wrong colour. Don't get me wrong, he's a sweetheart, but damn he's wound tight."

"Do you want me to walk you back?" I ask, oddly reluctant to leave his company.

He grins at me. "You're really putting a lot of effort into avoiding your family, aren't you?"

"For as long as I can." I nod, and he snorts.

"Come on, then. I'm sure we can find something for a hot firefighter to do in the shop. If you're going to be hiding out, don't think we won't put you to work."

We head back towards the hill and I find that, actually, I'm okay with that.

Chapter Four

Cookie

Colin's emergency turned out to be the fence around the back of the bakery crashing down. It had only been upright by the grace of god—due to winter storms giving it a good battering, some kids kicking balls at it had finished the job.

Quinn, in his mission to avoid his family and delay a long overdue conversation, had been all too quick to offer his manly services to replace the fence with a new, sturdier one. This has resulted in the sweet torture of a half-naked Quinn all hot, sweaty, and stripped to the waist in a tool belt and tight jeans while he hauls lumber around the very tiny backyard of Colin's bakery.

Over the course of the last few days of ogling that fine-ass man every spare minute I got, I'm now building up quite the spank bank repertoire. There's surfer Quinn in very tight Speedos, firefighter Quinn asking me to check his hose for him, and now sexy lumberjack Quinn showing me his tool.

Seriously, I haven't jerked off this much since I was a horny teenager. My dick's gonna fall off soon.

Damn, that man is hot, like supernova, surface-of-the-sun hot. If I get too close, I'm gonna burn, but I can't seem to help myself. I'm a sucker for punishment. I glance over at the to-go cup sat beside the cash register and smile at the little pinwheel propped up in it.

Reaching out a finger, I give it a little flick, unable to help the smile on my face as it spins. It's seriously the cutest gift a guy has ever given me, and Quinn's not even banging me. In fact, I'm still sure he's straight. Well, okay, maybe like eighty percent sure he's straight. I don't know, there are moments when I catch him looking at me that make me wonder.

The bell on the shop door rings. "Sorry, we're closing–"

I look up, the words dying on my lips when I see the blue-haired surf girl, Georgie.

"It's okay." She smiles easily. "I'm just here to see Quinn. Is he still banging away at Colin's fence? I don't know why he said he'd do it, I've never so much as seen him swing a hammer."

"There are probably a lot of things you've never seen him do," I snap defensively. "He's done a great job. Colin's really grateful."

Georgie laughs, oblivious to the daggers I'm shooting her way. "He probably has. Quinn's doesn't do a bad job on anything he sets his mind to. He's always been a bit of an overachiever and perfectionist, come to think of it. I'm just surprised Colin didn't go flutter his eyelashes in Garrett's direction. That man would have tripped over himself to get over here and handle Colin's wood."

268

I snort out loud, unable to help myself. Fuck, I really don't want to like her, not after the way Quinn looked at her and hugged her, which is ridiculous of me, I know. But I have to admit, she's cool and funny, and if it wasn't for my stupid unrequited crush on the six-foot wall of handsome currently hammering nails into the decorative trim, Georgie and I would probably already be besties.

"Quinn's out back."

"Great. I won't be long, just need to drop this off."

My gaze is drawn to the plain cardboard box in her arms, which clinks when she moves.

"What is it?" I ask curiously.

"A case of Ryan's most popular craft beer. These babies have won awards and were responsible for a very drunken trip to Vegas where Colin woke up dressed as a showgirl and with poker chips in his sequinned knickers. Beck was in a pair of ass-less chaps, and Jesse and Deke woke up married." Georgie drops her voice and winks. "There may be pictures."

My mouth falls open. "Are you serious?" She nods and grins. "And I thought Miami was wild."

"It's got nothing on the bay." She shifts the obviously heavy box in her arms. "Don't even get me started on the red double-decker bus Kyan bought on a whim and named Hank. Whenever he's over from the States, they take it out, and you seriously do not want to know the shit they get up to when they take the party bus out."

I nod enthusiastically. "Sounds exactly like something I do want to know."

The box wobbles in her arms again. "Did you say he was out back?"

"Oh, yeah. Sorry." I motion her back behind the counter and lead her through the kitchen to the back entrance and out onto a small patio area.

She drops the box on the small garden table by the door and stretches, rubbing her back. "Fuck, that shit's heavy when you're heaving it down that bloody big hill."

"Hey, Georgie." Quinn turns toward us, and I have to bite my lip from sighing out loud.

He's wearing his worn, ripped jeans slung low, with that damn tool belt riding his hips. His Adonis belt is visible above the waistband and his chest is gloriously bare. It's tanned and sweaty, covered in a fine dusting of blonde hair that tapers down to his belly.

"Fucking hell, Quinn!" Georgie's eyes widen. "Put some bloody clothes on. You'll have someone's eye out with those pecs. I have literally no idea how you went from skinny student to He-Man."

"What?" He grins and stands with his hip cocked and his hammer resting on his shoulder, making his bicep pop. "I like the look, it makes a statement."

"Uh-huh. Is that statement, 'By the power of grey skull'?"

I snort loudly again. Damn it, I really don't want to like her.

He nods to the table. "What's in the box?"

"Well, Brad Pitt, thank you for asking." She reaches in and picks out a bottle, holding it up for him to see. "Never let it be said I don't pay up."

"Pay up?" I repeat.

"Georgie lost a bet," Quinn says smugly.

"What was the bet?"

"It was a surfing thing." Quinn shrugs.

"Fuck off." Georgie wedges the lid against the edge of the table and smacks it with her palm. The beer pops open easily and she raises it to her lips, taking a long, satisfying pull while flipping him the finger with her other hand. Swallowing, she turns back toward the gate in Colin's brand-new fence. "I'm out of here." She unbolts it and lifts the latch. "Later."

"Loser," Quinn yells as the gate clangs shut.

Her voice drifts over the fence. "Fuck you. I hope Skeletor kicks your arse."

Sniggering, Quinn crosses the small yard and plucks a beer from the box, then holds it out to me. "Want one?"

"Thanks." I turn it over in my palm and read the label. "Tastes like Bad Decisions."

Quinn grins. "It's not for the fainthearted. Take a look at the alcohol content."

My gaze scans down the label and my brows rise. "That's a lot... for a beer."

"I'm pretty sure Ryan mixes it with moonshine or some shit like that." He pulls one for himself from the case and, retrieving his keys from his pocket, pops the top with a mini bottle opener keychain, then leans over and opens mine too.

"Well." I smirk at him. "I like to live dangerously." I clink my bottle to his in a toast and watch him take a pull. I can't help but admire the long line of his throat as he tilts his head back and swallows. Fuck, that makes my dick twitch.

"Uh, that hits the spot." He lowers the bottle and groans before fixing me with that unwavering blue gaze. "You done for the day?"

I try to find my voice and answer him, instead of what I

really want to do, which is climb him like a tree and lick the sweat from his neck... *for starters.*

Clearing my throat, I nod. "Colin's gone home. He's got candies he needs to make a start on for the Festival of the Seals or something."

"The Festival of the Sea." Quinn grins.

"Yeah, that's it. I said I'd close up for him once you're done." I look around the small courtyard at the brand-new fence.

"I'm done." Quinn turns to survey his handiwork. "Hopefully, they should hold up against gale-force winds and budding Christiano Ronaldos."

I huff a laugh.

"Didn't get in trouble for kicking footballs at fences when you were a kid?"

"Honey." I roll my eyes. "For starters, kicking is not what I'd do when faced with balls, and second, back then, I was the one jumping up and down with a pair of pom-poms. Seriously, I had the best high kick on our block, all the girls were jealous."

"With those legs, I have no doubt about that," he murmurs, his hot gaze travelling down to my thighs.

Okaaaay. The likelihood he *may* be straight just dropped to fifty percent.

"You hungry?" Quinn asks. "I'm starving and since we've got the place to ourselves, I thought we could sit out here where it's quiet, have a couple of beers, hang out."

My stomach jumps with excitement and the thought of spending more time with him.

"I could call Nat," Quinn offers. "Get some of his signature seafood tacos. My younger sister Juni is waiting tables at the restaurant tonight. If it's not busy, I'm sure she wouldn't mind running them over but if not, I can go grab them."

"That sounds great." I can't help my smile. "I'll just go make sure everything is locked up out front."

"Great," Quinn says, and I'm sure I'm not imagining his gaze dipping to my lips.

Forty percent.

Setting my beer on the edge of the table, I turn around and head back into the bakery before I do something crazy like throw myself at him and devour his mouth.

Colin had already finished up and cleaned down the kitchen before Georgie showed up, so I don't have to do anything there. I had brought in the few folding tables and chairs from out the front earlier and stacked them neatly inside. Hurrying through the main part of the shop floor, I lock the door. The cash register is emptied and the sales counted. There's very little left to do, so I box up the last few cupcakes I'd been saving for Quinn and switch out the lights.

By the time I eagerly make my way back out into the yard, Quinn's just hanging up the phone. My stomach flutters as he pulls one of the chairs out for me and gives me a sweet smile. Taking a seat, I slide the box onto the table, and his gaze falls on it.

He groans. "Please tell me that's what I think it is?"

"*Mijo*, you are too easy." I chuckle and pick up my beer. "But yes, your favourites."

His eyes light up and he goes to open the box, but I lightly slap his hand. "Uh-uh, dinner first."

He pouts and oh my god, how I want to suck on that

lower lip. Instead, clearing my throat, I take a casual sip of my beer and cough slightly. Boy, he wasn't wrong. I'm not usually one for beers, but this is strong shit.

"So, did you order the tacos?"

He nods. "Yeah, Juni said she'd run it down to us."

"She's one of the twins, right?"

Quinn grins. "Yeah, my parents must've been real bad in a past life to be saddled with two sets of twins and two singles. Anyone would think they liked having kids."

I smile at him softly. You can see the affection he has for all his siblings every time he talks about them.

"How old are the girls?" I ask.

"Twenty." He leans back comfortably in his chair and absently picks at the label on his beer. "Joss is training to be a vet so she can work with our brother Jesse. Juni is doing marketing thing. I'm not sure what, to be honest, just that it has something to do with social media. She went to college locally, but now she's doing some online courses because she wanted to stay close to home."

I toy with my beer. "Sooooo," I say casually. "What's up with you and Georgie?"

"Up?" He lifts a brow.

"Yeah. I mean, I kinda got the feeling the other day that, you know, you might"—I shrug a little too casually—"have a thing for her."

He leans back, rocking his chair onto its back legs, and laughs. "Oh, yeah. My crush on Georgie." He shakes his head in amusement. "I think I was twelve the first time I noticed her that way. Which would have made her sixteen, I guess.

No, seventeen? Anyway, I pined for her for years in a haze of angsty teenage drama."

"You never told her how you felt?"

He snorted. "She barely even noticed me. I was skinny with acne and braces and listened to way too much Muse. She was way too cool for me. Georgie was always comfortable in her own skin, and I both admired and envied that about her."

"Do you think she knew? About your crush, I mean."

"God, I hope not." He laughs and drains his beer, then reaches for another one. "Our families were tight. Our parents and hers were best friends their whole lives. They were godparents for me and all my sibs, and my mum and dad were Georgie's godparents. Georgie hung out mostly with Beck, Jesse, and Ryan. The four of them were pretty inseparable. In fact, she probably knew your friend Tyler if they're about the same age and they all went to school together. I was a few years behind them. They were mostly all going off to college by the time I got to secondary school."

"Do you still feel that way about her, then?" I ask, hoping that I sound casual and not like a potential stalker.

"Do I?" he mutters and takes a swig of his beer. "Hmm, I guess I haven't really thought about it."

"Some crushes die hard." I set my now empty bottle on the table, and Quinn pops the lid on a new one and hands it to me.

"I think I might've up until a few years ago, although it had faded by then. To be honest, I think after Dad died I was just trying to hold on to anything familiar, even an unrequited teenage crush."

"And now?" I sip my beer.

"Now." He hums thoughtfully and then frowns. "It's just not there anymore. Since being home, I... well, I'm happy to see her, but happy the way I am to see my brothers and sisters. No sweaty palms, jumpy belly, or teenage angst." He laughs. "The last few years I've made a lot of changes I wasn't even aware of. I guess it's called growing up. I've been so focused on my career that I haven't thought about relationships. Just hooked up here and there."

"And those hookups would be women or..."

"Women." He smiles at me and my heart sinks.

"So you've never–"

Suddenly, the gate rattles. "Quinn!" a feminine voice calls out. "Open the gate. I've got my hands full." Setting his almost empty bottle on the table, he pushes to his feet and unlatches the gate. "Oh my god, put some clothes on, you himbo," the young woman says when she gets a look at his bare chest. Quinn laughs and flexes his biceps. "You think that's impressive just because now you don't look like Shaggy from *Scooby-Doo*." She rolls her eyes and steps further into the yard, holding out a small cardboard tray containing two full paper bags.

"Cookie." Quinn closes the gate behind her. "This is Juni."

"Hey." She smiles, and I can see the family resemblance. She's probably about the same height as me, slim, and wearing black pants and a black shirt with *Sully's Bar & Grill* embroidered on the breast. Her blonde hair is pulled back from her pretty face in a neat ponytail, and her blue eyes sparkle with mischief like her brother's.

"Hey, Miss Juni, nice to finally meet you," I greet her as she sets the tray down on the table in front of me. A whiff of a heavenly aroma wafts up from the bags, which makes my mouth water.

"You too, Cookie." She grins. "I have to say, you've got the whole bay talking about these famous cupcakes of yours. I didn't think anyone would be able to outdo Colin, but even he says they're the best he's ever tasted."

"Oh, stop." I wave my hand. "And by stop, I mean please continue."

She laughs. "I'll have to come by the bakery when I get the chance and try them."

"Oh, here." I reach into the box on the table and retrieve one of my rainbow swirl unicorn cupcakes with my signature frosting.

"Hey!" Quinn whines. "Don't give her my cupcakes."

I shush him. "She earned it coming down here to drop off dinner for us."

"Thanks." She unwraps it and, keeping eye contact with her brother, smugly takes a deep bite. He sends her a dirty look, but I know he's just playing, just like I see the moment Juni's pupils pretty much dilate and she forgets all about teasing her brother. "Oh my god!" she moans. "I think I've just had a religious experience."

"Bless you, child." I nod piously.

"Do you have to speak with your mouth full?" Quinn sulks.

She stuffs the rest of the cupcake in her mouth and grins, her cheeks puffed out like a squirrel. I watch as she chews and swallows. "Amazing." She turns to me. "Ten out of ten, would definitely recommend to a friend."

"Thanks, honey."

"Anyway, I'm heading back now before the rush starts, need those tips tonight. I've got a date tomorrow."

"With who?" Quinn demands, and Juni rolls her eyes.

"No one you know, but she's gorgeous and the sweetest thing ever." Juni sighs happily.

Quinn blinks. "She?"

"Yeah, I like girls." She shrugs. "I just didn't feel the need to make a big coming-out announcement." She crosses her arms and stares down her brother, who still looks bemused. "I mean, why should I? I found someone I want to date, so why should it matter if it's a girl or a boy or trans or anything else? It's way past time this was normalised." She throws her hands up. "We shouldn't have to 'come out,' like we're asking for approval or some shit like that."

"Sing it, sister." I hold up my hand and she gives me a fist bump, then smiles.

"She's kinda quiet and really kind, but I've seen her in a bikini, and I'm pretty sure she has nipple piercings."

I wink. "It's always the quiet ones."

"I'm kinda crazy about her," Juni says nervously. "I just hope she likes me as much as I like her, even without the potential nipple piercings which, not gonna lie, are hot as hell."

"Just be yourself," I say gently.

Quinn unfolds himself from the chair and moves closer to his sister. "I'm happy you've found someone you like, but Cookie's right. Just be yourself and she'll love you."

He leans in, but she backs up a step, holding up her hands.

"As much as I'd love to have a touching brother-sister bonding moment, you're sweaty and half naked. Give me a call when you've showered and put a shirt on."

"Some people are so touchy."

"Okay, Rizzo, I'm gonna head back now before Mum sends out a search party, but thanks, Quinn, I appreciate the support." Juni heads back to the gate. "You kids have fun! And drink responsibly!" she calls over her shoulder with a laugh.

"What does she mean?"

"Last time my brothers got drunk on Ryan's beer, they all ended up in Vegas."

"I heard about that." I snigger and reach for my beer, draining the bottle and taking another one.

"I'm sorry I missed it." Quinn shakes his head, a smile tugging at his lips. "But then that's what happens when their best friend is rich and famous, with his own private jet named Todd."

"Todd? Would this be the same friend that owns a bus called Hank?" I ask curiously.

"Yep, that's Kyan. He's a rockstar, so very few people ever tell him no. Consequently, he tends to be very impulsive."

"Kyan? Oh my god, you don't mean Kyan Amos, do you?"

"That's the one." Quinn nods as he reaches for the food bags and begins to unwrap them.

"Your brothers are friends with the lead singer of Amos?" I gape in shock.

Quinn nods again and hands me a napkin. "He's actually

a really good laugh, and a good friend to Jesse and his husband Deke. Deacon's how we all met Kyan, they were friends first. Kyan actually comes back to the bay fairly frequently. He likes it here."

"Wow."

"Yeah." Quinn chuckles and hands me a taco. "Wait til you meet Finn."

"Finn?"

"Finn Gallagher."

"The movie star?" I blink. "Are you seriously telling me he visits here too?"

"Actually, he lives here. He's with Wyatt, Jesse's business partner."

"Looks like I seriously underestimated this sleepy little bay of yours." I shake my head in astonishment and bite into my taco, moaning in delight when the flavours burst over my tongue. "I love these so much. Ty and I ate at the restaurant the first night we were here and I had these. One bite and I was hopelessly addicted. When I move on again, these alone will be worth a visit back to the bay."

For a while we sit in companionable silence, too busy devouring our dinner, but gradually conversation starts up again. We talk about anything and everything. It's just so easy being around Quinn, and it's not just because he's hot and I'd love for him to rail me into next week. I *like* him. He's funny and smart, but there's an air of vulnerability about him that makes him somehow... relatable? Accessible? I don't know what the word is. What I do know is that we've made our way through over two-thirds of the case of Ryan's beer, and every-thing is looking pretty fuzzy.

The sky above is now a darkened blanket of indigo with bright pinpricks of starlight. The small yard is lit by the security light above the back door of the bakery. It's a weeknight so the bay isn't that busy anyway, but even the light foot traffic passing by the back of the bakery fades away into silence. Other than our conversation, the only sound I can hear is the constant crash of the ocean nearby.

"It's so peaceful here."

"Yeah it is," Quinn answers, and I jolt, unaware I'd spoken that last part out loud. Then he sighs.

"Whass wrong?" My tongue is weirdly numb so that first word slurs.

"I's juss thinkin' bout"—he hiccups—"havin' to tell my family I'm a bit of a liar."

"You's should write them a letter." I point at him and nod, which makes the world spin around me a bit.

Quinn blinks and then pats down his bare torso, frowning. "Don' have a pen."

I try to think for a moment, but my brain's kinda sluggish. "Email?"

Quinn brightens. "Thass genius! I should send an email."

He picks up his phone and presses and swipes at the screen before stopping and looking back at me with bleary eyes. "What should I say?"

"S'okay, *papi*, I gotcha." I sway in my chair but lean in closer. "Juss write this, 'kay?"

He nods, his head flopping unsteadily. "Shoot."

"'Kay." I squint as I think. "Dearest Mother–"

He blinks. "You been watchin' too much *Bridgerton?* Thass a bit formal."

"How'd you know about Bridg–" I give a little burp.–
"Scuse me. *Bridgerton?*"

"Iss got loads of sex in it." Quinn frowns. "'Course I'm
gonna watch it. Plus, iss romantic."

"Aww you're so cute," I coo at him, and he waves his
phone at me. "Oh, right, where was I? Dearest Mother."

"Iss too formal. Told you."

"I'm juss tryin' to sound English. Is not like you can put
hey, Mamita."

"How 'bout *hey, Mum.*"

I snap my fingers and point at him. "Perfec! Hey, Mom,
so you know you thought I was at uni the last couple of years?
Well, I wasn't. Surprise! I'm a superhot fireman."

"S-U-P-E-R-H-O-T FIRE-MAN," he mouths as he peers
blearily at his phone screen and taps away with his thumbs.

I nod. "Superhot fireman. And I'm a hero. I rescue cute
kitties from trees and wear a supercool outfit... and I have a
realllly long hose."

"R-E-A-L-L-Y LONG HOSE." Quinn makes exaggerated vowel shapes with his mouth.

"So don' be mad. I love my job and I love being aroun' all
the other superhot firemen. Plus, I get to slide down a big
hard pole all day."

"BIG HARD P-O-L-E ALL DAY," he repeats, still
typing.

"Love, Quinn, smiley face, heart, heart, hug, kissy face."

"K-I-S-S-Y.... Oh." he snorts. "You mean the emoji?" He
taps the screen a few more times, then stops and stares at it.
Then he bursts out laughing, and I can't help but join him. "I
can't send this!" He wheezes out a gasping breath and wipes

the tears from his eyes, then sobers. "I really don' rescue that many cats."

We stare at each other for a moment and then burst out laughing again. His phone slips from his fingers and clatters to the table. He picks it up and flicks off a stray piece of lettuce from the tacos. And stares at the it.

"What?" I blink.

He holds up the phone and shows me the screen, which I can't read from here due to a combination of poor lighting and the fact that I'm very drunk.

"I accidentally hit Send," he says. "Oops."

We both laugh even harder. My sides are actually starting to ache. Finally, I drag in a deep breath and so does he.

"Oh god." He rubs his face. "I'm sooo drunk," he slurs, dropping his phone on the table again. "You know what we should do?"

"What?" I hiccup loudly.

"We should go for a walk, burn some of the booze off."

"M'kay." I push myself out of the chair and the whole world tilts. I stumble sideways, fall on the floor, and start laughing again.

"Cookie?" Quinn's face appears above me. "You a'right?"

"No." I grin. "I think you might need to give me CPR."

He snorts and reaches down, hauling me to my feet. I stumble into him and shamelessly grope his biceps.

"Mmmm," I hum, "Firm."

"Why, thank you." He gives me a pleased smirk.

"Iss that a tool belt diggin' into my hip or are you real happy to see me?"

He laughs and unbuckles his tool belt, letting it drop to the ground.

"We should lock the door." I pat down the pockets of my shorts. "Where are the cheese?"

Quinn frowns. "Keys?"

"Thass what I said, ssush." I put my finger to my lips to shush him so I can concentrate. I find the keys on the table and, after a great deal of fumbling, manage to lock the back door.

Letting ourselves out of the back gate, Quinn locks it behind us and takes my hand. It must be really late because the streets and boardwalk are deserted. In the distance, I can even see that the lights of the restaurant are out.

"Race ya!" I whoop in delight and streak off toward the sand, running along the beach with the wind in my face and the roar of the waves in my ears.

I feel good.

Suddenly, strong arms wrap around me, lifting me into the air.

"Caught you." Quinn laughs, his hot breath fanning against the back of my neck, making me shiver.

He drops me gently to my feet and as I turn, I see that we've managed to cover a fair distance down the beach in our inebriated state. It's a quiet, deserted section with a small formation of rocks behind us, and I know from experience that a concealed pathway leads up the cliff face to the bluffs not far from the rental where Ty and I are staying.

Turning in Quinn's arms, I look up into his eyes. The moon shines over us, bathing us in a pale, silvery light.

"Now what?" I ask breathlessly.

"There's only one thing to do." He grins and pulls back. Next thing I know, he's yanking off his boots and tossing them to the sand. Then he unbuttons his jeans and shoves both them and his boxers down. Stepping out of them, he peels off his socks and throws them aside so that he's standing in front of me bathed in moonlight, gloriously and unapologetically naked.

Fuck me.

He's gorgeous. Miles of golden skin and thick muscles, and a dick that's perfectly proportioned and surrounded by a neat thatch of fair hair. *Oh, my god.* My mouth waters, and I'm desperate to drop to my knees and taste him.

"Well?" He challenges. "Perfect night for a swim."

"A swim?" I try to blink through the haze of lust and alcohol.

"Dare you."

I am not one to back down from a dare. Kicking off my shoes, I whip my T-shirt over my head and fling it behind me, followed by my shorts, then stand in front of Quinn just as naked and unrepentant as him.

I'm sure I'm not imagining the way he swallows slowly and his hot eyes trail down my body to pause on my dick... my very enthusiastic dick. Which decides to harden under his intense gaze.

I look down and to my delight, his starts to thicken in response. Praise Jesus, but just when I think I might be able to get on my knees for him after all, he spins around abruptly and heads for the water.

With a sigh, I follow, unsteady on my feet and the soft,

uneven sand, but as I reach the water's edge and the tide washes over my toes, I let out a yelp.

"Nope." I turn around and march back up the beach, but I barely make it three paces when those powerful arms wrap around me once more, lifting me up and slinging me over a broad shoulder. He doesn't seem bothered that we're both butt naked.

"Quinn, don't you dare–" I don't get to finish my sentence because he drops me, and all I can hear is the rush of the water as I go under in the icy waves.

Quinn

I dive in after him, keeping his body close. Even though I am well and truly wankered thanks to Ryan's beer, I'd never let anything happen to Cookie. I probably shouldn't have even suggested this, but I needed to do something. The way he stood in front of me, his hot body on display, and when I'd got a look at his hard cock, the blood rushed south so quickly I thought I was going to pass out. Heat and desire stronger than I'd ever felt before crashed over me and so help me, I wanted to reach out and touch him.

I wanted my lips on mine, his tongue in my mouth and fuck me, I wanted my fist wrapped around his cock. I wanted to feel him moaning into my mouth as I pleasured him. Wanted to feel his hot cum spilling over my skin.

I can't even blame the alcohol because I've had hot and sweaty dreams about him all week long. I've lost count of how many times I've wanked over the thought of him, of those long golden legs wrapped around my hips as I fuck into his tight hole.

I've never really thought of myself as bi before. Sure I've found other guys hot, but I've not really thought about doing anything. Although to be fair, I've not really thought about sex much at all beyond one or two hookups. I haven't had the head space for it, but now all I want is him.

My brain keeps trying to tell me all the reasons why this is a bad idea: I have no experience with guys, neither of us is staying in the bay, I have too much going on in my life right now that's unresolved. But whenever I'm near him, all those reasons disappear and all I see is him.

His head breaks the surface of the water and instead of looking pissed, his eyes flash dangerously and his mouth curves into a wicked smile.

"Oh, you in trouble now, *papi*." He launches himself at me and wraps his arms and legs around me like a spider monkey. I can feel his dick, now softened from the cold water, pressed against my stomach, and my hands automatically grasp his tempting arse.

He throws himself back, using his weight to pull me off-balance and dunk us both under the water. We wrestle back and forth, hands all over each other and bodies touching. Laughing and playing but with an undercurrent of desire.

Eventually, we begin to wear out, and I find myself just holding him. We've edged out into slightly deeper water, too deep for him to put his feet down and touch the bottom, but the water only comes up to my shoulders.

His legs are still wrapped around me, his arms wound

around my neck, and our faces are close together. The water is calm, the waves gently lapping around us as we stare at each other in the pale moonlight.

"Quinn," he whispers.

I can't help myself. I lean in and press my lips to his. His fingers tangle in my hair as he opens his mouth against mine. I pull him in tighter, sliding my tongue between his lips. I can feel the cool dampness of his skin and the slight rasp of his stubble. His flat chest is pressed to mine, the tiny hardened nubs of his nipples rubbing against my wet chest hair. I can feel his dick and his balls rubbing against my stomach as he writhes against me.

There is no doubt, despite the fog of alcohol, that I'm making out with another man, and holy hell I've never been so turned on in my life.

All I want is more. More of his taste. More of his body. More of... him.

Still carefully holding him to me, I head towards the shore as we continue to eat at each other's mouths. We've barely made it out of the water when the sudden lack of buoyancy and the alcohol catch up with me. I stumble forward, dropping to my knees but careful not to crush his smaller frame as I lower him to the sand.

Cookie spreads his legs, cradling me between his thighs, and I gasp into his mouth when I feel his hard cock press against my own.

"Quinn," he pants against my mouth, clutching my arse cheeks with desperate hands forcing me to rut harder against him. "Please."

The waves are still rushing and breaking gently over my

feet as we grind hungrily against each other. God, he tastes so fucking good, sweet like his cupcakes we ate earlier.

I've never felt so out of control, driven by pure primal pleasure. My cock is so hard, my balls drawn up tight and aching with the need for release. His tongue tangles with mine, and his fingers dig into my skin as he urges me on. Our cocks slide together, heat and pressure, and a bite of friction that is borderline painful but still just the right side of intense pleasure.

Suddenly, he cries out, and I feel his cock pulse before hot wetness slicks my stomach. His orgasm triggers my own, and I come all over his cock, unloading in throbbing spurts. Jesus, my cum is all over his dick and balls, and fuck me if that isn't the hottest thing I've ever experienced in my life. My body shudders as he wraps his arms around me, and we lie there panting in the sand.

After a moment, I roll off him, afraid I'm crushing him with my size. We're so close that there's barely an inch between us. His hand finds mine and our fingers interlace. Neither of us says anything—I'm not sure either of us can. The world still spins but not just from the alcohol anymore. I look up into the vast starlit sky above us, Cookie's warm body beside me.

I've never felt so content in my life.

About the Author

I write MM Romance and love all things spooky and supernatural. Inside my pages, you'll find fantastical realities filled with sassy ghosts, witches, and demons. Take a wild journey through the dangerous streets of Victorian London, and for a bit of a relaxing break, head to a little Cornish bay for some contemporary love stories.

Feel free to step into my worlds and explore, but fair warning! Once you enter, you may never want to leave!

Direct Store: **https://vawncassidystore.com**

Newsletter: **https://crafty-trader-8895.ck.page/ed9e4867b5**

Instagram: **https://www.instagram.com/vawncassidyauthor/**

Sweet On You

Colette Davison

Chapter One

Cameron

I browse social media apps on my phone while I wait for the school bell. Since I became the responsible adult in the house, I've made sure to be here at least five minutes early. Me. Responsible for taking care of my ten-year-old brother while our dad is away with work. I'm still wrapping my head around it. Hopefully, I'm doing a good job. Dad wasn't keen on the arrangement—he thinks it's a lot of responsibility for a twenty-five-year-old—but Elliott didn't want to get dragged to Hong Kong for six months. Dad's been away for a month, and the two of us are doing just fine. Dad checks in whenever he can, and his best friend, Euan, is next door if we need anything.

Euan. I go weak at the knees just thinking about him. If only he'd been my drama teacher when I was in secondary school. His son, Peter, is the same age as Elliott. They're best friends, and because I'm an awesome guy, I've been picking Peter up after school so he and Elliott can hang out until

Euan gets home from work. Getting to drool—I mean *see*—Euan five evenings a week has nothing to do with it. Nothing at all.

The shrill bell rings. The teacher opens year six's cloakroom door, and the kids rush out. Now they're in year six, the teacher doesn't wait until they've spotted a child's parent or guardian to let them go. At least half of the kids in Elliott and Peter's class walk home alone now.

Elliott and Peter slam into me in their enthusiasm to hug me. Elliott waves a letter.

"Woah, slow down there." I pat them on the back.

"Bake sale. You'll make cupcakes, won't you?" Elliott asks.

"Cupcakes?"

"Yeah. Everyone's parents are being asked to make cakes."

"Or buy them," Peter says.

Elliott rolls his eyes. "That's cheating. Besides, you can bake cupcakes, can't you, Cam?"

"Uh—" I stare at him, wide-eyed.

Elliott nudges Peter in the ribs with his elbow.

"Dad could help. You could team up and bake them together," Peter says.

Now, there's an idea.

"Won't your dad be too busy?"

"Nah, he's got a teacher training day on Monday."

"Won't he have to—?"

"—Work? Nah. It's disaggre-something," Peter says.

I raise my eyebrows. "Disaggregated?"

"That's it. They do three evening sessions and get to take a day off."

"But we'll be at school. So we won't get in your way." Elliott gives me a butter-wouldn't-melt smile.

A whole day baking cupcakes with Euan. Sounds fun. Not that making it happen is as simple as they're making out.

"I have clients on Monday." I'm a mobile hairdresser. I love it, and I get to work whatever hours I want, which has been perfect for picking the boys up from school.

"Cancel them," Elliott says.

I laugh. "Just like that?"

"Yes."

"Don't you want to bake cupcakes with my dad?" Peter asks.

Yes, yes, I do.

We wander out of the school gates and turn up the hill towards home. It's about a twenty-minute walk. I pick them up in the car when the weather is bad, but today is what Dad would call T-shirt weather.

"The real question is, why are you two so keen for me to bake cupcakes with your dad?"

They glance at each other.

"We think you'd make a good team," Elliott says.

"One of you has to know how to make cupcakes," Peter says.

"Or you could learn together." Elliott grins.

"Uh-huh. Why do I get the feeling there's more to it?"

They turn on their most innocent expressions, which makes me even more suspicious.

"Well, assuming I can shuffle my clients around, I'm happy to help your dad make cupcakes. Also assuming he wants my help."

"Leave that to us."

"Riiiight... What are you two up to?"

"Nothing," they say in unison.

Suspicious.

"We'll ask him when he picks me up," Peter says.

"Wait. When do you need the cupcakes by?"

Elliott shoves the letter into my hand, crumpling it in the process. "Tuesday."

"Handy. I assume we're also expected to buy cupcakes at the bake sale?"

"Of course."

I roll my eyes. "Of course. It would be faster to buy cupcakes from the supermarket." And there would be less risk of me giving anyone food poisoning. I'm not a bad cook, but baking is a whole different ball game.

"That's cheating," Elliott says.

"Everyone will know if you bought them," Peter says.

"How?"

"It's obvious."

"How?"

"The shop-bought ones always look—" He clamps his jaw shut.

"Better?" I offer.

"No. I wasn't going to say that."

"I bet you weren't."

"Samey," Elliott says.

"Machine made," Peter says.

"Nice save there, boys. How was school?" It's time to change the subject.

"Okay," they reply.

298

"What did you do?"

"Don't remember," Elliott says.

"Peter?"

He shrugs. "Don't remember either."

"Did you do maths?"

"We do maths every day."

"English?"

"Every day," Elliott says in a bored tone.

"Hey, English is a great subject."

He feigns an over-the-top yawn. "If you say so."

"It is! It was always my favourite subject at school." I enjoyed writing stories the most.

"I bet you liked maths too," Peter says.

"Maths was—"

"Boring?"

"I was going to say *okay*."

"But not great?"

"No. Not great."

"What about break and lunchtime?"

Elliott's eyes light up. "We played football at lunchtime."

"I scored a goal!" Peter runs ahead, pretending to dribble a ball and kicking it into a goal. He thrusts his hands into the air in victory.

Elliott dashes after him and gives him a congratulatory hug. "It was an epic goal!"

I laugh. "Did you score any goals?"

Elliott releases Peter and holds up two spread fingers, his palm facing me. "Two and I kicked the ball so hard it went straight over the fence."

I wince. "Oops."

"One of the dinner staff had to go and fetch it for us."

"She didn't mind," Peter says.

"Uh-huh. How is it you can remember every minute detail of break times but forget all the work you do?"

Elliott shrugs. "Break times are fun."

They chatter amongst themselves until we get home. They sprint down the short path to our red front door. Elliott has a key, so he opens the door, letting us in.

They chuck their bags on the floor, shed shoes and jumpers, and head for the stairs.

"Homework first," I call.

Elliott pauses halfway up the stairs, turns, and gives me a pleading look. "Aww, can't we have a break first?"

"Fine. Half an hour and then homework."

He crosses his heart, and they run up the stairs and out of sight. His door slams shut. Which game will they end up playing? I set a timer on my phone for thirty minutes. And then change it to forty-five so I can claim to be the cool big brother who doesn't stick rigidly to times like an army general.

After tidying up their bags, shoes, and jumpers, I wander into the kitchen and browse Dad's cooking books. He has books with one-pan meals from around the world, air fryer recipes, healthy slow cooker recipes, and meals for fussy kids, but no baking books. None. Zip. Nada. I guess Dad is as enamoured with baking as I am.

Thinking about it, all our birthday cakes were shop-bought, except on special years—one, ten, sixteen, eighteen, and twenty-one—when he paid someone to bake something special. Not that I can remember my first birthday cake, but I do recall Elliott's. It was a tall, blue cake with sugar craft zoo animals on and around it. Dad took us to the zoo. Elliott loved the penguins the most and was frightened of the lions when they roared.

Elliott's tenth birthday cake was decorated to look like it was out of a comic book. The way it was iced made it look two-dimensional. He adored it.

For my twenty-first birthday, Dad had a Pride cake made for me. Not that you could tell at first glance. The top was covered in plain white icing with gold numbers and sprinkles, but when I cut into it, I discovered every layer was one of the colours in the Pride flag, in order. Yeah, that cake was special and made me feel accepted.

I look up a cupcake recipe on my phone and rummage around for everything we'll need. I come up short. Funnily enough, the house that never bakes does not have cupcake cases, a cupcake tray, or a cooling rack. Nor do we have vanilla essence, icing sugar, food colouring, or caster sugar. We do have eggs, milk, and flour. I always have that combination of ingredients for making cheese sauce. It's my speciality, which is useful, as lasagne is one of Euan's favourite foods. I should make it for dinner tonight. Will he have any of the cupcake things I'm missing? Not that he's agreed to bake them with me. Will he? I cross my fingers and toes.

I make a list of the things I'm missing. I'll show it to Euan after whirlwinds Peter and Elliott have convinced him to bake cupcakes and, more importantly, to bake them with me on his day off. Knowing my brother and his best friend, they *will* convince him. Look how easy it was for them to twist my arm behind my back. They're a dangerous tag team. So dangerous I'm positive they'll convince Euan to spend his day off baking cupcakes.

I find my appointment book and call Monday's clients. Whatever happens, I will be baking cupcakes. What remains to be seen is whether I'll be flying solo—or crashing and burning solo, more like—or if I'll have the help and company of the sexiest drama teacher in England.

Chapter Two

Euan

I pull onto the drive, get out of the car, dump my stuff in the house, and jog next door. Cameron opens the front door before I get the chance to ring the doorbell.

"I'm so sorry I'm late," he says.

His kind, cheerful smile reaches his sparkling brown eyes. "No worries. The boys are fed, and they're just finishing up their homework. Oh, and I made an extra portion for you, so you don't have to worry about cooking tonight."

I stare at him. Cameron is truly amazing. He's stepped up while Lewis, his father, is away on business. I'm starting to wonder what I ever did without Cameron helping out by picking Peter up from school and ensuring he gets his homework done.

"Thank you so much."

"It's my pleasure." He has a dazzling smile. Which I shouldn't notice.

Not only is Cameron ten years younger than me, but his dad is also the closest friend I have.

He steps aside to let me into the house. The rich scent of meat, tomato, and cheese hits my senses.

"Lasagne?" I guess.

"Yes. I know you like it."

I do. He makes every layer with a rich, homemade cheese sauce. It's probably not good for my waistline, but it's delicious. To be fair, the red sauce is packed full of hidden vegetables. Even the boys love it, and ten-year-olds have a habit of being notoriously fussy. At least, my ten-year-old is.

"Fair warning, the boys got a fundraising letter from school today."

"Ugh. What do they want us to do this time?" I'm silently hoping for a non-uniform day. They're the easiest. Unless they add that the kids need to wear a specific colour or a football strip or dress up like someone they admire. Then it gets tricky. Fast.

"Dad!" Peter runs out of the kitchen and barrels into me with the force of a cannon ball.

"Oof!" I'm winded, and my chest is a little sore from the tackling bear hug he's giving me. I embrace him and ruffle his hair. "Did you have a good day at school?"

"Yes."

"What did you do?"

"Can't remember."

Cameron laughs. "That's all I got out of them too."

"Honestly, I think I'd be more worried if Peter could give me a blow-by-blow of his school day."

"Right? I'd be wondering who had replaced my kid brother and what they'd done with him."

Elliott, who is leaning against the kitchen doorframe, sticks his tongue out at his older brother.

"Cameron said you have a letter to give me," I say to Peter.

"Oh, right. I'll go get it." He dashes off, almost colliding with Elliott in his haste. He returns seconds later, not panting despite his exertion, and hands me the letter. "Year six are having a bake sale on Wednesday next week. They want all the parents to send cakes in by Tuesday."

I scan the letter. "Oh, no problem. I'll pick some up from the supermarket on Sunday."

Peter pulls a face.

"What?"

He clasps his hands behind his back and swings from side to side. "I was hoping you'd make them this time."

"I don't think—"

"Cam's going to make cupcakes, aren't you?" Elliott asks.

Cameron blushes and rubs the back of his neck. "They kind of talked me into it."

"I'm not sure I have the time. I have a lot of coursework marking to do." Plus, I've never made a cupcake in my life.

"You're a drama teacher. How much marking can you have?" Elliott asks.

"El!" Cameron says.

"What? It's true. It's all prancing around, pretending to be a tree." He holds his arms out like branches.

Peter joins in, and together, they dance around the hallway.

I can't help but chuckle. Loudly. "It's more than pretending to be a tree, and my students do have to do some writing."

Cameron mock gasps, which makes me laugh harder.

"Anyway..." Peter draws the word out as he stands in front of me, hands clasped in supplication. He wouldn't look amiss in a performance of a Greek tragedy.

"I'll buy cupcakes," I say decisively.

"But you have Monday off." Peter pouts.

"And a mountain of marking to get through."

"Cam's going to be baking cakes on Monday. You could do it together. Teamwork makes things faster, right?" Elliott says.

I glance at Cameron to gauge his reaction. Would he want to spend the day baking cupcakes with me? Not that it would take a day. An hour at most. Surely? Besides, I shouldn't want to spend time with him. Alone. Without the kids. I tug my shirt collar.

He smiles and shrugs. "How hard can it be to make a dozen cupcakes?"

"Two dozen," Peter says.

"*Two* dozen?" Cameron asks.

"A dozen each."

"And decorate. You *have* to decorate them," Elliott says.

Are they trying to talk me into it or give me more reasons to opt for the shop-bought option?

"I'll do my best. What do you say? Want to team up? It won't take all day. You'll still have plenty of time to do your marking," Cameron says.

I should say no. "Um, sure. Why not?"

Cameron grins. "Great. I made a list of the things I don't have, which is quite a lot. Do you want to take a look at it and see if you have any of the missing things? I can nip to the shops at the weekend and get anything else we need."

Is it me, or is Cameron talking a little faster than usual? His cheeks are flushed. Don't read anything into it. He's ten years younger than me. He's Lewis's son!

I moved in next door when Peter was four. I'll admit I chose to move to the catchment area of a better school. Yes, I put stock in OFSTED gradings and school league tables. It didn't take long to discover that Lewis was also a single dad and even less time to realise that Peter and Elliott were the same age. Lewis suggested Peter and I should come over for a playdate, and two firm friendships were forged. Peter and Elliott. Me and Lewis.

Meanwhile, Cameron was nineteen and at college, studying for an NVQ in hairdressing. The first time I truly noticed him—when I absolutely shouldn't have—was when he quit working at a local hairdresser's and set up his own mobile hairdressing business. I offered to be his first client and write him a testimonial. That was a year ago. Now I frequently have to remind myself not to notice his smile, the sparkle in his eyes, or how good he looks in an unbuttoned denim shirt and a white T-shirt.

I absolutely should not be agreeing to spend any time alone with him. Not even in the name of raising money for the school my son goes to.

"Euan?"

"Oh, the list. Yes, of course. What are you missing?"

"Come this way." He walks towards the kitchen.

"Hey, Peter, do you want to play some more games?" Elliott asks.

"You bet!"

The boys leg it up the stairs, sounding more like a herd of elephants than two children.

"Any idea why they're so keen on us baking cupcakes together?" I ask.

Cameron shrugs. "No clue, but it'll be fun. Don't you think?"

"Erm, I suppose so."

"How messy do you think cupcake making is?"

I don't want to think about it at all.

He laughs. "I guess we'll find out. Right, here's what I'm missing." He pushes a list across the breakfast bar towards me.

I scan it. "I don't think I have any of that. Although I do have a baking with kids book my sister bought me one Christmas. It will probably have a recipe in it."

"Great. Wait. Have you never made anything from it?"

"A couple of things. But I was put off by the amount of stuff I'd have to buy to make anything. I know, I'm a terrible dad."

He snorts. "Hardly. If parents are rated on whether they bake with their kids, Dad would score nil points."

He says *nil points* in a French accent like he's giving out a score at the *Eurovision Song Contest*. It's funny but also a stark reminder—like a slap across the face or a bucket of ice-cold water being tipped over my head—that Cameron is my best friend's son.

"Anyway, no worries. I'll pick up everything we need. Your place or mine?"

I blink. "I'm sorry, what?"

"Do you want to bake cupcakes here or at yours?"

"Oh, right, of course." Is it getting hot in here? "I don't mind. Do you have a preference?"

"Nope."

"Nor do I."

He chuckles. "We could go back and forth like this all evening. Why don't I come to yours?"

"Fine by me." I think.

"Great." He taps the breakfast bar.

Am I supposed to be saying something? "I should get Peter home." I walk to the bottom of the stairs and call him.

Cameron lounges in the kitchen doorway, watching while Peter runs downstairs and grabs his things. Elliot comes downstairs too, and before Peter walks out the door, they do an elaborate series of fist bumps, finger hooks, and high fives that only a pair of ten-year-olds would be able to remember.

"I'll see you on Monday," Cameron says.

"To make cupcakes," I reply.

He grins. Is it my imagination, or does he have a mischievous glint in his eyes?

He clicks his fingers and dashes into the kitchen. He returns holding a glass dish with a plastic lid, which he gives to me. "Don't forget this."

The dish is warm. My mouth waters. "Forget lasagne cooked by you? Never. I'm looking forward to it."

His grin softens into an expression I can't name. Contentment? No, that's not right. Pride? Happiness? Perhaps a cross between all three. Not that it matters. What matters is that beautiful smile turns my legs to jelly.

I clear my throat. "I'd better go. See you on Monday."

"Monday."

Chapter Three

Cameron

Before Dad went to Hong Kong, he and Euan would take turns driving the boys to the school's breakfast club every school morning. Now that I'm in charge, Peter comes to ours for breakfast, and I walk them to school in time for registration.

At least, that's the usual plan.

This morning is different.

Euan and I walked the boys to school together.

We're standing in the playground while Elliott and Peter dash around, running off excess energy before school starts.

"I got everything we need for cupcakes," I say. "At least, I hope I did."

"Supermarket-bought is the backup plan if baking goes wrong, right?" Euan asks.

I laugh. "Absolutely. But hey, how hard can it be to make cupcakes?"

His expression twists into something caught between horror and 'you'd be surprised'.

It makes me laugh harder. I put my hand on my aching side. "At least we'll be able to say we tried."

The bell rings, and all the children rush to their lines.

"You can go now," Elliott says as he runs past us.

"Yeah, go and bake cakes, Dad," Peter says.

Euan arches an eyebrow. "I think we've been given our marching orders."

"Definitely."

Their class teacher arrives and walks down the line, saying hello to every child and asking them how their weekend was. I nudge Euan, and we slip away, ambling up the hill towards home.

"Decorating will be the hardest part," Euan says.

"You reckon?"

"Yes. I have no idea how you make those fancy swirls. Do you think we can just dollop the icing on with a spoon?"

"I watched a YouTube video. You need a piping bag and fancy tips. I picked some up when I got everything up. It looks pretty easy."

"In my experience, things that look easy when experts do them rarely are."

I snigger. "Sounds like you have experience with that."

His face turns beet red. What did I say?

"And it sounds like you had to spend a lot of money so we can make two dozen cupcakes."

"Eh, a bit. It's fine."

"Tell me how much, and I'll give you half."

I shake my head and wave my hand. "It's fine. A lot of it is stuff I'll be able to use again next time."

"Next time? You're optimistic that this is going to go well."

I shrug. "Maybe it will, maybe it won't. Either way, it'll be fun." I grin.

At least, I hope baking cupcakes with Euan will be fun. It'll be the most time I've spent with him alone. It'll be the only time I've spent alone with him. Deep breaths. Don't get too excited. We're making cupcakes. Nothing else.

Euan's house is a mirror image of Dad's, although the decor is more traditional and less modern. The kitchen has lots of warm shades from the wooden cabinet doors to the walls and floor tiles. Like Dad's kitchen, it has a breakfast bar dividing the kitchen and dining spaces. After collecting everything we need from Dad's, I arrange the ingredients and equipment on Euan's breakfast bar. He opens the recipe book he mentioned and pops it on a green plastic stand that folds shut like a book. We stand, shoulder to shoulder, reading the recipe. Being close to him makes my heart beat faster. Act cool, Cam. Don't let on that you think he's the most gorgeous man alive.

He has thick, dark brown hair, swept to the right like he's stepped out of a romantic forties movie. He has a widow's peak, and although his hair doesn't have a trace of grey, his hairline is receding a little at the temples. His grey-blue eyes fit his kind face perfectly. He has laughter lines around his eyes and a short beard, which is barely longer than stubble. He's wearing a blue-and-white-checked shirt with a grey scarf tied around his neck, making him look like a quintessential drama teacher. He's a couple of inches shorter than me, with a perfect dad bod I've fantasised about hugging, even though I shouldn't. Why would he even look at me in the way I look at him? I'm ten years younger than him. He's my dad's best friend.

"Do you have a food processor?" I ask.

"No. Do you?"

"Nope. I guess we're doing it all by hand." I chuckle. "It says here you should get your child to put the cupcake cases in the cupcake tray while you turn the oven on."

"I'm short a child helper right now."

I grab the box of cupcake cases. "Looks like I'll have to be the stand-in." Ugh. What a stupid thing to say. He'll never see me as the adult I am if I act all goofy.

And yet he watches me as I place two dozen rainbow cupcake cases across two trays.

"The oven?" I prompt.

"Oh, right, yes." He checks the recipe book and turns the oven on to heat up. "Now what?"

"Now we measure everything out."

We gather a collection of plates and bowls and carefully measure all the wet and dry ingredients, quickly covering the breakfast bar in supplies. Euan finds a large mixing bowl from the back of one of the cupboards, washes and dries it, and puts it on the countertop with a satisfying thud.

"Hopefully, this won't take too long. I know you have lots of marking to do," I say.

"Lots might have been an exaggeration."

"To get out of making cupcakes?"

He clears his throat. "Maybe."

I laugh. "Why, Euan, that's devious. I like it."

"Don't tell Peter."

I pretend to zip my lips shut. "Your secret is safe with me."

"Wait. We need to double the recipe."

"Oh, shit, yeah. Thanks for remembering."

"Teamwork."

His smile is so contagious I grin from ear to ear.

Another round of weighing and measuring commences until, finally, we're ready to start mixing. I put the butter and sugar in the mixing bowl and, using a fork, attempt to mash them together.

I frown. "Maybe we should have warmed the butter up somehow first?"

Euan glances at the microwave.

"I think it's too late now we've added the sugar."

"True, it will probably caramelise. Want me to take over?"

"I'm good for a few."

I mash the butter and sugar until my hand and arm get tired and then hand the bowl and fork to Euan. I lean against the breakfast bar as he takes a turn. The butter is a lot more malleable now. Euan's concentration face is perfect. He wrinkles his nose and pinches his lips together. I could kiss him. I won't, obviously, but I want to.

Euan catches my eye. "What are you thinking?"

Heat flushes into my cheeks. "Oh, nothing."

He smiles. "It wasn't nothing."

I can't tell him what I was thinking. Think, Cameron, think. "I was thinking you've got a much better hand technique than me." What was that?

It's his turn to blush. "I don't know about that," he stammers.

Now I'm thinking about whether he *does* have a good hand technique. I bet he does. Now I'm imagining him in the shower, rubbing one out. My pulse increases. Blood thunders in my ears, racing towards—oh no. Think unsexy thoughts. Quick.

"Do you think this is ready?" Euan shows me the contents of the bowl.

I check the recipe book. "It says the mixture needs to be light and creamy."

Euan carries on mixing the butter and sugar, whipping it until it's light and creamy. I shouldn't watch the movement of his hand and wrist intently, but I do. I shouldn't let my imagination run riot, but I do. At this rate, I'm going to have to stand on the other side of the breakfast bar so he can't see my groin. I'm staving off a hard-on by keeping my breathing slow, even, and calm. How long will that work for? Being alone with Euan was a bad idea. I cannot keep my crush in check around him.

"What next?" he asks.

I'm captivated by the movement of his lips and the crinkles around his eyes as he smiles.

"Cameron?"

"Huh? What?"

"What do we do next?"

"Oh, right." I shake myself and turn my attention to the recipe book. He could easily have read the next instruction, but I guess he wants to keep me involved in the process, which is super sweet. He's amazing. "We need to beat"—my voice catches. I'm suddenly hot and sweaty. I clear my throat. "We need to beat the eggs in one at a time."

"Do you want to do that?"

Do I want to beat—? He's talking about eggs. Beat the eggs into the mix. One at a time. Not beat him off. Although yes, please, in a heartbeat. Ask me to beat you off, Euan. Please?

"Sure." I take the bowl, crack one egg into it, pick out a couple of stray pieces of shell, and beat everything together into a less-appealing gooey mess.

I get hotter as I realise Euan is watching me while I work. He helps by cracking the second egg into the bowl.

"You're good at that," I whisper.

"Huh?"

"You didn't get any of the shell in the bowl."

"Oh. It's a talent."

"I bet you have lots of talents." Shut up, Cameron. My voice sounds weird. Lower than normal. A little husky. Bit by bit, my body and mind are betraying the crush I've kept hidden for years. I've dreamt about being with him. About kissing him. Heck, I've even fantasised about being the one he comes home to. But here? Now? All I want is *him*.

He smiles and looks away. He uses his finger to read the next part of the recipe. Am I making him feel uncomfortable? That's the last thing I want.

"We need to sift the flour in next." His voice is a little odd too. Stilted.

"You sift, and I'll stir?"

"Sure."

He sifts the flour through a sieve slowly while I keep stirring the mixture. Gradually, it looks more appealing again. Not that I have a clue what cake batter is supposed to look like or what the recipe book means by a 'soft dropping consistency'. I lift the spoon. The gloopy mix drops off the spoon and plops into the bowl. I puff my cheeks out.

"We're supposed to add a bit of milk and the vanilla essence," Euan says.

"Go ahead."

He adds a teaspoon of vanilla essence and slowly pours some milk in while I stir. Every so often, I lift the spoon. He stops adding milk when the batter drips off the spoon in thick splodges. And now all I can think about is something else thick, sticky, and dripping. I shiver and lick my lips.

"It does look good," Euan says.

His voice brings me back to the moment. "Oh, yeah, it does. Teamwork." I raise my hand in a high five.

He hesitates, then strikes my palm with his own. "Hopefully, they'll look even better once they're baked."

Between us, we spoon the mixture into the cupcakes. It's a messy job. We manage to splatter cake mix on the baking trays and ourselves. I want to lick the batter off his fingers and then suck them into my mouth. Oh, fuck, I need a cold shower. I adjust my jeans as surreptitiously as I can.

Euan puts the trays into the oven and sets a timer for fifteen minutes. He smiles. "I guess we've got some time spare now. What do you want to do?"

Chapter Four

Euan

I noticed Cameron adjust his jeans, and now it's taking every ounce of willpower I have not to glance down. Instead, I maintain eye contact with him while he stares at me like I've asked him to solve the world's hardest equation. His lips are still damp from when he licked them a few minutes ago. He has a plump lower lip, perfect for sucking on or nipping between teeth. What am I doing? I should not be having thoughts like that about my best friend's son.

And yet it's impossible to miss how Cameron has become increasingly flustered while we've been making cakes. It's impossible to forget some of his comments, which could have easily been taken in less than innocent ways. And fuck, is he beautiful, not to mention energetic and vibrant.

"What do I want to do?" he asks.

"Yes."

"I dunno. What do you want to do?"

My mind stutters. I rub the back of my neck and mess up my hair to buy myself some thinking time. He follows the movement of my hand with his eyes and then stares into mine once more, his gaze intense and—No. I must be imagining it. Why would his stare be hungry for me? Hungry for cupcakes, sure. But not for a man ten years older than him with a receding hairline and a few extra pounds around the waist.

"We could lick the bowl," he says.

I blink. "I'm not sure we're supposed to because of the raw egg."

He snorts. "Really? Isn't that advice from decades ago?"

I shrug. "I don't know. Maybe."

He runs his finger around the bowl and sucks the batter off it. All I can do is stare at his finger disappearing into his mouth and the way his cheeks hollow as he sucks. Do not imagine him sucking anything else that deliciously. Do not.

"It's nice." He holds the bowl towards me.

"No, thanks."

"Are you sure?" His voice sounds innocent, but the way he scoops up more batter onto his finger and sucks it off isn't.

I can't breathe. My pulse is going haywire. If he keeps doing that, he won't be the only one who needs to adjust his clothes. Before I realise what I'm doing, I'm glancing at his crotch. At the curve of his dick through his tight jeans. They must be uncomfortable.

I force myself to look up, straight into his eyes. He's still sucking his finger. Or maybe he's sucking his finger again. I'm not sure. His stare tells me he knows exactly what I was looking at. Exactly what I am looking at. He can't want me. He can't. And I shouldn't want him.

He scoops more batter onto his finger. This time, instead of holding the bowl to me, he sticks his finger in my direction, tantalisingly close to my lips. "It's nice."

I'm sure it is. I'm also sure it would be even nicer if I licked or sucked it off his finger. His finger has been in his hot mouth.

I take a deep breath. "Maybe we should do a bit of washing up so there's less to do at the end."

He shrugs. "Maybe." And keeps on wiping the bowl with his finger.

I swallow. I'm generating too much saliva. I'll be drooling before I know it. I want to suggest he licks the bowl with his tongue. Wouldn't that be a delicious sight?

"You've got—" I gesture to the corner of my mouth while staring at the same spot on his face. He's managed to transfer some of the gloopy beige batter there.

He wipes the wrong side of his mouth.

"The other side." I point.

He wipes but misses it. Is he doing it on purpose? I grab a piece of kitchen towel and, despite my better judgement, step into his personal space so I can clean the corner of his mouth. Heat rises off his body. His breathing is sharp and a little ragged. I glance up. His pupils have shrunk to almost nothing. He is so beautiful. So sexy. So out of my league. So off-limits. My head knows that. My body doesn't care. It reacts to being close to him. Blood rushes to my cock, which plumps up within the uncomfortable confines of my chinos. Why did I choose to wear something so constricting today?

"I wish you'd used your finger to do that," he whispers.

I widen my eyes.

"Oh, shit. Forget I said that." He waves his hands and back-pedals away from me. "I am so sorry."

I wish I had too. I take a deep breath. I need to get this situation under control before I lose my head completely.

"It's fine. No harm done." I turn to check the oven timer.

Less than five minutes have gone past since I put the cupcakes in. I crouch and peer through the glass door. The batter is starting to rise. As I stand, I adjust my chinos, but not subtle enough for the action to escape Cameron's notice. His stare lingers on my crotch. On my obvious erection through my clothes.

He swallows. "I could help you with that." His voice is raspy. "I *want* to help you with that."

I sway and grasp the counter to steady myself. "You—?"

"It must be obvious that I'm into you." He smiles apologetically. "I've been trying to keep it secret."

"Trying—? Secret—?"

"It's just...well"—he rubs his bright red face—"I've been sweet on you for years. I mean, look at you. You're—" He gestures at me vaguely, encompassing all of me with a shaky sweep of his arm. He drops his arm to his side. "I'll go. I'm sure you can decorate the cupcakes alone. I'm so sorry for ruining your morning. I'm sorry for—"

"Don't go." What am I doing?

"I think I should. I've made things super awkward."

"Maybe a little."

He snort-laughs and holds his thumb and finger a few millimetres apart, then spreads them as wide as he can. "A little?"

I run my hand through my hair. "I had no idea."

322

"That I like you?"

I nod. "Why?"

"What do you mean, why?"

I gesture to myself.

He flicks his gaze from my head to my toes. "All I see is a sexy drama teacher."

With a hard-on.

"I'm—"

"Sexy."

"Older than you."

"So? Older means more experienced."

"Not necessarily."

He scratches the corner of his mouth and smirks. "I like older guys."

"Your dad is—"

"Thousands of miles away."

I suck in a breath. "What are you suggesting?"

"I dunno." He steps closer. "You're the one who asked me to stay. Why?"

I told him not to leave, which isn't the same thing at all. Is it? He's gone from acting like he wants to run away in embarrassment to openly telling me he has the hots for me. What am I supposed to do with that information?

Once again, my head and my body are at odds. My head is telling me to let him down gently and then make up an excuse for him to go. Marking. Yes. I have to do marking today. He'll understand. Except my body is begging me to take him up on his offer of alleviating my erection. It doesn't help that he's attractive. It doesn't help that I haven't been entertained by anything but my hand in well over a year. It doesn't help that my chinos are far too fucking tight and his smirk is far too suggestive.

I should tell him to leave, but I don't.

He steps into my personal space, picks up the bowl, and turns the inside to me. A few traces of batter remain, more than enough to coat a finger. Or two.

"Try some," he says.

It's like being offered the forbidden fruit. I know it's wrong to take it, but that doesn't stop me yearning for it. It doesn't stop the offering from being tantalising. If I trail my finger through even a smidge of cake batter, I'm going to be opening a door I won't be able to close.

I should tell him to leave, but I don't want to.

I meet his sultry stare and trail my index finger around the edge of the bowl, gathering sweet, sticky batter onto it. I raise my finger to my mouth. Cameron catches hold of my hand and, still staring into my eyes, brings my finger to his lips. He pauses as though waiting for my permission. This is my last chance to put the breaks on. My last chance to be sensible. I don't take it. Instead, I nod.

Chapter Five

Cameron

I put his finger into my mouth, clamp my lips around it, and slowly suck and lick it clean. Does he realise I'd gladly do this to his dick if he wanted me to? His lashes flutter, his pupils shrink, and he releases the most glorious little groan. I suck and lick long after the batter is all gone, then finally release his finger. I lick my lips, swipe some of the batter onto my fingertip, and smear it across his lips. I lean forward, waiting until he nods, then lick his lips clean and kiss him. The moment I pull away, he hooks his finger through my belt loop and pulls my body against his. He smashes his mouth over mine, kissing me hard. Our lips part. Our tongues battle. His beard tickles my clean-shaven jaw. I tangle my fingers through his hair and bring my hand to rest on his nape. I grab his hip, pulling him harder against me so the hard heat of his erection burns against mine through our clothes.

"What are we doing?" he gasps.

"Don't think."

The moment he does, this will end. He'll realise he's made a mistake. He'll realise he doesn't want to fool around with a younger man. Scratch that. He'll realise he doesn't want to fool around with his best friend's son. Will Dad be mad at me? At Euan? No. Don't think. Dad isn't here. It's just me and Euan. Alone in his kitchen. My cards are on the table. This could be my only chance to be with him. I have to take it. I'm going to take it.

"Cam—"

"Just kiss me."

He does. His breath puffs against my skin. The kiss is rough and desperate and needy. My pulse is going crazy. My cock aches to be freed from the confines of my jeans. I want to touch him, kiss him all over, put my mouth around his dick. Every fantasy I've ever had about Euan I pour into the kiss. I groan into his mouth and suck on his tongue. He pinches my bottom lip between my teeth, driving me wild.

"Oh, fuck, Euan, you have no idea how long I've wanted to kiss you for."

"We shouldn't—" His hands sweep over my body, tickling me through my T-shirt.

"I want to. Don't you?" I slide my hand around his body to cup his arse. Oh, it's a lovely handful.

"Yes, but—"

"But what?" I kiss his jaw and neck and then find my way back to his lips, plunging my tongue into his hot, wet mouth.

"But—" He sighs and holds me tighter. "Don't think."

I laugh against his lips. "Good plan." I reach between our

bodies and press my palm against his hard dick, squeezing it through the firm fabric of his chinos.

He groans and shivers.

"Want me to take care of that for you?" I ask.

I hold my breath. I need his permission.

"Yes," he rasps.

I kiss him again, which quickly turns into him kissing me with equal passion, and knead his erection through his chinos. I swipe my other hand over his chest, circling my palm over his nipples until they're firm enough to be visible beneath his shirt. I tug his shirt out of his trousers and tickle my fingers over his delightfully soft stomach. He squirms and gasps but doesn't stop kissing me. If anything, he kisses me harder.

I tear my lips from his and, staring into his eyes, sink to my knees. The tiled floor is hard and unyielding, but I don't care. I don't take my eyes off his as I unfasten his chinos.

".He-here?" he stammers.

"Relax. We're behind the breakfast bar. No one can see me."

Besides, the kitchen faces the back garden, which has a six-foot fence and tall bushes around it. I push his chinos and underpants down his hips, freeing his cock. Finally, I tear my gaze from his so I can feast my stare on his cock. He's leaking clear pre-cum, which I don't hesitate to lick. It's salty, especially compared to the overwhelming sweetness of the cake batter.

He leans against the breakfast bar and grips the edge of the counter with his hands. His breathing is a harsh, staccato rhythm. He stares at me, his eyes wide, his damp, swollen lips parted. His expression radiates surprise like he can't believe this is happening. Like he can't comprehend that I'm about to suck him off in the middle of his kitchen.

I grip his cock, rubbing the bottom of it while I stretch my lips wide enough to take the head. It's heavy on my tongue. He's a real mouthful. I lick and suck greedily. I might never get this chance again, so I'm going to damn well enjoy it.

"Cameron—"

I glance up. He tips his head back and releases a satisfied sigh-groan. I suck harder, taking his length up to my hand. I spiral the tip of my tongue over his veiny, rock-hard shaft and bob up and down, moaning to show him how good he tastes. I suck harder. Bob faster, inhaling whenever his pubes tickle my nose and chin. At first, I hold his hip, but after a while, I move my hand to cup and massage his heavy balls.

He gasps. "Oh, Cameron." His voice is deep, throaty, and wonderfully needy. "Oh, fuck."

I smirk around his shaft. Would he want to fuck? Or is he going to throw me out the moment this is over?

"Cameron, I—"

I ignore his warning and suck harder. He shoots his load down my throat. The cooker timer goes off, its shrill beep filling the room while I suck him dry and then suck him some more. He pants and gasps and shudders. His knees sag. I keep sucking. Keep licking. The timer keeps beeping. I swear it's getting louder and more irritating. Finally, I pull off his cock, rock onto my heels, and draw the back of my hand over my wet lips.

I meet his heavy-lidded stare and smile. "How was that for perfect timing? The cupcakes are ready."

Chapter Six

Euan

I turn the timer off. Cameron, grinning lazily, tucks my damp, flaccid cock into my underwear, pulls my chinos up, and fastens them. He stands while I turn on wobbling legs to inspect the cupcakes in the oven. They've risen nicely and are golden brown on top. I turn the oven off, put oven gloves on, take the cupcake trays out of the oven, and place them on heat-proof mats.

Cameron doesn't help. Instead, he kisses my nape. The tender brushes of his lips create a chain reaction of desire within my body. Racing pulse. Thrashing heart. Fluttering stomach.

I take the oven gloves off, lean on the counter, and sigh. What have we done? I can't take back the last few minutes, nor do I want to. I really needed the releases he just gave me. It's been so long since anyone has sucked my cock I'd almost forgotten how good it felt. And Cameron is very skilled at fellatio. I tremble just thinking about how amazing his hot mouth felt around my cock as he sucked, licked, and stroked my aching shaft. And now he's kissing my neck like a lover. He presses against my back, the hard bulge in his jeans against my arse reminding me that he needs release too.

"What next?" he asks between kisses.

"We—" I pant and lick my lips. I can't think straight. To be fair, that's probably a good thing. If I let my brain kick in, I'll realise how foolish all this is. "We have to let them cool in the trays for a few minutes before—" His lips tickle my skin delightfully. "Before transferring them to the cooling racks."

"I wonder why."

"I don't know. Maybe they'll lose their shape if we take them out too soon."

"I guess we should trust the recipe book."

"Yes."

"They smell delicious."

So does Cameron. "Yes."

"I wish we'd made some extra cupcakes."

The air gets trapped in my throat. "Why?"

"For us to enjoy, covered in gooey icing. I could have peeled the case off one and fed it to you."

An image of him straddling me, naked, feeding me a cupcake pops into my head. I groan. My cock twitches as blood pumps into it, but I'm too spent to get hard again so soon.

"This is wrong," I whimper.

He puts his hands over mine and rests his chin on my shoulder. "Why?"

"We're getting frisky while making cupcakes for the boys."

"It's fun."

Yes, it is. Hot, sexy fun.

"I'm—"

"Sush." He kisses me behind the ear and sucks my earlobe into his mouth. "I know all the reasons we shouldn't. But we have, so enjoy it. Unless you'd rather I left?"

I wouldn't. It's foolish and wrong, but heaven help me, I want to enjoy this virile young man while I've got the chance. Before he realises he's not as into me as he thinks he is. He told me I was sexy. It sounded like he meant it. If this is my only chance to be with him, why shouldn't I take it?

Because I'm ten years older.

Because his dad might find out.

He's an adult. He can make his own decisions. Right now, he's choosing me.

He holds my hips and rubs against my arse. "Have you stopped thinking yet?"

"I'm trying to."

"I think kissing me might help."

He gives me enough space to turn around before pushing against me and slamming his lips against mine. Oh, fuck, he tastes divine. His lips and tongue are sweet from the cake batter and salty from my cum. For the first time, I understand why people like sweet and salty popcorn. I wrap my arms around his lower back and pull him hard against my aching body. I devour his mouth, feasting on his eager tongue and pliant lips.

A small voice in the back of my mind urges me to stop or, at the very least, slow down and *think*. But I don't want to think. I want to feel and do. I want to give in to temptation and passion and enjoy Cameron, like he clearly wants me to.

"Cupcakes," I whisper.

"Oh, right."

We wash our hands and transfer the still-warm cupcakes to a cooling rack.

"How long will they take to cool?" Cameron asks.

I consult the recipe book. "It doesn't say. It just says we should wait until they're cool to ice them."

"Huh. Well, they're only small, so I guess they won't take too long."

"I don't know. They could take a while."

He grins and plays with the buttons on my shirt. "Are you suggesting we should go somewhere more comfortable?"

I swallow. Am I?

"Like your bedroom?" He raises his eyebrows.

Holy fuck.

He walks his fingers down my chest and stomach and up again. "We could have a lot more fun up there." He undoes the top two buttons of my shirt. "We could get naked. I want to see all of you." His voice is warm with desire.

A shiver snakes down my spine. My thoughts fly apart and struggle to come back together into anything coherent. What is he suggesting? More fooling around? Sex?

"What are we doing?" I ask.

Giving in to sweet temptation, that's what. The cake batter wasn't the forbidden fruit. Cameron is.

"Having fun. You are having fun, aren't you?"

When I'm not second-guessing everything we're doing, yes. But what's going to happen later, when Cameron is gone, and the gravity of this encounter hits me in full force? Will we keep it secret? Will we indulge again, or is this a strict one-off? I should ask, but the potential answers scare me. It doesn't help that I don't know what I want. A secret one-off would be the best option, but a part of me wants him to want more. Being desired by him is electrifying. Knowing he's just scratching an itch and nothing more would be mortifying.

"Euan?" Concern flits through his gaze. "Do you want to slow down? I'm sorry. I'm being pushy. It's just—"

"You're young and horny?"

He throws his head back and laughs. "Well, yes, I am."

"Have you really been—How did you phrase it earlier?"

"Sweet on you for a long time?"

"Yes. That's such an archaic term."

And yet it's utterly adorable coming out of his mouth.

He laughs harder. "What can I say? I like old movies. They're romantic."

"They don't go straight to finger-sucking and blow jobs in old movies."

"No. There's no sex either. Only chaste kisses. I fill in the blanks in my imagination. In my head, all those black-and-white characters are going at it like rabbits as soon as the screen fades to black."

I hold his hips and stroke his sides with my thumbs. "Maybe we should watch your favourite film while we wait for the cupcakes to cool."

"Is that what you want?"

What I want is to take him upstairs and... Well, what I want isn't sensible. We should slow down. If he were someone I'd met in a bar, I wouldn't hesitate to go straight to sex if they wanted to as well. Assuming Peter wasn't in. Of course if Peter were in, I wouldn't be at a bar hooking up with anyone. There's a reason I haven't had sex in over a year—and only sporadically for the nine years before that. One advantage of living next to a fellow single dad is that Lewis and I babysat for each other on occasion. The boys loved having sleepovers, so it was a win-win situation. But neither of us wanted to impose on the other too often, so we didn't.

It might be silly of me to turn down the offer of sex, but sleeping with Cameron would be complicated, to say the least. Not that letting him go down on me hasn't already made things complicated.

"You're thinking," he says like he's accusing me of something.

I sigh. "Yes, I am."

"Film?"

"Film."

"Okay. But we're watching *your* favourite. Not mine."

"Why?"

"Because you already know the type of films I enjoy. It's my turn to find out something I didn't already know about you."

Chapter Seven

Cameron

It turns out Euan likes drama, suspense, crime, and thrillers, which works because I enjoy all those genres too. He picks a film I haven't seen. We sit, not too close, in his living room, watching it while the cupcakes cool. I want to kiss him again so badly, but I respect his desire to slow down. I did come on kind of strong, but can you blame me? I might never get the chance to do anything sexy with him again.

"Icing," Euan says once the film is over.

"I watched a bunch of YouTube videos about how to ice." I follow him through to the kitchen.

"So you said."

"It looks pretty easy."

"Uh-huh. You said that earlier too." He leans against the breakfast bar, arms folded.

"What are you doing?"

"Letting you take charge. You're the expert."

I snort. "Hardly."

"You know more than me. Honestly, I'd just add a bit of water to some icing sugar and dollop it on with a spoon."

"Uh-uh. We're making buttercream icing. Oh, except you don't have a stand mixer, do you?"

Euan shakes his head.

"Maybe I should have bought one."

He raises his eyebrows. "You're taking this pretty seriously."

"Making cupcakes?"

"Looking after Elliott."

"Well, yeah. Dad's relying on me. I don't want him worrying while he's away. I don't want to let Elliott down either."

Euan smiles. "You won't. You're a great big brother."

My cheeks get warm. "I try." I clear my throat and find a buttercream recipe on my phone.

Next, I weigh out the butter and icing sugar—even spooning it into a bowl creates clouds of fine white powder—and beat the butter with a fork.

"This would be much easier with a stand mixer," I say once my arm is getting tired.

"Let me take over."

"Gladly." I resist the urge to comment on how good at beating he is, even though that's exactly what I fantasise about. His hand on my cock, beating furiously until I come all over him. I tug my T-shirt away from my chest and fan my too-hot skin.

His cheeks flush red. Can he guess what I'm thinking about?

Once the butter is fully whipped and almost white, I take over mixing while Euan slowly adds the icing sugar. Sweet dust gets everywhere despite his best efforts. Pretty soon, everything within a foot radius is covered in a fine sheen of white powder, including us. It makes me want to kiss him more. The taste of him, plus the sweetness of the icing sugar, would be a divine combination.

"I'm buying a stand mixer if I ever make cupcakes again." I flex my aching arm.

Euan chuckles. "Let's hope this is the last time we have to. They'll be in secondary school soon."

"True."

We have a batch of buttercream that's hopefully big enough to ice twenty-four cupcakes. I split it into six bowls, which is messier than I thought it would be, and then mix a few drops of icing colour into each one, so we have a rainbow of colours.

"Do you have any cling film?"

Euan frowns. "Cling film?"

"Yeah. It's a trick I saw on—"

"YouTube," we say in unison.

I crack up laughing. "Yes! It's less messy, and you can combine the colours more easily to make multicoloured swirls."

"I'll take your word for it."

I arrange sausage-shaped dollops of the icing side by side on a sheet of cling film and roll them into a larger sausage.

After snipping the end of a piping bag, I slip one of the fancy nozzles I bought inside. It falls out the bottom through the hole I cut.

Euan arches an eyebrow but doesn't say anything.

"It's the first time I've done this."

He waves his hands. "You're doing a better job than I could. I would be using a spoon right now."

I get a fresh piping bag and cut off a smaller amount of the end. This time, the nozzle fits just right. Next, I cut the end of the cling film icing sausage and put it into the bag.

"You certainly look like an expert," Euan says.

I poke my tongue out and gingerly hold the bag over a cupcake. "Then the idea is you squeeze gently in a spiral and... Voila!" I stare at the crooked, not even remotely neat spiral of icing on the cupcake. "It looks a bit like a unicorn took a shit."

Euan laughs. "It looks great. Better than I could do."

I grin. "Let's find out." I hand him the piping bag.

"I think I'd rather let you handle the icing."

"No chance. We're making these cakes together."

"We have no idea if they taste nice."

I hum. "True. Maybe we should try one."

"We didn't make any extras."

"Also true. But do you think the boys would miss one cupcake?"

He scratches his jaw. "Probably. But you're right. We should taste-test one."

"At least one. In the interests of quality assurance."

He chuckles. "Quality assurance, huh?"

"Yes. It's very important."

"Well, the one you iced looks half-decent. So we can try the one I'm about to put icing on."

I fold my arms and tut. "Pessimist."

"I prefer to call myself a realist."

I roll my eyes. "You're a drama teacher. You should be an optimist."

"Where's the logic in that?"

"Because theatre involves suspending imagination. Believing in the magic of what you're seeing on stage. Creating something out of nothing."

He stares at me, his expression unreadable.

"What?" I ask.

"Your eyes lit up just then. They were—" He blushes and looks away.

What was he going to say?

He takes a deep breath and squeezes icing onto a cupcake. It's more of an artistic dollop than a swirl. He ends up with three times as much icing as cake.

"As I said, things that look easy when experts do them rarely are," he says.

"I think you did an awesome job."

"If awesome has suddenly become a synonym for terrible, then I agree."

"Aww, come on. You'll get better the more you do. We both will. Practice makes perfect."

He gestures at the cupcake. "As this one isn't suitable for public consumption anyway, we should taste-test it."

I smirk. "I think you did a terrible job on purpose."

He sighs. "If only." He puts the icing bag down and picks

up the cupcake. He stares at it for several long seconds, barely breathing.

I wait not so patiently. What is he thinking about?

"You—uh—mentioned something about—" He squeezes his eyes shut and takes a deep breath.

"About—?"

He opens his eyes. "Peeling the case of a cupcake and—" He stammers over the words.

"And—?"

"You know what you said."

I do, but I need him to say it. I need him to ask me to do it. I need him to make the next move because I promised I'd slow down. I'm trying to behave.

He stares at the cupcake, licks his lips, and then makes eye contact with me. "Feed it to me."

"Is that what you want me to do?"

He holds the cupcake towards me. "Yes."

"Are you sure?"

"God help me, yes."

Smiling, I accept the cupcake. I take my sweet time peeling off the case, showing him how much time I'd care I'd take over peeling off his clothes. If he'd let me. I brush the cupcake against his lips. He parts them, allowing me to slip the soft cake into his mouth. Icing flakes off on his moustache and lips.

He bites the cake in half, lashes fluttering. "It's good. You should try it," he says around his mouthful.

Instead of bringing the rest of the cupcake to me, I go to it, kissing him in the same motion. He grabs my hips and pulls me against him. Somehow, we manage to eat the spongy cake and sweet, sticky icing while kissing one another.

"It is good. We should try another."

"We shouldn't."

"We can always make another batch. We have time."

He picks up the cupcake I iced, takes the wrapper off, and puts it to my lips. We eat it *Lady and the Tramp* style, our lips meeting in the middle.

"This isn't slowing down," I say.

"No."

"What made you change your mind?"

"You."

"I was trying to be good."

"You were, but you're also mesmerising, beautiful, and irresistible."

His praise makes me shiver. "Mmm, so are you, but we still have twenty-two cakes to decorate."

He runs his hand up and down my side. "Can they wait?"

I loop my arms over his shoulders and clasp them against his nape. "I like this version of you."

"What version is that?"

"A man who knows what he wants and takes it."

"I want you, Cameron," he says huskily. "I shouldn't, but I do."

"Well, you've got me. What do you want to do with me?"

"Kiss you."

I moan as he devours my mouth, licking any last remnants of icing from my lips, twirling his tongue against and around mine.

"Touch you." He pushes my T-shirt out of the way so he can skim his hands over my skin.

I tilt my head back. He kisses my throat, his lips soft, his beard tickly.

"Oh, that's so good. What else do you want to do with me?"

He grinds his groin against mine, reawakening my cock, which had gone limp during the film. "Make you come."

"Mm, yes, please. What else?"

He chuckles. "Isn't that enough?"

"It's a good starter." I nip his jaw and lip. "But what about the main course?"

"Sex?"

"Yes." I squeeze his arse through his chinos. "I would love to slide my cock deep inside your arse."

His pupils shrink.

I wince. "Too much, too fast?"

He cups my cheek tenderly and kisses me softly and slowly. "No. It's just been a while since I had sex. I'll need to douche." His eyes gleam mischievously. "Why don't I do that while you finish icing the cupcakes?"

I gasp and swat him across the chest. "That was your devious plan all along, wasn't it?"

"No." He whispers the words against my lips and kisses me again, this time with a lot more toe-curling passion.

"Liar," I tease.

"Do you want me to douche or not?"

I whimper. "You know I do." I push him away, turn him around, and smack his arse. "Go on. I want you all nice and clean for me by the time I'm done down here."

342

He heads towards the door.

"And naked!"

He glances over his shoulder and smirks. "I'll be ready and waiting for you."

"You'd better be." I pick up the piping bag and get to work.

I'm all hot and bothered again. Fingers crossed Euan hasn't changed his mind by the time I get upstairs.

Chapter Eight

Euan

I finish showering and douching, get dried, and stand in the middle of my bedroom, staring at the bed. Shit. I invited Cameron up to my bedroom for sex. My heart is pounding, my skin is tingling, and the prospect of having his hands running over my body has made me hard. We shouldn't be doing this, but I can't stop myself wanting him. I won't stop myself from having him.

He wants me naked. How long will he be? Should I lie on the bed and try to look sexy? Should I sit? Should I wait in the bathroom until I hear him coming? Should I hide under the quilt? Should I put my dressing gown on? No. He'll think I've changed my mind. I plump up my pillows and lie on top of the quilt. I want to look sexy, but have no idea how to arrange my body, so I try out a variety of positions like a drama student moving from one tableau to the next. I feel silly. At the very least, I need to look like I want him, so I rub my cock until it's hard. It doesn't take long.

"Well, hello there." Cameron lounges against the door-frame, rubbing the pad of his thumb against the corner of his mouth. "You are even sexier than I imagined."

Am I?

"And I feel overdressed." He takes his T-shirt off and walks towards the bed.

He is stunning. Long neck, waxed torso, and slender hips, with pronounced V-lines disappearing beneath the waistband of his jeans.

He rests one knee on the edge of the mattress and undoes his belt. "I thought you might have changed your mind."

I don't blame him for thinking that. I've been blowing hot and cold on him all morning.

I shake my head. "Have you?"

He rakes his teeth over his lower lip. "No." He pops open his button fly and slides his jeans over his hips, revealing tight, white underpants and the long, thick, hard outline of his cock.

"Fuck."

He grins, steps out of his jeans, and tugs his socks off. "Did you enjoy your shower?"

"Yes. How did the icing go?"

"Eh. Let's just say I got better with practice. The twenty-fourth cake looks amazing."

"Twenty-second. We ate two. Or your twenty-third. I decorated one."

He sniggers. "You're talking really fast."

"I do when I'm—" What? Nervous? Flustered? Gagging for it?

He cocks an eyebrow, resting his hands on the waistband of his underpants. He's teasing me.

"Waiting for a gorgeous guy to do wicked things to me," I say.

"You do that a lot, do you?"

"No. It's been over a year since I've been with anyone."

He widens his eyes.

Heat rises to my cheeks. "I told you it had been a while."

"Are you sure you're okay for me to top you?"

"Yes." I'm breathless with desire. "I want you to." I can't explain why, but there's something sexy about wanting a younger man to fuck me. About wanting to surrender myself to him. "Let me see you."

He pushes his underpants down a fraction, allowing me to see neatly trimmed pubic hair.

"More."

A little farther, giving me my first glimpse of his length.

"More."

He pushes them down his thighs. His cock springs up, the head briefly grazing against his stomach.

I suck in a breath. "Gorgeous."

"Me or my cock?"

I can't speak. Every word dies in my throat in an awkward, embarrassed squeak.

He laughs, which makes his cock bounce, and steps out of his underwear. He stands, hands on his hips, letting me stare at his beautiful body.

"It's hot that you think my cock is gorgeous."

"All of you is gorgeous." Have I redeemed myself?

He crawls onto the bed, coming towards me on his hands and knees. He straddles me, moving closer until he can kiss me. "You're gorgeous too."

346

I twine my fingers into his hair and pull him into another longer, more passionate kiss. I cannot get enough of kissing him. He still tastes of cake and icing. The saltiness of my cum is long gone.

He moans and kisses me harder as our tongues tangle. "So fucking sexy." He glances around my room.

"Is it what you imagined?" I'm breathless.

"Mostly. Neat. Organised. Like you. To be honest, my fantasies focused on you rather than your bedroom. Please tell me you've got lube and a condom?"

"Yes."

He scoots away while I turn awkwardly and scrabble in my drawer until I find supplies. They were shoved at the back, unused for months. I check the expiry date, sighing when I discover the lube and the condoms are good for several months. I would have cried if they'd been out of date. I hand them to him.

He kneels, staring at them. "We're about to cross a line."

"We already have." We've kissed—lots. He's sucked me off. In my kitchen! No one has ever given me a blow job in my kitchen before.

He meets my stare, eyebrows pinched together. "There are lines, and then there are lines."

My stomach churns. "Having doubts?"

"No. Just making sure you're not."

I suck in a breath. Is this wrong? We're consenting adults. We want each other. How can it be wrong? What will Lewis say when he inevitably finds out? Will I ever be able to look my best friend in the eye again?

"Euan?"

I'll cross that bridge when—and if—it comes to it. I want Cameron. He wants me. Right now, that's all that matters. My cock aches. My skin tingles. My heart races. My body is telling me this is right. My head doesn't get a say.

"I'm not."

He relaxes and grins. "Well, okay, then. Do me a favour, handsome. Get on all fours for me."

A thrill runs through me. His bossy tone excites me. I get on all fours, my arse pointed in his direction, and spread my knees as much as is comfortable. The mattress depresses. He strokes my lower back and releases an approving sound.

He squeezes lube over my arse. I shiver from the sudden shock of cold. He runs his finger over my pucker tenderly. My muscles tremble and quiver in response.

"Thank you for trusting me with your arse," he says.

I laugh. He slips his finger inside me, taking me by surprise. Oh, fuck, it feels so good. I'd almost forgotten how good arse play feels.

"Nice?" he asks.

"Yes."

I allow my trembling arms to collapse so I'm leaning on my elbows and forearms instead of my hands. I bow my head and groan as he fingers me slowly. The tip of his finger brushes over my prostate. He cups, squeezes, and rolls my balls with his other hand. I gasp. At this rate, I'll spill my load before he gets his cock anywhere near me. I've already come once. He hasn't orgasmed at all.

"Cameron!"

"Yes?"

"I—" I grip the sheets. "You're going to make me—"

He chuckles. "It has been a long time, hasn't it?"

I whimper, nod, and then groan as he releases my balls and slips two fingers inside me. It's glorious. My arse hugs his fingers. He moves them smoothly and expertly, teasing me, warming me up, getting me ready to receive his cock. I want him so badly. I can't remember ever wanting someone this much. Shit, I've desired him for a long time. Far longer than I've ever admitted to myself. I was in denial every time I got lost in his smile or struck up a conversation simply to hear his voice. I'm not in denial any longer. I want Cameron. I *need* Cameron.

"Fuck me!" I cry.

He tuts. "So impatient."

"I need you, Cameron. Please."

"You need to be patient." He slips a third finger inside me on a satisfying squelch of lube. "I've wanted to do this for a long time." His voice is low and husky. "I'm going to take my sweet time."

I tremble. Half of me wants him to take all the time in the world so I can enjoy him for as long as possible. The other half wants him to fuck me hard and fast. Right fucking now. That half craves the high of release, the buzz of having a man come inside me. That half needs him to take control and fuck me without restraint. But I'll be patient. I'm giving myself to him. Surrendering to his whims.

He slips his fingers out of me and kisses the small of my back, right over my spine. "Now you're ready." He slides his cock over my crack a few times, giving me a taste of what's to come.

He rustles the condom wrapper and rips it open. I glance

over my shoulder. He rolls the condom onto his engorged cock and applies plenty of lube. I lick my lips.

He waggles his eyebrows. "Ready?"

"Oh, yes."

"I'm really looking forward to this."

"Me too." I press my forehead against the mountain of pillows and take deep, slow breaths.

He nudges the head of his cock against my hole, teasing me, causing my muscles to flex in response to his presence.

"Please fuck me," I whine.

He grips my hips, digging his fingers into my flesh. It's divine. He pushes inside me, sighing deeply.

"Oh, you feel so fucking good, Euan."

"Yeah? So do you."

His hard length fills me up nicely. He stays still for several seconds. Is he savouring the sensation of being inside me? I'm back to being torn. I love the feel of him simply being inside me, warming his cock while my arse gets used to his presence, but I want him to thrust his hips. I want him to ride my arse. Oh, fuck, I want *him*.

"How do you like it?" he asks.

"However you want to give it to me." I grit my teeth. I sound needy. I am needy. "Just fuck me."

He laughs, holds my hips tighter, and fucks me. Slowly at first, each stroke strong, long, measured, and deep. He quickly picks up pace. Soon he's grunting as his balls and thighs slap against my arse. I rock in time with him, hollowing the small of my back so he can get deeper. So he can brush the head of his cock over my prostate on every wonderful thrust. I pant and groan. I clutch the pillows with my fingers. I enjoy every wondrous second of this stunning man pounding my arse. This is really happening. Cameron is fucking me, and I'm enjoying it so fucking much I can hardly bear it.

"That feels so good, Cam." It's the first time I've ever used the short form of his name. I don't think I could manage his full name right now. Too many syllables to spit out when all I want to do is groan and moan and tell him how fucking amazing this is. "Harder. Please harder."

"You want it harder?" His voice is light and breathy.

"Yes!"

He thrusts into me like a drill sergeant sprinting. His rhythm is hard, fast, and perfect. I let out a long moan, which quivers and vibrates with every snap of his hips.

"You like it like that, handsome?"

"Yes!" I like him calling me handsome too. It makes me feel good.

He presses his palm against the small of my back. Manages to bury his cock deeper and deeper. He cups my balls and rolls them, then grasps my cock, stroking it in time with his desperate, noisy, wonderful thrusts. I'm beside myself. My balls are heavy. My groin quivers. My cock aches.

"Cameron, I—" My orgasm explodes out of me, soaking his hand in sticky cum, leaving me shivering and shaking.

He releases my cock and holds my hips like he's riding a bucking bronco. He thrusts until he comes with a satisfied grunt and a loud, happy sigh, his cock shuddering inside me.

"Oh, wow." He pulls out gently.

I summon up the energy to roll over, facing him.

He's taken the condom off and is tying a knot in the end. He drops it on the bedside table to be dealt with later and lies beside me.

I stroke his face, his collarbone, his chest. "Thank you."

He smiles. "You tired me out."

I raise my eyebrows. "I tired you out?"

"Yes! Wanting it hard and fast like that. Phew! I need a few minutes to recover."

I laugh. "Only a few minutes?"

"Hey, I'm in my twenties. I recover fast."

Faster than me, no doubt. Ten years makes a big difference. I don't want to think about that now. About the years between us. About Lewis and what he might think. I lay my head on Cameron's chest. His heartbeat thrashes against my ear.

I brush my hand over his cock, which remains flaccid. "Let me know when you've recovered, and I'll make you come again. I owe you for earlier."

He kisses my nose. "You don't owe me anything, Euan. I enjoyed sucking you off and drinking you dry."

I shiver.

"And I enjoyed fucking you." He flops his hand over his forehead and stares at the ceiling. "What now?"

"We cuddle, and we recover."

"And then?" His voice has a worried quiver to it.

I sigh and move so I'm mirroring his position. "I don't know."

He rolls onto his side, props himself on his elbow, and runs his fingers through my hair. "Do you want to do this again?"

"Sex or baking cupcakes."

"I was thinking of sex, but I could be down for baking more cupcakes."

"We shouldn't."

"Bake more cupcakes?"

I chuckle. "Have sex again. Do any of *this* again."

"Why?"

"What if your dad finds out?"

"I'm an adult. He doesn't get to dictate who I fuck. Or who I date."

Date. The word hangs between us. He was making a statement, so why did it feel like a question?

"It's not that simple, Cameron. This could ruin my friendship with your dad."

He wrinkles his nose. "If it does, it wasn't much of a friendship."

If only that were true. Oh, to be able to see the world through the eyes of a twenty-five-year-old again, when you're convinced everything is yours for the taking and that nothing is complicated. Sadly, life is complicated. Friendships are complicated. Relationships even more so.

"Let's not worry about it now," I say. Which is a cop-out if ever there was one.

"Just enjoy the moment?"

"Yes."

"All right."

It's not all right, but apparently, we're also willing to bury our heads in the sand.

"What about your marking?" Cameron asks.

"Forget the marking. I want to stay in bed with you."

"Sounds wonderful." He snuggles against me.

I wrap my arm around him and hold him tight. For the next few hours, I intend to forget that anything outside this room exists. For the next few hours, it's just me and Cameron.

Chapter Nine

Cameron

The moment we leave Euan's bedroom to pick the boys up from school, something shifts between us. The flirtiness is gone. We maintain a reserved distance from one another. We're careful not to glance at the other for too long. To not make eye contact. I hate it. I want to kiss him. I want to hold him. I want to run my fingers through his hair. It's the not knowing what—if anything—is going to happen next. We avoided a much-needed conversation in favour of pretending the outside world didn't exist, but it does. I don't care what Dad thinks about me and Euan hooking up, but Euan obviously does. Does my age bother him too? Was telling him I liked him a dumb idea?

The boys race up to us. It's refreshing to only have one of them tackle-hugging me at a time.

Elliott bounces on the soles of his feet. "Did you make cupcakes?"

I smile. "Yes."

The boys jump and fist-bump the air.

"You're the best. Dad." Peter hugs Euan. Then he hugs me. "And you, Cam. Thanks a bunch."

"We have invitations." Elliott takes an envelope out of his bag and hands it to me.

I pull a space-themed card out of the envelope and read the invitation. "A sleepover party?"

"At David's. For his birthday. It's a week on Friday. Can I go?"

"Can I go too?" Peter gives Euan an identical invitation.

Euan frowns. "It says the party starts at five. I'm not sure I'll be home in time to give you a lift."

"I can take them," I say.

Euan smiles at me. The skin around his eyes crinkles beautifully, his blue irises appearing lighter and brighter in the afternoon sunlight. He is so damned gorgeous, and he's staring right into my eyes, and I'm falling for him all over again. I am doomed.

"Thanks, Cam."

Cam. It's only the second time he's called me by my nickname. The first time was while I was buried deep inside him. My knees sag. I'm swooning like the women in my favourite black-and-white movies.

"Did you have fun making cakes?" Elliott asks.

My cheeks flush with heat. I rub the back of my neck. "Uh, yeah. It was fun." I catch Euan's eye again, even though I shouldn't.

He blushes too.

"Did you get your marking done?" Peter asks him.

Euan clears his throat. "Cupcake-making took longer than we anticipated."

The boys glance at each other, smirking. Elliott pats Peter on the arm, and they run ahead, whispering to each other.

"What's that about?" I ask Euan.

"No clue. They're probably plotting something."

"Yeah, but what?"

He shrugs. "Hopefully, we won't ever find out."

"Euan—"

Elliott stops and waves to us. "Hurry up! We want to see the cupcakes."

I sigh and pick up the pace. Now isn't the right time to talk to Euan anyway. The boys could overhear. The trouble is, we're unlikely to get a moment alone anytime soon. I guess that's it, then. One and done. I should be grateful I got to have him at all. I *am* grateful. It was amazing. But our encounter hasn't done anything to work my crush on him out of my system. If anything, I want him more. Is there a chance he might want me too? Not for another one-off. Truly want to be with me. If he did, I'd want to be open and honest about it. I wouldn't want to pretend I'm not crazy about him.

Peter unlocks the door to his house. The boys dump their belongings by the door and dash into the kitchen. Out of habit, I pick up their things and hang them up, even though it's not my house.

"You didn't need to do that. We should have called them back to do it," Euan says.

"It's fine. I don't mind."

We follow the boys into the kitchen, where they're scrutinising the cupcakes.

"They look good," Euan whispers.

It's the first time he's seen them decorated because we stayed in bed together until the last possible second. More orgasms were had. I was correct: he has an excellent hand technique.

"Why are there only twenty-two?" Elliott asks.

"We had to taste-test them," I reply.

I'll never forget how the icing crumbled onto Euan's beard and lips or the taste of cake and icing on his tongue as I kissed him. I shouldn't be thinking about it right now. I do not want to get a hard-on in front of my ten-year-old brother and his best friend. Think unsexy thoughts. Think unsexy thoughts.

"They look great," Peter says.

"You can tell they're not shop-bought. You know what this means, don't you?" Elliott asks.

I shake my head.

"You've got no excuse to make cupcakes next time."

"Next time? What next time?"

Elliott shrugs. "School are always doing things to raise money."

"They ask us for ideas of what they can do."

"We suggested a cupcake sale."

I narrow my eyes.

Elliott bounces from foot to foot. "You could make me a birthday cake! I've never had a homemade birthday cake!"

You and me both, kid.

"Could you make *me* a birthday cake, Dad?" Peter asks.

Euan looks terrified.

The boys glance at each other.

"You could work together to make us birthday cakes," Elliott says.

"That's a great idea!" Peter says.

"We can talk about cakes when it's your birthday," I say.

"I think baking and decorating a cake would be a lot harder than cupcakes," Euan stammers.

I fold my arms. "Do you have any homework tonight?"

"No," the boys reply in unison.

"Then why don't you go play in Peter's room while we box up the cupcakes to take to school tomorrow?"

Elliott nudges Peter. "See? I told you they'd make a good team."

"No. *I* told you they would."

They continue arguing as they leave the kitchen and head upstairs.

Euan breathes out and sags against the counter.

"They're a pair of whirlwinds, but at least they approve of the cupcakes," I say.

"I'm surprised they didn't ask to try one."

"Each."

Euan chuckles.

I lean against the opposite side of the breakfast bar and tap my finger against the counter. "Euan, we should talk."

He glances up at the ceiling.

"Relax. They're probably playing a computer game or creating something out of Lego."

"This afternoon was fun."

I smile. "It was."

Why isn't he making eye contact with me?

"But—?" I ask.

"It needs to be a one-off."

"Because of Dad?"

He nods.

"Is he the only reason?"

"You're ten years younger than me, Cameron."

"And?"

"You'd have more fun with someone closer to your age."

"I think that's for me to decide, isn't it?"

He still doesn't look at me.

"You realise Dad is ten years older than *you*? I guess age gaps only matter when it's someone you want to fuck." I'm careful to keep my voice low. Am I being unfair? Maybe. It won't stop me from getting the hurt in my heart out in the open. "You don't even know that Dad *would* have a problem. You're just assuming he will, and you're too scared to find out."

Euan clenches his jaw and bows his head.

I knock my loose fist lightly against the counter. "I'm not a kid, Euan. Please don't treat me like one."

"I'm sorry, Cameron."

I hunch my shoulders. The truth is, I knew it was going to come to this. I knew I was playing with fire. I did it willingly. I should be happy I got to be with him at all. Why wish for more? It was never going to happen.

"I won't tell Dad what happened between us. Send Elliott home in an hour, please. I'll have dinner ready for him."

"Cameron—"

I turn my back on him. "I'm sorry I encouraged you to cross a line you didn't want to cross." I walk out without

360

giving him a chance to speak. I don't want to know what his response would have been.

Instead, I go home, nursing my wounded pride and bruised ego. At least I have hot memories of my sexy next-door neighbour to console me.

Chapter Ten

Euan

I've made a mistake.

It turns out it's not the mistake I thought I'd made.

It wasn't a mistake to kiss Cameron. It wasn't a mistake to let him feed me cupcakes. It wasn't a mistake to take him to bed.

It was a mistake to tell him it had to be a one-off. To make excuses about his dad or his age. All right, maybe they're not excuses, but do they need to be obstacles?

I haven't stopped thinking about Cameron. Every morning, I've woken up from erotic dreams about our encounter, my cock hard as a rod. I wanted to talk to him but told myself there wasn't a good time. When I drop Peter off before I go to work in the morning? No. The boys are there. When I pick Peter up after work in the evening? No. The boys are there. I haven't even made eye contact with him because I know if I do, I'll want to kiss him.

I was a coward when I told him our post-cupcake

encounter had to be a one-off. Now I'm pathetic *and* a coward.

It's Friday evening. It's been a long two weeks. Usually, I leave work promptly on a Friday, but tonight, knowing Cameron was taking the boys to their sleepover party, I stayed late and got all my marking and planning for the following week done. It'll be good to take the whole weekend off for a change.

It's almost seven when I arrive home. By some miracle, I'm able to park outside my house, right in front of Cameron's car. I stay in my car, staring at his house. Lewis's house. What would he think of me and Cameron hooking up? What would he say if we wanted more? Not that I have any reason to hope for more. Or rather, I can hope but not expect. I upset Cameron with my cowardice. Why would he want anything to do with me now?

With a sigh, I gather my things and get out of the car. I hesitate at the end of the path to my front door. I could talk to Cameron. Explain I was wrong. Tell him I miss him. Let him know I still want him. But why would he listen? I straighten my back, roll my shoulders, and lift my chin. I'm being a defeatist. A pessimist. What was it Cameron said? I'm a drama teacher, so I should be an optimist. I'm still not sure I follow his logic, but his words—and the earnest expression on his face—captivated me. He's captivating.

I let myself into my house, drop my things inside the front door, lock up, stride next door, and ring the doorbell before I can second-guess myself.

Cameron opens a few moments later. He blinks, brow

furrowed. "Oh, hi, Euan. Peter's not here. Did you forget? The boys have a sleepover party tonight."

"I didn't forget. Peter was very excited about it this morning."

He smiles. "So was Elliott. I think we'll have two very tired boys tomorrow."

"I think so too."

He runs his finger over the inside of the door frame. "Why are you here?"

"Can we talk?"

His frown deepens. "What about?"

"Monday. Us."

He folds his arms. "You made it quite clear there isn't an us."

"Can I come in? Please?"

He nods and steps backwards, away from the door. I go inside, shutting the door behind me. I can't miss the tension in Cameron's body. He still has his arms folded, his fingertips tucked under his armpits in a defensive gesture. His chin is lowered, and he's glaring at the wooden flooring.

"Why are you here, Euan? Did you fancy a booty call?" His voice drips with sarcasm.

I gape at him. "That's not why I'm here."

"Then why?"

I spread my fingers wide. "To talk. To apologise."

He raises his chin a little and makes eye contact with me. "I'm sorry."

Now I'm here, close to him, I want to hold him even more. I want to kiss any hurt away I've caused. Heck, I'd welcome him taking out his anger, annoyance, whatever on me via hard, rough sex if he wanted. Unlike on Monday, I need to make my head rule my cock. He's just told me he's not interested in sex.

"I was a jerk on Monday. I shouldn't have shut down the possibility of us the way I did. The truth is, I want to be with you."

"But?"

"But I'm scared."

"About Dad's reaction?"

"Yes."

"And my age bothers you," he says flatly.

"I don't understand what you see in a guy ten years older than you."

"That's the thing. I don't see the age gap. I see a gorgeous, creative guy, who I've been sweet on since the day I met. And yeah, maybe I did see the age gap six years ago. There was no way you were going to look at a nineteen-year-old. But I'm twenty-five now. I'm not a kid."

"The age gap hasn't changed."

"No. But I have. I've grown up. I know who I am. You know what hasn't changed?"

I shake my head.

"My crush on you. The more I got to know you, the more I fell for you. Not that it matters."

I catch hold of his wrist. "It *does* matter. You're amazing, Cam."

He hunches his shoulders.

Right. It's only the third time I've called him that. He must associate it with the intimacy we shared. I don't blame him.

"It doesn't matter if you can't see past my age. If you can't even bring yourself to find out what Dad might think about us. I'm fine with keeping a one-off secret but beyond that? If you truly want to be with me, it needs to be out in the open. You need to be proud to be seen with me. You need to be willing to tell Dad we're together." He wipes his hands over his face. "I'm running a million miles ahead. You came to apologise. Not ask for a second chance."

I run my hand down his arm and thread my fingers through his. "I do want a second chance. If you're willing to give me one."

He stares at me.

"You're amazing, Cameron. I haven't stopped thinking about you and how good we were together."

"We did make awesome cupcakes. They all sold, you know."

"It was your decorating skills that made them look appealing."

"It didn't hurt that they tasted great."

Especially when I was kissing crumbs and icing remnants off his lips and sucking them off his tongue.

"We can thank the recipe for that," I say.

"Nah, it was our execution of the recipe."

I laugh and then clear my throat. "I want to see where this thing between us might lead. Will you give me a second chance?"

He scuffs his foot over the wooden floor. Seconds tick by, turning into a minute. Waiting is excruciating, but I deserve to squirm.

"No secrets?" he asks.

"No."

"You'd be happy for me to tell Dad who I'm seeing?"

It's his nonnegotiable. The thing I have to agree to if I want to be with him. I do want to be with him. I could try to negotiate. Suggest we wait a month, two, or maybe even five, until Lewis is back in the country. Why potentially risk ruining our friendship or his relationship with Cameron over something that might not last? Which is a pessimistic view-point, if there is ever one.

I raise my chin. "Yes. I want to be with you. It turns out I'm sweet on you too."

"You are, huh? Isn't that an archaic thing to say?" He smiles, which makes his eyes twinkle beautifully.

"Maybe. But it's true. Tell me what I need to do to prove it."

"You can shut up and kiss me."

I widen my eyes.

"Right now." He taps his lips.

I pull him into my arms and ravage his mouth with my tongue. Damn, he tastes even sweeter than before. He holds on to me tightly, returning my kiss with equal passion. It's not long before we're whimpering and moaning against each other's lips. My pulse races, my cock hardens. His erection presses against me.

"Do you want to talk more?" I ask, breathless. "Watch a film? Make dinner together?"

"I want you to take me upstairs."

"I thought you weren't interested in a booty call."

"I wasn't. But this isn't that."

"Oh. What is it?"

"How about a date?"

"A date?"

He chuckles against my lips. "You know what a date is, don't you? Two guys enjoying getting to know each other better while enjoying a rare evening without kids around."

"It sounds nice."

He hums as he kisses me. "It does, doesn't it?" He takes my hand and tugs me up the stairs, somehow still kissing me. "I hope you're feeling energetic tonight, handsome. Because I intend to take full advantage of having you all to myself."

I squeeze his hand, desire brimming in my heart. "I can't wait."

Chapter Eleven

Cameron

"Hi, Cam, what's up?" Dad asks.

So far, every time we've video-called, Elliott has been with me. Today, it's just me. Euan offered to talk to Dad with me, but I decided this was a conversation we needed to have from father to son. Besides, if Dad reacts badly, I want to be able to give Euan a heads-up. So I'm calling him now while Euan is picking the boys up from their sleepover party.

"Has something happened?"

"Nothing bad." I wipe my hands over my thighs.

"Then why do you look so nervous, buddy?"

Buddy is the nickname Dad gave me when I was three or four. I don't remember. He means well, but it never fails to reduce me to feeling like a kid. Except I'm not a kid. I'm an adult, and I need to act like one.

"I've started seeing someone. It's very new, but I thought you should know."

Dad purses his lips. "I'm sure Euan would be happy to babysit every so often if you want to spend time with your new boyfriend, especially if you offer to repay the favour. We used to do that quite a bit."

I half smile. "I remember. Dad, the thing is, Euan *is* the guy I'm seeing."

He widens his eyes.

I flinch and brace myself for whatever his reaction might be.

"You've liked him for a long time," Dad says.

I gawp at him. "You knew?"

"It was obvious." He scratches his beard. "I didn't realise he liked you."

"Nor did I. Elliott and Peter convinced us to make cupcakes together for a school bake sale, and one thing led to another. Please don't be angry, especially not at Euan. I came onto him."

"I admit it's a little odd to think about my son and my best friend." He shakes his head. "Maybe I shouldn't think about it. There's quite the age gap between you."

"Ten years. The same as you and him. Those ten years haven't stopped you from being friends, have they?"

"No. It matters less the older you get. We had a lot in common, Cam."

"You're both single dads."

"Yes. Through choice."

He makes it sound like they made the same decisions. They didn't. Dad was twenty, and his girlfriend was eighteen when she got pregnant with me. She chose to go through with

370

the pregnancy, but she intended to put me up for adoption. Dad offered to take care of me instead. He's told me a hundred times or more that he never regretted that decision. Elliott was another accidental pregnancy. Once again, he stepped up and took on the role of sole parent without hesitation or reservation, and honestly, he's an amazing dad.

As for Euan—he wanted to be a dad. He had a friend who didn't want kids of her own but offered to be a surrogate. They went the IVF route.

"You and Euan have less in common," Dad says.

"I like him, Dad, and he likes me. I don't know if this is going to turn into anything serious, but it would be easier to see where things go if we know you're okay with it."

He puffs his cheeks out and stares off somewhere to his right. It's evening in Hong Kong. Is it dark out already? Is he looking out his window at the city lights? One of the first things Dad did when he arrived was take a photo of Hong Kong out of the window of his temporary apartment. It looks amazing.

"I've got five months to get used to it," he says eventually.

My heart sinks. "You don't approve."

"I didn't say that. What I did say is that it's odd, and it is going to take some getting used to. All I've ever wanted is for you to be happy, Cam. Do you think Euan will make you happy?"

"Yes."

"Long term?"

I shrug. "I don't know. Maybe. I don't have a crystal ball."

"True. He's got a son."

"Uh, yeah, I know."

"My point is, if things do get serious, being a stepdad is very different to taking care of your younger brother for six months."

I take a breath. His comment should terrify me. Is that why he said it? It doesn't. Peter is a great kid. "We're a long way off stepdad territory, Dad."

He smiles. "I know. But it's something to think about. You can't get into a relationship with a parent—however casual—without considering their child."

"I know."

"Do the boys know?"

"Not yet."

"But you'll tell them?"

I nod.

"They might be a tougher audience than I was."

My jaw drops. "You think so?"

He laughs. "No. I think they'll be excited at the prospect of getting to have more sleepovers."

I laugh along with him. "Probably."

"Do you have any more bombshells to drop on me?"

"Nope."

"Then tell me everything you've been up to since we last talked. I want every detail."

I grin. "Sure thing, as long as you tell me everything you've done."

"Are you sure you want details of every boring meeting?"

"Eh, no. You can skip work stuff. But tell me everything else."

"Deal."

When Euan and the boys get home, I meet them at the front door. Elliott and Peter have dark bags under their eyes. Not that Euan and I are faring much better. We spent a lot of time talking, cuddling, and fucking last night. We did eventually get to sleep an hour or so before dawn. I would love a nap later. Especially if I can spend that nap in Euan's arms.

"Hey, how was the party?" I ask.

"Great!" Elliott replies.

"How late did you stay up?"

"David's parents hid all the sweets and snacks and turned the lights out at ten."

"But—?"

"Michael had snuck sweets into his bag. When we were sure David's parents were asleep, we played Monopoly," Peter says.

I smack my hand over my face. "You are never having a sleepover party here," I tell Elliott.

"Aww!"

"Nor are you." Euan ruffles Peter's hair.

"Dad!"

"Can we go play games?" Elliott asks.

"Wouldn't you rather have a nap?"

"Nah. I'm too wired to sleep."

"It'll be all that sugar," Euan says.

I laugh. "Probably. Go ahead."

The boys dash past me up the stairs.

I beckon Euan into the kitchen and close the door.

"Did you speak to Lewis?" he asks.

"Yes."

"And?"

I put my hands on Euan's hips and pull his groin against mine. "He was fine with the concept of us."

Euan widens his eyes and lifts his eyebrows. "He was?"

I bob my head from side to side. "He said it would take some getting used to, but as long as we're happy, he's happy." I lean my forehead against Euan's. "Relieved?"

"Yes."

"Me too."

"We should tell the boys."

"Yes." I kiss him tenderly.

"Before they walk in on us and catch us kissing."

I laugh. "Uh-huh. But right now, they're playing games."

I kiss him again, pulling him as close as I can so his body is sandwiched against mine. I walk him to the breakfast bar and press him against the counter.

"They could come down at any moment, looking for a snack." He slips his hands beneath my T-shirt and runs them up and down my back.

"I think they've had enough sugar for now." I stroke his tongue with mine and moan into his mouth.

"They're growing boys. They're always hungry." He slides one hand to my arse and squeezes.

"True." I tangle my fingers through his hair and tickle his nape.

"We should stop."

"Absolutely." I pull away and wipe the back of my hand

over my damp lips. "You need to stop being so irresistible, handsome."

He jabs his finger against his chest. "Me? You're the irresistible one, Cam."

"No. You." I smile and brush my fingertips over his beard.

"We should speak to the boys."

"Yup."

We go upstairs and knock on Elliott's door.

"Come in!"

The boys are sitting on the floor, with their backs against Elliott's bed, playing a cartoony racing game on the game console.

"Could you pause that for a moment?" Euan asks.

They do.

"What's up?" Elliott asks.

"We need to talk to you about something," Euan says.

Elliott and Peter exchange glances. They grin.

"You kissed, didn't you?" Elliott asks.

Peter clasps his hands in a pleading gesture and whispers, "Please, please, please."

For a moment, I can't do anything but stand and stare at them. Euan does the same.

"Well? Did you?" Elliott demands.

"It was on Monday, wasn't it? When you made cupcakes together." Peter unclasps his hands.

I glance at Euan. He looks at me.

"If we had kissed, would you be okay with it?" Euan asks.

The boys roll their eyes.

"Uh, yeah. We were counting on it," Elliott says.

"Why else do you think we were so keen on you baking cupcakes together?" Peter asks.

My mind is racing to catch up.

"We set you up," Elliott says.

Euan laughs.

"Why?" I ask.

"Because you've liked Euan for ages," Elliott says.

"And we thought it would be cool if you two got together," Peter says.

"Especially while Dad is away."

"Why?" It's the only thing I can spit out at the moment.

"More sleepovers!" they chorus.

Dad called it.

"So, did you kiss?" Elliott asks.

"If not, why not?" Peter asks.

Euan slides his fingers through mine. "We kissed."

They fist-bump the air and whoop.

"Awesome. Anything else, or can we get back to our game?" Elliott asks.

"That was all," Euan says.

"Hey, Dad, can we sleep over tonight?" Peter asks.

"That's not really up to me."

Elliott fixes me with a pleading stare. "Say yes."

I throw my hands up. "Yes!"

"But no playing Monopoly and gorging on sweets at midnight," Euan says.

"We're too tired for that." Peter yawns, proving his point.

They turn back to their game and play again. Euan and I back out of the room, closing the door behind us.

We go downstairs into the kitchen, where I immediately press Euan against the wall so I can kiss him.

"Relieved?" I ask.

"Happy." He cups my face and caresses my shoulder. "And looking forward to seeing where this thing between us goes."

"Yeah, I'm looking forward to that too."

Epilogue

Euan

We're at the airport, waiting for Lewis to get through security. The boys have made 'Welcome Home' banners. As a result, my house looks like it's been hit by a glitter bomb.

Cameron and I stand hand in hand. Exploring our mutual attraction has led to five amazing months of getting to know each other in new and wonderful ways. I've never been happier, and judging by the way Cameron smiles at me every day, the same is true for him.

Despite Lewis giving us his blessing—so to speak—I can't deny I'm nervous about seeing him face-to-face for the first time since Cameron and I got together.

"There he is! There he is!" Elliott exclaims.

He and Peter bounce up and down, waving their banners. Multicoloured glitter drifts onto the floor around their feet. Lewis is wearing a casual linen suit. He has a rucksack slung over one shoulder and is pushing a large suitcase. His skin is tanned. He has a few more grey hairs and crowfeet than I remember but overall looks happy.

As soon as he's close enough, he puts his bags down, holds out his arms, and crouches. Elliott abandons his poster and hurls himself into his dad's arms. Lewis hugs his youngest son tightly. When Elliott finally lets go, Lewis stays where he is, arms outstretched once more, and winks at Cameron.

"Oh, no. I'm too big for that," Cameron says.

"You're never too big for hugs." Lewis stands and gives Cameron a hug combined with a pat on the back. "It's good to see you, buddy. I've missed you all."

"We've missed you too, Dad. But hey, the house didn't burn down while you were gone."

Lewis laughs nervously. "Good to hear it. Is it still in one piece?"

"In one piece. Clean, tidy, with a fully stocked fridge."

"Impressive." He turns his attention to me and shakes my hand.

It's a more formal greeting than I was expecting. What was I expecting? A handwave, perhaps. Maybe even a brief hug like the one he gave me when he left for Hong Kong. But a firm handshake?

"How have you been?" he asks.

Oh, you know, enjoying kissing your son. Enjoying running my hands all over his body. Enjoying having his— Never mind. "Great."

He glances at Cameron. "Are you taking care of my son?"

What do I say to that?

Lewis laughs. "Relax, I'm kidding."

"You've got used to the idea of there being an us, then?" Cameron asks.

Lewis shrugs. "I didn't have much choice, did I? Are you making each other happy?"

Cameron and I stare into each other's eyes for far too long a moment.

"Yes, they are," Peter and Elliott say in unison.

"I've never seen Dad happier," Peter says.

"It's the first time Cameron hasn't dated a loser," Elliott says.

"Hey!" Cameron objects.

"It's true."

Cameron cups my face. "I'm not going to confirm or deny anything about my past boyfriends, but you're definitely not a loser." He kisses me. In front of his dad. It's not a peck on the lips either but a long, passionate kiss with tongues.

I stop caring about Lewis's presence after the first few seconds. I close my eyes and kiss Cameron just as hard.

"They do that a lot," Peter says.

Cameron and I break apart.

Lewis's eyes are sparkling. "You do seem happy together. Now, as wonderful as airport reunions are, can we get home? I'm looking forward to sleeping in my own bed tonight."

"It's still morning!" Elliott says.

He and the boys walk away, trailing their posters and glitter behind them. Cameron and I linger a little farther behind.

"That went well," I say.

"Did you doubt it would?"

I shrug. "I wasn't sure until the moment we saw him.

Video chats are very different to seeing a relationship in person."

"Why do you think I kissed you like that?"

I smile. "Because you like me?"

Cameron pulls me round and to a halt so we're facing one another. "I more than like you, Euan."

I blink.

"This is probably the least romantic place in existence to say this, but here goes. Somewhere along the line, I fell in love with you."

I gawp at him, eyes wide. My tummy flutters. My head spins. My pulse races. Cameron loves me?

He smiles nervously. "Say something."

"You—?"

"Love you. And Peter."

My heart does a loop-the-loop. The fluttering in my stomach transforms into giddy bubbles that spread through my body, making me feel so light I could float into the stratosphere. I smile so wide my cheeks ache. I know, deep down, in that instant, how I feel about Cameron.

"I love you too, Cam."

He grins.

I pull him close for a searing, lip-tingling, toe-curling kiss, which leaves us gasping for air.

He rests his forehead against mine. "We should catch up with the others."

We glance in that direction. Lewis and the boys are standing twenty or so feet away, grinning.

We hold hands and walk towards them. They carry on

before we reach them. Are they purposefully giving us privacy?

How are things going to change now Lewis is back? Will Cameron want to continue living under his dad's roof? Before the Hong Kong trip came up, Cameron was all set to move out. He'd put a deposit down on a flat. If he doesn't move out, would I feel comfortable spending the night there, with Lewis in a neighbouring room? On the other hand, it would be easier for Cameron to spend nights at mine.

"Penny for them," he says.

I blink and stare at him. "Who says that anymore?"

"The guy who likes old black-and-white movies." He winks.

Over the last five months, Cameron has shown me all his favourite films. I've never been enamoured by that era of film, except the ones that included song and dance, but I've grown to appreciate the ones he loves, helped along by his infectious enthusiasm for them.

I squeeze his hand. "Would you think about moving in with me?"

"Are you serious?"

"Yes."

"Have you talked to Peter about it?"

"No. I've only just come up with the idea."

"You should."

He's right. I should. It isn't just my house. It's Peter's too. Every decision I make—especially one as monumental as asking the guy I love to move in with us—has to involve Peter.

"I will."

"When you have his blessing, ask me again."

When we get to the car park, the five of us squeeze into my car. Cameron sits in the passenger seat, and Lewis sits in the back between the boys, who fire questions at him about Hong Kong and the flight the whole drive home. Cameron rests his hand on my thigh throughout the drive.

Once we're home, I put my hands on Peter's shoulders before he has a chance to dash into Lewis's home with Elliott.

"We should give them some space," I say softly.

"Aww."

"Plus, I need to talk to you about something."

"What?"

"You'll find out. Let's go."

We wave Cameron, Lewis, and Elliott goodbye and enter our house. I go to the sitting room, sit on the sofa, and pat the cushion beside me.

Peter joins me. "What did you want to talk about?"

"How would you feel if I asked Cameron to move in with us?" I hold my breath.

Peter purses his lips. "Would it mean fewer sleepovers?"

"Not necessarily. Elliott could sleep over here, and I'm sure his dad would be happy for you to sleep over there. Not every night, mind."

Over the last five months, Cameron and I have kept sleepovers mostly to Friday and Saturday nights and school holidays.

"Well, what do you think?" I ask.

Peter grins. "Sure, Cameron can move in. I like him."

"I love him."

"Does that mean you're going to get married?"

My heart flutters. "Maybe. One day. Let's start with

seeing how we all get along with Cameron living here first, okay?"

"Will he sleep in your room?"

"Is—is that okay?"

"Uh, yeah. It would be weird for your boyfriend to sleep in another room."

I ruffle Peter's hair. "Thanks, buddy."

He stands, grabs my arm, and tugs me up.

"What are you doing?"

"We need to ask Cameron to move in with us."

"Now?"

"Yup."

"You don't want to make another poster?" I'm joking, but Peter's eyes light up.

"Good idea! Give me half an hour." He releases my hand and runs off.

Oh, well. Aside from the fact that my house will be even more caked in glitter, it'll give Cameron, Lewis, and Elliott more time to catch up. I'm going to ask Cameron to move in with us. Will he say yes?

Almost an hour later, we ring next door's doorbell. Peter is holding a huge sign with the message facing towards him.

Elliott answers the door. "Hey, do you want to come in?"

Peter shakes his head. "Go get Cam," he whispers.

Elliott stares at Peter, the poster with its message hidden, and then me. "Okay." He leaves the door open and runs into the house, calling Cameron's nickname.

Cameron approaches the door a few moments later, smiling. "Hello, strangers. Do you want to come in?"

384

Peter turns his poster around and yells, "Move in with us, Cam!"

I nudge him. "You're supposed to ask, not demand."

Cameron laughs.

"Will you move in with us?" Peter asks.

Lewis joins us at the door. "What's going on?" His gaze drifts to the sign. He hooks his arm around Cameron's shoulders. "Trying to steal my son away, I see?"

Heat rises to my face. "It's not like that," I splutter.

Lewis laughs. "You need to relax, Euan. I've got used to the idea of the two of you being together. If it helps, I officially give you my blessing to date my son *and* ask him to move in with you. Just don't break his heart."

"Dad!" Cameron rolls his eyes.

"I don't intend to. Ever," I say.

Cameron blushes.

"Well? You didn't answer our question," Peter says.

"Will you move in with us?" I ask.

Cameron steps over the threshold and grasps my hand. "I would love to move in with you and Peter."

"Pack your things," Peter says.

"Now?"

"Yes, now. Chop-chop."

Cameron cracks up laughing. "I love this kid. Who says that?"

"My kid, apparently." I pull Cameron to me for a swift kiss. "Seriously, though, there's no time like the present. Move in with us. Now."

He kisses me back. "Gladly."

About the Author

Colette's personal love story began at university, where she met her future husband. An evening of flirting, in the shadow of Lancaster Castle, eventually led to a fairytale wedding. She's enjoying her own 'happy ever after' in the north of England with her husband, two beautiful children and her writing.

You can find all the ways to connect with Colette here: https://smart.bio/colettedavison/

All's Fair In Love and Pizza

Lane Hayes

Content Warning

Past bullying and derogatory language

For Bob, my carb-loving superhero and my original tall, dark, and dreamy. Love you to the moon and back!

Chapter One

Mateo

Boardwalk Pizza's lunchtime rush was the usual medley of starry-eyed tourists, loyal locals, and a smattering of students and faculty from the nearby college. Like now.

A family of five sporting sweatshirts advertising the roller coaster at the pier studied the menu on the wall behind the register while the old man with a newspaper folded under his arm and an unlit pipe in hand chatted with the professor of humanities. A gaggle of female students huddled at the end of the line, gazes locked on their cellular devices.

The family was currently vacillating between the extra-large meat lover's pizza and my cousin Sal's special with double pepperoni. They couldn't decide which sounded better, which meant they'd probably drag me into the decision-making process. I'd happily push the meat lover's, but I was feeling a little stabby that I was running the register at all.

I was supposed to be in the office, finalizing tomorrow's grocery list. This was Giovanni's job.

Where the hell was he?

"Everything just looks so good. What would you suggest?" the middle-aged mom asked, fluttering mega lashes at me.

See, I told you so.

"The meat lover's. Hands down, my favorite." I flashed a flirty smile, ignoring Mr. Smith's eye roll. The old geezer got testy when forced to wait too long for his daily slice of 'za and a side salad...hold the onions.

"Sold!" The woman twittered. Thankfully she and the rest of her family knew what they wanted to drink.

I rang her card and pushed a plastic marker across the battered wood counter. "Thank you. Here's your number. Your pizza should be out within ten minutes or less."

Mr. Smith toddled forward, his signature deadpan expression in place. He stuffed his newspaper into the front pocket of his tweed coat and tapped his pipe on his thumb. "I'll have the usual."

"You got it." I narrowed my eyes mischievously. "You sure you don't want to try Sal's special?"

"The last time I tried Sal's special, I had heartburn for three days. No, I'll stick to the usual." He pulled a ten-dollar bill from his pocket. "Keep the change."

Our prices had gone up a couple of times since the older man had last bothered checking—however, no one corrected him. Mr. Smith had been a regular for forty or so years, which meant that other than on my days off and during my short stint after college playing pro football, I'd seen this man more often than I saw some family members. He was a bit of a curmudgeon, but he'd played poker with my grandpa and had coached Little League with my uncle once upon a time, so yeah...I wasn't about to let him know he owed me an extra five bucks on the daily.

"Thanks, Mr. S." I held my hand up for a fist bump, chuckling when he raised his brow and shuffled off.

The college girls were next. No problem. I locked and loaded my most charming smile just as Vanni rushed in, tying a marinara-stained apron around his slim waist.

"Sorry about that. I had some snoopin' to do. You're not gonna believe who's moving in next door, Cuz." Vanni bumped my elbow and grinned like a fool at the pretty girls waiting at the counter.

My cousin was a little scatterbrained. However, he was great with customers. I let him take over, hanging the new orders on the line for Sal and Jimmy in the kitchen. I should have ducked out and made a beeline for the office, but I poured drinks and made myself useful instead. And yeah, I was curious.

"Who?" I asked, arranging a tray of drinks.

Vanni closed the register, waiting for the counter area to clear before he replied, "A football buddy of yours."

"Really? From Haverton?"

"Yeah, a big guy—a linebacker, I think. Rob something or other? He was standing outside with an inspector, talking about permits. I said hello, all friendly like. Introduced myself. He says, 'Nice to meet ya. I'm opening a bagel shop.'"

"Rob? I don't know who—oh, Rob Vilmer?"

Vanni snapped his fingers. "That's the guy. Rob's makin' bagels. Not regular bagels, either. Savory ones. Whatever the fuck that means. Heya, Mrs. Sanders. What can we get started for you today?"

Rob Vilmer. *Huh.* Talk about a blast from the past.

I delivered the drinks to table fourteen, pausing to inquire about their meals. How was the pepperoni today? Do you need any parmesan? That kind of thing. I made my rounds, strategically stopping near the entrance with the tray tucked under my arm to open the door for a group of students, then sneaked outside to peek at the flurry of action at the neighboring store.

The former owners had operated a candy emporium for decades. You know, the kind with big barrels of saltwater taffy and walls filled with classic treats—Pop Rocks, Abba-Zabas, and Sugar Babies. It had been a staple of my childhood, and my cousins and I had been sad to see it go. The Corcorans had given us first right of refusal three years ago, and though I'd appreciated the gesture, we hadn't been in a position to buy them out. My dad had just passed away, and keeping the pizza parlor afloat with my cousins had seemed daunting as fuck at the time.

It made me sad knowing that Dad had always wanted to expand, but paying our employees had been the number one goal that first year after he was gone. We'd been in mourning, and taking on additional debt had been the last thing on anyone's minds. The pressure had eased a bit in recent months, and that For Sale or Lease sign had taunted me.

Seriously. Just three weeks ago, I'd worked on a spread-

398

sheet and outlined a proposal for expansion. My cousins, Sal, Vanni, and Jimmy were interested too, and that had me fired up. This could be real. After three years of sadness and nonstop struggle, we might actually do something positive.

We'd talked about tinkering with the menu, tearing the wall down, and modernizing the space. The old, pockmarked linoleum floors, seventies' paneling, and dull lighting could make room for fancy tiles, leather booths, and contemporary accents.

Or not.

The agent had regretfully informed me that the property had been leased. Okay, that was a bummer, but I figured it might be the universe's way of letting me know the timing wasn't right. I had to hold on, be patient. Trust me, that was easier said than done lately. It pissed me off knowing we'd never get a chance like the one we'd just missed out on again.

All because of...bagels.

And Rob Vilmer.

We'd never been friends. Not really. Just teammates. I hadn't seen Rob since graduation. He'd been drafted and had played pro for a few years, and now he was back in Haverton...selling bagels. Color me curious.

I peered through the window at the cavernous space with a brick façade on one side, black-and-white tiled flooring, furnished with nothing but a cardboard table littered with rolls of design plans. Two men stood in the center: a shorter, balding guy pointed at the ceilings while a tall, massive dude with shaggy brown hair nodded, his arm draped over the shoulders of a woman with bouncy blond curls.

"Mateo, honey. Are you lost?"

I pivoted, rolling my eyes at the stout older woman with a jet-black bob who was decked out in her signature gold chains, hoop earrings, and leopard pantsuit. I kid you not.

"Hi, Aunt Sylvie." I kissed her on each cheek and tried not to wince when she reached up to smooth my wild hair into place, her bangles smacking my temple. "We have a new neighbor."

"Oh, go say hello." She shooed me with a red manicured hand toward the door and held up a pastry bag before hurrying to the pizzeria. "I brought cannolis for you boys. Better hurry, or they'll be gone."

"Thanks, I—"

"Mateo Cavaretti. Is that you?" The shaggy-haired bear of a man stood in the doorway with his arms crossed and his head cocked inquisitively.

Well, I was stuck now.

I transferred the tray to my left hand and offered my right. "Yeah, that's me. Rob, right?"

He shook my hand, nodding. "How've you been, man?"

"Uh...good. You're back in Haverton?" Captain Obvious. I know.

Rob smiled and damn, he had a nice smile. It met his twinkling blue eyes and gave him a warm, welcoming aura. "Yeah, I'm in the midst of a career change. Football to bagels. I guess we're neighbors."

I nodded, letting my gaze wander over his massive shoulders and thick chest. His navy sweater stretched at the seams around his biceps. He'd definitely grown since college. His face had matured too. Baby fat and wispy facial hair had given way to sharp cheekbones and a beard Paul Bunyan

400

would be proud of. Rob looked like what he was...a newly retired professional athlete in great shape, probably with plenty of money in the bank.

And in my red-checked shirt and stained apron while wielding a tray like a shield, it was fairly obvious that the past eight years hadn't been as kind to me. Don't get me wrong, I was proud to carry on the family business. I just hadn't intended this to be my whole fucking life.

Bitter much? Ugh, that wasn't a good look.

"I guess so," I agreed. "Why bagels?"

"My grandfather had a bagel business in Philly. I loved that place. I have these amazing memories of shaping the dough and watching it rise in boiling water. He had classic flavors...plain, sesame, everything—and he made these incredible breakfast sandwiches. I was thinking about investing in someone else's business, but when I heard about the candy shop closing, it was like a sign from above." Rob grinned. "College kids love bagels. And pizza. I bet they'd love pizza bagels."

Screech.

"Uh...come again?"

"My partner and I are gonna make savory bagels. Bagels with a twist. We'll sprinkle those in with my grandpa's tried and true recipes. Should be fun." He glanced at his watch and tipped his chin. "Hey, I gotta run. I'm sure we'll be seeing a lot of each other. Just like old times."

"Whoa. Wait up." I held my hand like a stop sign and stepped into his space. Bad move. I had to tilt my head to meet his eyes now, and that was weird. I was six one—not exactly a small dude, but that asshole had sprouted at least another two inches since college. I'd bet he was six foot six. And yes, he was an asshole. I hadn't thought so until a minute ago, but now... "You can't sell pizza bagels next to a pizza parlor."

"I can't?"

"No, you can't. It's brand assimilation or something. It's illegal."

"Illegal?" he scoffed. "I don't think so, Mateo. Bagels are bagels, pizza is pizza. But I was only kid—"

"Yeah, but a pizza bagel is a piece of dough that's dressed up to look like something it isn't. It's shady advertising, not to mention blatant customer poaching. Sell all the bagels you want, but don't sell pizza bagels. That's a great way to get off to a rotten start. You know what I'm saying?"

Rob regarded me for a long moment. "Are you threatening me?"

"Threaten is a strong word. I'm suggesting that you do the right thing."

"Or what?"

I snort-laughed in my most derisive, supremely irritating fashion. It was the kind of insincere and dismissive gesture that had pissed off opponents on the field years ago and still probably got under my cousins' skin. Nothing to brag about, but hey...I'd learned how to play with the big kids early. Rule number one: never show fear. Rule number two: never back down or give someone else the upper hand.

"I 'spose you'll find out." I turned on my heels, tray clenched to my chest as I sauntered next door.

Yeah, yeah. Look, maybe Rob wasn't the enemy. Maybe it

was a quirky act of fate that he'd happened to lease the property next to mine. The one I wanted.

Fortune had shined upon him and that was nice and all, but Boardwalk Pizza was an institution in this town. We were the experts, we were the ones with decades of experience, and we weren't going anywhere.

So Rob could shove his goddamn pizza bagel up his ass.

Chapter Two

Rob

Steam had to be billowing out of my ears. Was that asshat serious?

Definitely. And he was just...rude. And mean-spirited.

I didn't like Mateo Cavaretti. Not one little bit. That was disappointing 'cause I'd actually admired that prick in college. He'd been a great quarterback—cool under pressure with sharp instincts and a keen, strategic mind. If you'd have asked anyone from our team which one of us would have had a career in football, they'd have said Cavaretti. No question. He was a talented leader...who now ran a pizza parlor.

No shame there. I'd personally been biding my time for years so I could move on from the pros and start over. In Haverton.

Life had been sweet and simple in this town. I'd naïvely counted on slipping into that easy familiar rhythm and leaving the constant stress of the spotlight behind.

Apparently, stress just looked different here. Like a tall, dark, sinfully handsome hunk with a bad attitude. Great.

"Oh, wow. Dreamboat meeting! I'm so jealous you got to chat with him first. Is he as yummy up close?" Amber winked before craning her head as if hoping for one more glimpse of the pizza jerk.

"He's an asshole." I strode toward the plans the designer had left for the construction crew and pretended to study them in a weak attempt to get my temper under control.

"What? No!" She slumped against the doorjamb theatrically. "Why are the hot ones always either taken or horrible? Or lovely, but gay?"

"I highly doubt he's gay, but he's definitely horrible." I filled her in on our accidental meeting, finishing with an annoyed growl. "So now we need a recipe for pizza bagels."

Amber met me at the small table in the middle of the empty store, sweeping a golden curl from her eyes as she fixed me with a confused expression. "Pizza bagels? Since when are we making pizza bagels?"

"Since he threatened me like a thug. Screw him."

Amber joined me at the table, her hands on her hips. "Spite bagels. I see..."

It was hard not to chuckle at Amber's tough-chick energy. She was a pint-sized dynamo who'd never met a challenge she didn't like.

We'd been best friends since our senior year at Haverton, and it wasn't an exaggeration to say that she was the only person on the planet who really knew me. She'd been a calming constant during some turbulent times.

Sometimes, I felt as if I owed my sanity as well as my

undying gratitude to her. Sure, that sounded dramatic, but being a closeted gay athlete had been tougher than facing the league's biggest, meanest defensive lines.

Amber had stepped in as my plus one or my faux girlfriend or whatever the occasion called for more times than I'd like to admit.

"I don't mind. You can return the favor," she'd insisted. "I'll be a celebrity with my family if you spend one Thanksgiving with the Petersons, and if you agree to sit next to my super obnoxious brother-in-law and my Uncle Carl—who'll ask a hundred and fifty questions about the NFL—you'll achieve rock-god status."

I'd rolled my eyes. I mean, c'mon...I could discuss football all day long. What I couldn't do was let the world know that I was gay. No chance. Hell, I'd done my best to ignore my queerness until I was in college and by then, my career had already been on a trajectory that surpassed my wildest dreams. And once I'd hopped on that ride, there was no turning back.

The way I'd seen it, the closet had been my only choice. I'd been freaked out of my mind worrying what my teammates would think if they knew. Guys like Mateo. *Jesus.* I'd thought he was a solid dude in college and even though we hadn't been friends, he'd seemed trustworthy—like the kind of guy who wouldn't have ostracized me if he'd known my truth.

Incorrect.

I'd listened to my gut and was glad I'd kept my secret to myself. It had been excruciating at times but the right choice for me. Now...I was finally ready to come out. My parents, sisters, and a few close friends knew. But Amber was the only person who'd known about me all along.

How? Well...that was an embarrassing story.

She'd sat in front of me in English Lit at Haverton College and used to lend me pens or give me a piece of paper...whatever I'd forgotten that day. Objectively speaking, Amber had always been a cute girl with a halo of curls, apple cheeks, and pink lipstick. She'd worn cardigans and jeans rolled at the hem. And best of all, she'd been bubbly and easy to talk to.

So when my teammate had reminded me that I'd needed a date for a banquet that very evening, I'd panic-asked her out.

It went something like: "I know you don't know me very well, but will you go out with me? Not on a date-date. More of a friend-date."

"A friend?" she'd repeated.

"Yeah."

Amber had stared at me for an uncomfortably long time, sizing me up as our fellow students had weaved a path around us. "I get it."

"Get...what?"

"You need a beard."

I'd choked and stuttered through my denial, finally settling on, "I just need a friend."

And that knucklehead had said "Yes" or "You got it" or "Don't we all."

After college, I'd been drafted to New York and by sheer chance, Amber had been offered a marketing job in Manhattan. I'd played at the highest level with a new team in the N-

F-fucking-L. I'd had a cool apartment and access to anything my heart desired at the snap of my fingers—private jets, elite parties, quality drugs, beautiful willing women. I'd liked the apartment, but the rest...not my thing. Having a friend nearby who knew my secret and got me had made all the difference in the world.

We'd weathered our fair share of storms—the meaningless hookups, my secret relationship with a "straight" politician, her secret affair with a married man who'd sworn he was separated from his wife, her miscarriage and the emotional aftermath.

When I'd been traded to Dallas, I'd talked Amber into moving with me. She'd needed a fresh start, and I'd selfishly wanted someone I could trust nearby. She'd moved again with me to LA, enrolled in cooking school, and a year later, we'd begun hatching a business plan. Something we could open in Haverton.

Personally, I'd gotten tired of packing my shit every other year, tired of nursing my battered body, and tired of hiding. The idea of returning to a simpler life in a Northern California seaside town where fishing, tourism, and the small private college on the hill were the main draws appealed to me. No New-York-style nightlife, no Dallas bling, no LA-movie-star energy.

Haverton was a quintessential beach town. One turn off the freeway led to the boardwalk and a plethora of stores selling ocean-living accents, like picture frames embellished with seashells, sea-breeze-scented candles, and Haverton's famous pier and fun zone emblazoned on tea towels, coasters, and welcome mats. There were a couple of bars, a fifties-inspired diner, two bistros, one "nice" restaurant that always used fancy tablecloths and served amazing surf and turf, a yogurt store, a market, a laundromat and dry cleaners, a coffee shop, a post office...oh, yeah, and a fucking pizza parlor.

But they didn't have a bagel shop.

So here we were, eight years post-graduation, back at the starting line, ready to take on a new challenge.

I couldn't speak for Amber, but this place had always felt like a warm hug to me with its fresh air, clean streets, and plenty of interesting things to do. The college's proximity to town kept it from being too sleepy in the winter months, so I had every reason to believe a bagel store would do well.

The only snafu so far was the new neighbor.

"I didn't think Mateo was still here," I grumbled. "Such a jerk."

Amber snickered at my cranky face. "Oh, c'mon Robby. He can't be that bad."

"He is."

"Well, I vote for not antagonizing our new neighbor. Let's get this shop lookin' pretty and get those bagels rollin' out the door. What d'ya say?" She held her hand up for a high five.

I smacked my palm against hers and nodded.

"But we're still making pizza bagels."

Chapter Three

Mateo

I called a meeting with my cousins immediately after my run-in with the bagel boy. They thought I was over-reacting.

"Cuz, bagels and pizza are like apples and bananas. You can eat 'em both. One's superior," Vanni said. "But you know what I mean."

"It's more like Froot Loops and mac n' cheese," Sal interjected.

I was surrounded by lovable bozos, but maybe they were right.

According to my family, I was a hothead, and was it possible that Rob had just rubbed me the wrong way? Yeah, definitely.

Still, I kept an eye on the hullabaloo next door all fucking summer.

Two months of annoying pounding on walls, accompanied by the grind of a saw and delivery vans blocking the curb in front of our shop. Two whole fucking months. But I had to admit, it looked good.

The logo on the new black awning was sophisticated, the contemporary lighting, refurbished tile flooring, and the steel-and-glass cases were classy as fuck. And the smell of fresh bagels was mighty pleasant first thing in the morning.

And as my mom reminded me, "Any new business in town brings new customers our way."

Maybe this wouldn't be so bad.

The invite to the soft-opening soiree arrived on an ordinary Tuesday in September. It was one of those fancy engraved numbers with thick paper I associated with weddings. And get this...it was for Friday night—the busiest night of the week for us. What were they thinking? People ate bagels in the morning. No one wanted a bagel at six p.m., but I wasn't gonna miss this. I needed to know what we were up against.

I left Vanni and Jimmy in charge of the store and traded my apron and red-checked shirt for a black V-neck sweater and a nice pair of jeans. I wasn't trying to impress anyone, but I figured I should step up my game.

And I could tell this was a bougie event. A cascade of balloons framed the front door, and jazz music drifted from the speakers as waiters circled the room, passing out flutes of champagne and bagel-ish canapes.

I nodded to an acquaintance as I plucked a glass of bubbly from a tray along with a cream-cheese-and-lox everything bagel bite dusted with caviar. Holy crap, it was tasty. I grabbed another, then moved on to a feta-and-cucumber combo garnished with delicately shaved red onion that should have been gross but was equally amazing.

I mingled amongst the locals as I feasted on a variety of interesting concoctions, not one of them resembling a piece of pizza. Good. My ego had taken a beating over the past few years, and this minor concession felt like a win.

And since Rob the football hero had made an effort to be cool, I could do the same.

I spotted him at the far end of the shop, chatting with Coach Malveney and his wife and the pretty blond I'd assumed was Rob's wife or girlfriend until she'd set me straight last month.

"No, no. Rob and I are best friends and business partners. That's all," Amber had clarified.

Vanni had been happy to hear that. He thought she was cute and nice, and that I was an idiot for making enemies when I could have been angling for a sweet discount.

Whatever. I liked Amber fine, but Rob...

Well, now that pizza was off his menu, I could be cordial.

I set my empty flute on passing waiter's tray and approached the group. "Coach, Mrs. Malveney, it's nice to see you."

"Mateo! Oh, heavens! How are you?" Coach's wife threw her arms around me and kissed my cheek. I was afraid she was about to ruffle my hair for old times' sake, but she just beamed like a proud parent. "You're as handsome as ever."

"This guy has a big head, honey. Don't give him any reasons to strut like a peacock." Coach punched my biceps and pulled me in for a gruff, one-armed bro hug. "How ya doin'? Long time no see, kid."

"You need to eat more pizza, Coach," I joked.

"You think?" The older man patted his ample belly before gesturing between Rob and me. "What are the chances of two of my guys setting up shop next to each other? I feel like I should be yelling at you to remember curfew."

"Time flies," Amber singsonged, flashing a pretty grin my way. "Hi, Mateo. I'm so glad you made it."

"Congratulations," I said, managing a sincere smile.

She motioned between Rob and me. "I know we all went to college together, but it was ages ago. Sometimes I forget that you and Rob played football together."

I slid my gaze toward the big guy standing behind her. Rob wasn't exactly handsome—his jaw was too strong and his nose had been broken more than once. However, his size and build made you take a second glance. And as much as I hated to admit, he cleaned up well in a navy sport coat, blue oxford shirt, and jeans.

"We did. Thanks for the invite."

"Of course." Rob tilted his chin in acknowledgment. "Glad you could make it."

Coach slapped my back and chuckled lightly. "It's a treat to be able to brag that two of my star players are business owners in town. You're a great example to a younger generation."

And with very little prodding, he launched into a trip down memory lane involving a fourth-quarter Hail Mary at a championship game. Not gonna lie, that was one of my best throws ever, but reliving college glory days with a guy who'd taken his career to the next level was a little humbling. Unfortunately, it was impossible to walk away from Coach without being rude, and the man had always been good to me.

Amber and Mrs. Malveney drifted into another conversation, but just as Coach had settled into storyteller mode, a parent of one of his current players interrupted. Rob and I waved off his apologies and stepped aside. And okay, maybe I should have left well enough alone and let the guy enjoy his party, but I was curious about the renovation. We were definitely going to need to make some improvements next door, and it seemed like a harmless conversational segue.

"What's your new kitchen like?"

He didn't reply right away. Instead, he motioned for me to follow him, deftly maneuvering through the press of bodies. The brick wall dividing the store from the kitchen provided a nice sound barrier. I could actually hear myself think as I studied the stainless steel ovens, the large kettle for boiling bagels, the commercial-grade refrigerator, and the ample workspace with a twinge of envy.

Rob spread his arms wide. "This is where the magic happens."

"*Huh.* Well, this is really—" I stopped short and pointed at the congested counter. "That's a fucking pizza bagel."

Yep, lo and behold, there on a large silver tray were dozens of pizza canapes—sausage, pepperoni, a sprig of basil, feta, goat cheese, pine nuts. They looked gourmet, and damn it, they looked delicious.

"Try one," he urged.

"No, thanks."

"C'mon, don't be a dick." Rob picked up a pesto, goat

cheese, and sausage bagel bite and offered it to me on a napkin.

"I refuse on principle," I growled. "I told you not to—"

He shoved the bagel bite into my mouth.

The fucking nerve. And you know what was worse? It was delicious.

Of course, that was beside the point.

I glowered as I wiped the corners of my mouth. It might have been my imagination, but I could have sworn his gaze followed my tongue with the kind of attention that gave me all the wrong ideas. And what the actual fuck was I thinking? Rob Vilmer was off-limits, all caps. Not only was he most likely straight as an arrow, he was a minor celebrity *and*...he was a jerk.

"Good, isn't it?" Rob's smile didn't reach his eyes. It was predatory and dangerous, and damn, that did something for me. All the wrong things.

"It's edible."

He barked a laugh. "You're a piece of work, Cavaretti."

"Me? You're shamelessly poaching my business!"

"I'm not poaching your business. For fuck's sake, man. I never intended to make pizza bagels, but—"

"You did. So, congratulations, you've just started a pizza war."

Christ, I sounded like a moron or a child who was pissed at the meanie who'd called dibs on his favorite swing at recess. I hated coming across as a dumb jock to someone who used to know me as being relatively cool under pressure. Now...well, I wasn't at my best.

Rob shook his head in undisguised amusement. "A pizza

war. That's a new one. And how does that work? Are there rules in a pizza war, like...only five pepperonis on each slice or a quarter cup of mozzarella and it has to be from a specific region in Italy or—"

"Funny. Very funny. Hey, I came tonight 'cause I was curious. I'd hoped you'd done the right thing, but no, you actually made the pizza bagels."

"So what? You're not gonna bully your way into setting *my* menu. Nice try, but I don't work for you."

"It's called common fucking courtesy," I growled, stepping into his space. "It's called not being a jackass."

Rob lips twisted unpleasantly as he nudged the toe of his shoe to mine. "How am *I* the jackass here?"

"You're openly competing with an established business in a small town. That's fucking hostile."

He knit his eyebrows fiercely. "I'm making fucking bagels. Bagels don't compete with pizza."

"Until they do," I countered.

Geez, his eyes were the clearest shade of blue and his lips were full and— *Oh, no. No hate-lusting after the enemy allowed.*

"You're out of line or out of your mind...or both," he huffed.

"Right...to you, this might be a joke. To us, pizza is a legacy that my family has carried on for generations."

Rob rolled those fucking pretty eyes and paced toward the refrigerator. "I never said or insinuated that this was a joke. But I will say that I wouldn't have asked Amber to come up with new pizza recipes if you hadn't basically challenged

416

me to do it. So now...you bet your ass I'm making these bagels."

"Two can play that game." I shot him a condescending smirk and showed some restraint by not grabbing another bagel bite on my way out the door. "It's on, Vilmer."

"What's that supposed to mean?" he called after me.

Fuck if I knew. I was spouting gibberish and digging a nice hole for myself.

Yeah, in string of lows, I'd officially hit a new one.

Chapter Four

Mateo

"Pizza bagels? What the fuck?"

"Should be easy. We just do the dough different. The rest is the same," I bluffed.

My cousins treated me to a three-way blank stare from across the counter. It was almost comical since they all looked alike. Well, not exactly. Sal was heavyset and balding, Jimmy was a gym rat with copious tats, and Vanni reminded me of a skinny rock star. But the Cavaretti genes were strong. We all had olive skin, dark hair, prominent noses, and some mystery family trait that made it obvious that we were related.

Sal broke the silence. "What are you up to, Teo? You don't just up and start making bagels. You gotta do the research. We lack some crucial equipment that costs money."

Vanni nodded. "Yeah, we don't have that thing they use. What's it called?"

"A kettle," Jimmy replied. "You gotta boil them in water,

and there's the dough, and who's gonna do it all plus make the pizza?"

"You could ask Ma," Vanni suggested.

"You kidding me? I'm not working with Ma. Or Aunt Therese...no offense, Teo. I love your mom, but this"—Sal gestured between the four of us—"this is ours."

"Fuckin' right it's ours."

"No one said it's not and..."

I held my hands up in surrender, or defeat, as the three brothers talked over each other, Cavaretti-style. Dinners at Aunt Sylvie's or my mom's were noisy affairs, and that was putting it mildly. There were a lot of us, and no one was particularly reserved. I was an only child, but Uncle Sal and Aunt Sylvie had three daughters plus these three dingdongs, ten grandkids and counting. Not to mention the in-laws.

A little Cavaretti backstory: Our great-grandparents had immigrated from Italy in 1900 and opened a restaurant in Brooklyn. One of their sons inherited the business, and the other moved west to Haverton. So I hadn't been kidding when I'd told Rob this was a family legacy. Boardwalk Pizza had been passed on from generation to generation. This place had been Dad's and Uncle Sal's pride and joy. But they were both gone now, and it was up to us to carry on.

Jimmy and Vanni were closer in age and argued about everything while Sal and I were the practical ones. My degree in accounting from Haverton pushed me into the business portion while Sal oversaw the kitchen. The others pitched in to do whatever was needed. We had a few non-Cavarettis on the payroll, but the four of us made all the big decisions.

Like bagels.

I put two fingers in my mouth and whistled. "We agreed to bring the pizzeria into the twenty-first century, and maybe we can't make all the changes we wanted to right away...like busting the wall open, but we can start with a few adjustments to the menu and have some fun with it. What d'ya say?"

Sal frowned. "I hate it."

"Me too," Jimmy agreed.

"Sorry, Cuz. I'm with them. Why are we fixin' something that's not broken, ya know?" Vanni checked his watch. "Are we done here? I got a date."

I ignored Vanni and continued. "I found a used kettle online, and it's a great deal. I propose that I handle the pizza bagels. We'll do some taste testing and if they're good, which they will be—we'll stick 'em on the menu."

Another three-way glance.

This time Vanni and Jimmy nodded in acquiescence. "Fine, why not?"

A couple of fist bumps later, they headed home or out for the night, leaving me with a suspicious-looking Sal. I pulled the till from the register and took it to the office, unsurprised when he followed me.

"What's wrong?"

"You tell me, Teo. Seems like a lot of fuss for a small gain. I'm trying to figure out where your head is at," he replied, crossing his beefy tattooed arms as he leaned against the jamb.

"Healthy competition never hurt anyone."

"Right," he drawled, his voice dripping sarcasm. "Why I do I think this is about football, not pizza?"

"Huh?"

"Rob's the guy who got drafted, played for New York, Dallas, LA. He went to the fucking Super Bowl. Impressive career. And maybe you're a little bummed it wasn't you."

"Fuck you, Sal and good night." My smile was smarmy at best, but unfortunately, it didn't encourage him to move on.

Sal's gaze wandered to the photo on the wall of our dads standing in front of Boardwalk Pizza, arms around each other, shit-eating grins on their faces as if they had the world at their feet.

"Healthy competition is well and good, but sometimes I think you're in competition with yourself, looking for one play that's gonna change your life and put you in the win column."

I fixed him with a blank stare. "What do pizzas and bagels have to do with winning at life?"

"You tell me, Teo. You tell me."

I didn't have an answer for that. At least not one that sounded sane.

But damn, I couldn't help feeling like I needed a win. For my dad, my uncle...my family. The years I'd lost had to mean something. I was aware that was a melodramatic take on what probably amounted to nothing more than an adult temper tantrum. Sue me.

The thought of a former teammate returning to Haverton like a prodigal son and setting up shop next door was so far under my skin, it wasn't funny.

Or...maybe it was funny and the joke was on me.

Chapter Five

Rob

Great H Bagels opened for business on a cloudy Saturday morning in autumn. The windows were so clean, they sparkled off the glare of the pendant lights over the counter. The glass cases adjacent to the marble counter were stuffed to capacity with a medley of flavored bagels: plain, poppyseed, onion, chocolate, everything—you name it, we had it.

We also offered specialty gourmet creations like the ones we'd served at our preopening party and a "build your own bagel sandwich" option, along with a variety of standard sandwiches ranging from breakfast to turkey, roast beef, chicken salad, and tuna.

Oh yeah, and we had pizza bagels.

I highly doubted we'd sell many, but I had no regrets. Every time I thought of that altercation or whatever the fuck had happened with Mateo in my kitchen, I got hot under the collar. Seriously. I wanted to punch a hole in the wall or punch his freaking gorgeous face. *Ugh*. As much as I hated to admit it, Mateo was hotter now than he'd been in college. Too bad he was a dick.

Back then, I'd used every superpower in my arsenal not to notice his chiseled features and sexy ass. I noticed now, and it pissed me off. Thus, the pizza bagels...which, by the way, weren't terrible.

They weren't flying off the shelves, though. Our best sellers so far were the baker's dozen, the breakfast sandwich supreme with scrambled eggs, avocados, red onions, and special secret sauce...oh, and our gourmet smoked lox and caviar was a big hit. In fact, in the two weeks we'd been open, business had been fantastic.

Haverton liked bagels.

Not that I was surprised. Amber and I had done our research. A college-slash-beach town practically required a bagel shop, and it was criminal that the residents had gone without for so long. Of course, I knew that to some degree, *I* was the novelty.

The name alone was a nod to the football team. Haverton Hawks were also known as the Great Hawks and the school itself, Great H. As an alumni and former player, I had no qualms with advertising my personal connection to the town. My jerseys from college and every pro team I'd played on had been framed and lovingly hung on the brick wall. It was a statement: I'm one of you. I belong.

Of course, if the bagels sucked, the novelty would wear off fast. But we'd hired a talented crew and with my grandfather's recipe book and Amber's marketing and culinary skills, we were in fine shape. Much to our neighbor's chagrin.

I still couldn't believe he was selling pizza bagels. Did I mention that Mateo Cavaretti was a dick?

"Mr. Vilmer, will you sign my shirt, please?"

I stepped away from the counter and smiled at the kid who might have been around ten or eleven. "Sure. Got a pen?"

His dad happened to have a marker on hand. I didn't recognize him, but apparently, we'd had a statistics class together in college. He wanted to talk football, though, so I obliged for a minute or so before moving on to greet the other customers in line.

I was the resident celebrity here, and I knew it was important to use whatever we had to get people in the door, but I wasn't naturally gregarious. I preferred being behind the counter, ringing up sales. However, the busier we were, the more distracting my presence was at the register.

Customers wanted a sporty side scoop with their bagels. What was Tom Brady like? Which QB currently had the best arm? Who was my favorite teammate? Where had I liked playing the best? I never minded answering questions, but being the focus of attention got old. I found myself dipping out of the shop for a breather, which inevitably led me to Boardwalk Pizza.

I didn't always go inside. No, I was more of a lurker.

Other than Mateo, they were a nice group. Vanni was a goofball, Jimmy was a cool dude who was a little full of himself, and Sal was reserved but always friendly. If Mateo wasn't at the counter, I'd say hello with a bag of free bagels and cream cheese on hand, order a slice, and shoot the shit for a minute or two.

Sometimes a growly Mateo would make an appearance and that was awkward, but whatever. I wasn't going anywhere, so he might as well get used to seeing me around.

Besides if there was a pizza-bagel war happening, I needed to know the rules.

I'd assumed his initial strategy would be to ignore me until he had a competitive product and I'd been right. Vanni had spilled the beans to Amber and me about the new kettle they'd purchased. He'd said it was bound to be a write-off, but a week later, Boardwalk Pizza featured their first ever pizza bagel...a basic marinara, cheese, and pepperoni number.

I'd wanted to buy one, but Mateo was at the counter that day.

Our conversation had gone something like this:

Me, tapping the glass: "I'll take one of those."

Mateo, shaking his head, a feral gleam in his eye. "I'm not selling you a pizza bagel. Sorry, champ."

"How mature of you. I'll pay double."

"No."

"Triple."

Mateo had turned away and returned with a slice of their pizza of the day. "Take it and beat it. Next in line, please."

Fucker.

Vanni had brought me a pizza bagel over an hour later. On the house. "Sorry about that. Teo's a hothead. We can use an expert opinion, but I gotta tell you, I think these are okay. Not as good as yours, but still decent."

I'd agreed. So had Amber, who'd laughed at the idea of our pizza-bagel war.

"It seems more like two jocks pissing on each other's cleats for funsies. Guys are so weird." She'd snorted.

True. But you know what? Mateo had started it, so when he'd slipped in the door to clandestinely check out *our* business, I'd given him a taste of his own medicine.

"Your money is no good here," I'd said in greeting, a phony grin pasted to my mug. "Anything you want is on the house."

Mateo had cocked his head and frowned. "I don't want anything."

"You're here. You must want something," I'd taunted.

"Yeah, I wanted to see if you'd come to your senses."

"Nope. I guess that means we're still at war."

"Guess so," he'd grumbled, turning on his heels.

Yep, the rules of war had been unclear. That was until Mateo renamed his pizza bagel, "The Best in Town."

It was a subtle dig, but I couldn't ignore it. I retaliated by sticking mini pennants in our pizza bagels, labeled, "The Original." And "The Best Ever." Hokey and childish? Yes. And I couldn't wait till someone told him.

Sure enough, Mateo stormed in the next day to scoff at my pizza bagel and made a snide remark about the pennants. "Gee, I wonder if the owner ever played football."

Fuck that guy.

Yet here I was, sneaking out of my own store to see what my unpleasant neighbor was up to now...because I kind of got a cheap thrill from winding him up. It was as if I'd tapped into a hidden power. Not as exciting as mind reading or an invisibility cloak, but knowing I'd needled my way under Mateo's skin was oddly gratifying.

426

If I were completely honest, there was more to this feud for me. Try not to laugh, but...I had the attention of the hottest guy in town, the most popular jock in college, the goddamn star quarterback.

Time had marched on. We were adults, and he was still straight. Plus, he didn't like me. *But* he noticed me.

Mateo peeked into my store window when he thought I wasn't looking. He asked Amber about me, mentioned me to his cousin. Mateo Cavaretti was thinking about me. Often.

I liked it.

And today, I was feeling brave.

I spotted Mateo behind the counter, sporting his ubiquitous red-and-white checked shirt and a grungy white apron. The combo should have given "picnic with a pig" vibes but instead was annoyingly sexy.

That could have just been him.

Mateo had a great smile, damn it. His eyes crinkled, his full lips parted and snagged on one of his incisors, and his dimples were the stuff of teen magazines. He was the very definition of tall, dark, and dreamy. Always had been. I hated that the sight of him made my pulse skitter, but it fascinated me too. After all this time, Mateo Cavaretti still got to me.

"Ah, look who's here. Business must be slow," he greeted me as I approached the counter.

"Nope. The line is out the door." Slight exaggeration, but we were busy enough. And so was he. There wasn't anyone waiting for service, but almost every table was taken.

"Good for you. If you're here looking for new ideas... don't. I've decided to trademark everything in the store. If you steal any—"

"Steal? Are you fucking joking?"

"Watch the language, Vilmer. This is a family establishment. My ma would smack you upside the head if she heard you talkin' like that. We keep it clean here."

I pointed at his messy apron. "Ri-ght...real clean. And who's stealing from who? You bought a bagel kettle."

"You made a *pizza* bagel! Pizza!" Mateo picked up a pizza box and tapped it obnoxiously. "Look at this...established in Brooklyn, New York in 1900, established in Haverton in 1958. Same year the Dodgers moved to LA. That means we've been here for well over sixty years. You haven't even been open sixty days, genius. So don't twist my words or—"

"Oh, look at you guys...getting along." Amber breezed into the restaurant, waving at Vanni through the kitchen partition before nudging my elbow at the counter.

"He started it," Mateo said.

She huffed. "Don't you think this feud is kind of silly?"

"No," we replied in unison.

"Well, it is. It's petty and ridiculous and—" Amber paused abruptly, pushing an errant curl behind her ear as she cast a wary glance between us. "Oh, my God. Why didn't I think of this sooner?"

"Think of what?" one of us asked.

"I have an idea. A great one!" Her mischievous smile made me nervous. Especially when she rubbed her palms together in scheming mode. "Can we talk somewhere private?"

Mateo skewered her with a puzzled look, but his

428

animosity for me didn't apply to Amber. And like me...he was probably curious.

He motioned for Vanni to take over, then led us to his office, located down a narrow hallway opposite the kitchen.

This was my first backstage pass to one of my college haunts, and I felt almost giddy with anticipatory nostalgia.

Like every other football player at Haverton, Boardwalk Pizza had been a post-practice staple for me. As Mateo had implied, it was as much a part of the town as the amusement park at the pier and the statue of Colonel Haverton that stood at the top of the hill on campus, a la Christ the Redeemer in Rio de Janeiro. But I'd never seen the kitchen up close or checked out the collage of family photos along the narrow hallway.

The kitchen was smaller than ours and full of well-used appliances. Sal minded one of the giant pots on the behemoth stove while Jimmy kneaded dough at the flour-strewn prep space. They were too engrossed in their work to notice us, or possibly couldn't hear anything above the din of the Springsteen classic on the radio. I wanted a closer peek at the small bagel kettle, but the collage wall was much more interesting.

The faded colors and styles of clothing hinted at the bygone eras. Grandparents, parents, aunts, uncles, cousins and more cousins...and Mateo. I spied a photo of him in his high school football uniform. The roguish smile and mischievous glint were still present, but his youthful cockiness had soured into mistrust and weariness now.

Still hot, though.

Mateo sat on the corner of a battered desk littered with

paper work and an old computer. "I'd offer you a seat, but...I don't have one."

"No worries. I'm tight on time." Amber pulled her cell from her pristine apron and typed a message.

"What's this idea?" I prodded.

"A bake-off." She had the nerve to grin like a loon.

"Huh?" Mateo and I shared matching befuddled glances.

"Mrs. Malveney put the idea in my head at the opening party and after weeks of listening to you two nitpick and one-up each other, I think it's time to do something positive with all this...testosterone." She circled her wrist meaningfully. "I have a degree in marketing, and I'm good at highlighting positives to sell a product. I've been wracking my brain on ways to spin your feud, and it's really so obvious. We'll advertise it as a fund raiser for the football team, but let's be honest, it's great for business for both of us. Local jocks duking it out over pizza and bagels...for charity."

"A charity bake-off?"

Amber beamed. "Yep! Brilliant, huh?"

"Wouldn't that contest be between me and you?" Mateo asked. "I thought you were the head chef."

"Yep! Rob's a total disaster in the kitchen," she replied, her gaze dropping for a moment to the phone buzzing in her hand.

"Hey!"

She slugged his arm playfully. "You know it's true, and that's what would make this fun. Okay, look, I gotta run. They need me next door. I'll come up with some ideas, but I'm loving the contest concept with a couple of friendly judges. Maybe a food blogger or two and members of the current Great H football team. It's October, and they're in the middle of their season. The timing couldn't be better. We've got to strike while the iron is hot...and all that jazz. Details to follow! Toodle-oo!"

She was gone in a blur of golden curls, leaving an awkward silence.

Mateo lifted one eyebrow, cartoon-style. "I feel like I just got run over by an eighteen-wheeler."

"That's Amber for you." I scratched my nape and exhaled. "Uh...it's not a terrible idea."

He nodded thoughtfully as he stood. "No, it's a good one. But she's your business partner, so I gotta think this is gonna be rigged in your favor."

"Is it possible for you to not be a dick for one whole minute?" I fumed. "Jesus, I don't remember you being a cynical fucknut with a martyr complex when we were teammates."

Mateo scoffed. "How would you know what I was like? We barely knew each other in college."

"Except we were on the same fucking team. I guess you were too busy shining your halo while the defense did your dirty work to notice anyone else."

Okay, I had no idea why I'd said that. It wasn't true. Mateo had been a great QB. It was a stupid dig designed to get a reaction...and it worked.

"*My* halo? Not sure where that's coming from, but it's rich coming from a blowhard linebacker who's got his jersey plastered on every inch of spare wall in a fucking bagel store." He lowered his voice, his lips twisted in an evil sneer. "And you're the one who wants to do cross-promo advertising. Why is that? It's like you need me or something."

Grrr. I leaned into his space—so close, I could see the vein pulse at his temple. Unfortunately, I also noticed that his eyelashes were ridiculously long and that his lips were full and lush and— *Stop.*

I clung to anger, stabbing my finger at Mateo's chest. "Nice one, but I don't need you. Unlike you, I'll figure it out myself. Must have been sweet to have a business handed to you, but gee, my daddy didn't give me a shop to run or—"

"You fucking prick." Mateo raised his fist as if to punch me.

I dodged him and collided with the desk. He spun around with his dukes up again. No thanks. I'd made a career out of wrestling on the field and had the battle scars to prove it. I had no intention of adding more. Besides, this wasn't how real adults dealt with frustration, for fuck's sake.

I captured Mateo's wrists and pulled him against me to keep him from using his legs or body weight as a weapon. He was strong, but I was stronger, not to mention bigger and thicker all over.

"We're not doing this," I growled.

"Like hell we're not. You don't know anything about me or my family or my..."

Shit, Mateo was on a roll now, and he didn't seem to have noticed that my grip had loosened in his tirade. I couldn't follow what he was saying. Something about family and pizza and blah, blah, blah.

Hey, it was probably interesting info, but the more fired up he got, the more I noticed *him*—his thick brows, the flecks

432

of gold in his brown eyes, his chiseled cheekbones, and that mouth—so angry, so tough, so fierce, so goddamn hot. I was staring and I knew it, but I couldn't look away.

After what felt like twenty minutes, he finally shut up.

I had to let his wrist go and say something...anything. I was frozen, though. So was Mateo. He didn't bother shaking me off. He narrowed his gaze slightly, lips parted. *So damn sexy.*

Heat rose between, us and wave upon wave of something potent yet undefined rushed in like high tide. I couldn't tell if I was in danger of combusting or drowning or in some kind of freefall, unmoored and unhinged. All because of him.

It pissed me off.

And just like that, my mouth was on Mateo's. And he welcomed me.

He thrust his tongue inside, my fingers in his hair, his fist clutching at my shirt. I couldn't think, and I could barely breathe. It was as if there were a system malfunction and I no longer had control of my body. This was all instinct—like it had been when I was in uniform, wrestling an opponent to submission. I didn't want to tackle Mateo now. I wanted to own him.

He dragged my bottom lip between his teeth and ravaged my mouth again, driving his tongue so deep he hit the back of my throat. He eased the pressure but not the intensity. I lowered my hands to his ass and drew him close. *Holy fuck.* Yeah, I'd been hoping for friction, but the feel of his hard cock through two layers of denim was too damn much. I was gonna come in my jeans.

I'd had some hot and uninhibited sexy times, but I'd

always been in control. Neither of us was now. The only saving grace was that I knew without a doubt that Mateo felt it too.

I held his face still in an attempt to resurface, licking his jawline and biting his earlobe. "Stop. We're not doing this here."

He blinked as if in a daze. "I—you. I didn't know you were..."

"Yeah. I am."

Mateo went perfectly still before pulling away and glancing toward the door. "This is...a new one. My cousins are probably debating which one of us is walking out of here alive."

I didn't know what to say to that or what should happen next. My God, I'd just tongue-fucked my neighbor-slash-rival and former teammate...who hated me. Talk about awkward.

"Right. Um..."

"I'm not gonna tell anyone, if that's what you're worried about," he assured me in a softer tone.

"I'm out. I mean...not all the way out, but it's in the works."

Mateo cocked his chin curiously. "In the works?"

"According to my manager, if I intend to come out publicly, I should tell the story myself and avoid giving someone ammunition to use against me. 'Pro linebacker, gay... read all about it.' " I shrugged uncomfortably. "I'm not sure who'll care, but I'll do it when I'm ready."

"Oh." He shoved a hand through his hair. "I'm out. The people who matter know, anyway. I stopped worrying about the rest of the world a while ago. I'm not a football star anymore. I'm just a boring guy who works in the family business. The same business you can't decide if you want to crap on or shamelessly copy."

"Has anyone ever told you that you're very fucking difficult?"

Mateo widened his eyes comically and gave a self-deprecating shrug. "Once or twice. But you're the one playing the big-shot card."

"What's that supposed to mean?"

"Mr. NFL, Great H alum. And like a true kiss-ass, you even named your store after the college. Then you emphasize your coolness with a few jerseys on the wall and oh, so slyly put a pizza on your menu. C'mon, Vilmer. The only thing I like about you is the part I just found out." He gave me a heated once-over, lingering on my crotch.

I knew I had to proceed with caution, but the bolt of desire threw me off guard. No one had looked at me with that kind of hunger in a long, long time.

With a speed I hadn't tapped into in a while, I pushed him against the wall and caged him between my arms.

"Same," I panted, dragging my erection alongside his.

Our noses brushed and our gazes held steady. If he were anyone else, I'd ask for his number so we could meet up later and get this out of our systems, but...Mateo? I didn't know what to do with him.

So I pushed away and headed for the door.

Noise from the kitchen and the pizza parlor came rushing in, effectively breaking the spell. What the hell had I done? This was a disaster in the making.

Chapter Six

Mateo

mber was nothing if not relentless. She'd been at the shop every day, chatting with Sal and me about the football fund raiser. Yesterday, she'd come with a spiel about getting the local paper involved and starting a social media campaign. It seemed like more effort than necessary, but then again, Boardwalk Pizza was woefully behind the times when it came to marketing.

My dad and uncle used to advertise in the yellow pages and in the church bulletin once a month. We always donated and gave back to the community, but not on a grand scale. And we'd certainly never had an ad campaign or done anything out of the box. Christ, we hadn't changed our logo in sixty-plus years.

So yes, I was intrigued by Amber's proposal. I might have been more jazzed about it if Rob wasn't involved, though. Now he was a baffling loose end, and I didn't know what to do about him.

436

Okay, not true. I wanted to fuck him. Or he could fuck me. I wasn't picky.

It was a classic conflict of interests. I was a pro at those. It was always a case of one thing being good for me and the other, my ruin. Or just a really stupid risk.

That hadn't kept me from wandering into his shop after hours every day this week with a thin excuse or a veiled complaint just to see him.

Your delivery guy blocked my truck in the alley this morning.

Your trash bin should be emptied earlier in the day.

The bagel line shouldn't cross our entrance.

I made sure Amber wasn't around. This shit was just for Rob. I wanted to test him and maybe convince myself that I'd imagined that scene in my office.

But guess what? It was real.

'Cause every night that I strutted into Great H Bagels, pumped with manufactured angst, intent on riling him, I ended up with my back to the wall, humping and grinding my boner against Rob's while we sucked face.

Like now.

I didn't have to say a word. He'd taken one look at me, locked the door, and marched into his office—which, by the way, was a hell of a lot nicer than mine. My list of daily gripes were forgotten at the sight of this big, burly former linebacker wearing a plaid shirt, worn jeans, and a scowl. He was my kryptonite, and he had no fucking idea. Tough, tall, and rugged...sign me the fuck up.

If we'd met at a bar or a club, I would've already offered my ass. No doubt about it. The vision of bending over Rob's office desk was my new fantasy. I wanted to climb him like a tree, suck his cock, and swallow every drop of him, but I couldn't tell him that.

This was a delicate situation and an unexpected development. I had to treat this with care.

So I admired his muscular biceps, messy hair, and his impressive package, then gestured in the general direction of the entrance. "Your sign is crooked."

Rob crossed his arms, his expression stony and unreadable. "Oh, really?"

"Really. You should fucking fix that."

"Make me."

A crackle of heat and anticipation rose in the charged silence. We could have been a couple of gunslingers in the Wild West, fingers on triggers, wondering who was going to strike first. It was me this time.

I pushed Rob's chest and pounced, slamming my mouth over his. My heartbeat rang in my ears as I devoured him with a ferocity that made my head spin. The scent of his cologne and sweat and something uniquely him hit me hard. I didn't understand my reaction to him. It was reckless and extreme. So not like me, it was scary.

And get this...I whimpered like a kitten when he hooked his fingers in my belt loops and yanked me closer. Here we were again, making out with hands roving, hungry tongues, and the sweet tease of friction.

I managed to unbuckle Rob's belt, but I moved slowly, giving him plenty of opportunity to stop me. He didn't. I unzipped him, hiked his T-shirt out of the way, and lowered his jeans. Then I gripped his shaft through his cotton boxer briefs, running my thumb along the head of his cock and the precum leaking at his tip.

Rob broke the kiss with a gasp, eyeing me curiously...or cautiously. I couldn't be sure. I stilled my hand and awaited the verdict—stop or go?

"On your knees," he commanded in a deep timbre.

That should have pissed me off. I didn't like being told what to do. I wanted to be in charge, wanted to call the shots. Not tonight.

I obeyed in a flash, shoving the elastic band over his hips to free his erection.

And holy shit, I was salivating. No joke. He was thick and hard and so damn perfect. I glanced up...for permission? Maybe. Again, that wasn't like me, but he'd set something in motion, and I sensed a power play that couldn't be ignored.

Rob inclined his chin, and it was all the invitation I needed. I gripped his length, squeezing his base slightly as I licked a path to his slit. I twirled my tongue at his crown, lapping up precum like a hungry cat before opening wide. He set a hand on my head and groaned, low and needy.

I hummed around his cock, sucking, licking, stroking. It had been a while for me and God, it felt so good to worship dick. No, not just any dick. This was Rob fucking Vilmer. My memories of him in college might have been hazy, but I'd watched his NFL games. I'd seen his powerful body in action, obliterating opponents like a warrior in battle. He was wildly strong and fierce, and nothing turned me on quite as much as knowing he was hard for me.

I couldn't drag this out and make him beg me. Not this

time. I wanted to deep-throat him, taste him, swallow every drop of—

Rob pushed my forehead in warning, pulling his cock free and panting as he met my gaze.

"I'm gonna come."

"Give it to me," I demanded.

He squeezed his eyes shut but didn't protest. I pumped his shaft, flicking my tongue under his crown and sucking it. Two seconds later, he erupted with a strangled growl. I took it all. Everything he had.

I sat on my heels, wiping the corner of my mouth as I looked up at Rob blinking his way back to reality. Was I feeling smug and a little satisfied? Fuck, yeah, I was.

"C'mere." Rob pulled me to my feet and held my head in his hands as he ravaged me.

I was so caught up in filthy dirty kisses, I barely registered that he'd undone my jeans until he was jerking me off. It was sensory overload in the extreme, and there was no way to fall apart with dignity. He silenced my roar with his mouth, softening the connection as I slowly returned to reality.

Oh.

Shit.

I just blew my neighbor.

Christ, a few days ago, I'd sworn I'd never touch Rob again, and look at me now. I'd folded like a house of cards.

There was no point in pretending we didn't know exactly where this was going, but I was me, so...

"We shouldn't do this." I plucked a few tissues from the box on his desk, head lowered as I cleaned up.

Rob straightened my collar, and met my glowering expression with a sunny grin. "No, but we will."

I frowned, unable to think of a single F U or a sweet comeback to put him in his place.

The best I could do was, "Do something about your crooked sign. This is a respectable neighborhood."

His melodic laughter followed me all the way out the door. And I couldn't blame him.

Not one little bit.

Chapter Seven

Mateo

The afternoon crowd had dwindled to a few regulars, a couple in the corner checking out a map on an iPad, and a few football players from Great H. I didn't advertise that I was once one of them. I didn't have to. My bigmouth cousin usually did the honors.

"You know who this guy is?" Vanni paused in the middle of ringing up Sal's special to hike his thumb in my direction. "Former award-winning QB for you guys. He took Great H to the championship three years in a row for the first time in like...forty-five years. And they won. Did you say extra cheese?"

"Uh...yes, sir." The fresh-faced kid politely smiled the way I probably had when introduced to someone who'd been relevant while I was in fourth grade and my biggest worry had been beating my cousins' scores at whatever video game we'd been obsessed with at the time.

I wasn't proud to admit that I'd gone through a period of

feeling ashamed that I hadn't achieved more after college. You might say I was a work in progress in that area, and yeah, Rob's presence had certainly ignited those old feelings of inadequacy, but I was getting better at letting go of the past.

Football wasn't my life anymore and hadn't been for years. That was okay. The trick was to figure out if running this pizza parlor was going to be enough for me.

But I'd save my heavier thoughts for after business hours. In the meantime, I fist-bumped the kid and wished him good luck at the game this weekend.

Vanni set the new order on the rack, raising his brows in question. "You goin' to the game?"

"Friday night? No, I'm working, genius." I filled drinks from the soda machine and set them on the counter.

"Oh, well...one of us could cover for you if you want to go," he offered.

"Thanks, but—"

"Yeah, yeah...another time," Vanni intercepted, quickly changing the topic. "I hear we're doing the bake-off with the bagel folks."

"No one agreed to a bake-off."

"Amber said you did, and—hey, what do you know? Here they come."

I turned to the entrance just as Amber swept into the pizzeria with a bemused Rob trailing in her wake. Damn it, he was hot. Twinkly eyes, broad chest, and muscles so thick his shirt struggled to contain them.

Less than twenty-four hours ago, I'd sucked him off, and my dick had definitely put the experience into the "good memory" box. I hoped my apron hid the swell behind my zipper—if not, this was going to be embarrassing.

"Oh, good! You're all here," Amber called in greeting.

"Speak of the devil." My cousin waved to the newcomers. "Yo, it's the neighbors. How's it going in bagel land?"

"Excellent! Listen, I need an answer today about the bake-off. I have the reporter lined up to do the interview, and I've created some titillating social media posts to get everyone fired up. Here. Check these out." Amber passed an iPad across the counter.

I scrolled through her slogans and reluctantly had to admit...it wasn't terrible. *Do you bagel or pizza? Bagel me this...or pizza me that. Bagels, morning, noon, and night. Can pizza do that?*

"These are good," I said.

"Thank you! Mrs. Malveney is so excited, it isn't even funny. This could be a gigantic fund raiser for the football program and—"

"Both of our shops," I finished. Christ, I'd heard Amber's spiel so many times, I could have recited it myself. "We know, we know."

"So...are we doing this or not?"

That was Rob, his gaze locked on me with an intensity that got my motor running.

If we were alone, I wouldn't have thought twice about plastering myself all over him. *Scary shit.* The last time I'd wanted someone this badly hadn't gone well. I'd learned my lesson, and I'd vowed not to do stupid shit with men I couldn't trust.

Except I sort of trusted Rob. I couldn't say why, but I

444

supposed it had something to do with knowing he was a semi-closeted professional athlete. Like I'd been. My story was old, but I could relate to some of the angst and fear I assumed he'd experienced. Even if I was wrong about that, I couldn't deny the physical pull between us.

Vanni and Amber stared at us expectantly.

"Jimmy and Sal are in, and I'm cool with it. What do you think, Cuz?" Vanni prodded.

I nodded slowly. "Yeah, we'll do it."

Heads turned as Amber squealed, punching her fist in the air triumphantly. "Yes! Awesome. The format will be a simple once-a-week sample contest, which will give us both a chance to advertise our goodies, and will culminate with a finale at the beginning of December. That's six weeks of—"

"Six weeks?" Rob and I sputtered in unison.

"It's all about the buildup," Amber explained. "We have to get the word out and get the frenzy going."

I frowned, skirting the counter to avoid disturbing our customers. "I thought this was a one-time deal. What are we going to do for six weeks? We have businesses to run."

"That wouldn't do justice to either of us," she argued. "We have to milk this through the entire football season and get our audience revved up. Here's an idea...Rob could make marinara from scratch. We could put it in small paper cups for customers to taste and rate. And Mateo could make everything bagel bites and do the same thing. I think both of our customers will go nuts!"

Huh. Sounded like extra work for yours truly, but she was right about one thing...it would draw people in.

"I don't know how to make marinara sauce," Rob griped.

"Too bad for you, 'cause I know how to make a bagel."

"No, you don't."

"Yes, I do."

"No, you—"

"Oh, for f—udge sake. Six weeks of this will be torture for all of us," Vanni huffed, smiling at the young family striding toward the register. "Welcome to Boardwalk. What can I get for you?"

Amber chuckled, a ringlet of curls snagging on her chin as she tucked her iPad under her arm. "I say keep it up, boys. The more angst, the better. Back to work for me. See you later, Mateo. And thank you. I think this is going to be great."

We watched her walk out the door before looking at each other.

"I guess that's something we're doing," Rob grumbled.

"Hmph. I hope you're ready to get your ass handed to you. I literally have marinara in my veins."

"Good to know." Rob nudged my elbow as he pulled his cell from his pocket. "What's your number?"

"Why?"

"I'm going to text you my address. We can trade recipes or..." He lowered his voice and leaned in. "We can finish what you started."

"Tonight?" I gulped.

"Tonight."

I wanted to tell him to fuck off for the sake of it, but when he pushed his phone at me, I typed in my number and shoved it at him...too strung out to argue. I needed some space. Stat.

"Unless you're buying, get outta here. We're busy."

Rob's lips tilted at one side as stepped a little closer. "I can't wait to take you apart and put you back together again. See you later, sunshine."

Oh, fuck.

That right there was a fine example of what was wrong with me. I wasn't the kind of guy who got twisted up over meaningless compliments and vapid praise. Nope. But the threat of having my insides rearranged? Yeah, that did it for me.

I shook my head in consternation and all I could think was, *Wow, you're one sick fucker, Cavaretti. I hope he's worth it.*

Chapter Eight

Rob

Before you judge...don't. I had no idea what I was doing. I could blame my sudden lapse in judgment on a myriad of things, but the simple truth was that I wanted Mateo. The popular quarterback was suddenly, possibly attainable. He'd let me touch him, devour him, and rub up against him the way I'd fantasized so many years ago. And then he'd blown my mind.

Sadly, once wasn't enough. I had to have more.

Amber's PR idea was a good one, but better yet, it gave us an excuse to spend time together. I'd happily subject myself to his wrath if it meant I got an up-close and personal view of those long lashes and full lips. And if there was a snowball's chance in hell he was willing to see how far we could go, I was all in. I wanted to be inside him...deep, deep inside him.

However, I'd been raised in a nice midwestern family who prized good manners above all else. There'd be no jumping Mateo's bones the second he showed up on my doorstep. No, I vowed to show a little restraint tonight and find some common ground that didn't involve sex or violence. Food was my best bet. Specifically...marinara sauce.

"Marinara?"

I motioned for Mateo to give me his leather jacket as he stepped into the foyer. "Yeah."

"What happened to taking me apart? Talk about false advertising," he snarked.

I lowered my head to hide my smile, draped his jacket on a bench, and headed through a maze of rooms to the family-style kitchen. "Can I get you something to drink?"

"Beer, if you have it. If not, I—holy freaking crap." Mateo marched to the wall of windows overlooking the sun setting over the Pacific. "This is a killer view. When they were building this place, I remembered thinking it was going to be some monster mansion, but it's really...nice."

"Thanks, I like it." I popped the tops off two beers and joined him at the window, handing him one. "I bought it from the contractor after the original investor pulled out."

"Does anyone else live here?"

"No, just me."

Mateo lifted a curious brow. "By yourself? Geez, it's fuckin' huge."

He was right.

But I'd earned a fuckton of money and had invested wisely in stocks and real estate. I still owned condos in Manhattan and Dallas, a house in Hollywood Hills, an estate in Indiana near my family, and this house, a five-bedroom beach chalet.

It was more house than I needed and I swore I wasn't one

to flaunt my wealth, but privacy was important. Some athletes were stalked like rock stars and while that wasn't me, I wanted to be insulated from prying eyes...to be on the safe side.

Besides, I'd always loved this stretch of beach. I used to come out here whenever I'd felt overwhelmed by college courses and football...and life in general. The miles of golden sand and the ribbon of blue that kissed the sky at the horizon had always calmed me.

"Where do you live?" I asked conversationally.

"Above the shop." Mateo shot a suspicious glance my way. "Why?"

"So I can throw eggs at your window later. Why else?"

"Ha. Ha."

I followed him to the kitchen and leaned on the island, sipping beer while Mateo poked his head into my oven and examined the built-in air fryer and the vent above the stove.

"Check out the fridge too. It's new."

Mateo opened the Sub-Zero and whistled. "It's bigger than my first car, and...it's empty. Don't you eat?"

I patted my belly with a laugh. "I think it's obvious I don't miss many meals."

His gaze went molten with desire and damn it, I couldn't breathe for a hot second.

"Quit fishin' for compliments. You look good, and you know it."

"Gee, thanks."

"*Mmm.*" Mateo flopped onto the nearest barstool. "You didn't really think I'd share a family recipe, did you?"

I took another slug from my bottle. "No. But I think we need to call a truce and figure out a way to be civil."

"And you went with sauce," Mateo teased, a ghost of a smile lifting his lips at one side. "Wow."

I picked up one of the bottle caps I'd tossed onto the island earlier and threw it at his head. "You're an asshole."

He caught it easily, flashing a wide grin. "Fine. Truce...we'll talk sauce. But just so you know, that's like asking for tips on salad dressings. There are too many kinds to list—thousand island, blue cheese, ranch. Same with 'sauces.' You can have pesto, alfredo, arrabbiata, Bolognese. Even a basic marinara varies between chefs. We still use my great-grandmother's recipe at Boardwalk, but if I told you the ingredients, I'd have to murder you."

I chuckled, charmed by his mischievous expression. Mateo still had that bad-boy vibe he'd cultivated in college, and damn, it was intoxicating.

"Keep your recipes, and I'll keep mine. However, in the spirit of a truce, I bought tomatoes and spices and pulled up a decent-looking marinara recipe online. I thought maybe you could give me some pointers."

"How'd we go from a BJ in your office to marinara tips? Your sexy game has taken a nose dive, Vilmer," he chided without heat. "Try again."

I snort-laughed. "You're right. How about a trade?"

"*Hmm*, like marinara pointers for a blowjob?"

He was joking, but...also...not.

That familiar telltale crackle of awareness was back. There was absolutely no way to ignore it, so I didn't bother.

I nodded slowly. "Yeah, something like that."

Mateo's gaze fixed on my mouth. He cleared his throat and stepped toward the bowl of tomatoes.

Good. Food was easy.

This...whatever was going on with us—not so much.

"We can't use these. They're not sweet or ripe enough. You can substitute quality canned tomatoes. If you do that, we can continue, otherwise you're outta luck with the *sugo*."

"What's *sugo*?" I asked, opening the pantry.

"It's Italian for juice or...sauce. My grandfather and my dad and uncle called it *sugo*. Or you say gravy, marinara, or spaghetti sauce or pasta sauce. It's the simplest thing to make —very few ingredients. Tomatoes, tomato paste, onion, garlic, bay leaf, salt, pepper, red pepper flakes, and a couple of secret spices Cavarettis never share."

"Understood. Found it." I held up a twenty-eight-ounce can of whole tomatoes and a smaller can of tomato paste. "This too?"

"Yep. Paste thickens the sauce. It's not mandatory, but some people like a thinner consistency."

"What do you like?"

Mateo waggled his brows. "I always go for the thicker option."

I snorted as I reached for a bottle of Pinot Noir. "Wine?"

"Sure, thanks."

I poured the wine, humming along to a series of instructions I had no hope of following. I was too distracted by him.

It wasn't just physical attraction, though. I was fascinated by Mateo's command of my kitchen. He literally took over, spreading ingredients across the island and barking orders like a...well, a chef. He knew what he was doing. There was no consulting cookbooks or Internet experts. I got the impression that the recipe he was sharing was one he'd memorized as a kid.

"When did you learn how to cook?" I asked, dicing onions on a cutting board while Mateo crushed tomatoes in a bowl.

"I've been in a kitchen my whole life." Mateo rinsed his hands, poured olive oil into the pan on the stove, and turned on the burner. "I have early memories of standing on a stool next to my *nonna,* chopping basil or stirring marinara. Her kitchen was always busy...lots of family around. My house was quiet and—you're gonna chop a finger off, Vilmer. Hold the onion like this."

He gave a brief tutorial, handling the knife the way he used to handle a football. It was tempting to argue that I knew how to chop a damn onion, but I didn't want to upset our fledgling truce. And every crumb of information Mateo shared made me curious to know more.

I scraped the onions into the pot per his instructions and stirred. "I can't imagine a quiet house. I have two sisters, Kate and Gwen—one older, one younger. There was always something going on. They shared a room, and I had my own. They're still bitter about it. They conveniently forget that they constantly hogged the bathroom. I was always late because of them. Evil."

Mateo shot an unreadable glance at me. "Now we add the garlic, salt, and red pepper flakes. This is a variation...right here with the garlic. We don't always add garlic. According to my grandparents, garlic and onion compete for flavor and too much garlic overpowers a dish. But that's a taste thing. Okay, add the tomatoes, a teaspoon of tomato paste, and...a bay leaf.

Cover the pot and let it simmer. In twenty minutes, it'll be ready."

I furrowed my brow. "Really? That seems too easy."

He swirled the content of his glass and shrugged. "I told you it's simple. It may need more salt and pepper, and personally, I like basil and parsley too."

"Do you use fresh or dried herbs?" I leaned casually against the counter and sipped my wine. And almost did a spit-take at Mateo's deadpan stare. He didn't crack a smile until I almost choked around a laugh, wiping tears from the corner of my eyes. "Asshole."

"So I've been told," he quipped. "You can use either, but I prefer fresh. Too many people buy dried herbs and never check the expiration dates. Then they put fifteen-year-old nutmeg in their gingerbread cookies and wonder why they taste weird."

"That would be my mom. I helped her clean out her pantry when Dad was in the hospital for gallbladder surgery last summer. She had cans of soup from the last century."

Mateo widened his eyes comically. "No."

"Yep. There's a strong possibility she's been serving expired soup for years. Kate and Gwen think the fact that we survived meatloaf surprise and Mom's chicken casserole with potato-chip toppings means we have cast-iron stomachs and are probably immune to most diseases."

He chuckled as he lifted the lid on the pan to stir the sauce. "Not a great cook, eh?"

"Nope. I love my mom, but if my sisters and I hadn't learned some basic skills, we'd have starved. And I do mean basic. I was the king of mac and cheese, omelets, and protein drinks in high school. You have no idea how happy I was that my full ride to Great H included a generous meal plan."

"You had a scholarship?" he asked, replacing the lid.

"*Mmhmm*. I wouldn't have been able to afford a four-year college otherwise. My folks are retired junior high teachers. It wasn't in the budget. The plan was for me to go to the local community college and transfer after a couple of years on my own dime."

"But you knew how to play football."

I inclined my chin. "Yeah. I had a short stint with flag football in elementary school and didn't play again till freshman year at Spring Creek High. I was a big kid, more chubby than muscular, though. They put me on defense, and it stuck. I wanted to try another position in college, but—"

"Like what?"

"Quarterback." I grinned at his faux glower and continued. "Or tight end. Coach wouldn't hear of it. He needed me to be a beast...so I was. No complaints here. Football has given me opportunities beyond my wildest dreams. The memorabilia in the shop is meant to be an acknowledgment of that, in case you're curious. I love this town. It's been good to me."

"I know I'm gonna sound like a dick, but if I'm hearing correctly, you just admitted to gunning for my job in college, having a limited skill set in the kitchen, and to moving back to town for a victory lap. Which means...I was right about you."

There was no malice in his tone. It was a straightforward assessment...very on brand for a man who didn't mince words.

"You're right about sounding like a dick. The rest...no. I

don't have your culinary lineage of amazing cooks from the mother land, but my grandfather owned a bagel shop. After he passed away, my aunt and uncle ran the business for a decade or so, but they're older now and not interested in the long hours, and there was no one else to pick up the torch. Including me. I could have moved home, but—" I stopped abruptly, surprised at how much personal info I'd shared. Had to be the wine. I gestured to the stove. "How much longer till it's ready?"

"Ten minutes."

"*Mm*, it already smells great. I'll boil some water for pasta." I could feel Mateo's watchful gaze as I filled a pot and set it on the burner next to the simmering sauce.

"Why didn't you want to go home?" he asked softly. "You're obviously close to your family. Your eyes crinkle when you talk about them...like you miss them."

"I do." I topped off our wineglasses to give my hands something to do. "Not all my memories were great, though. And maybe it's silly, but my least favorite thing about visiting home is running into shitheads who bullied me mercilessly in grade school and having to act like that crap didn't leave scars while I sign jerseys for their kids. My mom likes to say it's karma doing her work and that I should enjoy it, but..."

"You don't," he finished.

"No. I don't want to think about being scared all the fucking time and the daily mental ambush. I was too fat, too ugly, too stupid, my clothes weren't trendy, my backpack was a hand-me-down. I never fit in until I picked up a football. Even then, I was too soft—at first anyway."

456

"I'm sorry. Bullies suck." Mateo frowned, gnawing on his bottom lip.

"Yeah, I probably shouldn't be holding grudges on behalf of my younger self, but preteen me was a sensitive kid. Imagine my horror when I realized some of the things they said about me were true. Maybe everything. I *was* chubby, ugly, uncool, and...gay. That last one was a mind fuck. The kids in my town used 'gay' to describe anything unsavory—tacky shoes, a bad movie, a song they didn't like. I didn't want to be gay." I let out a humorless laugh. "It got better in high school because of football. Suddenly, I was valuable. My stats were amazing, coaches loved me, my teammates saw me as an asset, and no one made fun of my shortcomings 'cause they liked what I could do."

"That's good."

"Sure, but I was still gay...very gay. So you might say the accolades were tinged with the kind of fear that eats at your insides. If I wasn't on a football field, I was a wreck, constantly worrying that someone was gonna figure me out."

"Sorry. I know how that feels."

I nodded. *Yeah, I bet he did.*

"It was a bad time, but plenty of kids have it tough in high school." I shrugged ruefully. "College was my reset, and this town gave me what I needed to start over—self-respect, confidence, acceptance. No one here gives a shit if you're gay, bi, trans, pan, or whatever."

"Yet you're still technically in the closet." Mateo raised a hand. "Not that I'm judging. Hey, I didn't come out to my mom or my aunt till my dad died. My cousins knew, but Dad...nope, couldn't do it."

"Oh. Was he..."

"A bigot? Sort of. He tried to be open-minded, but he was from a strict Catholic Italian family. He had old-fashioned ideas and I was his only son, only kid..." Mateo waved dismissively. "It wouldn't have ended well, but that's old news. I'd rather talk about you brown-nosing the whole fucking town with bagels."

I snort-laughed. "You're an asshole, Cavaretti."

"But you knew that," he singsonged, a cocky grin tilting one corner of his mouth.

I hid my smile as I opened the bag of spaghetti. I plucked the lid off the pot of boiling water and lowered the heat, then took a handful of dried noodles and broke them in half. A choked gasp interrupted me. I spun toward a wide-eyed, apoplectic Mateo.

"What's wrong?"

He grabbed the noodles from me, his mouth open in shock and dismay. "What do you mean, 'what's wrong'? You're murdering spaghetti! You don't break them in half. Stop. This is...sacrilege!"

I widened my eyes, wisely stepping aside as Mateo dumped the rest of the noodles into the pot, muttering in Italian. "They're going to the same place and let's face it, it's easier to eat shorter pieces of spaghetti."

Mateo's deadpan stare was on point. "There is so much wrong with that sentence that I don't know where to begin."

I snickered. "Oh, come on."

"Come on? Pasta is shaped as it's supposed to be eaten. Breaking it like a heathen is disrespectful. You're lucky my mom and my aunt didn't see that."

I raised my hands in surrender. "Lesson learned."

"Hmph." Mateo stirred the sauce, adding a smidge of salt.

"You speak Italian."

He set the spoon down, checking his watch as he turned to face me. "Yeah. My mom was born there. Her family moved to California when she was thirteen, so she grew up speaking both and made sure I did too. Funny thing...my dad's Italian was terrible."

"Really?"

"Yeah, he tried but it was painful sometimes. And none of my cousins learned. After so many generations here, some things get lost and the definition of home changes. Let's test these poor broken noodles." Mateo declared them perfect and assembled two heaping bowls of spaghetti.

And damn, it was delicious.

We sat at the island and steered conversation toward neutral topics—the new mural at the lifeguard headquarters, rainfall this season, and my thwarted attempts at surfing.

"I spend more time getting tossed in waves than I do standing on the board," I griped, twirling spaghetti around my fork. "It's painful, but I swore I'd finally learn how to surf after I retired, and I'm not giving up."

"It's all about balance," Mateo said matter-of-factly.

"You surf?"

"Yeah. I'll come out with you sometime. Give you some pointers."

I snorted. "Yeah, I bet you will. I'd rather not end up as shark chum."

Mateo set a hand on his heart as if wounded. "I thought

this was a truce. If so, you're gonna have to trust me...just a little."

He was right. And like it or not, I was more interested in him than ever. His strong family bonds, his culinary prowess, and...he could surf too? Yep, very interested.

"Okay."

Mateo grinned. "Okay."

We made plans to surf that weekend, and later, I blew him in the kitchen, slipping a digit in his hole till he came. Call it a thank-you for the meal or call it what it really was...lust.

Pure and simple lust. With a little curiosity and yes... admiration thrown into the mix. Mateo fascinated and confounded me in equal measure. Sure, there was a bagel and pizza war to win, but at the moment, I was more interested in winning him over.

Chapter Nine

Mateo

Waves cascaded onto the shore, fiercely one moment and almost gently the next, as if the gods of the sea hadn't agreed on a mood for the day. The sun was doing its best to fight its way through the pewter gray skies, beaming the occasional ray of light through the clouds behind us on the empty beach. It was so peaceful, so still, so beautiful.

It felt strange to share this with someone, as if it were significant somehow, and that was just...silly. It was Rob, for fuck's sake. And we were surfing, not sucking each other off. Again.

Sex had been on the menu daily these past two weeks. Once that cat was out of the bag, there was no going back.

We were voracious. Ten-minute booty calls weren't enough anymore. We'd graduated to dinners at his place, chopping vegetables while debating NFL stats, sharing cups of coffee in our offices, discussing our favorite flavors of cream cheese or ice cream, and...surf lessons at dawn.

Let's talk sex for a second here, though.

I'd been with a lot of men and thought I'd done it all, but it was different with Rob. Get this—we hadn't fucked yet. We'd done everything else. Hand jobs, BJs, sixty-nine, rimming. It was all very fucking good. He'd used a dildo on me the other night. I'd thought it was a prelude, but it had been the main event, and I'd come so hard that it hadn't occurred to me to be disappointed that it wasn't his cock.

I was being edged to the brink of sanity, and I didn't mind. Which was nuts. I should have been restless, bored, and done with him by now. I was more of an in and out, move on kind of guy. I didn't feel that way about Rob. Once I'd gotten past the ick factor of being attracted to someone I'd thought was an opportunistic charlatan, I could admit that...I liked him. A lot.

I liked his dry sense of humor and the way his eyes lit up when he talked about his family and Amber. I liked that he wasn't afraid to discuss past struggles or credit the people and places who'd influenced him. Rob could be vulnerable without ever seeming...weak.

Take now, for example.

The dude wrestling his board into submission sported a big-ass grin as he trudged through wet sand toward me. If I hadn't known better, I'd think he'd just won a surfing competition, but I'd witnessed him lose his balance and plunge into the ocean over and over again this morning. He was either a glutton for punishment or he truly enjoyed falling.

462

"Did you see that last run?" Rob shook his head, spraying me with ocean water.

I fixed him with a death glare I had no hope of maintaining when he smiled like a kid in a candy store. I huffed instead and motioned for him to turn so I could help unzip his wetsuit. "I saw everything. You've improved."

"Thanks. I stayed on for a whole twenty seconds." Rob peeled his suit off his arms and chest before flopping onto the towel I'd spread out.

"Not bad." I handed him the thermos I'd packed on a whim. "I forgot how much I like being out here first thing in the morning."

Rob leaned into my side. "I thought you were a regular."

"Not since I was a teenager. Early football practices messed with my surf time in high school and college."

"*Hmm.*" He uncapped the thermos and sipped. "You were drafted after college too."

The sentence hung between us like a bubble I could pop and forget. Rob wouldn't pester me for details I didn't want to share. I'd learned that much about him. But if he could share bleak episodes, I should be able to do the same.

"Yeah, to Tennessee. I lasted five months...wasn't good enough. What worked for me in college didn't translate in the pros. It was a hard pill to swallow," I admitted, my gaze locked on the horizon.

"That sucks."

"It did. I felt like I'd let everyone down...my dad, my coach, the whole town. I could've stuck it out, but my uncle got sick and my family needed me here." I inhaled then slowly released the air from my lungs. "I also met someone in San Francisco and thought I was..."

"In love?" he supplied.

"Something like that. It wasn't love, though. It was an unhealthy secret that made me feel almost as sad and defeated as losing my shot at the pros."

Rob passed the thermos to me. "I've been there. I had a mutually beneficial arrangement with someone deeper in the closet than I was. I thought that was a good thing at the time, but I wouldn't do it again."

"Me either." I scrubbed my hand over my stubbled jaw. "He was a corporate lawyer, a little older, and bi. I was his low-risk experiment 'cause neither of us was out. But then he met a girl who fit the suburban lifestyle-dream he'd been spoonfed his whole life, and *boom*, that was the end of me."

"Ouch."

"Meh, he did me a favor. I just..."

Rob nudged my shoulder with his. "What?"

"I wished I'd been braver earlier. I wished I'd come out to my dad, my coaches, the whole damn world. If I was going to lose people and opportunity anyway, I wished I'd done it being a thousand percent true to myself. Hiding sucked. It felt necessary at the time, but...it still sucked. I guess I'm trying to say...I see you. I've been there. You're not alone, ya know?"

Okay, that was a terrible speech, and it sounded sappy as fuck when I replayed it in my head. I wiggled my feet in the sand, watching the waves with the intensity of a new life-guard while I ignored Rob's curious stare.

"Thank you," he said after a beat. "I think I needed to hear that."

I opened my mouth, a casual brush-off on the tip of my tongue. The sincerity in his eyes stopped me. For the first time in years, I set my protective armor aside and let myself connect with someone new. I reached for his hand. That was it. The smallest gesture, really, but it was a leap of faith for me and he knew it.

Rob laced our fingers and squeezed.

We sat there for a while, holding hands. And I knew without asking that it was a first for both of us.

Chapter Ten

Rob

Amber was one smart cookie. The bake-off, which was really more of a "vote for your favorite free bagel or pizza sample of the day" was a huge hit. Great H Bagels and Boardwalk Pizza had lines out the door every day, though at different times. We were busy from dawn to early afternoon, and Mateo and his cousins were swamped from late morning to closing.

The ad campaign was pure genius. Our interview with the local paper had been picked up by the *San Francisco Chronicle* and had made the front page of the sports section. Nice, but it was nothing compared to the social media frenzy Amber had ignited with a few reels featuring Mateo and me in uniform in college mashed with current clips of us in our respective shops, making bagels, slinging pizza dough, and proudly representing Haverton.

We were asked to attend a recent football game together

where we'd been surrounded by eager fans who'd wanted auto-graphs, selfies, and a chance to chat with a couple of OG Great H players. I'd drawn the NFL crowd for sure, but Mateo was popular with the locals. He was gorgeous and charismatic.

I overheard two old women twittering on the sidewalk outside our stores the other day.

"Oh, that Mateo is a looker, all right."

"What I wouldn't give to be fifty years younger."

They'd giggled like school girls and winked at me as I'd pushed open the door to the pizzeria. I wanted to tell them I was as smitten as they were. It was true. I had a big ol' crush on Mateo Cavaretti...a thousand times bigger than the one I'd secretly harbored in college.

Now I knew him. The real Mateo.

I could tell his real smile from the polite one reserved for customers. I knew how to tease him, make him laugh, and turn him on. I'd mapped every inch of his body, kissed his scars, and tasted him...over and over again. He was prickly yet kind, edgy yet somehow relatable. And he was so good with people—customers, family, friends.

His interactions with his cousins were always entertain-ing. They were like brothers to him, and his colorful Aunt Sylvie was like a second mother.

Mateo's mother, Therese, was a petite beautiful woman in her sixties with jet-black hair and sharp eyes. He looked so much like her, it wasn't even funny. She came by once or twice a week for a plain bagel with cream cheese on the side. An interesting order from someone who liked to give Amber and me tips about seasoning.

"Leave 'em alone, Ma," Mateo scolded when he stopped by this morning before heading next door.

It was part of our new routine. I made him coffee, toasted an oat grain bagel with lox and capers or a scrambled egg and we'd chat about sports and current events. It had quickly become my favorite part of the morning.

But this was the first time Mateo and his mom were here together.

"I'm being nice and neighborly," Therese protested in a lilting Italian accent, giving her son a suspicious once-over. "What are you doing here? Don't you have work?"

"On my way now. I just stopped by to say..." Mateo glanced my way and smiled. "Hi."

His mom darted her gaze between us, nodding thought-fully. "I see."

A stream of Italian later, she patted my cheek and grinned. "*Ciao.*"

Yeah, that was gonna stick with me all damn day.

"Does your mom know about us?" I asked later that night as I stirred the arrabbiata sauce simmering on the stove in Mateo's one-bedroom apartment.

Mateo chuckled. "Yeah, she thinks you're hot for me."

My blush was instantaneous. "Really? Should I be alarmed?"

"That's up to you. If you're worried, you should know my cousins are on to us too."

I set the spoon on the counter and turned the burner off. "Oh?"

"Yeah, but it's 'cause you laugh at my jokes, and I'm not exactly funny."

"Laugh at—what?" I sputtered. "I don't laugh. I wouldn't—"

"Relax. I'm teasing you. They know me, Rob. They know I'm gay, and they know we're friends now. They've also noticed how much time we spend together. It's just a matter of simple deduction."

"Oh."

Mateo leaned against the counter. "In fact, one of them probably saw you come upstairs with me thirty minutes ago, and might think that arrabbiata is some kind of 'hanky-panky' code. Does that bother you?"

I didn't have to think about it. "No."

"Are you sure? It's okay if you—"

"I'm very sure." I stepped between his spread thighs, crooked my forefinger under his chin, and fused our lips in an almost tender kiss.

It exploded seconds later as he grabbed my nape and drove his tongue inside. I tugged his shirt from his jeans and splayed my palm along his spine. His skin was warm and soft. I needed to feel all of him...now.

"Bedroom." I broke the kiss and licked my lips.

Mateo's place was a fraction of the size of mine. While my house was light and airy, decorated with the beach-themed prints and ocean-inspired colors my designer had deemed appropriate, there were no real traces of me. Mateo's living area was filled with family lore—sturdy furniture that had once belonged to his parents, walls decorated with action photos from ski trips and wedding receptions, pics of his dad, his uncle, and more cousins than I'd thought any one person had.

The bedroom was spartan in comparison—a queen-sized bed, a nightstand that doubled as a dresser, and that was it.

Mateo stripped his shirt off and unbuckled his belt. "Let me see you."

I yanked my shirt over my head, but that was as far as I got. I had to touch him. I pushed him onto the mattress, twirling our tongues as we rolled from side to side, making out and grinding in a furious quest for friction until I captured his wrists and straddled his torso.

"Fuck, you're strong," Mateo hummed, testing my grip.

"Don't fight me. I want you to do exactly as I say." I licked the shell of his ear and whispered, "Got it?"

"*Ungh*...yes."

"Good boy. Hold on to the headboard...just like that."

I tweaked his nipples and slid lower, making quick work of his belt and zipper. I tugged his jeans off with his shoes and socks, then crawled between his legs to look my fill. Mateo's olive skin was a perfect backdrop for his colorful ink. His muscles were toned and taut, and my God, the light trail of hair pointing south at the bulge in his black boxer briefs was mouthwatering.

I met his gaze as I slipped my fingers under his waistband.

Mateo's nose flared in approval. I lowered the fabric and fuck, he was beautiful—long, thick, and hard as nails.

I bent over his crotch, inhaling deeply as I licked a trail from his base to his slit. He groaned and lifted his hips. I did it again...and again. I sucked the head and played with his balls,

470

chuckling at his growl of frustration. Mateo was too proud to beg, and I was too wired. And too damn hungry.

So I opened my mouth and swallowed him whole.

"Oh, fuck! Yes, that's it. Oh, fuck, yeah..."

His enthusiastic moans reverberated in my throat and sent shivers up my spine. I bobbed my head, rolling his balls and tracing my thumb along his crease. I was pushing my luck and I knew it, but for some reason, I felt in tune to Mateo's body in a way I never had with anyone else's. Like I could read his every response from the tilt of his pelvis to the desperate tone in his plea for more.

When he grabbed a handful of my hair, I knew he'd reached the end of his rope.

I sat back and wiped my mouth. "Hands off, boy."

Mateo clenched his jaw and growled. "I need to fucking come. Let me suck you, let me—*oh...shit.*"

I devoured him again, picking up the tempo as I massaged a single saliva-slicked digit between his cheeks. He spread his legs wider, giving me better access. I released him with a pop to get a good look at him while I finished undressing.

"Show me that pretty hole," I purred, stepping out of my jeans.

He tapped his entrance. "Are you gonna fuck me?"

"Yeah. You ready for me?" I slipped my finger inside his tight channel before he could reply.

He gasped. "Yeah. More."

I obeyed, gently gliding my fingers in and out, in and out. "Stroke yourself, but don't come."

"Oh, my God." Mateo squeezed his cock at the base, his

eyes rolling in his head. "Just...just fuck me already. Don't make me fucking beg."

The self-control required not to just suit up, lube up, and mount him was on a superhuman level. After weeks of sensual exploration, I was vibrating with need. No begging necessary.

I added a third digit, working my fingers in and out of his hole a few times. Then I pulled away to grab supplies from his nightstand drawer.

My fingers trembled as I rolled on the latex and added lube. I was nervous, which was silly. This was just sex.

But it didn't feel like meaningless sex anymore, and that should have scared me. It didn't. At all.

I lined my sheathed cock at Mateo's hole and pushed. We moaned, our eyes locked as I inched my way inside.

I moved slowly at first, savoring him. He was tight and hot, and so damn sexy. I rocked my hips and steadily upped the tempo till the room echoed with the sound of squeaky bedsprings and our soft hums and grunted sighs.

The carnal give-and-take was a perfect dance. I'd learned his body well over the past few weeks, and I knew Mateo liked to play a little rough. I rested my forehead on his, pistoning double time as he wrapped his legs around me and slipped a hand between our sweaty torsos.

"I'm gonna—I'm close," he panted, jacking his cock faster still.

Fuck, I was too. I bit his bottom lip and licked it better. "Come for me, baby. Come."

Mateo roared, shooting ribbons of jizz on both of us. That was it for me, too.

I fell apart in a blinding rush of white light, collapsing on my lover, my body quaking through the most intense orgasm I'd ever had.

I panted for air, blinking through the residual haze of lust. "You okay?"

"Okay isn't a strong enough word," Mateo countered softly.

"I know. This is..."

"So good," he whispered.

I kissed his brow and nodded.

It was...beautiful. I didn't want to ruin the moment with sappy sentiments, but that didn't stop the smile from spreading across my face.

Whatever this was felt...real. The way I'd heard it was supposed to feel with the right person.

Chapter Eleven

Mateo

This was new.

And strange. Meaningless sex with a willing partner was the only sex I'd had in years. Until now. Until Rob.

I couldn't decide if this was complicated or not. I'd always been an expert at deflecting curiosity about my private life. I had to be. My family was nosy as fuck. Before I came out, everyone in my family had someone they thought I should meet. I used to go along with the charade, feigning interest to get them off my back.

But I hadn't had to do that in years. Not since Sal had caught me making out with a barista the year I'd been sent home from the pros and gotten dumped by my two-timing lover. He hadn't said a word—he'd just given me a quizzical look. I'd nodded, he'd nodded, and that had been it. I was out. My cousins officially knew.

And they'd kept my secret for years. I hadn't even considered coming out to my parents. But then my father died and the opportunity was gone.

I'd shared the story of how I'd blurted, "I'm gay" at Sunday dinner with Rob. I couldn't say why I'd done it, but my working theory was that I'd bottled up the truth for too long and it couldn't be contained any longer.

My mom and aunt had hugged me, my cousin, Lucia had wanted to set me up with a doctor in her practice. End of story.

I'd gained my family's support with very little fanfare, and I was grateful. Sure, Ma had still asked if I'd met anyone nice, but she wouldn't want to hear about guys I met on Grindr, so that was an easy no. But Rob...yeah, she definitely wanted to know all about him.

Ma began showing up at the bagel shop with a bejeweled Aunt Sylvie dressed from head to toe in her signature leopard print, timing their visits to bump into me. If I wasn't there, they'd come by the pizzeria and gush about the nice young man next door. And of course, they'd voted for our "bake-off" samples each week, and gave their two cents.

Aunt Sylvie, honest to a fault: "Your bagel is doughy, Mateo. I don't like it."

Ma, also honest, but with a lighter touch: "It's not bad. It's just...I think it's maybe not your strength, honey. But your marinara is far superior."

Aunt Sylvie: "Not even a contest."

According to Amber, after six weeks, we were tied at three wins each. If it hadn't been for the posters all over town, promoting our support for the Big H Hawks, we might have forgotten that we'd started this hating each other. This silly contest I'd sworn I'd win hands down didn't seem so important anymore. It was good for the community, good for the football team, good for...us.

But there was one more event. The finale.

The first Saturday in December also happened to be a big home game for the Hawks. Alumni had flown in from across the country along with a hoard of football fans and social media sycophants who'd been following Amber's campaign from the beginning.

Amber chose seven judges: Great H's current hotshot QB, Coach Malveney, three food bloggers, and two random fans from the audience gathered at Haverton Park for a parade-slash-holiday-boutique and yes...the championship installment of the Pizza-Bagel Battle.

Our online audience had set the challenge for each of us to make our version of the perfect pizza bagel. Great H Bagels and Boardwalk Pizza provided samples to feed the crowd that had shown up, but the pizza bagels the judges would taste had been made by us.

Let's keep it real: Rob's bagel was better, but my toppings were far superior. If combined, we'd have made the perfect pizza bagel, but separately, it was up to the judge's palates.

"I like this one," Coach stated, pushing the plate forward.

The QB milked his off-field moment in the spotlight, biting into one, lifting his brows to the delight of the audience, then frowning and moving on to the next plate before ultimately choosing one. "Yo, this one."

The crowd went wild.

Our two locals weighed in next.

"I think you're gonna win," Rob whispered, sidling close to me.

"For sure."

"Asshole." He nudged my shoulder and laughed, sobering a second later. "The truth is that no matter whose name they call, I'm the winner."

I huffed. "How does that math work?"

"I'm with you," he replied, clapping as the locals finished judging.

The three bloggers were next. Their spiel about consistency, flavor, and texture was nothing but static. There was something so raw and earnest in Rob's tone, and I couldn't ignore it.

"What do you mean?"

He turned to me, his eyes bright and filled with something that looked a lot like affection and...hope.

"I mean...I'm grateful to have you in my life, to know you, to be with you. If you hadn't instigated a damn pizza war, this might never have happened. I don't care about bagels or pizza. I just want you, Mateo."

I licked my lips, overcome with emotion. This wasn't the time or place, but damn it, the lump in my throat was the size of a grapefruit.

"First of all, you started the war. Not me." I stabbed a finger at his chest and gazed deep into his eyes. "And second, I want you too."

"Yeah?"

"Yeah. I like who I am when I'm with you," I admitted.

Rob caressed my cheek. "Fuck, I want to kiss you."

I grabbed his wrist. "Careful. If you keep that up, everyone's going to know."

Amber took the mike from the food blogger. I heard her thank the town, the volunteers, Boardwalk Pizza, my cousins, me, Rob. People were watching us. I could feel the curious stares, but it was white noise.

He was everything. The only thing that mattered.

"And the winner is...Mateo Cavaretti."

"Congratulations, my love." With that, Rob grabbed my face in his hands and crashed his mouth over mine.

A surprised hush fell, immediately chased by a whooping roar of approval.

I chuckled against his lips. "You realize that you just came out, right?"

"Yeah, I 'spose I did. I'm glad. I've wanted this for a long, long time."

"Me too, baby. Me too."

We kissed again, then turned to the crowd with our arms raised.

My heart soared in my chest. This was a real win. Me and Rob.

We were a touchdown in the final seconds of a championship game, a Super Bowl ring, and a billion-dollar lottery ticket all in one. He was a gift out of the blue, and I was going to do my best to make sure Rob knew I was in this with him all the way. Beginning with bagels and pizza and leading to...a new start.

Epilogue

Rob

Three years later

Bang bang bang
  I pulled my earplugs out with a sigh. Either I'd put them in wrong or they were useless at cutting out construction noise. Then again, there probably wasn't a quiet way to remove a brick wall. Thankfully, it looked like the crew was almost done for the day.

"Wow, look at that." Mateo shook his head in wonder at the jagged opening between Boardwalk Pizza and the old florist shop next door. "I can't believe we're finally doing this."

I set a hand on his hip. "I know what you mean. This is exciting, baby. I'm happy for you."

"For us," he corrected. "This is ours. You're family too, you know."

I grinned. I did know. Things had changed dramatically since our pizza-bagel bake-off. In a twist, the world took notice when a former athlete kissed his lover in public.

The media had swarmed Haverton, hoping for a titillating story that amounted to headlines like, "Football Star Meets His Match Making Bagels." Corny much? It was silly, but damn, it was therapeutic too. I hadn't realized how freeing it would feel to come out on a large scale. I didn't have to hide any part of my life. I was gay and proud, and I didn't care who knew or what they thought. From that moment, I'd vowed that the next chapter of my life would be lived out loud. With Mateo.

Don't jump to conclusions. We hadn't ridden off in the sunset after the bake-off in a fairy-tale-style happily ever after. We'd taken it one day at a time, slowly building a life together and in the community.

Mateo had moved into my house two and a half years ago. We'd both been a little nervous about it. Living together was a big commitment, but we'd known we were ready for it and were committed to each other. Every day we grew as a couple. We were friends, confidantes, lovers. He knew me in a way very few people did, and he let me know him. There were no walls between us, no secrets.

A year ago, the florist on the other side of Boardwalk Pizza decided to retire and offered the Cavarettis first right of refusal. The cousins had jumped at the chance, but real estate prices had risen significantly, and they'd been leery of the cost of renovating the two spaces. I'd offered to become a silent investor and after some intense haggling, I'd finally talked Mateo into taking my money.

"My boyfriend shouldn't be funding my business," he'd griped.

"I'm investing. It's different, baby."

"Hmph. I'm not putting bagels on the menu. That's a hard no."

I'd laughed and kissed him. "No pizza bagels?"

"We'll save those for special occasions."

And we did. The Pizza-Bagel Bake-off was now an annual event that attracted fans and tourists from across the globe. We didn't compete anymore. Instead, we hosted aspiring chefs in the area while still raising money for the community.

In fact, if we didn't hurry, we'd miss the opening festivities.

"We should go, baby."

"You're right." He didn't budge, though.

"You okay?"

Mateo nodded, slipping his hand in mine. "Yeah, I'm...I can't believe it's real."

"It's going to be amazing too. The plans are—"

"No, I meant...us. Everything we are, everything we've done, everything we're going to do. I just...I love you...so much."

I crushed him to my chest, holding him close. "I love you too."

He squeezed our fingers and smiled. "C'mon, let's go judge some pizza bagels."

"You're on."

Perhaps all was fair in love and war, and maybe in love

and pizza too. I preferred peace and harmony...and our new beginning.

About the Author

Lane Hayes lives in sunny Southern California with her amazing husband, who thankfully doesn't mind cooking, and their fabulous fox red Labrador, George, who's pure mischief. Both provide oodles of inspiration for the low-angst, humorous books Lane loves to write.

She's been telling stories about sexy, funny, sometimes geeky and quirky men who find love for a dozen years now and loving every minute. In her previous life, she sat at a desk and dealt with numbers, so yes...romance is much more satisfying!

Lane loves tea, travel, and chocolate...in any order. Add a book and she's set!

Join Lane's reading group, Lane's Lovers for immediate updates!

Cheesecake Roses

Becca Jackson

Content Warning

Off page death of a family member

Chapter One

Nate

Last year, I was at the height of my career playing baseball with the Funky Monkeys in the Banana Ball league. Then I got hurt, and instead of telling me it was over, they dragged it on and pretended as if I could get back to where I was. I just had to have faith and wait and see, but eight months of daily rehab didn't make a fucking difference, and my dreams were crushed. I couldn't stay out there in Savannah after that. It was too hard seeing all my friends living my dream. It's selfish, I know, but I think I deserve to be a little selfish after all that. So I moved back home to Philadelphia to try to figure out what to do next. The only problem is, I have no idea how to do anything but play baseball.

Life can be a cruel bitch when she wants to be. Case in point, my mother sitting in a giant conference room, with views overlooking the streets of Philly, waiting for a lawyer we've never met. They've set out coffee and pastries, but as if anyone would feel like eating at a time like this. I know my mother doesn't. She's hardly eaten in days.

"What is taking them so long?" I ask her as we wait for the lawyer to return.

"I'm sure they will be with us as soon as they can. It was nice that Jack thought to leave you something, and I'm so glad to have you here with me," she says, and I lay my hand over hers and give it a soft squeeze.

"I don't know why he's left me anything. You're his sister. Everything should just go to you." I couldn't care less what he's left me. I used to see Uncle Jack every summer as a kid, but I haven't seen him since I was, like, thirteen. Mom and Jack had a huge fight one summer. I remember them screaming but can't remember what the words were, and we just never went back.

"He loved you."

"He loved you, too, Mom. I know it has been a while but..."

"We started to talk again a few months ago."

"Really?" She never told me that.

"I was going to suggest we go see him during the holidays, like we used to, but then..." She sniffs and grabs her bag, rummaging through for a handkerchief. I have no idea what she's going through. I'm a single child, but just the thought of losing her, the one person I do have in my life that I love, sends a pang to my chest and forces a lump into my throat. I can't let this become about me, though. This whole year has been about me, and right now, this has to be about her. About showing her that she's not alone. She has me.

490

I wrap my arm over her shoulder and hug her to my side, leaning my head against her shoulder.

"He knew you loved him."

"Thanks, hun," she says, and I lean back in the chair. What could be taking this fucking bloodsucker so long? They've had this meeting on their books for a week now. You'd think they'd be ready to go on time. Nothing like dragging out someone's pain as long as you possibly can.

I know the feeling, not what Mom's going through exactly, but I know pain. I know loss, and I know about people delaying the inevitable.

"Sorry to keep you waiting, Mrs. Buxton," the lawyer says, strolling through the door with a small stack of yellow folders in his hands.

"Miss," my mother corrects. Something she's had to do plenty. Why do people always assume a woman with a kid is married? She never has been, and my father, well, let's just say his *donation* was all either of us got from him.

"Yes, sorry, Miss Buxton," he corrects, taking a seat directly opposite my mother. "I am so sorry for your loss."

I scoff, and my mother shakes her head.

"There's no need to be rude, Nate."

"Sure, you're sorry for our loss, but you'll still take your fees, right?"

"The firm will be paid for handling your late uncle's affairs, yes."

"Then let's just get this over with so my mother can try to start moving on. You've had us in here for twenty minutes."

"Yes, again, I do apologize for keeping you waiting. We

were hoping the third beneficiary was going to be able to be in attendance, but they couldn't make it."

"So we have to come back again?" my mother asks, and I'm about ready to blow, but he's shaking his head.

"No, they provided us with consent to go ahead with the reading of the will and then provide them an update afterward. So if you like, we can get started."

"Yes, thank you," my mother replies, and she reaches for my hand again.

The lawyer starts reciting the terms of the will. I'm not actually paying attention. Instead, I'm fixated on his hair. It's medium length and swept back, but whenever he tilts his head forward, it doesn't move. Not even a little bit.

"Nate," my mother says, nudging my side again.

"Huh, sorry what?"

The lawyer slides a photo across the table. "The Buxton Estate, surrounding grounds, and operational accounts have been left to yourself and a second beneficiary."

"They what now?"

"Well, isn't that lovely," my mother says, picking up the photo. She runs her fingertips down it slowly. "Your uncle loved this place."

"But why leave it to me? Does it say somewhere in there why he left it to me? I don't want an estate. What am I supposed to do with an estate? I thought he'd leave me like a coin collection or the old Ford that he used to drive around."

The lawyer shakes his head. "The terms of the will don't include his reasoning, I'm afraid."

"You used to summer here, do you remember?" my

mother asks, still clutching the photo. "Maybe you could run it?"

"You've got to be kidding. I don't know how to run an estate. I'd be better off selling it and then you could pay off your place in Philly."

The lawyer interjects before my mother can.

"Your mother's been left the death benefit and the balance of his personal accounts along with some shares, all together coming to a total value of one point three million dollars. In regards to selling your inheritance, the second beneficiary would need to sign off on a sale unless they chose to buy you out, which they reserve first option at market value. That part is stipulated within the terms of the inheritance."

"So, who's the second beneficiary? I don't have any cousins, and Uncle Jack was the only other family I thought there was."

"A Mr. Remigius Dubois now controls fifty percent of the estate. He will be notified of his share after our meeting today."

"I've never heard of him," my mother says, finally laying the photo down on the table. "Maybe if I had returned to the estate, I would have met them. So many things must have changed over the years. I should have gone back..." she trails off, her gaze moving to the window but not before I see her eyes glass over.

"We always think we have more time," I tell her, resting my hand on her shoulder. She places her palm over mine and takes a steadying breath.

"Then we have to learn from this. Both of us," she says, turning in the chair to face me. "Promise me."

I have no idea what exactly I am promising to do here, but I agree.

"Sure, Mom. I promise."

"There is some paperwork for you both to sign," the lawyer says, moving right back to business. I should be grateful he's not dragging this part out, but also, fuck man, read the room.

It takes longer to get through the paperwork than it did for him to read the will, and when all is said and done, we leave their pretentious offices and head to one of our favorite spots. Tillie's Bakery on seventh.

"I know you've been through a lot," my mother says before pausing to sip her tea. "But Jack left you the estate, and I think you should go."

"You want me to go to the estate, to do what?"

"To run it. Or half run it with this Remigius person."

"I have zero clue about how to run an estate."

"You're smart, you'll figure it out."

"Mom, the only reason I'd be going to the estate is to check out how best to sell it."

She sighs. "Then do that then. It could be a nice holiday for you."

"Really? You wouldn't mind if I sold it?"

"Jack left it to you, so you can do whatever you want with it. We just agreed to not wait to do something we want to do. Right? We won't wait for another day, when today can be that day."

"Okay."

494

"Okay, what?"

"I'll go check it out. But only to set up selling my half. Who knows, maybe this Remigius person will want to own the whole thing and I'll be back in a few days."

"Or this could be the thing you've been looking for. The new adventure now that—"

"Don't, Mom."

"Honey, whether you talk about it or not, it still happened, and the sooner you start living again, the sooner you'll find something else to love."

"I won't love anything as much as I loved playing ball."

"Maybe, but how will you know if you spend your days cooped up in your old room playing video games online with ten-year-olds?"

"They aren't all ten."

She cocks an eyebrow as she takes another sip of tea. "Okay."

I pull into the driveway of the estate. The large ornate gate that would have once kept the grounds closed off sits propped against the overgrown hedges, leaving the driveway open. From here, I can see the estate itself, looming in the distance, a huge white manor. As the car bumps along down the dirt drive, the tires kick up stones that rattle against the underside of the car, leaving a trail of dirt smoke behind us.

A giant oak stands in the middle of long grass to my left, a broken rope hanging from one of its branches, and memories of a tire swing come to mind.

It's kind of creepy keeping the rope hanging up there all

frayed at the end. That will have to come down before we list it for sale, and the lawns will need a proper mow, I think, before pulling up on the manor itself. I don't get out, just sit in the idling car, staring out the windshield at the enormous three-story house.

I remember walking up the large steps with my mother, dragging a suitcase behind me like it was the heaviest thing in the world, and I can't help but smile as I gaze up at the painted brick facade. Thirteen large windows overlook the grounds, most of them the same, shaker style with clear glass, but to the right where the building juts out a little like an L shape, there are two that are tinted. I guess if my room was on the ground floor, I wouldn't want people walking past to be able to see in either.

The huge white door has a stained glass window set at the top that runs completely across it and depicts woodland or at least trees of some kind, and the whole thing is framed by an ornately carved trim, also painted white. It's actually quite pretty. A memory flashes of my mother holding me up to peer through the glass. We used to truly love this place.

"No. This is not a trip down memory lane, this is a means to an end. I'm here to look over the place and figure out how to sell it, then get back to Philly to figure out what the hell is next in my life. The only thing I do know is, this is not it. I can't run a hotel. How would that even work?" I ask myself as I pull around back. While the front of the manor looks to have been painted at least within the last few years, the rear has definitely seen better days. The paint is peeling from the brick in too many places to count, and one of the upper windows has been boarded up in sections instead of replacing the small glass panels it's lost over time.

"Great, more work to do before this thing can be sold." I mean, I guess I could list it as is and see what offers come in, or this Remigius person might be keen to buy me out, but it *would* get a higher price if it was in better shape. While the windows at the front were set in even numbers, at the back, there's a long lower window to the right of the stairs of the back entry. No fancy stained glass on this side. The door is plain wood, but it does have two carved framed sections and a large brass handle that gleams in the afternoon light.

I pull in beside three other cars out back and switch off the ignition.

"Okay, let's get this over with so I can get back to..." I can't finish that sentence because as much as I hate to talk about what I've lost, I did lose it. Now I have nothing. No career, no job, nothing. Maybe this can at least be a distraction from the shit show that my life has become? An ache radiates through my shoulder, and I try to massage out the pain, but I know it's not going anywhere. It's been a constant reminder of everything I had to let go of. Everything I left behind in Savannah. My hopes, my dreams, fuck... my whole damned life. Well, one thing is for sure, nothing is going to change sitting in this car staring up at the place.

Time to see what this old place has to offer.

Chapter Two

Rémy

The kitchen feels different without Jack here. It's quieter, too. Normally, by this time through the dinner service, he's sitting on the wooden stool opposite me, dipping spoon after spoon into a ganache or pastry cream.

"Just one more taste, to be sure it hasn't spoiled in the last few seconds," he'd say. The memory brings a smile to my lips and a tear to my eye.

This place will never be the same again. And what's worse, I have no idea what it will be, because while I'm so honored that he thought to leave me part of Buxton Estate, he also left it to his nephew, Nate. I remember playing with him in the summers he spent here as a child, and my stomach does a flippy thing as the images surface. I may have had a little crush. But that was all it was. Maybe it could have been something, if we had continued to get to know one another better. But he stopped visiting during the summer and definitely hasn't been here in the last three years since I made the move to the US.

While he may have been content to leave this place behind him, I couldn't wait to get back here. And now Buxton Estate has become my home.

I was born in the States, or so I'm told, but grew up in France with my very proper French mother and father. They both worked hard. My father is a bank manager for one of France's oldest banks, and my mother teaches ballet. Neither of my parents could take eight weeks off work during the summer, and a trip abroad was a good way for me to perfect my English and gain what they referred to as real-world experience. I was eight the first time I traveled here. I didn't care what they called it. I called it an adventure on a plane to stay with my favorite person in the world. Aunt Seline.

She moved to the States to get married after falling in love with the former groundskeeper of the estate, my uncle Vernon. She worked here as a maid for almost thirty years, but now she manages the whole housekeeping team, six in total, seven if you count the new groundskeeper, which he won't, but she definitely will.

Buxton Estate is special. It's been in the care of a Buxton for generations; Jack was born here. Or out in the fields beside the large oak, as he used to claim. Surely that has to mean something to his nephew. But what if it doesn't?

I try to distract myself by working. The kitchen is always where I find myself happiest. And this one is perfect. It used to be an old butler's pantry, set off to the side from the main kitchen. It was being used mostly as another storeroom, but when my desserts started to encroach on Chef's bench space, Jack had it cleared out and I was free to make it my own.

There was already an old marble counter against the left wall, with an inbuilt farmhouse sink under a window that looks out to the front drive. The counter continues along the back wall and partly around to the right as well, and while the marble is old, it's also perfect for tempered chocolate.

When the Morris place a few miles up the road was sold, Jack found out the new owners were pulling down the main house, so before they could get in there, we were lucky enough to pull out their old kitchen island counter and oak shelving. Now they live here, with me, in this tiny room of sweet perfection. Hmm, I should get a sign made to put up on the doorframe to my space.

The island was a nightmare to get through the door. Chef was adamant it was too big for my small area, but I think he was just hoping I would take his smaller steel bench and he'd gain this prized gray marble beauty. But I was going to do whatever it took to make it work, and it does. True, it takes up about half the floor space, but with it set to the left and closer to the entry into my area, once I'm behind it, it's perfect.

A scattering of rocks under tires draws my attention, and out the window, I spot a silver Dodge slowly moving down the drive, nearing the house. I can't make out the person behind the wheel, but it must be Nate. His email said he'd be arriving this week, and we don't have any more real guests due to check in until tomorrow.

The timer chimes, and I pull the sheets of sponge from the oven on the side wall, slip them into the cooling racks and am surprised to find the car still out front when I'm done. He better not park there.

I'm contemplating going out and telling him to park around the back like the guests do when the tires start to turn again and he's moving on. Good.

First impressions matter, and while Jack may not have been great at staying on top of all the upkeep of the old place, the front was painted a few years ago and the groundskeeper tends to the border hedges daily. They run either side of the driveway in an arch until meeting the steps up to the front door. That is what we want people to see, not an old Dodge. And sure, we don't have anyone checking in today, but dinner service will be in just over an hour and we have a few extra reservations from people staying at places nearby.

It's amazing what social media has done for this place. Well, that, and a lucky visit from a food critic last year. His wife booked their stay at Buxton Estate last Christmas.

Chef Henry almost died when he found out the guy he'd been cooking for was a world-class food critic. But he didn't have anything to worry about. They loved the food, but I guess if we're being honest, they loved my dessert more. I wanted to do something really special for the holidays, so I started playing with sugar. Determined to know how I could make a dome, like on a snow globe, I worked on it for days, sure it would make the perfect holiday dessert. And it did.

On the base, I created a layered spiced rum cake with hazelnut buttercream and coated it in a dark chocolate ganache. Etched to look like a wooden base, it was chilled slightly before I added a mossy scene out of apple foam with three chocolate Christmas trees set in the middle dusted with powdered sugar like snow. Once the dome was on, I piped the edges with more buttercream to hide the seam and served it with a tiny hammer tied with a Christmas bow. Hmm, I should do them again this Christmas.

We had a rush of bookings after his review, and now I'd say we have a steady run of bookings. Well, not steady exactly, but enough that it keeps us going.

Tonight's dessert is one of Jack's favorites. A lemon cheesecake rose. The bases are half rounds filled with a lemon curd jelly that I'll turn upside down onto the plate before piping the cool whipped cheesecake mixture around it in petals. A touch of gold and lemon zest will finish it off and hopefully delight our guests.

I know it delighted Jack. How has it already been almost a month since his passing?

I couldn't get away for the reading of the will. With Jack gone, I've been making sure everyone has what they need so the place can keep running.

They sent the paperwork with a paralegal a few days after they met with his sister and nephew. The paralegal sat with me while I signed next to every yellow tab they'd placed, and to be honest, I could have been signing away my soul for all I knew. But it's done now. Or at least, it is for now.

The lawyer implied on the phone that Nate wasn't keen to keep things going, and judging by the valuation in the paperwork, I'm in no position to buy out his share, but maybe I can convince him to let me run it, and he can just take his percentage of any profits.

But could I run it? I was learning the ropes already with Jack, helping handle many of the things he did to keep the place running before he passed. I have been wondering lately if he knew he was nearing his time. Is that maybe why he first broached the subject of me helping to manage the place? He'd said he saw the same love for the estate in me that he had, and it's true. But I never thought it could one day truly be mine. I'm not a Buxton. But to Jack, I was treated like a son. And for that, I am forever grateful. Now I need to do whatever I can to convince his nephew to keep this place going, because if the Morris place is anything to go off, selling would mean the destruction of this house, and I couldn't bear to see it lost to a pile of rubble as if it was never here.

The door to the main kitchen opens and Lilah hurries inside, closing it behind her and holding it shut against her back. I almost laugh. Lilah is not the person you want manning the door if you actually want to keep anyone out. She's a tiny thing, maybe five feet, and has bouncy dark hair that she curls in an old-fashioned sort of way, perfectly suiting the feel of the estate. We hired her shortly after the review came out as a part-time concierge, helping on Friday evenings and on weekends.

She's also my best friend.

"Haven't I told you not to be running in here like an excited child? Chef Henry will have you if he catches you," I tell her, and she scoffs.

"Haven't I told you to wear your toques when you're chef-ing? Those curly blond locks might be gorgeous on top of that irritatingly perfect French head, but in someone's souffle, not so much."

"It's too hot. I'll put it on when I'm assembling. I promise," I lie. I am perfectly capable of ensuring my hair stays out of the food without the toques.

"But you look adorable in it. Don't you want to look adorable for all the eligible men who might come to stay? I mean, you'll always look adorable. Except what is that on your face? When did you last shave?" she asks with a frown.

"A few days ago, why? Don't you like it?" I ask, brushing my fingers over my slight scruff. "I thought it made me look more...dashing." I pick up one of the large metal spoons and try to take in my reflection on the convex surface. The slight scruff makes the angles of my jaw even more prominent, and the cleft in my chin and above my lip appears deeper. Overall, I think it makes me look more mature.

"I could never date a man with stubble on his face. It's clean-shaven or full soft beard for me, but you do you. Oh, wait. Please tell me we are not on your way to a full beard. I've seen those beard nets chefs have to wear. There is nothing sexy about a beard net."

I shake my head. "Did you storm in here to critique my appearance, or was there something else you wanted?"

"Oh, right," she says, looking behind her for a second as if she can see through the door at her back. "He's here."

Chapter Three

Nate

Walking through the back door to Buxton Estate, memories begin to surface. The carpet is the same dark wine color, patterned with some kind of red flower, and in stunning contrast with the striped dark green and gold wallpaper, it gives it an almost regal feel. I remember being about twelve, running through this hallway and steamrolling out to the yard with another boy. I can't see his face clearly, but my stomach does a weird swirly thing. The scent of sugar fills my nose and my stomach growls again. I should have stopped to grab a bite to eat on the way, but I was making good time, and at least now, I can grab dinner here and check out if the food is any good.

Another memory surfaces. One of me and this same boy again, sneaking treats from the kitchen. He is a little clearer now in my mind, with a mess of curly blond hair and a big dimpled smile.

I stroll up the hall, taking in the countless photos that

pepper the wall on my right. They're mostly shots of what I assume are guests of the hotel standing in front of the estate over the years, but there are a few of the grounds themselves, too, of the small vineyard alive with grapevines, and the large oak with unbroken tire swing sitting proudly in manicured lawns.

"Mom?" I pause at a portrait of a group of children sitting on the front steps of the estate. It is definitely my mother. She's got to be barely six in the photo, though, and I'm guessing one of the boys seated around her is Jack. I pull out my phone and snap a pic, sending it off to Mom.

NATE:

You've barely aged a day. Xoxo.

MOM:

You're sweet but a terrible liar. How was the drive?

NATE:

Not too bad.

MOM:

If you decide to keep the place,
maybe I'll visit in the spring.

NATE:

I'm here to find this Remigius
person and convince them to sell,
nothing more. I have no clue how to
run a hotel.

MOM:

You had no clue how to play
baseball either until you gave it a go
and look how that turned out.

Yeah. Exactly, I feel like messaging back. Look how fucking
messed up that turned out. All that work and all that effort
and time spent on becoming the best baseball player I could
be, and for what? To just have it ripped away from me when
it was just getting good. I don't send that back, though. My
shoulder throbs, and I massage the muscle, hoping it will ebb
the ache that seems to always be there. It doesn't.

NATE:

Love you. See you at home in a few
days.

MOM:

Love you more!

I follow the hallway, listening to the floor beneath me creak
with every step until I turn the corner and freeze when I lay
eyes on the back of the main door. The light from outside is
cascading through the stained glass window and throwing a
rainbow of colors through the space.

"It's pretty, isn't it?" a woman's voice asks, startling me,
and I turn toward her. She's an older woman, maybe sixties,
with graying curly hair tied back in a loose ponytail. She's not
wearing any makeup, but she has this classically beautiful
look to her like they had in old movies. She looks familiar, but
I just can't be sure after all these years away.

"Umm, sure, yeah, it is. I saw it from the outside, but it
didn't even occur to me it would look like this on the inside."

"There is much about this place that will surprise you,
Mr. Buxton."

"You know who I am?"

"Yes, we have been expecting you."

Of course. I emailed a few days ago, letting them know I
was coming.

"Right. I booked a room."

"Yes, but we've also met before. You were probably too young to remember. My name is Seline, and I worked with your uncle for many years. So sorry for your loss."

"Thanks," I say, though it doesn't sit well. I hardly knew my uncle. I should probably give my condolences to her; she probably feels the loss more than I do. I try to remember her from when I would visit here as a child, and a fuzzy memory resurfaces of me and that same fucking boy running around her as she hangs large white sheets on the line out back. Then she's not hanging them anymore, she's chasing us playfully through them like they're a maze. What is his name and why are all my memories of this place involving him?

"Seline, yes. I remember. It's lovely to see you again."

"I can show you to your uncle's suite if you would like to shower and change before dinner?"

"My uncle's what now?"

"His room. It's much larger than the others, and given we have some bookings this weekend and were unsure how long you might be staying, we thought it would be best to set you up in there."

"I won't be staying too long. I'm just here to..." It's maybe not the best idea to tell her exactly why I came. "Sort some things out."

She nods and smiles, gesturing toward the right.

"If you'll follow me."

I let her lead me down toward the main stairs, but instead of going up, she slips down beside them to open a door set underneath.

"Jack's room is under the stairs?" I ask as she turns the

509

ornately decorated gold knob. You would think I would remember that. Except, there was probably no reason for me to be going into Uncle Jack's room when I was a kid.

"It is. Was. Sorry. That will take some getting used to."

She pushes open the door, and it's nothing like what I was expecting. The door might be set under the stairs, but it's just where the entry is. A coat rack built into a wall greets us, with an antique mirror speckled by age reflecting the bags under my eyes from the long drive. I thought I handled it well, but my face disagrees.

She turns right at the rack, and I follow into a wide-open space. The odd long window I had seen when parking out back is right above where a gold metal-framed bed is set up with fresh white linens and far too many pillows for a single person to ever need. But I guess they set it up for me like it's a hotel room and hotels always have way too many pillows.

"We've reserved a table for you for dinner. Seating is at six."

"Seating?"

"Yes, we have a set four-course menu. I don't remember you having any allergies. Is that correct?"

"Nope. I'll eat pretty much anything."

"Good. Chef Remigius is making your uncle's favorite dessert tonight."

"*Chef* Remigius?"

"Our dessert chef. Hmm, I expect you two will have lots to talk about after dinner service. The staff may be nervous, but I'm excited to see what you two make of this place."

So Remigius is a chef. My uncle left half of this place to a chef on his staff. I wonder why. Could I even ask this

510

Remigius, though? Would he tell me? Maybe it's one of those situations where some young person cons an old guy into leaving them all his money? I let out a small laugh and shake the thought away. I've watched way too many movies over the last year.

"Umm, thanks, Seline. I'll see you at six then."

"It's good to have you here. Your uncle would be happy you came. He always said you'd be back here one day."

"He did, huh?"

She nods, offering that same sweet, knowing smile before leaving me to my uncle's room.

There's not a lot to the space. It's simple but cozy with a large desk against the far-right wall, and around the corner of the coat rack, there's another door leading to the bathroom. I pull my bag along with me, locking it before turning on the water.

Thankfully, the water pressure in this place is good, but I doubt the heat is continuous, so I stay just long enough for the heat to ease the ache in my shoulder, if only a little.

Showered and changed, I finger through a few papers on Uncle Jack's desk. It's mostly old invoices and a few past check-in diaries. Judging by these books, I don't know how the lawyer valued this place so high. With numbers like these, they have to be barely breaking even. Or it costs less to run this place than I think. I check the time. Not long now. I should head down for dinner. The hotel was eerily quiet when I arrived, but now the halls echo with conversations and laughter.

Seline waits for me by the dining room door and smiles that easy smile of hers when she sees me.

"Right this way, Mr. Bux—"

"Nate is fine," I say, and she nods and leads me toward a table near the back.

"Would you like anything to drink?"

"No, thank you, umm, I'm sorry, but I should have asked, what is it you do here, Seline?" I ask, gesturing to the seat opposite me for her to sit. She pauses for a moment, but then pulls out the chair and sits opposite me.

"I manage the housekeeping staff and reservations."

"Oh, cool. So how are the reservations for this place?"

"We fill up over the spring and summer. Winter is quieter, though with the specialty desserts, even during winter, dinner is usually fully booked each night."

"Specialty desserts?"

"It's easier for you to see them for yourself. The first course will be delivered shortly. I should probably check on the staff," she says, rising from her chair. "Can I get you anything else?"

"I'd like to meet with Chef Remigius after dinner, if that's okay?"

"I'm sure he'll be happy to meet you. He'll be excited to start planning the future of the estate."

"He will?"

"Oh, yes. Remigius loves this place as much as Jack did. Jack saw his heart was here," she says, letting her gaze scan the room, and it's like she's looking at an old friend. What if I convince them to sell and she has to leave here? What if they all have to? "I guess that's why he left it partly to him, too, so that he would always have it. I can have Remigius meet you in your room after dinner?"

"No. I mean. Umm, here is fine. I'll stay back when service is finished."

"Very well. I'll let him know now," she says and heads behind a wooden swinging door into the kitchen. I get a glimpse of the space, and of the golden curls of a man in a white jacket before the door swings closed.

Chapter Four

Rémy

I try my best to stay focused through dinner service, but every time that door swings open, I can't help but glance up to look at him. He's changed so much but still has that stunning bright smile that sent butterflies swarming through my gut all those years ago. He hasn't shaved in maybe a day, and light stubble covers his chiseled jaw. And while his hair used to be down to his shoulders, he's cut it short now, tapered at the sides but longer on top, and styled with some kind of product that makes it look wet. Or it is wet. He might have just showered. And now I'm thinking about him in the shower. Shit. I have to stop. I have to focus. The kitchen is the place where I feel most at ease, where the world makes sense, but with Nate sitting out there, I feel completely off my game.

Every dish that has landed in front of him has brought a smile that makes his eyes sparkle, and my dessert is up next. Then I won't be able to put off this conversation any longer.

"Hey, Rémy, man. Are these ready?" Lilah asks, reaching for the plates and pulling me from my haze.

"Oh, yes, thank you. This is the last of them."

She carries them out, balancing three plates on one arm like it's the easiest thing in the world, and when the door swings wide as she passes through and she places one down in front of Nate, his lips pick up in a grin of delight, and my stomach flips.

It flips in the same way it used to whenever we played as children and he would smile or laugh my way. Shit. I can't be crushing on Nate, not again. He wasn't interested ten years ago, and I have no reason to think he would be now. Besides, hitting on him would probably be a surefire way to get him to run for the hills. I have to keep this totally professional. Show him what a great investment this place is. How amazing it could be.

I walk out to the kitchen after cleaning everything and setting up for the next day, but Nate isn't sitting at his table. He's laughing with Lilah across the room as he helps her to reset place settings.

"You don't have to do that," I say, drawing their attention.

"I know, but I was here anyway, so I figured I would give Lilah a hand. I'm Nate. You must be Remigius," he says, picking up another water glass and setting it down in its place. He doesn't remember me at all, does he? My mouth doesn't move. I'm stuck. My mind and body are frozen in place just watching him. Lilah laughs.

She laughs a little and then shakes her head.

"Only his aunt calls him Remigius. We usually just call him Rémy, or Chef Rémy, and he's clearly had a big night in the kitchen. How about you guys go talk? I can finish this up."

My lips finally move.

"Oui. Yes, umm, you can call me Rémy. It *was* a big night. Did you like everything?" I ask, moving to sit at one of the booths on the far-right side. The booths were another addition to the space Jack and I reclaimed before it was destroyed to make way for something modern, shiny, and new. They were in the old diner in town. Jack and I would visit there every Tuesday and Thursday and eat cherry pie while going over my ideas for the estate. When the owner, Mr. Wellings, passed and the place was picked up by some city developer, we convinced his wife to let us take a row of booths before the sale. I run my fingers over the soft black leather, feeling the slight ripples of its age, and my nerves settle. This place is amazing. Nate will see that. He has to. This pace can't end up just like the diner and the Morris farm.

"So, I was thinking—" Nate starts, but I suddenly cut him off and blurt out.

"You can't sell."

His eyebrows rise. "I think I can do whatever I want with my hotel." He leans back on the seat and folds his arms over his chest, and for a moment, his jaw clenches.

"Sorry, but it's *our* hotel, and I know I can't tell you not to sell your share, but I'm hoping you will give me a chance to show you what this place could be. Jack and I had big plans for Buxton Estate. He's gone, but we're still here. We can still make his... Well, our dreams for this place come true. If you just give me a chance. Give me a chance to prove this place is too special to be sold off to some corporation who'll just tear it down." I can hear my French accent coming through thick. While I spent a lot of time in the States growing up and my English is great, whenever I get stressed or overwhelmed, it's harder to maintain the control needed to sound less French. Not that I want to be less French. But when the accent is too thick, people have a hard time understanding what I'm trying to say.

He's still frowning, but his lips have picked up in a quizzical kind of smirk.

"Have we met before?" he asks, leaning forward, resting his elbows on the table and linking his fingers together in front of him. "I feel like I know you from somewhere."

I contemplate lying. Pretending that he wasn't the first boy I ever crushed on. Pretending that I wasn't that awkward foreign kid who would follow him around the estate every summer, just waiting for him to notice me. But I don't.

"Umm, yeah, we used to spend summer here as kids. I think the last time was maybe ten years ago."

He studies me, eyes moving from one feature to the next, and fuck if I can't help it; when his gaze moves to my mouth, I lick my lips. He mirrors my action, and a slight blush rises to his cheeks as his eyes go wide.

"I remember. You're the blond kid."

Ouch. Okay, so he obviously made a bigger impact on me than I did on him.

"You used to visit your aunt. Your hair is still amazing."

I feel my cheeks grow warm as my stomach flips at his compliment.

"Thanks. You look pretty much the same as I remember, too."

"Wow, so you work here now?"

"Oui. This is where I fell in love with baking, so when Jack asked if I wanted to come on as his dessert chef, I made the move."

"That cheesecake, by the way, is the best I've ever had. How did you get it to look like a flower?"

"Secrets of the kitchen. You'll have to come watch me work one night while you are here."

"Definitely. Oh, hey we used to do that, didn't we?"

"What?"

"Sit in the kitchen while the other chef cooked. What was his name again?"

"Henry?"

"Yes, Henry. I remember we'd sit on stools watching, and then when he'd turn away, we'd try to sneak in a taste, right?"

I laugh. "Oui, yes, we did, many times. Jack used to do the same thing to me. I had to set out a cup of spoons just for him."

"Wow, I can't believe I remember that. I thought I'd forgotten this place entirely."

"Well, it has been a while since you've been back. Why did you stop coming?"

"Mom and Uncle Jack had a fight about something, and we just stopped. She says she always planned to make up with him and come back here, but she never got to it, and now... well, now it's too late."

"She can always come back here."

"She says she might, but I don't know. With Jack gone, it

will probably be too hard for her. The memories might just be too painful. I know I can't go back to Savannah after..." He trails off, the lightness in him drifting away, and the frown returning. "Maybe we should just sell. I saw that a few of the other places around here have gotten a pretty good price."

"I won't be selling," I say, standing from the booth. I can't sit here and do this right now. I'm tired, and he's tired, and it's just better if we leave it for tomorrow. After a good night's sleep, he'll see reason. "You enjoy your evening. I'll be in the kitchen preparing for breakfast at five. Chef Henry handles lunch and the first courses of dinner, so if you would like to talk more about the plans for Buxton Estate, we can maybe take a walk?"

"I don't think you will be able to change my mind," he says, tilting his head to look up at me. "I have no idea how to run a hotel."

"I can guarantee you've got more of a chance learning how to run this estate than you do convincing me to sell. Sleep well, Mr. Buxton."

Chapter Five

Nate

The way he said Mr. Buxton before storming out of the dining room had an embarrassingly strong effect on my body. I pretended to scroll on my phone for a few minutes until my reaction calmed down and then finished helping Lilah reset for the morning.

"So you want to sell?" Lilah asks as we close the doors to the dining room and make our way down the hall.

"You heard that?"

"It helps that I was trying extremely hard to eavesdrop. So yeah."

I laugh at her easy honesty.

"I have no idea how to run a hotel, and this place needs so much work. It would be better off in the hands of someone who knew what they were doing."

"You could learn, like Rémy said."

Okay, so she really did hear all our conversation.

"That would take forever."

"So it's not that you wouldn't want to, it's that you think it would take too long to learn?"

"No. Well, in some parts, yes. But..."

"Do you have another job to get back to?"

"No."

"A house, wife, husband, kids?"

"No. I sort of moved back with my mom."

"Sooo, what's stopping you from giving this a go, then?"

"Crippling fear that I'll fuck it up," I reply with a laugh, as if I'm joking. But in truth, that is the only reason I can think of right now.

"You should always do what you're afraid to do," she says, and I stop walking. "It means you care enough to succeed."

"Did you just come up with that?"

She laughs. "Nope, it's an Emerson quote. Or the first part is, the second bit is just something Rémy throws in whenever he says it, but in his French accent, it sounds way smoother."

I bet it does. I could listen to him talk for hours. I don't tell her that, though.

She turns toward the front door where the moonlight is sending soft streams of colored light through the stained glass into the hallway. "I better be going. It's getting late and I'm back here for breakfast."

"Sorry to keep you."

"No, it's fine. You helped me reset the dining room, so I'm getting out of here a bit earlier tonight. Besides, I only live fifteen minutes down the road. I'll see you in the morning."

"Yeah, see you then."

She leaves, and I head back to my room, sleep coming easier than it has in a year.

The old estate feels even emptier in the early hours of the morning. Rémy said he'd be in the kitchen by five. It's ten minutes to five, and I'm trying to look busy flipping through the bookings in the old leather diary. The reception desk is just inside the main doors and to the left. It's got only what it needs, I guess, with the diary, a landline phone, and a cabinet attached to the wall with the room keys on display. There's a hook for sixteen in total, and only six are missing. The books show another five guests are checking in today, and two on Sunday. The dining room was pretty packed last night as it was with people coming in from other places nearby, so I guess this place is doing better than I thought.

I hear a noise down the hall and follow the sound through the dining room, pushing open the swinging doors that lead to the kitchen to find Rémy standing on the other side of a long stainless steel bench, wearing a black tank top that shows off his toned arms perfectly.

"Sorry, I didn't—" I begin as I start backing out of the room.

"It's fine, I was just about to get started," he replies, pulling on a chef's jacket, and I pause halfway through the doorway, watching as he buttons it all the way to the top.

"Do you want coffee?" he asks, and I nod.

"That would be great. Milk, two sugars, please."

As much as I hate to see him cover up any part of that gorgeous body, Rémy somehow looks even hotter in his chef's jacket. His hair is a mess of blond curls, just like I remember them being as a child. Not like the perfectly tamed ones I saw last night. He's mumbling something under his breath as he pours the coffee that I can't make out.

"Sorry, what?" I ask, and he spills some coffee over his hand. He puts down the pot and blurts something in French as he moves to run his hand under cold water.

I jump up from the stool and meet him at the sink.

"Is it bad?" I ask, leaning in and reaching for his hand. His skin is warm and soft, and as the cold water slips through our fingers, his hand rests heavy in my palm. "I'm sorry."

He turns to look at me, piercing blue eyes shining bright in the morning light. "Why are you sorry? I was the fool with the pot."

"I distracted you. I..."

"You are a distraction, oui, but it was not your words." He looks away. "Do you truly not remember me?"

My memories of Rémy were in a part of my mind that I pushed way down, and only after coming back here, seeing this place, seeing him, have they started to somewhat surface. I remember running with him through the grounds, tormenting his aunt, and swimming in the river that cut through the Peterson's place down the road. My stomach stirs at the thought of them, in the same way it flipped seeing him half-naked in the kitchen. Did I have a thing for Rémy back then? I thought I only figured out I was gay in high school, but maybe it was sooner. Maybe Rémy was where it all started.

I study his profile, sharp jaw, clean-shaven, he must have done that this morning, and big pink lips, slightly parted, like he's trying to control his breathing. I know I am. I know that my heart doubled its pace when I took his hand and that the warmth that started where we touched has now spread through my whole arm and settled like a balloon around my heart.

"I'm starting to remember bits and pieces, but it was a long time ago. Maybe you can help me remember?"

He meets my gaze again, his stare moves to my mouth for a moment, and fuck me, but I lick my lips. Don't Nate. You can't flirt with the sexy chef, no matter how good he smells or looks or sounds. Just no.

"Maybe it's me who's forgetting. Maybe I made up the memories in my mind," he continues, looking back at his hand still under the running water.

"Why would you do that?"

"Back then, I might have had a little crush, small. Hardly worth mentioning. But maybe my memories can't be trusted."

"I'd still like to know what you remember, even if they're... what do you call a memory that isn't a real memory?"

"A fantasy."

My cock twitches, and I let go of his hand.

"Right, yeah. Umm. I guess you could call them that. So, your hand, is it okay now?"

He shrugs. "Probably. I've been burnt plenty of times in the kitchen. It's no big deal," he says, shutting off the tap and grabbing a towel from a stack beside it to dry his hand. "Let's try this coffee thing again."

. . .

Watching Rémy in the kitchen reminds me of what I used to be like when I was training with the team. The baseball field was my happy place, and this is very clearly his. I sit on a stool he's pulled over for me and eat the omelet he's made me while we talk, and he prepares the orders coming in hard and fast from the dining room.

"So you handle the breakfast and the desserts?" I ask as he cracks another two eggs into the frying pan.

"I love the idea that my food is the first thing a guest will eat when they wake and the last thing they do before they sleep. It has a nice completeness to it. They start and end their days with me."

"That's cool. This," I say, pointing down to my mostly eaten breakfast. "Is the best omelet I've ever had. How did you know I like mushrooms?"

"We used to pick them, remember?"

I shake my head.

"Where?"

"At the Morris farm, down the road. You'd always be eating more than you picked for Chef Henry."

Vague memories of wooden logs covered in the large fungi start to emerge, then comes a memory of Rémy, with his golden hair shining in the light through the trees, standing so close beside me as we pick mushrooms from the same log. I remember teasing him with one, holding it up to his face, daring him to take a bite and him scrunching up his nose at it, shaking his head before I bite off the top, and he laughs.

"I remember now. I was allowed to eat as many as I wanted if I picked them, but you don't even like mushrooms. What did you get out of going all those times?"

A flutter of something sweeps across me as he flashes me the same youthful smile I now remember so well.

"Time with you."

A flash of heat rises to my face.

"I can't believe I forgot so much of this place," I say, turning my attention to the plate.

"It's been a long time between visits."

Lilah joins us, tapping her wrist where a watch might normally sit.

"Have you got table seven's order up yet?" she asks.

"Just finishing off the eggs," he says, and she starts collecting the plates that make up the rest of the table's breakfast from beside us.

"Do you want help?" I ask, but she shakes her head.

"It's nice seeing you sit there. Jack used to spend his time in the kitchen, too. That was his stool, and he was the only person allowed to sit in here."

Rémy flips the eggs, then turns back to me.

"You still don't remember why you stopped coming?"

"No, not really. I mean, Mom and Jack had a fight, but that's all I remember. Then there was college and baseball."

"Your uncle loved watching you play," he says, passing the finished plate over to Lilah, who has three balanced on one arm. Impressive.

"He loved the dancing, too," Lilah says, leaving us to deliver her order.

My shoulder throbs, and I roll it back a couple of times to try to ebb the ache.

"It was so much fun, the best job in the world."

"Maybe that's why your uncle left this place to you."

"What do you mean?"

"So that you would have to come back and remember you had fun before there was baseball, so maybe you can have fun again."

I reach over and pick up a slice of mushroom.

"I'll tell you what, you eat this, and I'll agree to *think* about not selling my half."

He scrunches up his nose just like he did in my memory of him, and it's just as adorable now. How did I ever forget him? He takes the slice from me between two fingers and holds it up.

"You promise?"

"Yep. All you have to do is eat it. Oh, and chew and swallow it, no spitting it out."

His disgusted look gives way to a smug smile, and he pops the thing in his mouth, chews with a devilish grin, then swallows without even the slightest pause.

"What the fuck?"

"Oh, I'm sorry. Did you think I still hated these little things?"

He's laughing, and I can't even be mad because the way his face lights up when he does brings a warmth to my chest I don't want to let go of.

"I learned to love them, just as you will learn to love this place. Just you wait and see."

Chapter Six

Nate

Rémy walks me through the entire hotel, talking over the plans he and my uncle had for this place, and around every corner we turn, there's a new memory surfacing of my childhood summers spent here with my mother and with him.

"I remember this," I say, laughing and pulling open the door to the dumbwaiter that runs from the kitchen on the ground floor all the way up.

"You should. We got stuck in there for an hour when we were hiding from my aunt."

The memory of being squashed beside him in the dark, his leg against mine, face so close that his breath tickled the skin of my cheek when he turned to whisper to me.

"I can't believe we both fit in there," I say, sticking my head through to look down.

"We didn't, that's why we got stuck," he laughs, and a

voice clears their throat behind me, and I bang my head on the way out.

"Are you okay?" Rémy asks.

"Fine, it's just a tap."

Seline is standing in the doorway, arms folded over her chest, one eyebrow cocked. "No messing with the food elevator or you'll be carrying up the room service yourselves until it's fixed."

"I was just looking," I say, rubbing my head. There is a small bump forming.

"Dean called from the farm up the road to check on the order for the week. If you want to have enough to feed these guests, you might want to give him a ring," she says, and Rémy nods.

"We'll head down now and see them."

"We will?" I ask.

"They're our biggest supplier. It would be good for you to meet them."

"I don't know..."

"Look, you promised to think about not selling, and to do that, you need to know how many people make this place run. It's not just us, our staff, and the guests who visit. We have connections with farms and small businesses all over."

"So your plan is to guilt me into not selling?"

He shrugs. "Whatever gets you to see that you can do this, that we can, together."

I have no idea if he's right, but what I do know is that I haven't smiled like this in months, and if visiting this farm means spending more time with Rémy, then I'm in.

"Okay, I can drive."

He laughs.

"How about you let me handle the driving?"

Seline is shaking her head. "Be safe."

"Safe? What kind of car do you have?"

"I don't own a car."

The second he wheels out the old bike, my stomach is in knots. I have no clue how to ride a motorbike and this thing looks like it's been pieced together from several different ones and has a sidecar that's more like a wooden crate attached to one side.

"I won't fit in that," I say, and he laughs and tosses me a small round helmet.

"That's for the supplies. You'll be riding with me. Jump on."

"On the bike?"

"That is usually how it works."

"Behind you?"

"Oui, yes, behind me."

I strap on the helmet, my heart racing, as my whole body vibrates with anticipation. I swing one leg over the back of the bike, and while I was aiming to keep some distance between us, the shape of the seat forces my body to slide forward until my crotch is pressed right up against his ass. Shit. Okay, control your thoughts, you have to control your thoughts or the ride is going to be awkward as fuck.

He kicks the bike to start and then tilts his head over one shoulder.

"Hold on tight," he says, grabbing one of my hands and

positioning it around his waist. His body is so warm. Or is it that all my blood has moved to the areas we touch like a magnet drawn to him? I swing the other arm around him, trying not to be weird about it, but then he takes off, and I can't help but squeeze him tight, turning my face into his neck as the world zooms past us.

I breathe in his scent, sweet vanilla sugar.

"You okay?" he asks over the noise of the wind and rumbling engine of the bike.

"First time on a bike," I reply, lifting my head. The wind stings my eyes, and I want to bury my face into his neck again but force myself not to.

I should be cold, but being this close to him, it's impossible to feel anything but the growing fire in my gut and my groin. Shit. Keep it together.

On the left, we pass fields of long grass with fences and horses and cows just mulling about. A large black cow lies under a tree in the shade up by the next curve of the road, and as the engine revs and we zoom past, it doesn't even flinch. Must be nice to be that cool and collected. Wonder what that's like?

Amongst the old farmhouses, barns, and grain silos, it's impossible to miss one of the newer estates. A smooth tarred road leads up to a giant modern hotel. It's a stark contrast to the rich natural surroundings. Is that what would happen if I sold Buxton Estate? Something stirs inside me, but then Rémy zigzags the bike around a pothole, and I clench tighter to his shirt.

"Holy shit, careful, man," I call.

"That was me being careful," he laughs, and I spot a sign

for Beaker Brothers up ahead with an arrow pointing right down a red dirt road. Animal Control has an Alan Beaker, and I'm pretty sure his family has a ranch he and his mates went up to last break. It's probably just a coincidence. Rémy slows only slightly as we near the sign. He can't possibly be going to turn at this speed. But he does, and as the bike leans so low to the ground that the crate lifts on the other side a little, I squeeze him tighter.

"Fuuuck," I cry out as he straightens us up and the crate side reconnects with a skid of its wheels.

"You get used to it, promise," he tells me.

"I'll take your word for it."

I might not be ready to agree with him just yet, but he's kind of right. It's weird. The fear has been overtaken by an almost childish excitement, but my heart continues to thump in my ears, nonetheless. The ranch is growing larger, the nearer we get, with the world around us flying past, the wind whipping his curls from under his helmet and brushing against my cheek.

Finally, we slow, and he pulls us up to a stop out the front of a big barn set beside the main house, and I climb off.

The ground feels like water under my feet.

"Wow."

"Fun, yes?" he asks, and I nod.

"Eventually, yeah, it was."

He smiles, pulls his helmet off, and shakes out his curls, fingering through them with one hand. I wonder what they feel like. Nope. Stop.

"So what are we picking up from here again?" I ask,

trying to stay on task and not let my mind wander to all the places it wants to.

"Many things. Cheese, milk, cream, honey and eggs to start."

"Is it safe taking eggs back on that thing?"

He laughs. "I may have been going a little faster than I would normally on the way here."

"I knew it."

"You had fun, though."

I can't argue with that. There was something exhilarating about being on the back of the motorbike, arms wrapped around him, pressed up against his back, feeling the world fly past us. Suddenly, I can't wait to do it all over again.

"Come, let's find Dean."

I follow Rémy into the barn, the smell hitting me the second we're through the doors, grass, dirt and cows. Is cows a scent? If it isn't, it should be. It isn't terrible, not like you might think a room full of them would be, and it isn't loud either, only the soft whirring of the milking machines they are hooked up to and a few random moos. Walking the rows are three guys, all shirtless, all stacked, and all of them smile wide when they spot Rémy. Can you blame them? He's freaking gorgeous.

"Perfect timing, the girls are about to come off," the tallest of the three says, reaching us and shaking Rémy's hand.

Rémy gestures toward me.

"This is Nate Buxton," he says, and the eyebrows rise on this guy as he takes my hand and squeezes it just a little too tight.

"Dean Beaker. So you're the new Buxton, hey?"

"I'm *a* Buxton," I reply, and he releases my hand. "So this is your farm?"

"Yep, me and my brother took it over from our Gramps a few years back."

"Do you just milk cows?" If they are a milking farm, it can't be the same one Alan's brothers run.

"Nope, we've got horses, too. Last year, we built a few new cabins around the back of the main house that we rent out, but you can't see them from here. Oh, this is my brother, Nial," he says, pointing toward the middle guy who's disconnecting one of the cows. "And that's Connor. He's just giving us a hand today. Normally, you can't get him to leave the mini moos, but we're down a farmhand today."

"Mini moos?"

Rémy lets out a soft giggle and explains.

"They have a section of the ranch set up with the calves of these lovely ladies and some mini Highlands people come to cuddle."

"Oh, cool. Well, it's nice to meet you both," I say, and Nial and Connor nod as a way of greeting, then get back to doing what they were doing.

"Sorry, best get these girls off if we're going to stay on schedule," Dean says.

"I can help," I say without thinking. Because if I did take a second to think, I would have told myself, I have no fucking clue how to milk a cow and should keep my mouth shut.

"That would be great. Jump over here. I'll show you how to unhook them."

I follow Dean over to the row of cows on our left, leaving Rémy to stand and watch.

"So are they on these all day?" I ask.

"Hells no. Our lovely ladies are milked three times a day, and it only takes about five minutes each time."

"Wow, really? What are they doing the rest of the day?"

"Being cows." He laughs, and I lean down to where he's unhooking one of the milking machines. "Flick the valve to switch it off, then after you disconnect these, you take this cup here, and dip each teat in this solution. It will help stop any infections."

"Okay," I say, moving to the next cow on the row. She moos loudly beside me, and I pause.

"Don't worry, she's just saying hi." Dean laughs, and I reach out and run my hand over her large head. It's like patting a very big dog, and she tilts her head into my hand. "See, she likes you."

"Hi, to you, too. I'll just be unhooking you now," I tell her, and I hear one of the guys behind me laugh, but I don't care. I'm about to be touching her teats. I think she deserves me telling her I'm going to do it before I actually do.

The machine comes off easily, and I hand the hoses over the edge like Dean has done on the one before, dip her teats in the cup of what looks like iodine, and move up the row to get the next girl taken care of. Dean and I move along the row, him twice as fast as me, but we still beat the other guys clearing their sections.

"Thanks, you can open the door and let them out if you like," he says, and I pull across the sliding door at the end of the section, and the cows funnel themselves out without any prompting. I suppose if they are milked three times a day, they would be used to this.

535

"Thanks for your help. We should probably get your order loaded up now. Did you want to add on anything else?" he asks, looking past me to Rémy who's been following along the row as we worked, watching me. I could feel his eyes on me the entire time, and I almost asked him if he wanted to jump in and give it a go, too, but thought I better not. They aren't my cows after all.

"Do you have any of those lavender soaps?"

"Yes, Sarah sent down a whole box of them."

"Great, we'll take them, too."

"No problem. Hey, Conner, Nial, I'm grabbing the order. You all good in here?"

"Yeah," they reply, and I follow Dean and Rémy out of the barn and toward the main house.

"So, you don't have another brother, do you?" I ask, my curiosity getting the better of me.

"Yeah, we do. But he doesn't work the ranch. He's up in Savannah keeping an eye on Gramps and playing Banana Ball. Why do you ask?"

Rémy looks my way but doesn't say anything. I could say nothing, too. Rémy is staying quiet, and these guys clearly don't recognize me. I mean, why would they? I was pulled early in the first season with the Funky Monkeys.

"I played with your brother, on the other team," I say, surprising even myself.

"Oh, cool. Hey, I think I remember. It was in the first year, right? You had to take a break because you got hurt."

"A permanent break," I reply.

"Shit. Sorry, man. That sucks."

"Yeah. It does."

"Alan will start coming up here when he can't play anymore. It can't last forever, right?"

He's right. One way or another, it was always going to end. My career just ended a whole fucking lot sooner than I wanted it to.

"Gotta have a Plan B," I say and follow him into the house to collect the order. I didn't have a Plan B.

We collect everything we need, and Dean loads the crate on the side of the bike with more than I thought it could carry before he heads back into the barn to help his brothers, and we ride back to the estate. The ride back is slower, by far. But no less exciting. Without the fear of death, I'm able to focus more on everything else. Like the way Rémy fits against me perfectly, and how his skin smells like sugar and cocoa. I try not to imagine tasting him, because the slightest thought of just that had me thickening in my jeans, and I can't exactly hide a hard-on when it's against his ass on this bike.

We bring everything through to the kitchen through a side door, but on my trip back out to get the last of it, I notice another door in the hallway, and it's slightly ajar.

"Wasn't this a storeroom?" I ask Rémy as he walks back carrying the boxes of soap.

"It used to be. We had it renovated when I moved here."

"Renovated to what?" I ask, pushing open the door to find the small storeroom had been completely transformed into a livable space. There is a sort of small hallway; on the left, another door is open to a bedroom where a single bed sits against one wall, a tiny side table beside it; and on my right is a bathroom with a walk-in shower.

"You live here?"

"Oui, I do."

"You didn't want one of the bigger rooms?" I ask, looking again at the small bed. He would be almost as tall as it is long. Surely it isn't comfortable. He should have a bigger bed.

"It has everything that I need, plus it is close to the kitchen. I'll just put these down, then how about I make you something to eat?"

"I'll grab the last few boxes," I say and collect the final things while Rémy washes up. I get back into the kitchen and find Seline stretched up on her toes, trying to grab a few teacups and saucers to load onto a tray.

"Here, let me help," I tell her, picking up the last few she was struggling to reach.

"Thank you. We have a high tea planned in the garden today."

"Cool. Do you need any help with anything else?"

"No, I think we have everything in hand."

"Okay, well, just let me know if you do," I tell her, and she leaves.

"You are full of surprises, Mr. Buxton," Rémy says as I lean against the counter beside him.

"What do you mean?"

"You're always trying to help. Yesterday, you were helping Lilah, and now today with the cows and with Seline."

"I guess I figure why watch if I can help."

"But with the estate, you want to sell and not try to help it, to help me?"

My cheeks burn. He's right. I've always been the guy who gets in and lends a hand wherever needed. I never used to shy away from anything. Trying new things was how I found baseball to begin with.

My shoulder aches, and I massage the spot with one hand. Rémy turns me to face him and lays a hand over mine on my shoulder. I look up into his piercing blue eyes and wonder how I ever could have forgotten them. I guess it's the same way I forgot how to try anything new.

"What is going through that pretty head of yours?" he asks, and my stomach swirls.

"I guess when I stopped being able to do the thing that I loved, I stopped wanting to try anything new. Like, if I did and ended up loving it, what if it got ripped away, too?" I say, the words leaving my mouth and lifting a weight off my chest.

"Then you try again. Like today."

"I don't think unhooking cows is big enough to count as a new thing."

"Then try something bigger?"

My gaze moves to his mouth, and then I do something I know I shouldn't. I push up on my toes and kiss him.

Chapter Seven

Rémy

I think at first I'm imagining things. I've imagined grabbing Nate and kissing him so many times, this had to be a dream, too. But his warm soft lips press against mine, as his hands hold my waist and when my fingers slip up the hem of his shirt and touch the soft skin of his lower back, my whole body comes alive with the realization this is very real.

I pull him closer and slide my hand all the way up his back, holding him against me as his lips part and his tongue finds mine. I want to stay right here doing only this, but we're in the kitchen where anyone could walk in any second to start the lunch prep.

I reluctantly pull away and the disappointment in his eyes sends a pang to my chest.

"Not here," I tell him, taking his hand and leading him toward my room. His palm is warm, and it's like tiny vibrations flow between us, electricity generated by this connection we have. I turn and pull him to me the second I'm into the small hallway.

"Here," I say, and he pushes up and kisses me again, and I fumble behind him to close and lock the first door. His finger loops under the hem of my shirt, and I copy him, lifting his shirt up his back, feeling the ridges of his muscles until he breaks our kiss and lifts my shirt over my head. I peel his shirt off, too, his toned chest glistening, pleading with me to run my tongue over every mound, taste every inch. But before I can do any of that, he presses his palms against my chest, keeping us apart as his lustful stare trails down my body and then back up to meet my gaze.

He sucks in a breath.

"Fuck, you're beautiful," he says, then launches at me. I shuffle us backward as we kiss. It's raw, all lips and teeth and tongue and hot moans as we move through the door to the bedroom section of the space. I kick that closed, too, before I fall back on the bed, pulling him down on top of me.

His tongue fights mine for control as his fingers lace through the curls at the nape of my neck, sending shivers through my entire body. I'm rock hard already. Truthfully, I was hard the second he kissed me. Nate always did something to me, even as kids. It was like he could just look my way and my whole body would switch on.

He's holding himself slightly above me, pushing up on one hand, and I roll him to the side and wedge us closer by linking my leg over his and pulling him in. His hard cock is like a rock against mine, and I grind a little. He lets out a soft moan between kisses.

I want him so badly, but can I do this? Should I? I break our kiss, and he locks on my gaze with those bedroom eyes.

"Are you sure?" I ask.

"I want this," he says, brushing a curl behind my ear and leaning forward. "I want you." He drags his lips softly across my jaw, peppering kisses down my neck until he reaches the crease at my shoulder. "What do you want?"

"You."

"Then take me," he says, and I reach between us and unbutton his jeans, his hard cock tenting the thin fabric of his boxers. He's unbuttoning my pants almost as fast, while his other hand is in my hair and his lips are on mine.

I work his jeans and boxers down, over his tight round ass, grabbing it in fists and moaning into his mouth when he pulls me out and wraps his hand around my length, giving it a slow soft stroke.

I release his ass, moving to take a hold of him, too, but he pulls back.

"I got you," he says in a fucking sexy rasp that makes my cock twitch.

Then he spits into his hand and reaches between us, and I suck in a breath as he positions his cock beside mine, the soft skin igniting a million nerves and sending a rush of electricity through me.

"Oui, yes you do," I breathe and clench his ass tighter.

He softly swipes the pad of his thumb over my cockhead.

"Oh god," I moan, and he does it again, collecting the precome he's brought out of me and then slides his hand down and back up again. He works us slowly in firm strokes, sliding the soft skin over my cockhead and then

542

back down, teasingly slow. I'm desperate to kiss those pouty lips of his.

I thrust into his downstroke, and he lets out a deep groan from his chest encouraging me on, and I thrust again, careful not to push him off my small bed.

He jerks us, as I explore every muscle of his ass and back, and lift my hips into every stroke. He nuzzles my neck, burying his face into the soft skin, moaning kisses down until he sucks the crease at my shoulder. The pressure inside me builds, and all I can think is, harder, faster, tighter as his grip on my hair tightens. He lifts his head, panting, eyes locked on mine.

"Holy shit," he breathes as his chest heaves up and down. I keep my gaze locked on his, trying to stave off the building orgasm, but as his desperate stare bores into mine, my balls tighten and the electricity pulses through me.

His ass flexes in my grasp, and then his head tilts back. Lips parted, he breathes in short grunts, completely blissed out. It's my breaking point. Seeing him so far gone, my high hits hard and fast, balls pulling up tight, thighs tensing as I unload between us, my come coating his fist, our cocks, my chest, and then his heat joins mine, and he shudders against me.

He buries his face in my neck, his warm breath like a perfect summer breeze against my skin, and we lie there in each other's arms until our breathing has returned to normal and the noises of the kitchen start to filter through to my room.

"I should go," he says, and a lump forms in my throat.

"You want to leave?"

He pushes onto one elbow and smiles that big gorgeous smile and cards his fingers through my hair.

"Not forever, just to my room to shower and change."

"I have a shower here," I say, looking past him to the door.

"Yes, but you also need to shower, and I don't think we'd both fit in there. I peeked inside before. It doesn't look that big."

"Do you want to get lunch together? We can talk more about what renovations the place needs?" I ask. What I actually want to say is we can talk about how amazing this place will be when we are both running it, but even after this, I don't know that he will stay, and I wouldn't want him to think I only did this to get him to. I've known there was something special about Nate front the moment we met as kids, and seeing him again, all these years later, only reignited those feelings like pouring gas on a bonfire.

"Lunch sounds great. Do you have any more of those cheesecakes?"

"Oui, but I'm making something else for dessert tonight."

"Then I can have whatever you have left, if you aren't going to be serving them."

He rests his chin on my chest, peering up at me through his thick lashes with a cheeky grin.

"I suppose it would be a shame for them to go to waste. Shower first, then dessert."

"Some might call what we just did, dessert?" he says, and I blush.

"It was the highlight of my day so far. Dessert should always be the star."

"Well, the day is only half over. Maybe we can...have dessert again later tonight. In my room?"

I lean forward and kiss him softly.

"I can't wait."

He cleans off and dresses, sneaking out the side door and back to his room to shower while I do the same. Leaning against the tile as the hot water streams down my back, I revisit the memory of his mouth on mine, his hands exploring my body, gripping my hair, jerking me off and I'm half hard again. As much as I could probably get there on these memories mixed with fantasies of what else we will be doing later, I want more than a fantasy. I want to taste the real thing, and tonight, I'll get to do exactly that.

I make my way to the kitchen. Lilah is collecting plates from Chef Henry and eyes me suspiciously.

"Where have you been?"

"I collected the order from the Beaker Brothers Ranch."

"Yeah, but then you dumped it all in here and disappeared. Are you feeling sick? You look a bit flushed."

I shake my head and then quickly turn into my space to grab the leftover cheesecake roses from my small fridge for Nate.

"Good," she calls after me. "We'll have no hope of convincing Nate to stay on if you're holed up in your room sick."

"Who's sick?" Nate's voice comes, and I plate the last of the cheesecakes.

"No one is sick," I reply as he moves around the island to where I'm plating.

"Good. It would be a shame to miss out on dessert

tonight. Are you still okay to go over the hotel stuff with me after dinner service? It would be nice to start getting the hang of things," he says, and Lilah's eyes go wide behind him as she mouths, "*Oh my god, yes.*"

"After dinner. Oui," I reply and slide the plate of three rose cheesecakes over to him and pass him a spoon. He sits on the stool that used to be Jack's and takes his first bite, eyes closing for a moment as the cream hits his tongue.

"Hmmm, so good. Oh, we should meet in my room. There are a bunch of papers and things in there that make zero sense to me. Is that okay?"

"Your room," I repeat, and Lilah is nodding her head furiously behind him. "Sure. I can meet you there, say about nine?"

"Nine works," he replies, licking his lips. "I can't wait to see what you have to show me."

Lilah strides through the doors to the dining room happier than I've seen her since Jack passed, and the staff behind Nate are smiling widely, too. I know Nate is using the hotel to create a cover story for me going to his room, but to them, this is a sign that he might do this, help run this place, and it's nice to see them happy, even if it's only for a little while.

"Hey," Nate says, placing a hand over mine. "What's going through that pretty head of yours?" he asks.

"It's nice seeing them happy again," I say, and he looks over his shoulder for a moment and comes back to me.

"We better make sure this place stays open then, so they can stay that way."

"Wait, really?"

He shrugs. "I still have no clue how I'm going to do it, but sure. If you think we can, I'm up for it. Let's give this thing a go."

I lean forward to whisper, "This isn't just because we... you know?"

He blushes, letting out a soft laugh.

"While I'd like to also see where that goes, no. You were right. Maybe Jack knew what he was doing leaving me this place. I've been in a haze of pain and anger for so long now, this place showed me I could smile again, I could find joy, and I'm willing to bet that's what he had here, too, with them. With you. I want that, too."

"Then it's yours."

"No, it's ours," he says, taking another bite of the creamy cheesecake topping. I grab a spoon and go to get some when he pulls the plate to the side. "But this is mine."

"You don't strike me as the selfish type," I tell him, and he purses his lips, pondering that for a moment before he spoons a small half spoon and holds it out to me.

"I'm an only child. We don't particularly like to share."

"I'll teach you."

"It could take years," he says, swinging the spoon slowly back and forth in front of me teasingly.

"Promise?"

About the Author

Becca Jackson writes MM romance that delivers heart, heat, and happily ever afters for some totally adorkable and fabulous guys.

Becca's books have all your favorite tropes, from small town romances, bi-awakenings, there's some sports, friends to lovers and enemies to lovers too, but no matter the trope that takes your fancy, you'll always find a happily ever after.

If you want more from Becca Jackson, and those cheeky Beaker Brothers, check out, Home, Hearts, Hooves book one in the Beaker Brothers Ranch Series here: https://geni.us/HomeHeartHooves

Prefer your men playing sports, check out Nate's former teammates in Becca's Love in Play series starting with Totally Ducked, read it now here: https://geni.us/TotallyDucked

Or if small towns are your happy place, check out where the connected universe all begins in Textual Connections, Love in No Man's Land Book One, read it now here: https://geni.us/Textual

Thank You

Thank you so much for reading *Delicious*, we really hope you had as much fun reading it as we did putting it together. Although we're sorry if you're now very, very hungry!

We'd like to say a huge thank you to all the authors involved with this project, and we're so grateful to them for crafting such beautiful stories.

All the profits from *Delicious* will be divided between two wonderful UK charities: Switchboard, the national LGBTQIA+ support line, and akt, the national LGBTQ+ youth homelessness charity. We're so excited to support these amazing organisations as they continue their vital work supporting the LGBTQIA+ community.

Thank you again for your support, it really does mean the world to us.

Thank You

With Love From,
  Charlie Novak & Charity VanHuss
  May 2025